Discovery

Leslie Schweitzer Miller

With a Foreword by
ROBERT H. MILLER

This is a work of fiction and, as such, there are characters and incidents that are wholly the invention of the author's imagination; and then there are historical characters and events used fictitiously. Any similarity to people, living or deceased, events, organizations or locales not otherwise acknowledged is coincidence.

ISBN: 978-0-9677480-8-5

Published by
NOTRAMOUR PRESS
Blairstown, NJ 07825

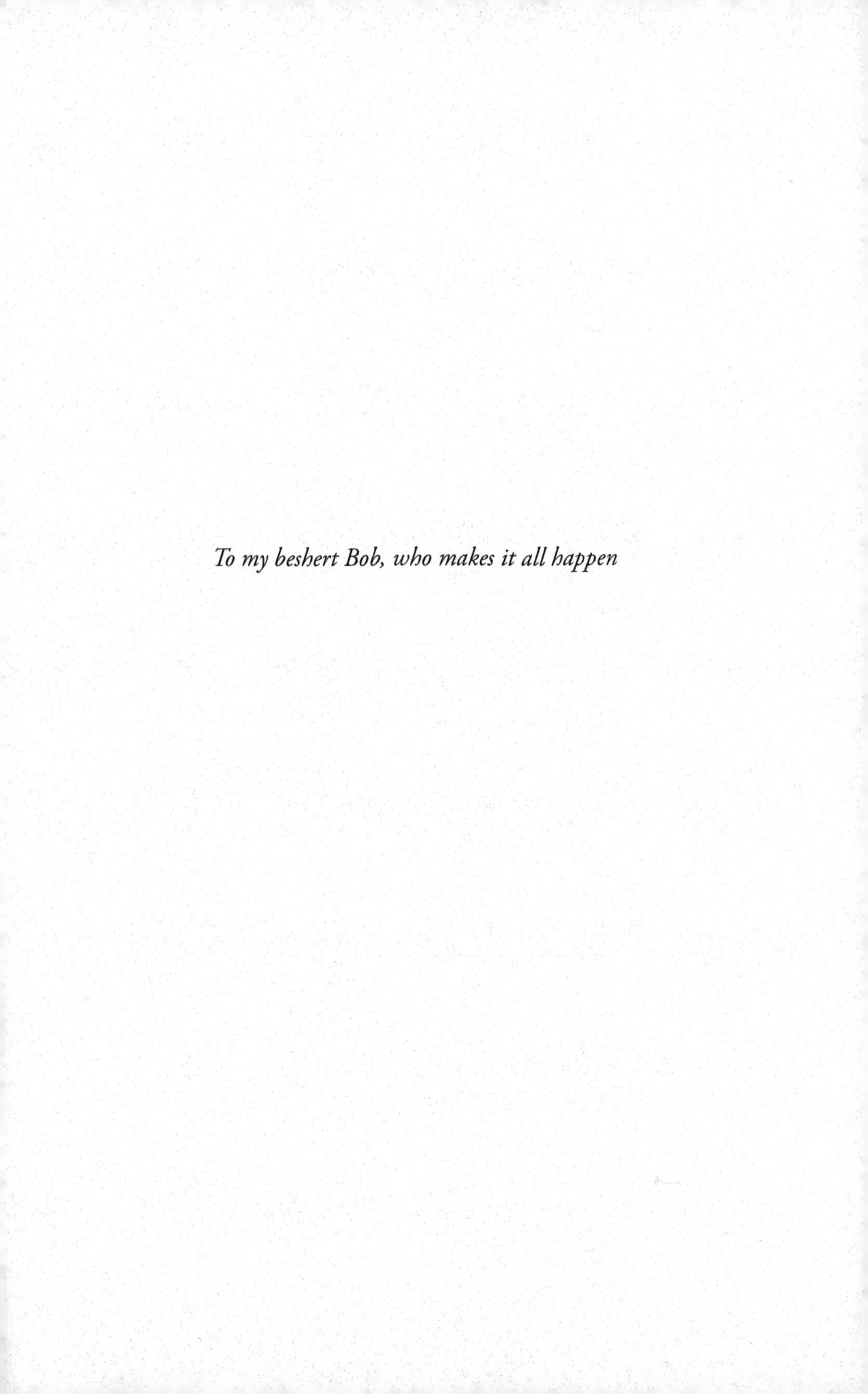

To my beshert Bob, who makes it all happen

The world is violent and mercurial—it will have its way with you. We are saved only by love—love for each other and the love that we pour into the art we feel compelled to share: being a parent; being a writer; being a painter; being a friend. We live in a perpetually burning building, and what we must save from it, all the time, is love.

Tennessee Williams

Just as no one can be forced into belief so no one can be forced into unbelief

Sigmund Freud

FOREWORD

By
Robert H. Miller

IN 1982, AUTHOR and speculative theorist, Michael Baigent, novelist, Richard Leigh, and writer and documentary presenter, Henry Lincoln, published their book *Holy Blood, Holy Grail*, which postulated that Jesus and Mary Magdalene were married and had a child. In its positive review of the book, the Los Angeles Examiner referred to the work as the " 'What If' school of historical speculation." But the book was also subjected to considerable criticism from the Anglican and Catholic Churches, which considered the book's conclusion wild speculation at variance with the truth reflected in the Gospels. But as the authors countered, the Gospels are a theological, not historical truth.

Appalled by what she considered blasphemy expressed in that book, Roman Catholic scholar, Margaret Starbird, set out to refute that conclusion, but instead uncovered new and compelling evidence that Jesus was, indeed, married to Mary Magdalene, which she revealed in *The Woman with the Alabaster Jar: Mary Magdalen and the Holy Grail*, published in 1993.

More recently, a three-time Emmy-winning Israeli-Canadian documentary filmmaker and widely-published writer and lecturer, Simcha Jacobovici, and a professor specializing in early Christianity, Barrie Wilson, came to the same conclusion in their 2014 book, *The Lost Gospel: Decoding the Ancient Text that Reveals Jesus' Marriage to Mary the Magdalene.*

Despite their differing approach, all arrived at their conclusions by reference to newly discovered documents and/or by interpreting previously discovered documents based on their coded or hidden significance instead of what they were formerly understood to mean. They had looked back at the early years of Christianity and the existence of conflict among many diverse groups, each of which practiced the religion differently. By the second century CE, the Church, as we know it today, was in its early formation and vehemently opposed to those who saw Jesus and his message in a different way. Towards the end of that century, Irenaeus, the Bishop of Lyons, wrote *Against Heresies*, a treatise in five volumes, dedicated to the *Detection and Overthrow of the False Knowledge*. Essentially, it was a refutation of Gnosticism, which was based on personal religious experience as opposed to the orthodox, or Catholic view, of the structured church.

As the Church's view became dominant, non-conforming discourse was deemed heretical and documents containing such material were destroyed when found. Gnostic writers then used hidden meanings and symbols to conceal their true significance. Documents known as the Gnostic Gospels, were hidden away, only to be discovered, centuries later. They disclosed information of life at the time of Jesus that had been excluded from the New Testament, for example, the Gospels of Thomas and Philip discovered at Nag Hammadi in Egypt and the Gospels of Mary and Pistis Sophia discovered elsewhere. The Gospel of Philip revealed information about the special relationship of Jesus and Mary Magdalene:

> *As for the Wisdom who is called "the barren," she is the mother of the angels. And the companion of the [...] Mary Magdalene. [...] loved her more than all the disciples, and used to kiss her often on her mouth. The rest of the disciples [...]. They said to him "Why do you love her more than all of us?" The Savior answered and said to them, "Why do I not love you like her? When a blind man and one who sees are both together in darkness, they are no different from one another. When the light comes, then he who sees will see the light, and he who is blind will remain in darkness."*

Having ignored or specifically excluded the importance of Mary Magdalene and her relationship with Jesus, one can readily understand why the Church went to great lengths to destroy any document, person or group that communicated a message other than the one it sanctioned. That reflexive action continued well into subsequent centuries and notably, in the Languedoc, an area in the south of France where its residents widely believe Mary Magdalene came after the Crucifixion and lived the remainder of her life. It is the Languedoc also where the story continues with the Cathars and, later, the Templars.

The Cathars were Christians who opposed the Catholic Church, believing it to be morally and spiritually corrupt. Unlike the Church, they conducted their lives as Jesus did, without structure or sacraments and considered women the equal of men. They rejected the doctrine of the Trinity and believed Jesus was married to Mary Magdalene.

The Church considered them heretics and, at first, attempted to persuade them by force of argument of the error of their ways and the need for conversion to the Church orthodoxy. But this failed to stop the Cathars' spreading influence. There was also concern the Cathars had in their possession some ancient Gnostic Gospel that had escaped earlier destruction, which revealed information damaging to the Church. Alarmed by such a blatant challenge to the Church's authority, and concerned that Catharism would spread even further, in 1209, Pope Innocent III called for a formal crusade to eliminate this heresy. He enlisted the nobles in the north of France to make war against the Cathars, permitting them to confiscate Cathar lands and those owned by their supporters, which included many noblemen in the south.

Thousands were killed in the subsequent massacre throughout the Languedoc. Though the war officially ended in 1229, the heresy continued. In 1234, the Inquisition was initiated to find and eliminate the remaining Cathars. Finally, in 1244, the Cathar fortress at Montsegur was overrun and more than 200 Cathar Parfaits or Perfects—the name given to the Cathar Monks—were burned to death in a huge fire at the foot of the castle. It is believed that a small group of Cathars escaped from Montsegur with "le trésor Cathar"—the Cathar treasure—speculating that it was a sacred Gnostic text or Cathar wealth, perhaps even the Holy Grail.

The need to eradicate heresy as seen by the Church did not end with the Cathars. Early in the twelfth century, the French knight Hugues de Payens created a monastic order of knights to protect the lives of pilgrims traveling to the Holy Land. He was granted a headquarters in Jerusalem in a wing of the royal palace on the Temple Mount in the captured Al-Aqsa Mosque, believed to be above the ruins of the Temple of Solomon—thus, the name, Templar Knights, or Templars.

Initially the Order had few financial resources and survived on donations, but after obtaining the blessing of the Church, it received money, businesses, land and sons of noble families willing to help advance the fight in the Holy Land. Later, a Papal Bull exempted the Templars from all taxes and authority except that of the Pope. As a result, they were able to move beyond that of just a military order. They built ships, engaged in commercial trade and banking and accumulated great wealth and influence in the process. They were the first real multinational organization and became principal financiers to the Kings and courts throughout Christendom. Not subject to any authority other than the Pope, they were literally a state within a state.

When the Templars were forced out of the Holy Land in 1291, many returned to France. Despite no longer having a military mission, they continued to amass even greater fortunes and continued to honor Mary Magdalene as "Our Lady," a Gnostic Apostle of Jesus, which was not how the Church viewed her. Pope Clement V became concerned that the Templars' power and influence represented a threat to Church orthodoxy.

At the same time, Philip the Fair, King of France, who was deeply indebted to the Templars, became envious of their power and wealth. Many believe that the desire to eliminate his financial obligations as well as seize the Templars' valuable assets and property were the real motivation behind the passage of a new law resulting in their prosecution. Acting on rumors and witness statements, the Templars were accused of performing secret rites and rituals of Satanist worship in their palaces, and engaging in immoral relationships, forbidden practices and other wrongdoing, blasphemous to Christianity.

Pressured by Philip—though perhaps with little resistance—Pope Clement V called for papal hearings to determine the Templars' guilt or innocence. As expected, they were found guilty, and in 1312, the Order was declared illegal throughout Europe. Tortured by the Inquisitors, they confessed to their heresy, though once freed, many recanted their testimony. Though the Grand Master and others were eliminated and many captured Templars punished, the movement was not destroyed as thousands went underground and continued their activity in England and Northern Europe. Their "treasure" was never found.

The Church was concerned that not only would the Cathars and Templars' failure to adhere to Catholic orthodoxy spread, but there was an underlying fear that both groups possessed documented proof relating to the relationship of Jesus and Mary Magdalene that varied significantly from the narrative advanced by the Church since its inception.

Which brings us to the end of the nineteenth century when Father François Bérenger Saunière became the parish priest in the mountaintop Village of Rennes-le-Château. Though he arrived penniless, a few years later he began renovating the church, followed by the construction of a magnificent and very expensive estate. Many theories have been advanced to explain the source of his funds. They include Saunière finding the Visigoths' missing treasure from their sack of Rome in the fifth century, or the missing treasures of the Cathars or Templars. Another theory is that during the renovation, Saunière discovered certain documents very embarrassing to the Church and was paid to keep them secret—perhaps documents that would reveal Jesus and Mary Magdalene were married.

Discovery, the novel, builds on this theme and with a foundation of real life characters and incidents, creates a plausible narrative of events that move between the present day and earlier centuries to provide the reader a new and different perspective on this controversial subject.

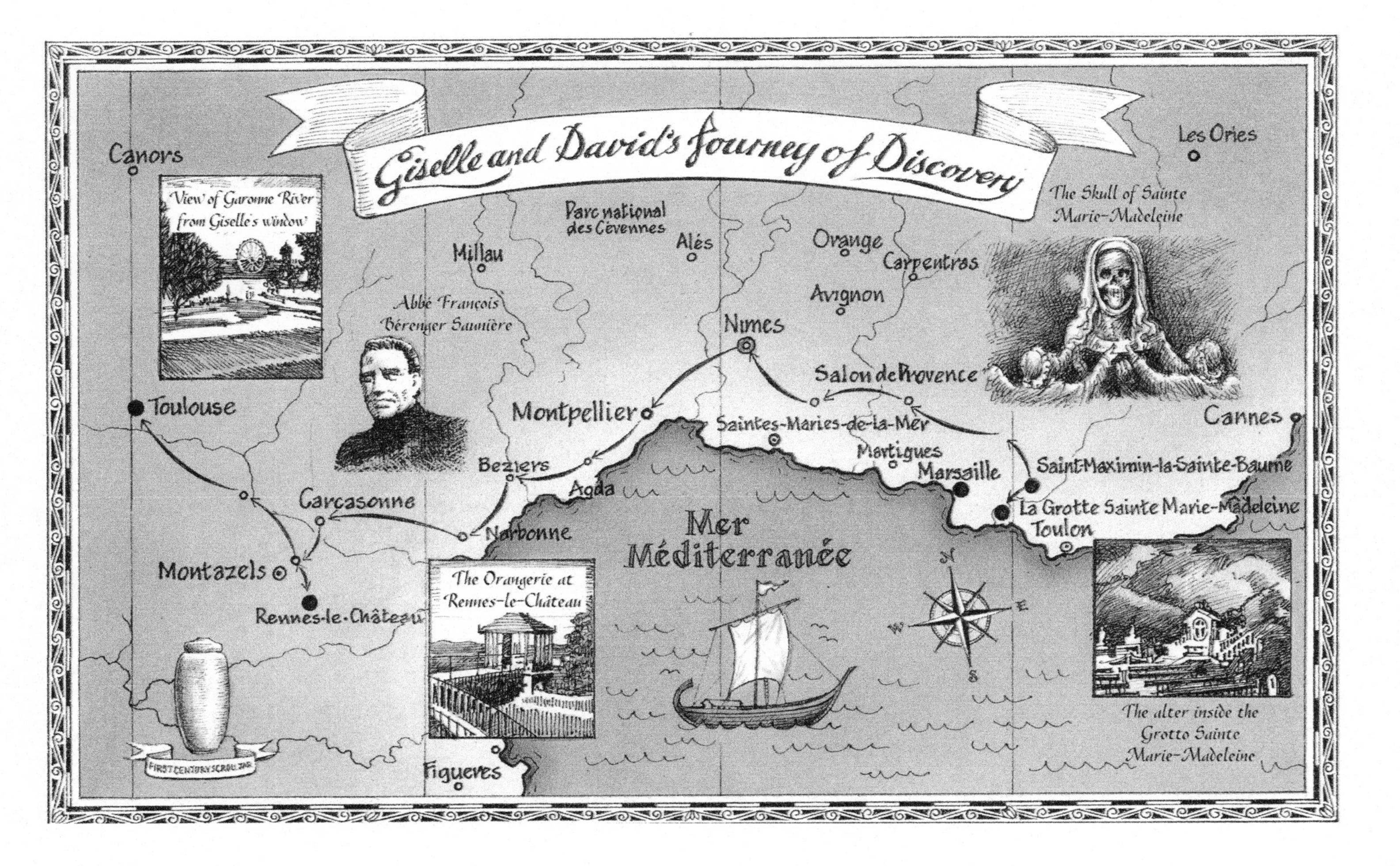
Giselle and David's Journey of Discovery
Canors
View of Garonne River from Giselle's window
Parc national des Cévennes
Alés
Orange
Carpentras
Les Ories
The Skull of Sainte Marie-Madeleine
Millau
Abbé François Bérenger Saunière
Avignon
Nimes
Salon de Provence
Toulouse
Montpellier
Saintes-Maries-de-la-Mer
Cannes
Martigues
Beziers
Agda
Marsaille
Saint-Maximin-la-Sainte-Baume
Carcasonne
La Grotte Sainte Marie-Madeleine
Narbonne
Toulon
Mer Méditerranée
Montazels
The Orangerie at Rennes-le-Château
Rennes-le-Château
N
E
W
S
The alter inside the Grotto Sainte Marie-Madeleine
FIRST CENTURY SCROLL JAR
Figueres

1

RENNES-LE-CHÂTEAU, FRANCE

JUNE 1885

TWO HOURS BEFORE sunrise, Father François Bérenger Saunière crept out of his parents' house as silently as a shadow, relieved to get away without any last-minute drama. It was a maneuver he'd perfected as a boy when he'd sneak a book under his shirt and hide in a massively overgrown blackberry bush, ignoring the thorns and inevitable bloody scratches on his arms and legs. Today, he headed directly toward the horse-drawn milk-cart waiting for him behind the fountain, a silhouette in the gloom. All his valued possessions, including a treasured copy of *Les Misérables*, were neatly packed into a large satchel carried in his left hand while he absentmindedly brushed his cassock with the right, as if telltale berries from the past might give him away.

"A morning such as this is a blessing," he murmured, hoping to appear calm and composed, as he climbed up to join the driver on the rough-hewn wooden bench. It would be unseemly to let this stranger get a whiff of the elation he felt. "It should be a pleasant journey."

Without even a grunt of acknowledgment, the cart began to roll.

Thick gray mist blanketed the ground and drifted over their route as if a magician had tried to obscure the border between road and vegetation. The plow horse inched along, oblivious.

"If we could float above the clouds and gaze down from the heavens, I imagine it would look something like this," the priest mused. No response. Perhaps he was speaking too quietly. "What I mean is this might well be an angel's view of earthbound mortals," he said, raising his voice. Nothing. *The*

Lord will do the fighting for me, and I need only to remain silent and calm, he decided and closed his eyes, amused at the irony of Exodus 14:14 floating into his mind.

Spring rains had gouged large furrows and treacherous holes the size of ripe melons in the earthen road, causing the cart to lurch and groan dramatically as it slowly bumped along, but Saunière had tuned it out and retreated into an impenetrable, meditative daydream. It wasn't until the morning sun warmed his face that he opened his eyes and saw the towering walls of granite, signaling his arrival.

He leaned his head back and forcefully filled his lungs with fresh mountain air, holding his breath for a minute to savor the sweet fragrance of pine and dew moistened grass. It was pure joy.

Without a word of warning or change of expression, the driver pulled on the reins and the cart rolled to a stop. Father Saunière had never had occasion to visit Rennes-le-Château—few people did—but he knew the village, *his village, his new parish,* was somewhere high above them, on top of one of these forested limestone massifs.

"This is where we part ways, Abbé," the driver said brusquely, pointing his pudgy index finger in the general direction of a narrow path that could have been easily mistaken for a gully between the towering evergreens. "You can't get lost. Walk uphill. When you get to the top, you're there."

Saunière could ignore being overlooked, but this abrupt dismissal and deliberate disrespect was an obvious slap in the face; still, it took a lot more than that to provoke a man whose personal code of behavior dictated he turn the other cheek—the first time.

"I've been told carriages are able to travel that road," he said amiably, wanting to sound as if he'd misunderstood.

"I regret any inconvenience." The driver waved the back of his hand toward the forest as if his passenger were debris he was trying to sweep off the narrow seat.

Saunière nodded as if he believed in the sincerity of the sentiment. There was nothing even vaguely reminiscent of regret in the snide tone, but he had no idea what had generated the palpable hostility. "No problem. I'll walk," he said cheerfully, "but I'm curious. You seem to be trying to tell me something."

The driver cleared his throat. "To begin with, it's barely worth my while to make this trip at all, and I only agreed out of respect for your father. Heloise, pathetic old nag that she is, wouldn't make it up there pulling both of us behind. One of us would have to walk with her, lead her, you know, so there's no point in that. And"—he emphasized the word—"you're a strong, strapping young man. In fact, my sister in Le Clat says she has it on good authority that you have the energy and strength of a stallion"—he paused, as if his implicit accusation needed time to hang in the air before he continued—"so the climb shouldn't be a problem for you. Anyway, best get used to it, I say."

Nodding again, Saunière climbed down, back straight, head up, with as much dignity as circumstance allowed, and waited for his satchel to be handed down to him. Had he not been a man of the cloth, he might have been tempted to offer a condemnation of busybodies and gossip, but he was a soldier of the Church and felt obligated to be charitable in all things.

"Bless you, my son," he said to the driver, making the sign of the cross. Turning to the horse, he added, "And bless you, Heloise. Every living creature is in the hands of God."

The road up the mountain was easy to find, and as he began to climb, the melody of a Gregorian chant—he always thought of it as a plaintive melody—began running through his head. Could he create a chorus of echoes? A few solitary notes in his rich baritone didn't quite produce the choir of his imagination, but it was good enough. No one, certainly not his family or his fellow seminarians, would ever comprehend the pleasure that coursed through him when he heard he was being sent to this inhospitable, impoverished village; but they'd never understood anything about him, and certainly never approved of his free, unconventional spirit. He'd never been the sort to obey rules that weren't compatible with his sense of right and wrong, and he certainly had no intention of letting the Church hijack his manhood. He answered to Jesus alone, and Jesus had never asked for that.

As the dawn light found its way through the mosaic of branches and foliage overhead, the lavender-covered hillside was transformed into a cascade of quicksilver. He fell silent. The words of Romans 14 seemed to whisper to him through the trees: *Blessed is the man who does not condemn himself for doing what he believes to be right.* He was at peace.

The ancient stone church, now his—his!—was in ruins, and there'd be no presbytery to call his own, not even a meager salary; he'd have to depend on the charity of parishioners who had agreed to provide for him as best they could. It had been made clear that being relocated—exiled—here had been intended not only as a punishment, but also as an opportunity to prove he could stay in line and follow the rules, but that wasn't his agenda now, any more than it had ever been. Rennes-le-Château was his to inspire. He would share ideas that mattered in the modern world, great ideas, idealistic ideas he'd gathered from his books, not only the Gospels. The pulpit was his, and he would use it to share what he knew to be true and encourage his flock to think. It was a thrilling prospect.

Growing up as the well-educated son of the mayor of Montazels, he'd felt entitled to dream, and dream he did, imagining a life in the arts among the intellectuals who gathered in Paris. The years spent reading under the blackberry bush had fostered his fantasies, but some part of him always knew he was deluding himself. His mother had a different agenda for her firstborn, and his father was useless when it came to doing battle with her. None of the realistic alternatives—apprenticeship in the trades, teaching—appealed to him any more than the priesthood, so with great reluctance and a heavy heart, he chose to make his mother happy and entered the Grand Séminaire in Carcassonne.

He rose quickly through the ranks and was made Curé of Le Clat barely three years after his ordination. It was a stepping-stone with a trajectory that should have landed him in the stratosphere of the Church, but his modern ideas and, ultimately, rumors of an inappropriate liaison—or two—eventually reached Carcassonne. The Bishop liked him but couldn't look the other way. Now here he was, deposited where the hierarchy thought his opportunity for mischief would be limited.

Last night he'd made the long journey to Montazels, knowing it would be some time before he saw his family again. He owed it to his mother. Her vision of seeing him ordained as a bishop, a cardinal, maybe even pope, was ruined; distress and disappointment was evident in her eyes when he knelt in front of her.

"Bérenger, my sweet, sweet, beautiful boy; my gift from heaven. I beg you, do not yield to temptation," she'd pleaded, withdrawing the lace handkerchief she kept tucked in her sleeve and dabbing the corner of her eye. "Cast your story books aside and give up your rebellious ways. I can't bear the shame. You're being sent away, and no one will tell me where my firstborn, my joy, will be saying Mass."

"Rennes-le-Château, Maman." She was the last to know. Her reaction was a foregone conclusion that he would have avoided indefinitely, had it been possible.

Madame Saunière, who had sunk back against the chair cushions in a show of despair, straightened up and stared haughtily at him; disdain dripped from every word. "That place barely qualifies to be called a village," she sniffed. "I've heard they all live in rubble like vermin, and there's nothing there. Nothing! No one of any consequence—oh, I had such hopes for you."

"You worry too much, Maman," he'd said lightly, praying some maternal intuition hadn't given her a hint of his excitement. "Remember, Jesus said, 'Blessed are the poor in spirit, for theirs is the Kingdom of Heaven.' There are good, worthy people everywhere. Have faith. I do." He'd kissed her on both creased, dry cheeks and, as his six brothers and sisters gathered around, he'd gone off to bed without a twinge of remorse, eager to leave the next morning while everyone was still asleep.

And now, barely nine hours later, he was standing awestruck at the top of the mountain. He slowly turned a full three hundred and sixty degrees, intoxicated by the breathtaking panorama and the illusion he was standing alone at the top of the world.

A narrow dirt path lay straight ahead up a small incline, past a road on the left that led to the sleeping town. The cemetery could be plainly seen a few meters ahead on the right. His pulse quickened as what remained of the Church of Saint Maria Magdalena, rebuilt in the twelfth century on the footprint of one erected in the eighth century, came into view.

He stood still at the vestige of the entrance, imagining how beautiful it must have been, and how magnificent it could be, would be, again. He bowed his head. "It's a daunting task, Lord, but you sent the right man. I may not be the most pious, but I am as capable and imaginative as any. With your help I will find a way," he whispered.

"The town will be grateful." The words traveling through the murky gloom were not much more than a sigh, and Saunière's first thought was that he'd created the answer he wanted out of the whoosh of a startled nesting bird flying away through the open roof.

And then she walked toward him.

2

AMSTERDAM

JULY 22, 2012

GISELLE SLID ONTO the only vacant barstool and ordered a chardonnay. The hotel's cocktail lounge was just the sort of cozy hideaway she loved; its worn timbers and exposed old brick announced its vintage as unapologetically as a dignified dowager. The bartender brought her wine quickly, and she smiled and lifted her glass in a silent toast. *Here's to the art of aging gracefully*, she thought.

The discreet buzz in the background was undoubtedly coming from colleagues who, like her, had found their way here on the eve of the Annual Conference of International Biblical Scholars. The program seemed particularly dry this year, but even in the best of years she wouldn't have described the meeting as exciting. Well, maybe last year qualified.

"My dear Dr. Gélis, beautiful as ever," a familiar voice oozed before kissing her on each cheek and insinuating himself into the space a hairsbreadth from her knee. She'd seen Charles, a fellow faculty member from Toulouse, yesterday morning. Two other regular attendees, both Italian, quickly joined them, giving Charles the perfect excuse to squeeze in even more and press his thigh firmly against the length of her bare leg. *Gross.* She closed her eyes for a moment, and tried to distract herself by listening to the music playing softly in the background; it was an old American World War II song, one of her father's favorites. Tears came so quickly she wasn't sure she'd be able to hold them back, but she gave her head a quick shake, took a deep breath, willed her eyes open and swiveled enough to get a look at the room behind her.

A man was standing motionless at the threshold of the two-foot thick doorway that kept the lounge sequestered from the twenty-first century. The figure was an indistinguishable shadow in the dim light, but he obviously recognized her, and without a moment's hesitation came striding across the room.

"Excuse me, gentlemen," he said firmly, as he reached between the two Italians and offered her his large, tanned hand.

The mischief twinkling in his eyes was an invitation to play along, and she put her hand in his, startled that his touch would make her heart race. *David...I didn't expect to see you,* she thought, wondering if her momentary lack of composure was as obvious as it felt.

"Sorry I kept you waiting," he said, sounding remarkably sincere.

"I was early." The perfect response came out of her mouth before the thought was fully formed.

He gave her a quick conspiratorial wink before turning to face the men. "Thanks for keeping Giselle company until I got here, but we have dinner reservations elsewhere and we've got to run. You know what sticklers the Dutch are about being prompt."

She was ready and willing. "Perhaps I'll see you at one of the meetings, Charles, or when we get back home," Giselle murmured softly to the thin-lipped, mustached man who had back-combed several long, brown strands of hair over his otherwise shiny scalp. Her hand remained in David's, making her intentions clear.

Charles took one small step to the left, leaving barely enough space for her to squeeze by, ensuring she'd have to press her body tightly against his in the process. She shook it off with a little shiver, slung her bag over her shoulder and, as elegantly as a runway model, walked briskly through the brick archways and marched out of the building with David beside her.

Barely twenty feet down the herringbone brick road, she slowed her pace and glanced over her shoulder. Following her gaze, David turned also; Charles was standing in the restaurant doorway, fists clenched, mustache twitching like rat whiskers at the scent of cheese, as the overhead entry light illuminated his face, now blotchy and purple with rage.

"Just keep walking," David whispered, as they turned the corner and continued side by side without another word, not stopping until they reached the metal guardrail along the Singel Canal.

She turned to him, making no attempt to hide her amusement. "My, my Dr. Rettig," she said playfully, "I didn't know you did hostage extractions on the side."

"Considering it was my first attempt, I thought it went very well," David replied. "By the way, your friend Charles has the makings of a first-class pervert—I'm relieved you can make light of it."

"Oh, he's mostly bark, although there are times, like tonight, it feels like a bite. He likes to think of himself as someone special—to me— probably because his family and mine go back centuries in the Languedoc. Anyway, it was totally my fault. I knew he'd be there, and I was prepared to be social, but then an old song started playing and totally changed my mood."

"Music can do that," he said. "What was it?"

"Oh, one of those poignant love songs written just before the war; you probably wouldn't know it."

"Try me."

" 'I'll be seeing you…' " Just saying the words brought tears.

" 'In all the old familiar places,' " he said, pulling a neatly folded white cloth handkerchief out of his pants pocket and offering it to her. "Those lyrics are meant to pull at your heartstrings, especially if you've lost someone you love."

"I guess I shouldn't be surprised to find an old soul in an archeologist's body," she said, blotting her eyes. "Thanks."

She handed him the handkerchief and brushed a wayward strand of gleaming, copper hair over her shoulder. Enough, she decided; enough of this melancholy. Her father would've been the first to tell her to let it go. "So, what brings you back to this year's meeting? I distinctly remember you saying that being an archeologist among biblical scholars made you feel like a Roman soldier trying to infiltrate the ranks of the apostles."

His grin was infectious, charming, and hard to resist. *Careful,* she told herself, as she returned his smile, *remember he lives in Israel, two thousand miles from Toulouse, and even if he knows the words to an old song, his world is diametrically opposed to yours.*

"I'm surprised you remember that, but yes, that's exactly what I said to Charles at the wine-and-cheese party after we had a little…um, let's call it dispute; I offered a premise I thought would be interesting to discuss, and he slapped me away like a pesky fly."

"That's a little dramatic," she said, laughing. "I think you proposed that biblical scholars should embrace archaeological discoveries even when they don't support biblical narrative, and Charles adamantly disagreed."

"Exactly. And you shocked me by coming to my defense. It was the highlight of the entire conference, and I haven't been able to stop thinking about you since. Really. That's why I'm here."

"I assume that's a boldfaced exaggeration, but I'll take it as a compliment anyway," she said. "As to my defense of you, my father was a biblical historian and he had lots of heated arguments about the same issue. But I was impressed that an archaeologist would take the time and trouble to educate himself on the hot topics in our little esoteric universe."

"Thanks, that's good to hear. I wish you'd been impressed enough to accept my dinner invitation. I was destroyed."

"Mon Dieu, that's laying it on a little thick!" No one had pursued her with such single-minded focus in a long, long time, but then again, she rarely ventured beyond the confines of her narrow, insulated world. It would have been easy to dismiss the hyperbole, except for something in his voice, something that didn't sound flip. "I didn't think it would matter to you. If it did, if I hurt your feelings, I apologize. It was a"—her voice trailed off and she looked away briefly, searching for a bland phrase—"a difficult time for me."

"I'm sorry to hear that. I hope things have gotten easier, and the future looks brighter."

"For the most part. The only cloud on the horizon is a promise I made to look into an old family tragedy, and I'm sort of dreading it. "

The startled look on David's face made her add, "I think your flare for the dramatic must be contagious. I don't know why I mentioned it. It has nothing to do with you."

Dusk had given way to a velvety navy sky, and the streetlights bouncing along the surface of the inky water created a cinematic special effects background. David stood next to her, staring at it as though it were a performance art piece that required his total focus. A canal boat full of passengers quietly floated by, gaily festooned like a Christmas tree.

After an uncomfortable minute, he broke the silence. "Well, assuming you find persistence a positive quality, I'd like to ask again. Please join me for dinner tonight."

She hesitated. "Don't take this personally, but I think I'll go back to my room and call room service. I do admire persistence, and I'm in a much better place, as you Americans say, than I was last year, or even twenty minutes ago—but that whole episode in the bar must have upset me more than I realized. I don't think I'd be very good company, and I hate disappointing people."

David put his hand over his heart, "Honestly," he said, "the only way you could disappoint me is if you refuse to let me take you to dinner tonight. In fact, I'd be more than disappointed; I'd be really hurt. And bewildered."

She lowered her gaze for a moment. Then she lifted her head and looked directly into his clear, blue eyes; the gold flecks in hers were smoldering. "I wouldn't like that," she said. "I'm not a tease, and I'm not cruel."

"I would've guessed that," David said, adding, "which is why I expect you to give me a chance. As for me, my mother always said I play well with others; I have all my hair—and most folks think I'm a pretty nice guy."

"You forgot to mention persuasive," she said, as her resolve melted away. "No expectations?"

He quickly nodded in agreement. "None. Scout's honor." He held up two fingers, making the pledge.

"Then I'd be happy to join you, but," she paused, before delivering the punch line, "we probably can't have dinner in the hotel restaurant."

As they both began to laugh, he said, "Not unless you want to see a lynching. Fortunately, when I checked in, the concierge mentioned a little place called Seasons. It's supposed to have really good food, but it's about a fifteen-minute walk…" He looked down, but it was too dark to see her feet. "If your shoes are comfortable enough for a long walk."

How clever of you, she thought. "I was a fool to turn down a dinner invitation from a man who understands that not all shoes are meant for walking. As it turns out, all I have with me are comfortable shoes. Once a woman gets to a certain age—well, comfort trumps vanity. Lead the way."

"Maybe you could define a certain age for me, because unless you have a portrait in your attic—or your face cream actually does perform miracles—I don't think you qualify."

"Actually, I do believe in miracles, but not the kind promised by face creams." *Something about this man makes me want to confide in him*, she cautioned herself. Again. "I should've realized an archaeologist is never satisfied until he knows how old everything is, even people. The fact is I'm forty-five, but I'm the kind of woman who's cared more about being comfortable than fashionable my entire life."

"In your prime."

"If my mother was still alive, she'd say I withered on the vine waiting to be picked."

"Not a sentiment I share," he said quickly, "and maybe it's none of my business, but in the words of my favorite playwright, I suspect you need to 'scape the serpent's tongue.' Let's leave her behind and get to know each other better."

"You seem like a very insightful and determined man," she said.

"You have no idea," he replied, and reached for her hand.

3

AMSTERDAM

JULY 22, 2012

CYCLISTS WHIZZED BY as if pedestrians were no more than holograms, prompting David to put his arm around Giselle's shoulder and guide her out of harm's way. "This is a city that would benefit from sidewalks," he commented.

"Perhaps, but I should have stayed more alert, instead of focusing over there." Giselle gestured to the iconic houses that lined the canal. "When I was a girl I used to spend hours alone, drawing houses that all stood in a row, just like those. And I'd make up stories about the people who lived in them."

David nodded and took her hand again. "And I make up stories about the people who lived in the places I excavate. I knew you and I had something in common."

Minutes after reaching the restaurant they were seated at a tiny table for two in the rear. Giselle settled into her chair with a small sigh.

"It sounds like this meets with your approval," he said.

She nodded. "Earlier, when you said this restaurant had good food—which I admit is important—I immediately wondered about the ambience. That cocktail lounge was a jewel, and I would've been happy with just about anything they served me."

"Good to know," said David, "but I have to admit my priority is the meal."

"Well," she motioned to an enormous arrangement of fresh tulips dominating a baroque table along the wall, "I'm happy. Hopefully, you will be, too. Sometimes, when the world is kind, there's no need to strike a bargain or choose one thing over another, because everything is as it should be…if only for a little while. Do you know what I mean?"

"I do. That's how I would describe being here with you tonight," David said, and quickly added, "and, by the way, that's not a line. Shakespeare said, 'All the world's a stage, and all the men and women merely players,' but he didn't know me. I'm not a player."

She wagged her finger at him, laughing softly and said, "I don't think that's what he meant Dr. Rettig, but I'll take it on faith that it's true. Anyway, I like the wordplay." She paused and looked down briefly before meeting those blue eyes directly again. "You're something of a surprise."

"As are you. Not many non-native English speakers would use the term 'wordplay.' "

"That's probably true. And I'm guessing there aren't too many archaeologists who go around quoting Shakespeare."

"Full disclosure. I majored in English literature."

"And I spent the first seven years of my life in New York, and then returned for graduate school."

"Well, that explains it," he said, and signaled the waiter, who quickly brought the menus and a wine list. After placing their orders, David got a faraway look in his eye, and stopped speaking.

"A euro for your thoughts," she said. No matter how irrational it was, she couldn't help reading criticism into silence.

"Sorry." He smiled apologetically. "I didn't mean to ignore you. Sometimes I take threads and patches of random thoughts and weave them into a cautionary tale. I was thinking that it's great to have a chance to get to know you better, and then I started a prosecution of my good fortune. A therapist friend once told me it was my way of preparing for disappointment. He was probably right."

"Well, I did warn you."

"I don't mean you! Nothing about you is a disappointment," he said emphatically. "It's just that I started thinking about religious beliefs, and how they can come between people. I was hoping we're not those kinds of people."

"I'm a believer," she said simply. "And I seem to remember that you're a professed doubter." She held out her hands as if to say the conclusion was self-evident. "Religion is part of the fabric of my life. I teach full time at the Institut Catholique de Toulouse, a world away from Israel and the carbon-dated olive pits you spoke about last year. It's not exciting or innovative, but it suits me—you know, work as a distraction from life."

"It's true that my work relies on verifying things," he said slowly, sighing and pausing as if he was searching for the words he wanted, "but, like you, I suspect there's a lot we can't make sense of, a lot that can't be explained…" David's voice trailed off.

She nodded in agreement. The thought crossed her mind that he might be telling her what he thought she wanted to hear, but there was no point in challenging him. It wouldn't make any difference in the scheme of things.

"I agree," she said, "I believe in lots of things that can't be explained, or proved, and I don't think that makes them any less true, or meaningful. If you asked my sister, she'd say I hide from life outside the Bible because my reality is"—she searched for the right word—"uninspired."

"Well, maybe you've been waiting for me to come along."

"I think I need to remind you, and I'm paraphrasing, pride goeth before a fall. On the other hand, you're partially right; I have been waiting for something. I can't tell you what that is, but I sincerely doubt you and I will ever have a meeting of the minds."

"Don't be so quick to rule that out. I haven't. You believe in miracles and I believe in kismet. Same church, different pew, so to speak." He grinned at her as though the logic of his statement was unassailable.

"You'd make a good politician," she said, smiling into his eyes. "You're charming in spite of being overconfident, and I am charmed."

"So, I have to ask about Charles," David said. "You implied he feels entitled to some special place in your life. Why?"

"Ah, Charles." The question was totally irrelevant. "He's been sweet on me for years and expects to be the one left standing when the music stops. Rest assured, that will never happen. He's the kind of man who despises that which he envies."

"And that would be me."

"Well, you did spirit me away from right under his nose."

"True."

"But you're in good company. My father—I don't think I mentioned he died two years ago—used to come to these meetings with me, and Charles despised him as well, though he tried to hide it. But it was reciprocal. My father used to tell me Charles had a dark soul and dead eyes."

"I'm sorry to hear you lost your father, but at least you have a sister," David said softly.

"True, to a degree. We're close, but not geographically. She lives in New York with her husband and her two little ones. I love them dearly, but long-distance relationships aren't..." She stopped.

"Aren't what?"

"Well, I don't think they work. You can't depend on someone who lives an ocean away, even with the best of intentions."

The waiter arrived and poured the wine. After twirling it around in the glass, David took a small sip, savoring the aroma with a dreamy look on his face.

"Here's to you," he said softly, holding his glass aloft and gazing into her eyes with unexpected tenderness, "and to what can only be understood by the human heart."

"A lovely, romantic sentiment," she responded gently, lightly touching the rim of her glass to his and hoping she didn't sound too harsh, "but even what the heart understands has to be tempered by reason."

"Take it from a card-carrying romantic," he said, "the brain is fueled by reason, but the heart is powered by magic, and we all need a little magic in our lives."

He reached over, covered the hand she had resting on the table with his, and began to gently stroke her wrist with his thumb.

Giselle almost gasped out loud; if the surge of electricity she felt at his touch had sent actual sparks flying across the table, she wouldn't have been a bit surprised. "That's quite a statement," she mumbled, flustered at the cascade of unanticipated excitement coursing through her body.

When dinner was over, and the wine bottle was empty, they left the restaurant and slowly ambled along the quiet street holding hands, without saying a word. David's body next to hers heightened the effect of the wine, relighting a sexual flame Giselle had forgotten long ago. It was a delicious sensation, and she was grateful he wasn't the kind of man who was easily discouraged and pushed away. At Wolvenstaat, he stopped walking and turned to face her.

For a blink, before she backed away from the edge, she wished she could let go and give herself over to the moment. "All in all, it's been an enchanted night," she responded huskily to the question in his eyes, "but I meant what I said about no entanglements. I can be forthright, but not impulsive or reckless. You've made me feel something I haven't felt in a long time, and I'm grateful, but we live thousands of miles apart and we're at a conference where it's hard enough to be taken seriously by some of these men. You know the apostles trashed Marie Madeleine's reputation even though she was one of them, and my colleagues are not so different. But that aside, we're on the same team."

"And I'm not."

She gazed down at her shoes, which had suddenly become the symbol of who she was and who she had always been; practical, predictable, and an inevitable disappointment to anyone who believed in magic. She looked back at him. "As I said before, you're a charming man, but as for you and me—it would be too complicated."

He nodded. "Just thought I'd let you know I'm not a giving-up-without-a-fight kind of guy. How about coffee during a break in the morning schedule, which will give you time to realize I'm quite a catch and you're crazy to reject me. No pressure. But just to remind you, you're the reason I came to Amsterdam."

She smiled at him. "Oh, you're good," she said, sighing, as the crescendo of desire slipped away. "I'll sleep on it."

4

RENNES-LE-CHÂTEAU

OCTOBER 1885

HER NAME WAS Marie.

"I'm named for Saint Marie-Madeleine," she explained with obvious pride shining in her dark eyes, "and you, Abbé, will be living at our house, right on top of me." She giggled and looked down at the ground. "In the attic," she added.

Rays of summer sunlight reflected by her glossy black hair created a blue glow reminiscent of raven feathers. She couldn't be more than sixteen, he thought, a girl practicing being a woman.

"And you must be Marie Dénarnaud." He'd been startled but recovered his composure immediately and wanted to be absolutely certain she couldn't misunderstand or feel encouraged. No laughing along, no approval—or disapproval—not even an acknowledgment of her attempt at what he assumed was meant to be flirtatious. "I'm pleased to meet you. Perhaps you'd be kind enough to show me the way to your home."

"It would be my pleasure. I set out at cock's crow because I wanted to be the first person you met in Rennes-le-Château." The womanly intensity in Marie's eyes was disconcerting. "Some say I'm a little brazen, but really it's just that I know what I want, and I speak my mind."

Saunière nodded. He was all too familiar with those qualities. "I look forward to hearing your thoughts after my sermon on Sunday."

The fire left Marie's eyes and she looked like a girl again. A crestfallen one. "I'm being sent down mountain to live with grand-maman. She's old and I'm the only granddaughter. I don't mind; in fact, I was excited to go, but I wish I could stay to hear you preach." She stopped speaking, and a small smile played around the corner of her lips. "And I will, maybe not right away, but I won't be gone forever."

In the four months since, Saunière had established himself like a fast-growing willow tree, sending down deep roots and claiming the terrain as his own. Marie hadn't returned, and he rarely, if ever, gave her a thought. Madame Dénarnaud treated him like royalty, and most of the parishioners went out of their way to let him know he was appreciated and admired. Intent on returning their love, his sermons became increasingly passionate and inspiring. Without an office or presbytery, he encouraged parishioners with something to discuss to join him in a glass of wine at the Dénarnaud's kitchen table, which is where Augie found him.

"Pardon me for disturbing you, Father, but I had to tell you that my uncle from Coustaussa has come up the mountain so he can be here to celebrate Mass with us on Sunday."

"Well then, Augie, I'll be sure to make the sermon something special." The boy's face lit up, and Saunière laughed, adding dryly, "I wouldn't want to let you down." He pointed to a plate of freshly baked cookies that had been left for him on the table. "Have a cookie."

Before taking a bite of his cookie, Augie dramatically clapped his hand over his heart. "You never let me down, Father, not me or anyone. Uncle Louis wants to hear you preach about the election. Pardon me for saying, but he says listening to Father Gélis is like taking a sleeping powder; Father Gélis recites the Mass, but that's it. He's old and cranky, and he never speaks about books, or art, or politics. Just sticks to scripture, even though everyone knows he reads those other books himself. He has a library, but he doesn't like anyone but him to touch anything in it. Maman tried to explain what you told us about the government, how they're interfering with the Church, but Uncle Louis didn't understand what she was saying, so he came to hear it direct from you. I told him clear; it's important to vote for the Royalists, and he doesn't even know who they are! Can you believe it?"

The squeaky adolescent voice held more than a touch of smugness, sending an immediate surge of pride through Saunière. *You're arrogant*, he told himself, trying to find a shred of contrition but coming up empty. *But Augie has a right to sound superior, and I have a right to say what I think. Sometimes breaking the rules is justified, and this is one of those times.*

There was nothing complicated or confusing in what the government's minister of religion expected from parish priests like him. He was required to follow clearly defined policies and expected to abide by them; yet, despite three letters of reprimand, he simply couldn't bring himself to comply. He said daily Mass, he heard weekly confession, taught a catechism class, baptized the occasional baby, and eulogized at funerals just as he was supposed to, but he chafed at being told to confine himself to those activities when he saw it as his obligation, his unique purpose, to bring the complexities of the larger world to Rennes-le-Château. If he didn't enrich the minds and spirits of his flock with the ideas of Dumas, Rimbaud, and Hugo, if he didn't share the brilliance of Manet, Degas, and Cézanne, who would?

"Well, Augie, my boy, I see you've been paying attention."

"Of course, Father." The boy looked genuinely horrified. "Maman says if we don't drink in every word, it would be a sin. Jesus sent you, and we have to make sure He knows we're grateful."

"You're a good, smart boy. Please tell your uncle he's always welcome here." They sat silently for a few minutes before Saunière decided to add, "you know, Father Gélis is my friend." He waited for the boy to nod, before continuing, "and I know for a fact he means well; the truth is, he follows the rules better than I do."

"No one in our village cares if you break the rules, Father. Oh, I almost forgot…" Augie pulled two letters out of his pants pocket. "Sorry they're a little crumpled, hope it's good news."

Not likely, Saunière thought, watching the boy head out the door. Putting the letters in his cassock pocket, he climbed up to the attic room, where he could open his mail in privacy. Using his treasured silver letter opener, an ordination gift from his mother, he slit open the first envelope, bearing the Church insignia. The letter was brief and unequivocal. Because of his "unrepentant defiance," he was being relieved of his duties and would spend a little time at the seminary, *more like a correctional facility,* he thought, before being reassigned to teach there—under supervision.

He sat perfectly still on the edge of his narrow bed, filled with fury, mentally damning meddling bureaucrats who understood nothing of human needs or spiritual sustenance, and cared less. *Narrow-minded, inflexible, dogmatic, rigid charlatans. Minister of religion, hah. Jesus must have been thinking of men like you when he said man-made rules learned by rote only give lip service to honoring Him while their hearts are far away. My heart is here, and I am doing right by the souls entrusted to me.*

He'd go; he had no choice. *But I'll find a way to come back,* he promised the humble room, before slitting open the second letter. It was written on fine linen paper emblazoned with the gold crest of the Countess de Chambord.

All his clenched muscles began to relax as he read and reread the message from the Countess. *The Lord taketh away and the Lord giveth,* he thought with amusement.

5

RENNES-LE-CHÂTEAU

JULY 1887

TWO LONG, TEDIOUS, mind-numbing years. And now, thanks to the Countess de Chambord, he was returning with the financial means to start rebuilding the church. Augie, who had probably been waiting with his donkey cart since dawn, was a small figure in the distance, his welcoming committee. *If I were a drummer boy strutting down the road in advance of a king's carriage, all decked out in red velvet and a plumed hat, I don't think Augie would be more excited.* The Bishop had assigned a substitute to recite Mass, but the village had remained loyal and petitioned for his return. Augie's mother had led the initiative, believing that her prideful bragging—she knew it was a deadly sin—was responsible for the entire village being penalized. He was returning as a hero, and he loved it.

Without bothering to address the perpetually sour coachman, he shouted a greeting to Augie and waved enthusiastically with both hands. No doubt his triumphant return irritated the driver but scowling petty-mindedness wasn't going to suck the pleasure out of this joyous moment.

"Beautiful morning," Saunière announced exuberantly, addressing the coachman. "I know you're not one to traffic in rumors"—he couldn't resist the sarcasm—"so I want you to hear the facts directly from me. I chose to return to Rennes-le-Château, and I'm here with the Bishop's blessing. As to the idle gossip that the Countess de Chambord has given me a gift of three hundred francs, well, I have to admit, it's true." The wicked glimmer in his eyes was meant to offer just enough innuendo to ignite the coachman's most voyeuristic fantasies. "Tell your sister in Le Clat the Church of Saint Maria Magdalena will be the envy of the Languedoc when I get through with it, and I'll be happy to welcome her—and you, of course, when it's complete."

The driver's mumbled response was lost over Augie's shouts and hoots as the carriage pulled up to let the priest climb off.

"I think you've grown a foot," Saunière said to the skinny boy. "Now you've got to put some meat on those bones."

"Tell Maman. She'll do whatever you say, now you're back." Augie loaded all the priest's belongings into the back of the cart and indicated that Saunière should sit in the driver's seat.

"I think I'll walk with you. I haven't been getting enough exercise." He patted his flat abdomen. "You know I like to stay fit."

"I know, Father." He cleared his throat. "Everyone says that royal lady really likes you."

"She does, Augie. And she's been very generous."

"It's like Maman says: The Lord made you handsome and smart for a reason."

"Well, if that's true, Rennes-le-Château is the reason." The priest stopped, filling his lungs with the sweet scent of lavender and pine, as if this would obliterate the years of stale classrooms and smoke. "Breathe deeply, Augie, my boy. There's no other place on earth that smells like this. It's a gift from Jesus."

"If you say so, Father. Everyone is waiting for you at the Dénarnaud's. They planned a little celebration to welcome you home. Except for Marie. She was here for a while, but she's off to Toulouse to learn a trade from Madame's sister. And if you think I grew a lot, wait till you see her. Anyway, my Maman baked for two whole days."

"I'm touched and honored, Augie, but it will have to wait. When we get to the top, take my things to the Dénarnaud's and tell everyone to come back at Vespers. I want to go to the church and be alone for a little while. It's a day to give thanks."

Augie nodded and Saunière continued to walk in silence, pleased that the boy was following his lead and had enough self-control to keep additional questions for another time.

Once at the summit, Saunière continued into the deserted remnants of the church, stopping at the center of the ancient apse. He stared up through what was left of the roof to the brilliant blue sky beyond, marveling at the series of events that had orchestrated this unique, perfect piece of providence. This church would be a love song—his love song—to Marie-Madeleine; the image of what it would be again flooded his imagination, and he was filled with gratitude that, among all men, he would be the one to make it happen. His life would be whatever he could make of it.

He crossed himself and walked outside, climbing over little mounds of loose pebbles and through the underbrush toward the knuckle of the mountain a few hundred feet behind the church site. His heart soared with pride of ownership at the scene around him. The smoky mountain peaks fanning out across the horizon, the forested slopes and the verdant valley below were part of his personal estate.

"Thank you," he said simply, before kneeling down, crossing himself again and reciting some lines from one of his favorites psalms. "I will give thanks to the Lord, with my whole heart, in the company of the righteous and in the congregation. Great are the works of the Lord; studied by all who delight in them. His work is full of splendor and majesty…"

After the last line floated out on the warm summer breeze over the mountain's edge, he stood, carefully brushed off his cassock, and started down the dusty path toward the village. As a seminarian, it had been impossible for him to believe he could live the life he dreamed, utilizing his talents and intellect while in the harness of the priesthood. But he'd been wrong. Today, with the generous support of the Countess and Bishop, God's logic was revealed. He'd done penance during his time away, and he'd been a model of decorum. But Augie was right, when the Lord gives you gifts, like intelligence, or charm, or good looks, it's a sin to waste them, and that wasn't among the sins he was planning to commit.

6

AMSTERDAM

JULY 25, 2012

GISELLE REACHED OVER and slid her finger across the bottom of her phone to silence the buzzing alarm but made no effort to move any other part of her body. She had allowed herself enough time for a quick run along the canal before showering, dressing, and getting ready for a day packed with meetings, but she was tempted to stay exactly where she was, engulfed by the fluffy down pillows. To do what, daydream? She had only known David three days, and she was already contemplating a change in her organized routine. Not good. Without vacillating another minute, she threw her legs over the side of the bed, stretched her arms toward the ceiling and, picking up a small elastic band, tied her hair back at the nape of her neck.

Running and daydreaming aren't mutually exclusive; sometimes it's not either/or, and having a smart, sensitive, sexy man in my life is certainly the stuff of daydreams, she thought, startled that the inner voice of truth had given David the triple S stamp. It was Simone's label, and Matthew had been the only one to ever earn it. And now there was David. After three nights of dinners and conversation, of him stroking her wrist and smiling seductively, sending him back to Israel without planning to see him ever again seemed ridiculous. And unnecessary.

They were meeting up later in the morning when his small group seminar took a coffee break, and she was far more excited by that than the panel she was planning to attend. It felt normal. After pulling on her running clothes and tying her sneakers, she was just about out the door when she stopped abruptly and made a quick detour to put on a little lip gloss, laughing at herself as she did. *Vanity, vanity.* She could hear her sister cheering.

It was common for attendees at the first meeting of the morning to arrive carrying disposable cups filled with coffee, sipping quietly while they waited for the caffeine to ease them into full attention. This morning, however, there was an unusual and palpable buzz in the room, clearly not generated by the presenters, who easily could have filled in for eulogizers at a state funeral.

"Have you noticed, there's a lot of whispering going on," David said sotto voce into Giselle's ear as they stood in line for a second cup of coffee during the break. "There's a lot more excitement in the air than I remember from last year, but I'm obviously not in the loop. Have you heard anything?"

Her eyes were dancing as she turned to face him. "Actually, when I was in the ladies' room just now, I heard the most astounding little tidbit. I bumped into someone I know from New York who told me that Professor Karen King of Harvard Divinity School was given a papyrus fragment that refers to the wife of Jesus. You may not know of her—Dr. King, that is—but she's an unimpeachable scholar and an expert on the history of early Christianity. She's written several books, including a very interesting one about Marie-Madeleine. She thinks there's a compelling case to be made for women to be accepted into leadership roles in the Church. This new fragment found its way to the right person."

"Wow! That'll certainly shake up a lot of people. Dr. King's name is vaguely familiar to me, but I don't know her work. Of course, I'm familiar with the idea that Jesus was married; that's been swirling around a long time, and some very smart people believe that the ossuaries discovered at Talpiot Tomb confirm it, although plenty of others disagree. Biblical scholars—present company included, no doubt—are a tough audience."

Giselle nodded. She obviously understood the reference but didn't offer her opinion. The tomb had been unearthed in 1994 and was found to contain ten sets of bones. One of the ossuaries had been inscribed *Yeshua bar Yehosef*, or *Jesus, son of Joseph*, while another was marked *Judah, son of Jesus*. Several others displayed names known to be male relatives of Jesus; connecting the dots was irresistible for some, but this was not a place she and David would have a meeting of the minds.

"Well," Giselle said, "you're not the first person I've met who finds the Talpiot Tombs intriguing, but from my perspective they're inferential at best. This papyrus is another thing entirely. Dr. King is about as highly regarded as you can get, and she wouldn't be planning to present her findings if she wasn't convinced the fragment was authentic and meaningful."

Although he was trying to pay attention, David was having a hard time staying engaged with the conversation. Giselle's legs were bare beneath her dark, knee-length skirt, and her hair was severely pulled back and pinned up into a French knot, although some wispy cinnamon-colored tendrils had escaped. *That silky white shirt makes her look like a Raphael Madonna,* David thought, *or a professional woman posing for a glossy magazine ad—a knockout, either way.* Tailored, buttoned-up women didn't usually appeal to him, but this strictly business side of her was a total turn-on.

"Have you heard where the findings will be presented?" he asked, forcing himself to focus on the conversation.

"Yes, at the International Congress of Coptic Studies in Rome this September."

"So I assume it's written in Coptic," he joked. He sounded inane. "Not one of my languages. What about you?"

"I hope the Israelis appreciate your keen powers of observation and astute conclusions, Dr. Rettig. Yes, it's written in Coptic, which is one of my languages, along with Aramaic, Hebrew, German, English, and French, of course." She took a few steps back and looked at him. "You seem distracted. Did you hear me…boasting?"

"Um, of course." The longer he stood next to her, the more her physical presence, even her fragrance, diverted his mind from Dr. King and the fragment. They had succeeded in keeping a professional distance and demeanor during the past three days, but it was difficult; the electricity between them was enough to power a small city. *Absurd,* he thought, *after all these years when I could take it or leave it, to feel so excited about a woman I barely know.*

Making a conscious effort, he put the distracting thoughts aside. "There'll be controversy no matter how solid Dr. King's evidence is, that's for sure. But as far as I'm concerned, a married Jesus would make him more believable as a man of his culture at that time. He was a nice Jewish boy, so it makes sense that he would've taken a wife, or that a suitable marriage would've been arranged for him. That's what they did in those days, and the Orthodox still do. But my team isn't playing. I'm a fallen Methodist and I have no religious stake in the story. How will you feel if it proves to be true?"

"Well, it's certainly not what the sisters taught me at Collège Stanislas de Paris," Giselle said. "Sister Jeanne-Marie would be outraged if she ever heard about this." She looked up at David, and seeing the question in his eyes, she added, "It's one of the best private schools in Paris, but very, very conservative, Catholic and traditional, at least when it's not rocked by scandal. It's where I went to school when we moved to Paris. But to answer your question, I'm prepared to keep an open, but critical, mind."

"Somehow, I don't think the Holy See will be quite as open-minded as you, my scholarly companion."

"I can't even imagine. It would contradict what the Gospels imply, and most Catholics—although not all—love the story just the way it's come to be told. I suspect the average churchgoer doesn't realize there were other Gospels—namely the Gospels of Mary, Philip, Thomas, and Pistis Sophia—excluded from the New Testament. Still, His teachings are the same, married or not."

Noting that people were beginning to drift back into meeting rooms, David looked at his watch. "See you in the lobby at seven," he said discreetly, as he turned to leave for an afternoon at the Rijksmuseum.

"*Parfait*," she said over her shoulder, and walked toward the elevator bank.

7

AMSTERDAM

JULY 25, 2012

AS SOON AS David saw Giselle step off the elevator into the lobby he turned and headed for the exit. She followed at a leisurely pace, nodding pleasantly to colleagues as she walked by, but feeling like Eve chasing forbidden fruit. *You are seriously disturbed; having dinner together is a secret, but all secrets don't have to be about something forbidden,* she chided herself, *even if it is delicious.* After a phone consultation with her sister, she'd decided to brush her hair out and allow it to cascade loosely over her mother's St. Laurent silk blouse. There had been a time she believed a woman over forty should either cut her hair short or wear it pinned up. Now that she was there, the idea seemed out of date and more than vaguely anti-feminist.

Exchanging a silent nod, they started walking over the herringbone-patterned brick, quietly chatting as colleagues would. A casual passerby taking note would have described them as innocent friends at best, but creating that fictional impression unwittingly heightened the voltage between them.

"In case you think I didn't notice, you look stunning tonight," David murmured evenly, without looking at her directly.

Giselle smiled. "I suspect you notice pretty much everything," she said. "But thanks. It's always nice to hear. And thanks for making all the dinner arrangements. As you know by now, if it weren't for you I probably would have had every meal in the hotel. My sense of direction is terrible."

"So wandering in the desert probably wouldn't appeal to you."

"Actually, I love wandering around, but that's when I have no particular destination in mind and getting lost is part of the plan. Right now, I'm content to let you lead the way, as you've done every night, and be sure we'll get where we're going."

"Walking in this city is like wandering into an elaborate video game where we need to avoid all the obstacles in our path," David said as a group of cyclists flew by at an alarming speed. "It's got the makings of a sci-fi adventure."

"Yes, it does," she said, "and how does it end?"

"No spoiler alerts from me. I think we'll need to collaborate on the ending."

It would be their last dinner together in Amsterdam, and David had spent a lot of time finding what he hoped would be the perfect spot for cocktails.

After strolling along on Keizersgracht for several blocks, he stopped in front of their unimposing destination, The Hotel Toren.

"The reviews said it was discreet, charming, and private," David whispered, as they climbed three steps to the entrance of an old row house, flanked by two large topiary trees.

"Private?"

"Off the beaten track. Hopefully, no one from the meetings had the same idea."

Nineteenth-century Netherlands greeted them on the other side of the door. There was no real lobby to speak of, only a narrow hallway lined with Persian carpets leading to a short flight of stairs. On the left was the entrance to a postage stamp-size room and registration desk, behind which a couple of friendly young faces were waiting to be of service. The bar and spacious but cozy little cocktail lounge was visible immediately on the right, looking as if it had been that way for hundreds of years, only better.

There were plump, down-filled velvet-covered bergères and love seats pulled up to small tables, each far enough away from other groupings to ensure conversation did not travel. The flocked burgundy-and-fuchsia wall covering muffled any sound and hit just the right note between bordello and Victorian boudoir. Except for one other couple seated near the extravagantly draped windows and the bartender, a discreet distance at the far end of the connecting parlor, the room was empty.

"A place created for seduction," Giselle murmured as she sank into a small burgundy-red settee nestled against the wall. "It's wonderful, really wonderful; it makes my heart sing. You're certainly a master when it comes to discovering hidden treasures."

"I was motivated," David said, enormously pleased, as he sat down across from her and took her soft hand in his large, calloused one. "I wanted to see your face look exactly as it does right now. Glowing with pleasure."

"You know, part of me loves being pursued." His touch was sending bolts of excitement through her again. "But I know how painful it is when it comes to an end."

He brought her hand to his lips and kissed it lightly. "Charles Dickens said, 'the pain of parting is nothing to the joy of meeting again.' Parting doesn't have to be the end. There are probably lots of things that could come between us, but why not take a chance and see what happens? These four days have felt like a fairy tale; maybe it has a happy ending."

The waiter approached discreetly. Giselle withdrew her hand and the sexual tension of the moment evaporated as they placed their drink orders and waited for him to return with a vodka tonic and apple martini.

David raised his glass and said, "To putting aside the past, and imagining a future."

"I'm not there yet," she said, "but it's tempting. How about a toast to believing in fairy tales?"

"You are an extraordinary woman." He tapped her glass and made no attempt to hide the desire in his eyes. "To fairy tales."

"You know, I never thought of Amsterdam as a romantic city, and maybe it's because of you, but...I've fallen under its spell," she said. "The buildings look like chorus girls, all lined up, leaning against each other and admiring their reflections in the canals; of course, it's sort of straitlaced compared to Paris. I know Amsterdam has a reputation as a little risqué, but you'd never find bawdy Parisian streetwalkers neatly assembled in a red-light district. And the canals—well, they're not the Seine." She sighed and held out her hands to indicate any description would be inadequate. "The Seine is magic. Something I know you understand."

"I do, and I'd love to soak in that magic with you one day, but this city isn't lacking in romance."

"I suppose people can bring romance to any city, but everyone knows Paris loves lovers," she said, with a far-off dreamy expression.

"Fred Astaire sings that to Cyd Charisse in an old movie called *Silk Stockings*. 'Paris loves lovers, for lovers know that love is everything,' " he said quickly, laughing at the shocked expression on her face.

"My goodness! I can't believe you know that," she said, looking at him with a mixture of awe and respect. "The surprises keep coming, in a good way. I haven't thought about *Silk Stockings* in…I don't know how long. Even after four days, you don't seem the *Silk Stockings* type."

David closed his eyes for the flicker of a minute. "It's my mother's legacy. She loved musicals; we'd watch movies like *Silk Stockings*, *An American in Paris,* and *Singin' in the Rain* over and over, and we never got tired of them. When the first VHS players went on the market, my dad surprised her with one, and I think it was her most treasured possession. She cried the first time we all sat down together and watched *Brigadoon*. It was always about the romance, Gene Kelly singing, 'You were meant for me.' Unlikely couples finding each other and refusing to let any obstacle keep them apart. Love always triumphed—as it should."

"How lucky to have a mother like yours."

"Yes. No son was ever luckier. She's gone now, but she was afraid a big guy like me might easily turn out to be too tough, and she was determined to help me become comfortable with what she called my 'softer side.' She would've loved our story—two loners from different parts of the globe cross paths, and find they are drawn to each other in a way that seems too powerful and right to be mere coincidence.

She twirled her green drink around in the delicate glass. "Maybe it's the martini talking, or maybe it's your wily ways, but whatever it is, I feel unexpectedly happy and hopeful for the first time in a long time." *What was it about him?* Revealing herself to him had started to feel natural. "I don't understand it; what I feel doesn't make sense, really, and you put it exactly right the night we met. The brain tries to make sense of things, but sometimes that's just not possible. When I think about it, I realize I believe in lots of things I can't explain or quantify."

David turned to catch the eye of the bartender, extended two fingers, and said nothing until fresh drinks were delivered and they were alone again.

"Well, this skeptic is grateful you do," he said gently. "I'm always trying to reconstruct some indisputable reality that doesn't require a leap of faith to be accepted as true."

"But you've said you believe in magic and chemistry—and kismet."

"I know. And I do. It's a constant struggle for me to reconcile all those contradictions. What I can tell you is after we spoke last year, I knew I had to see you again. Why? Maybe because I know when I find something of value. Or it could be my mother's ghost telling me to trust my intuition. This"—he motioned to the space between them—"is a force field that shouldn't be ignored. So, tell me what your plans are, for next week, next month, next year—and if there's a way you can find some time to fit me in."

Giselle gave him a sad, apologetic little smile. "I'd like to, I really would, but I'm teaching a summer session as soon as I get back, and then I'm committed for the academic year. My only significant break will be at Christmas when I visit my sister in New York. And then, there's that promise I made to my father."

"You mean about the family tragedy?"

"Yes, but this doesn't seem like the right time to tell you about it. It's sort of macabre; certainly not a fairytale."

"I'll chance it," he said.

She sat up very straight and folded her hands together on the crisp white linen tablecloth. "My father's family goes back hundreds and hundreds of years in the Languedoc. There are Gélis relatives scattered around the whole region, and as Papa got older, and there was so much information on the internet, he became fascinated by them, particularly his great-uncle, my great-grandfather's brother, Abbé Antoine Gélis. As far as we know, he lived the life of a devoted priest, but he was murdered, bludgeoned to death in his presbytery in 1897. There were no obvious motives, and no one ever discovered why he was killed, or who did it. It haunted my father."

The articles she'd read had graphic descriptions of the body lying on the floor of his presbytery, arms folded over his chest the way the murderer posed him, white hair matted with blood, alone. She gave a little involuntary shiver.

David reached for her hand. "I'm sorry," he said, "I had no idea it would be this upsetting to talk about. You can tell me some other time. Or never."

"No, I'm fine," she said. "I just hate being reminded that people can be such savages. Anyway, the killer left a note near the body, scrawled on cigarette paper, that said 'Viva Angelina.' You probably know it means 'Long live the messenger' in Latin. My great-great-uncle wasn't a smoker, and it's obvious that whoever killed him was familiar with Latin."

"It's an awful story, and certainly not what I thought we'd be talking about, but I don't understand its relevance to us."

"Oh, of course not." She smiled and took a slow sip of her martini, wondering why mental burdens never seemed quite as heavy when you shared them with someone.

"This is the thing," she said. "Papa located a distant Gélis cousin and asked me to get in touch. I'm not sure what the point is, but I couldn't refuse."

"And you're related to this cousin via this murder victim?"

She nodded. Far from looking morose, David looked somewhat amused and relieved,

"My sweet, earnest, Dr. Gélis. I love murder mysteries, they have a certain sex appeal—and if I were thirty years younger I'd say it's hot. So, if you'd allow me, I'm ready to play Dr. Watson when you're ready for your family reunion at the end of the semester. What else do you know? Where did this murder most foul take place?"

"You are incorrigible," she said. "But to answer your question, in a little village called Coustaussa, in the Languedoc region of France, across the valley from Rennes-le-Château. Father Antoine had been Curé there for forty years, and was a close friend of Abbé Saunière, the priest of Rennes-le-Château. Do you know about him?"

David thought for a minute, then shook his head. "No, his name doesn't sound familiar."

"Well, that's a mystery in itself, but not for tonight. Am I correct in concluding that hearing about my murdered great-great-uncle acted as some kind of ghoulish aphrodisiac? The look on your face is unmistakable, in case you think you're being subtle. You're not a vampire or something like that, are you?"

"No, just a red-blooded American male in the company of a fascinating, complicated, beautiful woman who's flying off to France tomorrow while I fly south to the Holy Land."

Once again, he brought her hand to his lips and slowly kissed it. "There's a fine line between patience and passivity," he said, "and I want to be sure my attempt at restraint isn't mistaken for indifference."

She put her finger across his lips.

"I'm not very hungry," she said. This wasn't what she had planned, but it felt more right than anything she'd done in a long time. "My flight tomorrow night is at eight something, so I'm leaving for the airport right after the last meeting. Maybe I can stop in Paris after Christmas on my way back from New York, and we can spend some time together, or maybe by then we won't want to, but I'm willing to give this long-distance relationship a try. If I've learned nothing else in my four-plus decades, I know the future is unpredictable, despite the best of intentions. Hopefully, we'll have more, but at the very least we have tonight."

He rose from his chair, walked around the table and put his hands lightly on her shoulders. "If I have anything to do with it, tonight is definitely not all we'll have; it's the beginning of all that's to come. I've spent more than half my life looking for you and becoming the man you were waiting to find. Not to brag, but I'm very resourceful. We'll find a way."

She had no doubts as she rose to leave and looked around the room, memorizing the colors, the gleam of the mahogany armoire, the tufted pattern of the wallpaper, and the fragrance of lemon-scented furniture polish. A verse from Jeremiah 29 popped into her mind, validating her decision and making her smile, "*For I know the plans I have for you, said the Lord, plans that will not harm you, plans to offer you hope and a future.*"

Holding hands, they retraced their steps down the lamp-lit brick streets and over the canal bridges, back to their hotel.

8

RENNES-LE-CHÂTEAU

OCTOBER 1887

IT WAS ONLY during the fleeting golden light of dawn, before the distractions of everyday life had to be considered, before there were people to greet, before a response or a decision was required of him, that his thoughts were truly his own. That was the snippet of time Abbé Saunière treasured most—when his obligations and dreams existed together in harmony and a nascent melody of thought swelled into a symphony. Even today, with rubble around him, his church was the place that offered a contemplative refuge; it was here he could try to make sense of his life.

His entire perspective had changed in the past three months—could it be only three months—and he wasn't the same man who'd returned here in July with the funds to begin rebuilding the church. He hadn't thought of himself as naïve then, but his previous misgivings had now hardened into absolute skepticism and distrust of the Church hierarchy. *Lord, this is my October pledge*, he thought, *with your guidance I am resolved to use my own judgment as the final authority in all things.* He should never have doubted himself, and his belief that art, and music, and the beauty of the here and now, feed the soul. *And I never will again.*

The summer heat had been oppressive when he returned with the funds from Countess Chambord, but his unbridled enthusiasm had overcome any reluctance the workers had to get started and mix sweat into church foundation. Following advice he'd received from Bishop Billard, he'd begun the renovation by removing two pillars that supported the altar and needed to be replaced. The rotting wood had yielded without much effort, generating celebratory shouts of "hallelujah" from the workmen. It was common knowledge among the clergy that in centuries past, valuable documents were often concealed in the hollow space inside a pillar, so when he'd examined the pillars privately and found one there, rolled up and written in an obscure language, it hadn't come as a surprise.

"I assume it's been hidden in there for seven centuries," he'd told the Bishop when he took it to Carcassonne, "but I can't make out the language, not one word. I thought you might be able to read it."

"No, but it's intriguing." His Eminence held a magnifying glass, trying to make sense of the scrawl. "No doubt Antoine would be able to read it, but he's in Rome on that holiday he's been saving for all these years. Never mind. I suggest you take it to St. Sulpice."

"You mean travel to Paris? I've only just gotten back to Rennes-le-Château." It was a thrilling thought, almost too good to be true and totally unanticipated. Paris! The one time he'd been there, he'd been too young to walk the streets alone, or attend the opera, but he'd always dreamed of returning to the enchantment.

The Bishop had cleared his throat and put a hand on Saunière's shoulder. "This looks like it may be a genealogy, my boy. And someone, more than seven hundred years ago, thought it was important enough—or perhaps controversial enough—to make sure it wouldn't be easily found. Remember, the church altar hasn't been rebuilt since the Albigensian Crusade, when the Cathars were slaughtered like farm animals and war raged across the Languedoc. Thank Christ we live in more tolerant and enlightened times; the linguists at St. Sulpice will make sense of this."

The trip was quickly arranged and, barely two weeks after his triumphant return to Rennes-le-Château and the beginning of the church renovation, he'd taken the document, packed his satchel, and traveled to Paris, City of Light.

Now here he was, back in his modest, crumbling church, but the experience was imbedded in his soul, and had changed him forever.

As a boy he'd dreamed of studying architecture at the École des Beaux-Arts, sitting in a sidewalk café with intellectuals, sipping wine, arguing that

Voltaire was right, and a society should be based on reason rather than faith or Catholic doctrine. But the essence of living, breathing Paris had transported him far beyond the universe of his imagination. Strolling down any street, at any table where people were gathered, he overheard snatches of conversation—"we must question religious orthodoxy" or "the scientific method is the future of humanity"— making him wish he could pull up a chair and join the dialogue. And he was well aware that in spite of wearing the uniform of the Church, he still made sophisticated Parisian eyelashes flutter.

St. Sulpice had been his first stop. He'd handed his parcel over to a soft-spoken friar who politely informed him the translation would be a lengthy process. "Come back in about six weeks," he'd been told. "Perhaps we will have an answer for you then."

The City of Light had held out its arms and embraced him as if he were a long-lost lover, and he melted into the embrace. It was a city painted in rapturous color, a city that buzzed with excitement, where every avenue, every carriage that rolled by, every horse trotting proudly with a feather in its mane, flaunted elegance and the merits of beauty for its own sake. He'd spent several days in a rare books shop, pouring over a collection of exquisitely illustrated volumes of architecture; ultimately, he purchased a dozen, as well as gifts for several of his parishioners. Notre-Dame was grand beyond anything he could have imagined, prompting him to purchase good sketching paper and charcoal; he'd spent two entire days in a painstaking effort to reproduce details he thought could be incorporated in his lowly little church.

He'd made the grand tour, going from one church and basilica to the next, welcomed by colleagues, admiring all the sculpture and paintings on display and soaking up the nuances of classical versus neoclassical style. The medieval stained-glass windows of Sainte-Chapelle filled him with awe, as he knew they would, and he'd paid his respects at the relatively new and less impressive Église de la Madeleine, another church dedicated to Saint Marie-Madeleine. It was an exhausting, exhilarating, and altogether thrilling first week.

But that was before the piece-de-résistance. The opera. Even now, the memory of it was rapturous. The Théâtre National de l'Opéra had just moved to its newly constructed home, the grand Palais Garnier, where the Countess de Chambord had graciously offered her stage-level box and arranged for him to meet the soloists after the performance. He'd settled into the opulent, crimson velvet chair, cocooned in a magnificent structure beyond his conception, where people gathered solely for the pleasure of the experience. Every fiber of his being quivered as he waited for the curtain to rise, when the great soprano Emma Calvé would sing *Carmen*, a performance hailed as "bringing new passion and pathos to the role." Alone in the box, he'd leaned his arms on the gold-leafed balustrade, the only barrier separating his seat from the stage. Emma had noticed him immediately when she made her grand entrance in Act One, and it would have been impossible for him to be unaware that the fire flashing in her eyes was aimed directly into his.

As she accepted an armful of roses at her curtain call, she'd looked straight at him and smiled. Never in his life had he experienced such an immediate, visceral response.

He found his way backstage and was directed to her dressing room, crowded with the crème of Paris society. The moment he appeared in the doorway she subtly began to make her way toward him, stopping briefly to accept congratulations from well-wishers and laughing easily, but never taking her eyes off of him.

"Join me later tonight," she'd whispered, when she finally reached him and purposefully stood close enough for him to feel the heat of her body, her lips brushing his ear and her long black curls tickling his cheek. "A friend is giving a small, private soiree. Let me introduce you to the real Paris, Father."

Her fragrance had been intoxicating and he only considered resisting for a fleeting moment. The soiree that night had been a small, intimate gathering where Emma made it clear she was interested in more than introducing him to her friends. "Tomorrow night I rest my voice," she whispered, as the gathering was breaking up in the small hours of the morning. She slipped a small piece of paper into his hand, pressing her body against his shoulder so that he could easily feel the softness of her breast through his cassock. "Join me for a private dinner in my flat. Let's say eight o'clock?"

He was at every performance for the next five weeks, and in her bed every night. As the days went on, she suggested he move his few possessions from his room in the Ephrem Hotel, guesthouse of the Sacred Heart Basilica of Montmartre, to her flat. When they were alone there, waking together in the morning, he could almost imagine what it would have been like to live the life of an ordinary man. She wasn't the first woman to fall in love with him or find him irresistible, but she was the first—and only one—to beg him to leave the priesthood.

"Any man—any man who isn't a priest—would be a fool to walk away from you; you are everything any mortal man could want. You thrill me. You set me on fire. When I touch you, when I hear you moaning for me, I'm transported to another dimension. If I were free, I would never leave you, but my life is with the Church," he'd said gently. "It is my purpose, my calling, and I"—he stopped to kiss the tears rolling down her cheeks—"I don't belong in your world."

"But…" she'd said, "but…"

He put his finger across her lips. "Jesus didn't ask his disciples to be celibate, and it was well over a thousand years after his death that Pope Gregory VII issued a decree against marriage. I am a disciple of Christ, and I hold myself to being the sort of man he would have expected me to be. It must be obvious to you," he said, as she nodded at the question in his eyes, "that laws made by men, particularly those men impressed with their own power and politics—even popes—are of little interest to me. But I believe in Jesus, in his message, and his hopes for the human race. It is my calling."

"I love you," she'd said, her voice breaking.

"And I love you. You have given me enough joy to last a lifetime and there will always be a special place in my heart for you," he'd responded as he took her in his arms and felt her shiver as his bare skin made contact with her naked breasts. They made love again, and when their passion was spent, she curled up next to him and fell asleep in his arms.

Exactly six weeks after his first visit, he'd returned to St. Sulpice, and waited several hours before a young friar approached him and asked that he return the following day, when the bishop in charge could make time to speak to him. "Is the translation ready," he'd asked politely, "or do you need more time?" "I am not at liberty to discuss the matter," was the soft-spoken reply, "but I'm certain all your questions will be answered tomorrow."

The last night with Emma was bittersweet. She promised to visit him in Rennes-le-Château, and he promised to return to Paris. But he never did.

The Church of Saint-Sulpice, only slightly smaller than Notre-Dame, and therefore the second-largest church in Paris, was in the Sixth Arrondissement, an hour's walk from Emma's flat. Saunière arrived in time to hear the end of the daily organ recital and presented himself at noon in the anteroom of the bishop's office. Some urgent matter would delay their meeting, and he was asked to wait. Three hours later, the same friar who'd taken the document from him came through the door.

"The bishop sends his regrets," the friar said. "A matter of some urgency came up and he was called away unexpectedly. He had hoped to speak with you personally."

"These things happen," Saunière said. He was well aware that the Bishop of Saint-Sulpice saw a priest like himself as barely worthy of notice. All he wanted was his ancient document and a translation of what it said. He wasn't any more interested in socializing with the bishop than the bishop was with him. "If you can bring me the document I brought, and whatever information there is, I'll be on my way."

"Unfortunately, your document has been misplaced."

Saunière stared at the friar, stunned, praying he'd misunderstood.

"What does that mean? Someone must know where it is—perhaps the translator?"

"That is all the information I have. I wish I could be of more help, but I have nothing else to offer you. The bishop instructed me to tell you that the document you brought us is not and will not be available to return to you. It is gone. He wishes you well and suggests you return to your parish and continue your work there. Good day, Abbé." With that he'd turned and disappeared through a heavy, oak door.

9

RENNES-LE-CHÂTEAU

OCTOBER 1887

THE MEMORY WAS so vivid that when Saunière opened his eyes it took him several seconds to orient himself to the present. He stared at the boulder in the floor that had supported the old altar and pillars, remembering Emma's parting words that last morning. "You're an extraordinary man, mon amour. You are not destined to sing in the chorus; you are a Verdi baritone, a soloist, one of the special few whose voice soars above the rest and rises to the heavens."

She had been overly theatrical of course, that was her way. But she'd understood, as he now did, that he couldn't remain in the choir, never raising an objection; all his previous promises to himself were validated. Whatever conclusions and decisions he came to, from small matters to large, would be his own. Paris—Emma—were almost inseparable in his mind, and would always be with him; but so, too, would St. Sulpice. Bishop Billard, Father Henri Boudet of nearby Rennes-les Bains and Father Gélis were like-minded friends he could trust, but aside from them, there was no one—not even his brother Alfred, who'd followed him into the priesthood but routinely drank himself into a stupor.

All future decisions, personal and professional, would be his and his alone: what to say and what to advocate; what to leave in the church and what to replace; how to maintain the character of this ancient building but bring it into the looming twentieth century; what to reveal and what to hold close. Whether it was Emma, or St. Sulpice, or a combination of the two, he had become his own man.

His church would never be as grand as the churches of Paris or Saint-Maximin-la-Sainte-Baume; they were overwhelming in their magnificence but, in his eyes, lacking in simple spiritual inspiration. He was determined to create a soulful place of modest beauty and harmony. It was his aria to interpret and sing. Every stone and crevice would have to be examined and repaired from the foundation up to assure its intact survival for future generations—a building structurally solid but visually delicate and nuanced that could withstand any catastrophic event nature might hurl. *Not only restored,* he thought, *gloriously restored, reimagined, and resurrected to splendor; the Saint deserves nothing less.*

He knelt down on the altar stone. "Holy Father, Blessed Mother and Saint Marie-Madeleine, I am your humble servant Bérenger. I have been tested and I have returned, ready to restore your church to glory and to provide spiritual sustenance to your faithful. Show me the way and I will not waver. Whatever secrets you reveal will remain safe with me."

As his clasped hands made a steeple over his eyelids, an image of the Basilique of Marie-Madeleine in Saint-Maximin-la-Sainte-Baume appeared in his mind. He remembered descending into the crypt below the church altar to see Marie-Madeleine's blackened skull, sheathed in gold—and her sarcophagus.

A crypt. This church must have a crypt. How could I have been so blind?

"Are you okay, Father?" Augie had arrived and remained at a respectful distance, but apparently thought it was time to make his presence known.

"Praying for your mortal soul, my boy. Did your mother send some of her fresh-baked croissants?"

"I left them in a basket at the door."

The priest got to his feet and whacked his long black cassock several times, sending up a cloud of dust. "There's some heavy lifting to be done today, so I hope you've had a hearty breakfast. I've decided the altar stone has to be removed."

"You mean that boulder." Augie pointed his spindly finger at the massive rock on which the priest had been kneeling. "That will be damn—excuse me, Father—heavy. Too much for me and skinny Rousset—and those old guys won't be no help neither."

"Better get some strong boys then. While I was kneeling down I got a sign, a kind of prophecy. It was a message to look under that rock, and there's no arguing with that."

"You mean Jesus came to you!" Augie sounded stunned.

"Actually, I think it was the Blessed Saint, Marie-Madeleine. But it wasn't a real vision, Augie, like the one Bernadette had in Lourdes. The clues were already in my mind and I had to decipher them. I mean, I had to figure out what they were telling me. It's like a dream."

"Whatever you say, Father. Think on it and I'll go round me up some muscle. You were a blessing in our village before you got sent away, for sure, but since you come back from Paris with the Sunday gloves for Maman and the book for me, there's nothing you could ask I wouldn't do. If you and Saint Marie-Madeleine want that rock moved, I'm your man."

"We're all a blessing in the Lord's eyes, Augie, and we all have a purpose, but sometimes the Lord asks us to dig for it before it's revealed."

After Augie left, Saunière walked the few steps to the church's southern wall, which, despite human neglect and the forces of nature, had remained standing. He reached out and ran the tips of his fingers over the smooth, creamy surfaces of the hand-chiseled stones, caressing each cool plane with the reverence he would have given the polished Michelangelo "Madonna and Child" he had seen in Bruges.

One large stone wiggled like a loose tooth, and he eased it out cautiously rather than chance it becoming dislodged accidentally. Something in the empty crevice caught the light, glinting as he turned his head and tried to get a better view. At first, he was afraid it was a rat's eyes; nevertheless, he pushed back the sleeves of his cassock and reached in, prepared to be bitten but relieved to grasp a small, cylindrical case covered in an unidentifiable reptile skin. It was the size of a small rolling pin, fastened shut with a silver clasp that sprang open at the push of a little silver button. Inside, two yellowed pages were rolled up and nestled in a groove of pink satin. A surge of excitement tore through him as he quickly snapped it shut and walked to the main door with a racing heart. The aroma of freshly baked pastries drew his attention to the basket waiting at the entry, but his usually ravenous morning hunger had disappeared. *My resolve has been put to the test. People hide things for good reason, and whatever the little case contains is nobody's business but mine.*

Far down the road, past the cemetery, he could just make out the silhouette of a figure hanging clothes on a line in the morning sun, but not so much as a squirrel was moving on the path connecting the town to the church.

Assured that he was unobserved, he quickly turned and walked behind the building, disappearing into the shadow cast by the rear façade before touching the silver spring mechanism again. The first page was a formal letter written on yellowed paper and dated 1792, addressed to no one in particular and signed by Father Antoine Bigou, one of his predecessors, who had been the Abbé at Rennes-le-Château before the Revolution. It was written in precisely formed, flourishing French script that reminded him of the carefully written documents his father occasionally posted in the town square. He'd have no problem reading it. The second page, written in the same neat hand, appeared to be a long column of names, many familiar to him, alongside a list of objects and locations.

He read Bigou's letter word by word, like a beginning student, slowly sounding out each syllable, unaware that he was holding his breath or that his hands were trembling. If a crater had opened on the spot, in the middle of the mountain, and transported him to the center of the earth, into brimstone, or tossed him into the heavens in an explosion of molten lava, he couldn't have been more jolted. He leaned back against the sun-warmed stone, wondering if his mind was playing tricks on him, and reread the entire letter to assure himself this wasn't some strange delusion. There could be no doubt. The second page fluttered out of his grasp into a patch of overgrown weeds; he picked it up by the corner, placed it under the page gripped between his fingers and carefully rolled them up before replacing them in the pink nest of fabric.

Knowledge could be a burden—or a gift. A path to enlightenment—or destructiveness. The passage from Proverbs his grandfather used to read to him came to mind: 'when wisdom enters your heart, knowledge will fill your soul with joy; discretion will protect you, and understanding will keep you safe.' *Yes*, he thought, *perhaps the joy will come in time, but even in this moment I can promise discretion.*

Suddenly, he felt an urgent need to step out of the shadow and let the sun fall on his face, see the distant mountaintops, allow his heart to quiet and his breath to flow. One deeply inhaled lungful helped steady him before he slipped the little case in his pocket, knelt down for the second time that day, lifted his head, and squinted into the brilliant heavens. A dazzling sunbeam directed at his pounding chest was a golden sword reaching from paradise and anointing him. *Wisdom has entered my heart, Lord. I am a knight in the service of Saint Marie-Madeleine and vow to keep her safe.*

"Father, you're doin' a lot of prayin' today." Respecting the priest's deep reverie again, Augie stood quietly for several minutes before interrupting, but the boys he'd brought with him would quickly become curious, or impatient.

"I have a lot to be grateful for today, my boy." Saunière stood up without attempting to brush himself off. He tousled the top of Augie's head and began walking.

"I hope you brought some sturdy lads. That altar stone has to come out."

"Yes, Father. We're ready. And"—the priest stopped and turned, waiting until Augie finally blurted out—"Father Gélis has come up the mountain to visit you. He wanted it to be a surprise, so please don't tell him I spilled the beans. I hope I did right."

"You did indeed." Saunière patted his pocket. The little round case was secure. "Sometimes it's better to be prepared for a surprise."

10

RENNES-LE-CHÂTEAU

OCTOBER 1887

"ANTOINE!" FEIGNING SURPRISE, Father Saunière embraced the gaunt visitor standing in the Dénarnaud's kitchen. "What a lovely and unexpected pleasure. Please, make yourself comfortable while I find someone to brew a pot of tea. Or would you prefer a glass of wine? Some cheese?"

Father Gélis settled onto a chair at the kitchen table, smiled and lowered his eyes. "The first miracle Jesus performed was to transform water into wine. He knew what the guests would want to drink, and you can't do better than following in his footsteps, my boy."

Saunière laughed and went to the cupboard which had been built specifically to store his red wine. He was fond of his visitor, who was one of the few among the local clergy to accept and support him without judgment or a snide, superior attitude. But no one dropped by unannounced in Rennes-le-Château, and his curiosity was piqued.

"Straight from Paris," he said, pulling the cork out and sniffing it. "Let's give it a few minutes to breathe while you tell me what prompted you to come up the mountain, my dear friend."

"Are we alone?"

"I believe so. Today is Madame Dénarnaud's day to visit her sister, and the boys are still at work. Is something wrong?"

"If you mean wrong with me, no, I'm as well as a man of my years deserves to be." He stopped and cleared his throat nervously like a man about to make a public statement. "I assume you know I was in Rome for several weeks."

Saunière shook his head, affirming the news had reached him, while he took two wine goblets off the shelf, put them on the table, and filled the one he offered to Antoine. "You sound a little parched, my friend. Take a sip or two and relax. The sun is still high in the sky, and there is ample time to regale me with tales of your escapades."

"Ah, my boy, only you would put it that way, and hearing you lifts my spirits. But no, I didn't come to speak of escapades, and though I'd love to hear all about Paris, it will have to wait for another time. I traveled here today because I have something to say, something meant for you alone to hear, something I was fearful to write down on paper." The old priest smiled a sad, half smile and brought his glass to his lips with gnarled, rheumatic fingers. "Are you speculating that I've become senile, my boy?"

"Not at all," Saunière said quickly, wondering if his expression was that transparent. "I know you, and you wouldn't have taken this journey unless something was of the highest concern. Of course, I'll take you seriously."

"I want you to be aware that there are those in Rome, in the highest places, that are keeping an eye on you. A critical eye."

Saunière's first impulse was to laugh. The pronouncement was made with an executioner's somber tone. "Are you sure about this?" he asked, somewhat amused but not wanting to offend. "I'm nobody to them. A name on a list in a place they barely know exists. I don't talk about politics anymore and, in any event, I've always been supportive of the Church and the Holy See being independent of government. I have no disagreement with them on that." He searched his mind but couldn't think of any recent infraction that would rise to enough importance to catch the attention of the powerful in Rome. They couldn't know about Emma. It all sounded absurd. "You must have misunderstood—something."

Color drained from the old priest's face, leaving his skin as grey as his sad, faded eyes. He slowly shook his head back and forth, as he would with a small child who didn't understand him. "Ah Bérenger. You are so young, so idealistic, still so naïve. You break my heart. Our Church is no less political than the government, and no less ruthless when necessary." He withdrew his linen pocket square from his cassock pocket and dabbed at his eyes, before he continued.

"You are like a son to me. When we met at the seminary all these years ago, you were a breath of fresh air, with your curiosity and enthusiasm for life. I suppose I was flattered a little too much because you didn't treat me like an old, irritating rotting relative, and you thought I had interesting things to say."

"Well, you did. And you still do."

"So it makes me very sad to be the one to disillusion you, if that is what I have to do."

"Antoine, be more specific. Tell me what you're talking about."

"I have it on good authority that the Archbishop of Notre-Dame informed the Cardinal, who passed word to the Vatican, that you had brought a highly sensitive document to St. Sulpice. And that you were less than satisfied when it wasn't returned to you. Is that so?"

This time Saunière's face did give him away, and it was all the old priest needed to see.

"Be warned, my boy. You may understand about wine the way our Lord Jesus did, but he didn't understand about traitors, and neither do you. And look where it got him."

"Good Lord, Antoine. That's taking things into another realm entirely, and you do sound a little overly suspicious. Even if they have their eye on me, as you say they do, they're not going to have anyone, not me, not you, murdered! Reprimanded, or even removed, maybe; I can't even imagine defrocked, although I guess that's always a possibility as a last resort."

"You're right, you're right. I think old age has made me a little morbid, and I'm always afraid someone will learn a little too much about me and then—what would I do? I have nothing of my own, no family, no home. I don't want you to wind up in that position."

"Don't worry, my dear friend. I think you have very paternal, protective instincts and it's a pity you never had a son. It means a lot to know you're watching out for me. And I don't have much, but whatever I have, I'm happy to share with you."

Antoine stood to go, and Saunière embraced him, and patted his back. "I'll go get Augie to take you home. And here"—he took another bottle of wine off the shelf—"I was going to bring it the next time I came to see you, but there's no time like the present. I have a friend in Paris who'll send more when I run out."

"It sounds like a good friend."

"Oh yes." Saunière sighed, as he pictured Emma's smooth skin and black curls on the pillow next to him. "The best."

11

KHIRBET QEIYAFA, ISRAEL & TOULOUSE, FRANCE

LETTERS

DAVID TO GISELLE

JANUARY 20, 2013

Dear Giselle,

When we left Paris and went our separate ways, I decided that in addition to using whatever electronics work best for us, I'd write a few real pen-upon-paper letters. It seems far more personal, and if it was good enough for Robert Browning, it's good enough for me. You're right. A long-distance relationship will make special demands on us, because deprivation is baked into it. Just remember, when we're together and turn the oven on, the heat is intense.

I was hoping that after our time together in Paris, you might change your mind and invite me to spend a weekend in Toulouse; I still don't understand your reluctance, but I accept it, for now. (A high frustration tolerance is a prerequisite in my profession.) Even so, when I lie in bed at night, I think of that overcast, windy winter afternoon we spent walking along the banks of the Seine. Your cheeks and nose were red with the cold, and your hair streamed out behind you like Botticelli's "Birth of Venus." I fall asleep yearning to see your hair spread across the pillow next to mine.

Always,

David

GISELLE TO DAVID

FEBRUARY 17, 2013

Dear David,

I loved getting your letter. I don't think I mentioned Papa used to write to me when I was in graduate school at Columbia, even though we spoke on the phone. He'd remind me to be a critical thinker in the same sentence he'd tell me not to overthink every decision and go out and enjoy life. He'd probably tell me the same thing now.

I've heard from my cousin (his name is Gilbert). His letter was a little strange, maybe more than a little. He wants me to promise that everything he says at our "meeting" will be confidential. I told him I'd agree, but that my boyfriend would be joining us. Even an independent, modern woman can use a bodyguard on a weird occasion.

So if it meets with your approval, we'll spend the last week of June in the south of France followed by a week in New York. We can meet in Marseilles, drive to Saint-Maximin-la-Sainte-Baume, then La Grotte de Marie-Madeleine, Rennes-le-Château, do a little hiking, and wind up in Toulouse. We'll have to rent a car, but the scenery is breathtaking and visiting Rennes-le-Château and Marie-Madeleine's tomb at the Basilique will be fun.

The second week in New York won't be very private, but I'd love for you to meet my family. Simone is going to send me a list of current Broadway musicals she recommends, and Matthew will probably be able to get us house seats to whatever we choose. I think I mentioned he's in show biz, mainly movies, and he knows just about everyone. His films usually deal with controversial topics and he's currently working on something Simone says is very hush-hush.

You're probably not familiar with the Gospel of Mary, (the one attributed to Marie-Madeleine), but your letter reminded me of when she tells Jesus she saw him in a vision, and he answers, "Where the mind is, there is vision." It's so true, and the reverse is true as well. If you have a vision of me when you fall asleep, it's because I'm on your mind.

I just want to mention I love your handwriting, particularly the way you form the letter G. I picture your big, tanned hands gripping the pen, and then I remember how I feel when you stroke my wrist. That's the vision I fall asleep with and dream about.

As always,

Giselle

DAVID TO GISELLE

MARCH 1, 2013

Lovely Giselle,

Dream on. It's good for the soul, and our relationship. Did you know Freud said dreams always have wishes? Just thought I'd mention that tidbit.

The south of France sounds perfect. And by the way, since Amsterdam, I've developed a little soft spot for your Mary Magdalene. This trip will give me a chance to pay my respects, and, more importantly, there couldn't be anything better than doing it with an amazing woman who describes visiting a tomb as fun.

Don't worry about Gilbert. He sounds a little paranoid, but lots of family trees grow nuts.

I'm reluctant to put my pen down and go to bed. The nights are still cool here, and I can hear the night owls (yes, we have owls in the Holy Land) asking their ancient question: who? It's such a good question. Who am I, who are you, who are we to each other? Now I have the answer. I am the boyfriend; and you are who I knew you'd be—you are the woman I was meant to discover.

I'll see you in my dreams,

David

12

TOULOUSE

JUNE 16, 2013

GISELLE HAD PURCHASED several new outfits, and impulsively indulged in an impractical, but beautiful pair of strappy evening sandals, which, along with everything else she wanted to take, had to fit into her little suitcase. *Who,* she wondered, *had made packing light a virtue anyway? Maybe it was me,* a little voice answered. *Maman thought I was ridiculous for traveling with a backpack, and I thought she was vain and pampered because she wrapped all her outfits in tissue paper and left Papa to deal with the luggage. Lesson learned. Using a suitcase isn't one of the seven deadly sins.*

The knot in her belly tightened with each piece of carefully folded clothing she added. *I am ridiculous,* she berated herself for the millionth time in her life, knowing those sentiments wouldn't change a thing.The week in Paris was ancient history now, and after the intimacy of their letters, anticipating David's physicality and his expectations, made her extremely nervous. Again.

A photo of her father was smiling at her from the bedside table, and she smiled back at it. Even after three years, she still felt the urge to ring him up, ask his advice and fill him in. *You'd like David, Papa, I feel certain of it— but I wish I could hear you say so. Maybe I should have put your cell phone in the coffin.*

It had been almost twenty years since her fiancée left her standing at the alter, but she could still conjure up the pain and humiliation as if it happened yesterday. Had she been too touchy? Too uptight? She didn't know then and she didn't know now. Papa's arms and wisdom and ferocious love were her only solace. "You've had your heart broken by a boorish man who lacks a moral compass and I, for one, will never forgive him. Never. It will take time for your soul to mend, but if you're blessed, and you find your soul mate, he'll treasure you the way I do. In the meantime, live your life fully and hold your head high like Marie-Madeleine. There are worse things than being alone."

The truth of those words had never failed her—and now there was David. She couldn't picture a scenario where he would hurt her the way Armand had, but the longer they were involved, the worse it would feel if...*Stop*, she told herself. *It's a two-week holiday. Go and enjoy it.*

She stored the suitcase packed for New York in the foyer coat closet and looked around the sitting room, trying to see it through David's eyes. They would be stopping here overnight before leaving for New York, and picturing him here, sleeping in her bed, made the knot in her stomach twist violently again.

She loved her home—high bookshelves thick with a mix of novels, biblical references, art books, and odd found objects; a down-filled sofa built for comfort that invited someone to sink in and relax; small paned-windows with a view of the river. The Persian rug had been inherited from her grandmother; parts of it were threadbare, but she loved the connection to all the family members who had walked on it. Once she let him in, once he sat on the sofa and crawled under her down-filled quilt, he would become part of her personal, private space. *Stop*, she told herself again. *You're going. It's not a lifelong commitment, just a holiday.*

Taking one last look around, she smiled approvingly and rolled her suitcase into the tiny vestibule, locked the door behind her and stepped out onto Place de la Daurade. The June day was sparkling; people were gathered around little tables at the café next door and students were strolling along the river hand in hand. She began to hum quietly, and started laughing when she realized it was an American World War I song Papa used to sing: "the Yanks are coming, the Yanks are coming."

13

MARSEILLE

JUNE 16, 2013

AIR FRANCE FLIGHT 7666, the connecting leg from Paris to Marseilles, arrived seven minutes early at the Marseilles Provence Airport. David had left Tel Aviv at eight o'clock in the morning local time and arrived in Paris around noon, picking up a bonus hour during the trip. Traveling with only a backpack and carry-on, he walked directly to Hall 4, maneuvered through the human traffic, and finished purchasing some euros from a Credit Suisse machine just as Giselle came through the door.

Dodging other travelers and waving to get her attention, he quickly covered the distance between them and, before she could prepare, wrapped her up in his arms and kissed her.

"That's not the way French way," she protested, laughing, despite her professed discomfort, "at least not in public. It's a kiss on each cheek, sometimes a third for good luck, but not on the mouth. Mon Dieu!"

"God has nothing to do with it; it's just one of the things we Americans got right," he said, undaunted. "Just needed to reacquaint myself with those luscious lips. Now, let's go get the car you rented and get out of here. Do you have the paperwork handy?"

As she craned her head around to dig in the pocket of her shoulder bag, some intuition—some unconscious awareness—gave her the creepy sensation of being watched, and despite feeling foolish, she glanced across the room. Her heart began to pound and she grabbed David's arm to steady herself. "Look over your shoulder," she whispered hoarsely, "but try not to stare. It's Charles. He's standing in line at the information booth glaring at me with the most horrible look on his face. I'm sure he must have seen you kiss me that way." She felt stricken.

"I assume he knows you haven't taken a vow of celibacy," David said lightly. "I'm sorry, I would've been more discreet if I'd known we had an audience." He turned, made eye contact with Charles, and gave a friendly wave. It was ignored. Pivoting back to face Giselle, he said evenly, "You know, on second thought, I'm not sorry. Screw Charles. Let's go."

She could feel those beady eyes on her back as she and David gathered their bags and began walking toward the exit.

"What could he be doing here?" Giselle asked. "I don't want to seem overly suspicious, but it is a strange coincidence. He asked about my holiday plans at the last faculty meeting, but I was evasive, and now, here he is."

"It's really not that strange. It's summer. Thousands of travelers pass through this airport, going somewhere. Dr. Charles Abrisson is a just a pathetic man in the miserable position of seeing the woman he desires go off with another guy. Twice. But a stalker? That seems unlikely. I think it was you who said he is without fangs, or something like that."

Long after they had left the terminal, Giselle continued to glance over her shoulder, half expecting to see Charles lurking behind her. David stopped walking, turned to face her, and kissed her forehead. "Let's try to leave your inconveniently omnipresent colleague behind us. Agreed?"

She nodded.

"Excellent. So which car rental place will be the beneficiary of our patronage?"

"Europcar. It's an old-line company with good rates, and it offered free drop-off in Toulouse, so I took a chance."

"I think taking a chance suits us. A colleague said he thought I was taking a big chance planning a two-week trip with you, but I don't see it that way at all. After our week in Paris, well, Charles has good reason to envy me." Color instantly flooded Giselle's face, making her discomfort so apparent that David was prompted to add, "Look, we both know he wishes you were in his arms instead of mine, but let me assure you that you took a chance on the right guy, and if you don't remember why, I hope that by tomorrow morning it'll come back to you."

A small smile began to play at the corners of Giselle's mouth, and her eyes signaled she was ready to move on. "Well, that sounds a little presumptuous, but if you're sure…"

"I am," he said firmly, relieved the lighthearted bantering that ordinarily went on between them had returned.

"As a biblical scholar, I feel it's my duty to inform you that Proverbs says, 'do not boast about tomorrow for you do not know what a day may bring.' "

"Well, that only proves you can't believe everything you read," he said, giving her a wink, "not even if it comes from the Good Book."

14

SAINT-MAXIMIN-LA-SAINTE-BAUME

JUNE 16, 2013

BARELY AN HOUR later, they arrived at an easily overlooked little sign on a quiet residential road where an iron gate sealed off the foot of the driveway.

"I'm sure they're expecting us." Giselle flashed a quick smile, which did little to mask her anxiety.

"We probably need to buzz the intercom."

"Of course." She got out, pressed the button, and almost immediately the gate slid open.

A lushly planted driveway led to the crest of a hill, where the proprietors greeted them like treasured friends and showed them to a spacious, homey room connected to a private brick patio. Family heirlooms sat on tables, and mementos collected on their hosts' travels added to the illusion of visiting family.

"May I offer you some local wine and cheese?"

"Thanks," David said, after seeing Giselle almost imperceptibly shake her head. "I think we'll unpack first. Maybe later."

"What a great find," David said, once they were alone inside. "It couldn't be more perfect." He thought about adding "like you," but decided it would sound contrived, although it was exactly what he was thinking.

Giselle murmured "thanks," but continued carefully transferring the contents of her bag onto shelves in the armoire.

"Any thoughts about what you want to do tonight?" David stacked his few pieces of clothing onto the shelf Giselle had left for him and put his hiking boots out of sight. His only objective for the moment was to put her at ease and let her know he'd follow her lead, hoping that would relieve some of the obvious tension in her face. "Whatever you have in mind is fine with me. Option one, we can have some wine and cheese on the patio; option two, we can go out for wine or cheese, or go somewhere for a nice meal; option three"—he knew he was taking a chance, so he didn't add, 'my favorite'—"we can just climb into bed. I'm at your disposal."

"I know you must be totally wiped out," Giselle said. "We have two glorious weeks ahead, so if it's okay with you I'd like to sit outside, have a little something to eat and a glass of wine, you know, chill out and get reacquainted...savor the anticipation."

"I get it," he said, and he did. "I think I started the anticipation phase as soon as I got home from Paris, so you have some catching up to do. No worries, I'm a very easygoing, patient man, you may remember."

"I remember, and those are qualities I'm grateful for. I've been looking forward to this trip too, but we haven't been together in person for a long time and I get a little nervous. It's silly, but there it is. Anyway, a romantic evening is missing something without a little anticipation; picture putting sugar in water and stirring while it heats, waiting for it to thicken into syrup."

David started to laugh, but Giselle interrupted. "Don't laugh," she said. "I know I sound like a bad greeting card, but that's what happens sometimes when I'm stressed."

"Sorry. You can sound as flowery as you need to, and now that I think about it, you said something similar in Paris, so if you'll allow me to translate for you—you want a little time to get used to me again. But I have to say the image of syrup, heating slowly, stirred until it's the right consistency—is making my mouth water already."

He held out his arms for her, and when she came to him, he kissed her softly on the lips, brushed her hair over her shoulder and kissed the nape of her neck in the spot he'd learned was particularly sensitive, whispering, "I've waited for you all my life, for your special blend of reserve, and grace, and passion. You're right. Letting it heat up for two or three more hours will make it all the more delicious."

"Sit outside while I change," she whispered back in a lighthearted, teasing tone. "It's not the modesty thing. I want to make an entrance."

"You take my breath away," David said, when she opened the French doors and stood still, framed by the white molding before joining him on the patio. "You look like an angel."

"And you don't disappoint." She smiled and sat down across from him.

After declining an invitation to join the other guests, they sipped wine and ate alone under the stars on their secluded patio. The early summer scent of lavender and wild thyme hung in the still night air. Candles glowed while small birds, celebrating the arrival of balmy temperatures, provided background music from the trees.

"It couldn't be a more magical night," Giselle sighed, taking another sip before looking into David's eyes. "I have something strange to tell you."

He nodded and smiled, waiting for her to continue.

"Most people who live in this part of France believe, as I do by the way, that Marie-Madeleine came here by boat after the crucifixion. She could have landed at Marseilles or a little village on the shores of the Mediterranean called Saintes-Maries-de-la-Mer. Many experts think it's more than legend; after all, her bones were found here. But that's not the strange part."

Giselle stopped speaking and turned her gaze to the shadowy hillside, wondering if her idea was a sort of revelation, or whether she found it simply too appealing to disregard. She wasn't prone to religious reveries like some fictional cloistered nun, and yet, she felt as if a mystical truth had been revealed to her.

"I believe Marie-Madeleine brought us together," she said softly. "I don't mean because of our interest in the Jesus wife codex, or her, or anything that concrete, although in that sense it's true, too. What I mean is, I feel her presence, as if she's guiding us, as if she has a purpose for us being here, being together. It probably sounds a little weird to you, and I have to admit it sounds that way to me too, maybe more than a little, but...it feels right. It's not typical for me to sound like Teresa of Avila, the famous mystic, and maybe I've had a little too much wine..."

She stopped speaking and averted her eyes again, trying to decide how much more to say, particularly when David's eyes were masked by shadows.

She took a deep breath. "Marie-Madeleine was a brave woman, and I've always felt a special connection to her. It's not just because my father's family is from this region, or that Saunière was connected to my family and his church was, is, dedicated to her, but because she's an inspiration to me. The 'slings and arrows of outrageous fortune' didn't make her bitter; she spent her life spreading a message of love, and I think she would want me to tell you"—long pause—"I've fallen in love with you."

All these months, since Paris, maybe even since Amsterdam, David had held back, never saying those three little words, afraid he'd be rushing her, frightening her, pushing her before she was ready. But he'd put her in the position of having to say it first. He'd wanted to slip it into the letters, be honest and take his chances, but had decided to wait until he was certain she felt the same. *People are so fragile,* he thought, *always preparing for rejection and the pain that follows, protecting themselves from the script they write.*

"You know I'm a confirmed skeptic," he said softly, "but if you believe Mary Magdalene brought us together, who am I to say otherwise? How we came to find each other in this far-flung world of space and time is something of a miracle, a cosmic event of synchronicity, and if she's the angel who made it happen, I'm eternally grateful. As to the bigger issue, well, I've fallen in love with you, too, head over heels. Long since. And every minute we're together, every time I hear your thoughts, or see your face, the flush that crawls up your neck when you're uncomfortable, the smile that makes your eyes crinkle at the corners, the long strands of burnished hair glowing copper in the sun—everything—I think this has to be more than luck or chance. You have captured my heart. I love you, and I should have told you long ago."

He poured the last few drops from the bottle into her glass. The moon was barely a sliver in the sky, and beyond the reach of the candles, the night was thick and black. The birds had stopped singing, no doubt retired to their nests, leaving the lovers alone in absolute silence. David reached across the table and wrapped his hand around Giselle's slender fingers. "Let's go," he said. "I'm nowhere as patient as the Saint, but I think even she would give us her blessing by now."

15

RENNES-LE-CHÂTEAU

AUGUST 1891

THE IRRESISTIBLE AROMA of freshly baked, golden-crusted apple pie and cinnamon wafted through the presbytery, and Marie Dénarnaud knew it would only be a matter of minutes before the Abbé wandered in, unable to remain in bed when warm pie was calling to him from the kitchen. Now that her brothers had finished installing the fence and iron gates, she and Saunière could dig in the cemetery unobserved. She enjoyed the physicality of working beside him by lantern light, watching the muscles of his bare arms ripple and strain with each shovelful of earth, knowing that his secret and his arms were shared only with her.

Still, she had risen at first light to begin rolling out the crusts, wanting the fragrance of something delicious to ease the man she cherished into the new day.

Marie had been smitten at first glance that morning five years ago, and she had no doubt she wouldn't be the only one; women of all ages responded as she did to his dark good looks, commanding stature, and wickedly obvious sex appeal. Most of her friends had pretended they didn't notice, but they had all gossiped about him when he was called away, and when he returned, flirting outrageously had become something of a sport because they all felt protected by his vow of celibacy. Saunière was still living in the attic of her parent's house when she returned home, and her fantasies of him, sleeping in the room above hers, were overrun with images of her in his arms and in his bed. She knew she had blossomed into a beautiful, voluptuous woman with a quick mind and a bit of worldliness. There was no shortage of young suitors in the village, and she could have had her pick, but she didn't want a boy; she wanted Saunière. She had no reason to be skeptical of the titillating stories whispered about him from his days in Le Clat, and in spite of him remaining pleasant and friendly from a respectful and appropriate distance, she was convinced it was only a matter of timing.

Paris had changed him in a subtle but palpable way. He seemed at ease with himself, and she sensed a kind of longing and brooding hunger that hadn't been there before. Two months after his return she decided to let him know she was willing if he was interested. She'd taken a job as a milliner in a shop in Esperanza, and when he came by to purchase a hat as a Christmas gift for his mother, she'd met his seductive sensuality with the boldness of an unblushing girl raised with three brothers. On the first night of the New Year she had gone to him, creeping silently up the stairs to his room, her shiny black hair brushed out over her thin white nightdress. A sliver of moonlight escaped through the narrow slit where the curtains failed to meet, and fell on the bare wood floor inches from his bed. She stood there, illuminated by moon glow, and when he pulled back the down quilt she unbuttoned her nightdress and allowed it to slide down her naked body and puddle around her ankles. She would have gone had he sent her away, but his sharp intake of breath was followed by silence, and with a longing she had never known, she quietly edged under the quilt next to his warm, hard body.

When the time came for him to take up residence in the newly finished presbytery, not one parishioner was surprised that Marie moved with him as his housekeeper, confidante, and life companion, with her parents' blessing. The entire village, which by now referred to her as "the Priest's Madonna," went about their daily lives with a tacit understanding: Abbé Saunière heard confession and kept their secrets, and they would allow him to keep his.

"It's good to see you in such fine spirits," Saunière said, quietly coming up behind her in the kitchen and kissing the nape of her neck. "Later today I'd like to show you the sketches I've made for the Orangerie. It will make you breathe fireflies. On beautiful days you and I will sit up there, as if we're Jupiter and Juno on high, overlooking the entire valley, and watch until the sun sinks below the mountains."

"Whatever you design will be magnificent," Marie said, distracted, as she cut a piece of the warm pie and set the plate on the kitchen table. "Do you worry that such a display of wealth will make the Bishop of Carcassonne, uh"—she searched for the right word—"curious?" She didn't want to sound critical, but she felt it was her obligation to protect him from what she saw as recklessness—or arrogance. Any fool would wonder where he was getting the huge sums of money he was spending, acquiring statues and reliefs for the church of Maria Magdalena, then purchasing all the available adjacent land and commissioning the construction of the presbytery. Now he had even grander plans, and in her experience arousing envy was a foolish thing to do.

"You worry too much," he said, and pulled her to him. "Bishop Billard has no reason to be envious of me—at least not where money is involved. He will live comfortably for the rest of his life with the inheritance one of his parishioners bequeathed to him. As for us, what we do by lantern light is our business. Everyone benefits. One day I'll have a library full of great books, and the entire parish will be welcome to read them. My dreams of buildings and gardens to rival Versailles will materialize, and they will be glorious places for contemplation. The Bishop isn't interested in my personal business."

"Of course, I forget sometimes."

"Remember I told you that when I first began the church renovation, I removed the pillar that supported the altar and found documents hidden inside."

"Of course, and you turned the pillar upside down and put it in the little garden behind the church as a plinth for our Lady of Lourdes."

"Exactly," he said, smiling at her and taking his seat at the table. She remembered everything but had no inclination to pry or criticize, making her an uncommonly easy and loyal companion.

"Have a bite of pie while it's still warm," she urged, "and I'll pour some fresh milk. You had a restless sleep."

"Yes, I did," he replied, taking his first bite of the pie and smiling at her with appreciation. "I was lying awake, thinking about my trip to Saint-Sulpice."

"Yes, I remember the whole story; they didn't translate what you gave them, they didn't return it, and they treated you like a stray dog."

"That about sums it up," Saunière said, laughing. "You have a special way of putting things into perspective."

"I'm happy you can laugh about it. But why is it on your mind?"

"Well, digging in the cemetery made me think about the past, and the secrets that get buried and forgotten—and then I began to wonder about that document, and who had the power to decide it had to be kept a secret, not only from me, but from someone as prominent as Bishop Billard. I've never stopped wondering about what it said, and I've never stopped regretting handing it over to strangers. Father Gélis warned me to forget about it, but I can't, though it taught me an important lesson."

"It pains me to see you look so troubled, Abbé."

"My sweet Marie, you notice everything. That experience is the reason I keep the precious contents of the urn that was hidden under the altar stone a secret—except from you, of course. Abbé Bigou's letter was very clear. The urn was where he said it would be, and when I scraped the wax away, I knew, deep in my soul, that what had been entrusted to me was Marie-Madeleine's most valuable possession. I've seen what she carried from the Holy Land, and I've touched it with my own hands. Sadly, I don't know anything about the little parchment rolled up with it, or how it came to be there." The priest stopped speaking and took another forkful of pie. It still shocked him when he stopped to think about what had been secreted away in his church and found its way to him for safekeeping.

"I've been entrusted with a two-thousand-year-old secret, Marie. Sometimes I'm overwhelmed by the weight of it; I pray for guidance, and I believe the Thirty-second Psalm has a message for me: 'God will instruct me and teach me the way I should go.' After a great deal of contemplation, I believe I understand what he wanted me to learn. He sent me to St. Sulpice so I would understand I have to protect the irreplaceable objects I find, and to keep them from falling into the wrong hands."

He stopped again, replaying the arguments he'd been having with himself. "That second little parchment haunts me. Its importance to Marie-Madeleine is obvious, but why? What could it be? Sometimes I think my curiosity is a curse; it tortures me and takes hold of my mind. It's a hunger. I had the parchment in my hand, ready to put it back inside the urn with the papyrus, but I knew I couldn't forget about it. Last night I made a decision. I'm going to ask

Father Gélis to try to translate it. I trust him entirely. He reads Aramaic, and I know he has no love for the Church hierarchy; of course, Bishop Billard will have to be told as well, but he is one of us."

"Abbé, I hear the hesitation in your voice. Even though you trust the brotherhood, you're not sure you're doing the right thing."

"Exactly. I'm afraid that if we find out it's something important, I'll be overruled on what to do with it."

Marie remained standing at the sink; everyone knew Saunière was an exceptionally intelligent and learned man, but, in her opinion, there were times she understood people, including him, better than he did.

"You can see why I'm troubled," he continued, carefully shoveling the last piece of pie onto his fork and savoring the aroma before putting it in his mouth. Several seconds of silence passed before he asked, "Do you have any thoughts?"

"I do," she responded slowly, trying to decide how best to help him. "I could be wrong, but maybe you're afraid it will make him wonder if you're keeping other secrets from him, like why you're digging in the garden, and, well, you know…" It pained her to see this wonderful man, sitting in their kitchen with his head bowed like a child who had misbehaved. "I think you feel guilty for keeping secrets, for having the money to build whatever you wish, to own the land, to be happy…" She wanted to say, "And to have me at your side and in your bed," but that would have been immodest and boastful; it wasn't necessary.

"Ah, Marie, you're even better than a confessor; you don't just listen, you understand. Sometimes I think you can read my mind. Since St. Sulpice, whatever I imagine is colored by suspicion and betrayal—but Antoine would go to his death to keep my secret. Psalm 13 says, 'I have trusted in your steadfast love,' which of course refers to the Lord, but Marie, my Marie, it is also meant for you."

Marie walked the few steps across the spotless tile floor, and stood behind the priest, as the love she always felt soaked up his words and expanded, filling her entire being. A shoulder rub would tell him everything she wanted him to know, and she gently began to massage his knotted muscles with light, circular pressure, giving herself a few seconds to think through what she wanted to say. "I'm glad you know that, Abbé," she whispered. "My love for the Lord and for you is steadfast, and just as Marie-Madeleine devoted her life to Jesus, this Marie is devoted to you, and will be forever."

16

THE BASILICA, SAINT-MAXIMIN-LA-SAINTE-BAUME

MONDAY JUNE 17, 2013

WHEN THEIR ALARMS buzzed insistently at seven in the morning, David quietly got up as agreed and headed for the bathroom. In an attempt to avoid the crush of tourists who paid homage at the Basilica every day, they'd decided to make an early start, delaying the pleasure of a leisurely morning for later in the week. After having breakfast on the terrace with two other guests, they drove the short distance into town, parked in a designated area in Place Malherbe, and proceeded through the still sleeping village past the shuttered shops and windows on Rue General de Gaulle to the Basilica.

"When we moved back to France, my father used to bring us—Simone and me—to visit my grandmother—we called her Mamie—on school holidays, and we'd all go out for a leisurely stroll and wind up at her favorite boulangerie for warm croissants. Coincidentally, of course." Giselle smiled, remembering the innocent days she believed that to be true. "Looking back I'd say the greatest gift of my childhood was being allowed harmless illusions."

"Ah. My mother used to say, 'fly away on the wings of your dreams,' and I think I still do."

Giselle laughed and nodded. "Well, in my case it was Mamie who encouraged us to think creatively and be our own little people. She lived in a town very similar to this, and I used to tell her the houses looked like they had curly hair because I thought the red clay roof tiles looked like the Shirley Temple curls on one of my porcelain dolls."

"I can see that," David said, "but it's funny you decided Shirley Temple had red hair, like yours; I think her movies were all black and white. How did you happen to know about Shirley Temple?"

"Mamie. My grandmother. Actually I didn't see any of those films until I was an adult, but my Mamie gave me the doll, Veronique, and told me all about Shirley Temple. She said I was just as talented, just as smart, and even more beautiful. I believed her, of course. Love makes the heart gullible."

"Ah, that may be true, but I bet that's actually how she saw you. Yeats wrote, 'wine comes in at the mouth, but love comes in at the eye.' I'm certainly not impartial, but I have to agree with Mamie," he said.

"I don't tap dance."

"That's okay. You have other redeeming qualities."

"Well, here we are," Giselle said, taking the opportunity to change the subject. "I have some nonpoetic and nonsuggestive facts you might find interesting. The Basilique was built over the crypt where a marble sarcophagus containing Marie-Madeleine's bones was found in 1279."

She held up her hand before David could ask the obvious question. "They knew it was her because there was a papyrus inside, dated 710, that said so. And then about six months later, a tablet of wood smeared with wax was discovered with a Latin inscription essentially verifying it was her. Many reputable scholars date that tablet to the first century."

"Impressive. I'm convinced."

"And so are the people of France. We sent her relics to be blessed in Rome, and went to some lengths to protect them during the French Revolution. You probably know it took the Church until 1969 to officially state there wasn't a shred of evidence, not even a subtle suggestion, that Marie-Madeleine was a prostitute. It's outrageous, beyond disgraceful, that she was maligned for almost two thousand years! It was a malicious fabrication that often gets blamed on the general misogyny of the time, but I think some of the apostles, particularly Peter, are the ones who defamed her. He was dripping with jealousy, and he thought he could have the last word."

"Well," said David, "there were two strikes against her: she was a beautiful redhead and a favorite of Jesus. It wouldn't take more than that for Peter's ego to be wounded. You bear a striking resemblance to her, by the way, at least to the portraits I'm familiar with. Do people tell you that all the time?"

"It's been mentioned." She could feel the telltale blush beginning to creep up her neck. Comparisons to Marie-Madeleine had begun when she was a teenager, and they never failed to both embarrass and please her. "Actually, no one really knows what she looked like, but you're right; most artists paint her as a redhead."

"Well, I'm happy to think of her looking like you, hair flaming in the sun, irresistible, maybe even to Jesus."

"Shh, don't let the monks hear you say that; it's heresy," whispered Giselle in a teasing tone. "Did you notice the front of the building is unfinished?"

"I did, and you're obviously itching to tell me why."

"The Black Plague. This archway was supposed to be something grand, but they decided to leave it unfinished, with just this hint of what was planned. Anyway, I always picture Marie- Madeleine as a woman of simple tastes. Of course there's no way to know, but given her life as an apostle she wouldn't have had many worldly goods. I can't imagine her any other way, so sturdy wooden doors, sans carving, seems right. At least to me."

"Makes sense," David said.

As they entered the dimly lit interior, Giselle crossed herself and slowly walked ahead, just as the early-morning sun began to stream through the huge gothic windows. She motioned to David, and when he joined her she whispered, "We got here at the perfect time. Whoever built this must have studied the path of sun and known this..." She pointed to the pulpit, as shards of sunbeams shot at them, framing a painting of Mary Magdalene.

They stood together silently looking around; golden cherubs and angels created an elaborate altar and creamy marble arches paraded overhead, continuing down the entire length of the center aisle.

"Gothic churches like this always make me feel like I'm inside a giant stone caterpillar," Giselle whispered. "I'll never understand how they managed to build something like this a thousand years ago, but the floors look a little shabby—and sad."

"Yes, I noticed that, too. I hate it when buildings like this are neglected. This is a work of art and deserves better, but it's still magnificent, even with the cracked and missing floor tiles. With a little TLC it could rise to glory again. It's got an understated, elegance—sort of fits with your idea of the Magdalene."

"I agree. On the other hand, you may not feel that way about the presentation of her skull, but I don't want to spoil it, so I won't say another word."

On the landing halfway down to the crypt, a reclining plaster likeness of Mary Magdalene was on display in a small, lit alcove. She appeared desolate, propped up on one elbow leaning against a rock with an Excalibur-like cross thrust into it; a once-live plant, now dead and shriveled, was at her feet, and remnants of two candles long burned out added to the pathos.

"I want to light a candle," whispered Giselle, "it's painful to see it looking like this."

"I'll run back upstairs and buy a couple from our Lady of Lourdes," said David, quickly sprinting up the stairs and returning a minute later with two votives.

The narrow tomb in the bowels of the church was a dark, cool, claustrophobic space built entirely of stone, exactly wide enough to house the sarcophagus. A thick sheet of glass stood in front of a black iron and brass fence obscuring the contents of the niche. "I'm glad we're the only ones here," Giselle said, pressing her nose against the glass and peering between the black metal bars, bringing her face-to-face with the blackened skull of Mary Magdalene, who appeared to be smiling garishly.

"Don't be shy," Giselle whispered, and David followed suit.

Seeing the braincase right in front of them was unforgettable and creepy. The skull was wearing a solid gold wig, made to look both like hair and headscarf; it descended in flowing waves onto a graceful, sculptured golden neck. Her gold cloak was fastened with an ornate brooch embossed with the face of Jesus, positioned just above a gold reliquary that held a piece of flesh, traditionally attributed to the spot on her forehead touched by Jesus. Two sets of gold wings fluttered around the reliquary as if they were ready and able to take flight, and all of this was mounted on the sarcophagus, which contained the rest of her bones.

"It's mesmerizing. And grotesque. I know I said I was convinced, but now—do you think it's really her?" David asked.

"I do," was the immediate response. "I don't think she would've loved having her skull displayed in a glass box with all the gold stuff around it, but I hope she would've understood it was created out of love and reverence. I wish this horrible fence wasn't here, but I guess the Basilique has its reasons. Things have changed."

"Sad but true. But I'm glad we came, because if you're right, and she's the one who brought us together, I want to say thanks."

"It costs nothing to give her the credit."

"You did good," David said to the smiling skull, "and to paraphrase the Bard, my heart is replete with thankfulness."

"Mine too," Giselle said as she took David's hand and headed back upstairs.

17

HÔTEL LE COUVENT ROYAL SAINT-MAXIMIN-LA-SAINTE-BAUME

MONDAY JUNE 17, 2013

"BY THE WAY, I forgot to tell you I heard from Gilbert just before I left Toulouse," Giselle said, as she stood still outside the Basilica door waiting for her eyes to adjust to the brilliant light. She reached into her bag, fumbling for her sunglasses, and put them on. "I assume our dinner is still on, but he was—I don't know—reluctant to commit. I had to swear on my father's grave that I was really his cousin by blood and give him my word of honor I wasn't doing research for a book."

David took her hand as they slowly began to meander across the plaza.

"That sounds even more weird than what you described in your letter. Suppose you were writing a family history, or a memoir."

"I think he would've refused to meet me," she said, shrugging her shoulders, "but it's what I promised Papa. And it brought us here, so that's a bonus."

"It certainly is, and this is only the beginning. I'm looking forward to more."

"Gluttony is a sin," she said playfully. She barely recognized the woman she was in David's company; the freedom was exhilarating. "Maybe it's better to be satisfied with what we've got."

" 'Can one desire too much of a good thing?' " David asked.

"Are you quoting someone?"

"Shakespeare—*As You Like It.* And my answer to his rhetorical question is—absolutely not!" His grin broadcast the turn his thoughts had taken.

"Now you've distracted me with innuendo and I've forgotten what I was going to say."

David began to stroke her wrist, and his slowly circling thumb started a cascade of desire she didn't understand but couldn't deny.

"Hungry?" she asked to distract herself. "I know it's early but I thought it would be pleasant to eat outside. There's a restaurant in the convent connected to the Basilica—it's been repurposed, of course, and I have no idea whether the food is any good. Are you okay with that?"

"Even if I wasn't the most agreeable man you ever met, there's very little that wouldn't be okay with me this morning. We're together and your hand sends little electric shocks to my heart. I just got to thank Saint Mary Magdalene personally for bringing you into my life, and last night was magical." David looked at her suggestively. "You know I enjoy good food, but it isn't always my highest priority."

"Behave yourself. We're going into a former convent," she whispered.

Sexual innuendo that would have made her twitch in the past, or pushed her away, had become a private communication that only heightened the intimacy between them. David laughed and brushed his lips against her cheek. "I promise not to say anything that will make a nun's ghost blush," he said.

They were seated quickly in the cloister arcade at a little table for two, quite a distance from other diners. The sky was the spectacular Mediterranean blue, which, she pointed out, was unique to this region, and the exact color Cézanne, Van Gogh, and Matisse had successfully captured. Beyond the towering adjacent Basilica, the mountains provided a purple backdrop worthy of a Hollywood soundstage.

"Did you notice there was a statue of a monk sort of guarding the menus inside?"

"Seems like a respectable and important post. Maybe he's praying we'll like the food," David suggested, with a grin.

"Well, I hope it doesn't require prayers, but if it does, I pray his are answered."

David excused himself, and on his way back stopped for a moment to kiss the top of Giselle's head, murmuring something about finding her irresistible. When she felt him behind her, and heard his barely perceptible words, it occurred to her that being jilted had been a blessing.

"Let's have some wine and celebrate the moment," she said. "It's amazing to feel I don't want to be anywhere else in the entire world or with anyone else. I love being a couple...with you. We are a couple, wouldn't you say?"

"I would."

"Well, I'm making a conscious effort to let go of the past and focus on the present, despite the irony that so much of this trip is about times gone by."

"I'm so happy to hear you say that. I was afraid you were getting a little morose down in the crypt."

Giselle laughed. "True enough, but if not in a crypt, where? I couldn't help thinking about poor Marie-Madeleine, stuck behind an iron fence and bulletproof plastic. But so what if she's trussed up with a horrible gold wig—looks aren't everything, and certainly not when you're two thousand years old. She was an extraordinary, inspiring woman."

The waiter approached as quietly as the monks who'd walked on these stones before him, poured the white wine chilling beside the table, and discreetly glided away.

"A toast," David said, as he raised his glass and touched hers lightly, "to the people we treasure from the past, and a future we have yet to discover."

"I guess archeologists are always hoping to discover something, no doubt something important."

"Of course," he said thoughtfully, reaching for her hand across the table and smiling into her eyes, "but right now, all I'm interested in discovering is you—what you think, what excites you, and what we can be to each other. I want to discover that my mother was right when she said the most powerful force in the world is love. I may be a particularly foolish mortal, but I know when I've made the discovery of a lifetime."

18

ON THE ROAD TO THE GROTTO, SAINTE-BAUME

JUNE 18, 2013

THE ALARM RANG at five thirty. Giselle turned it off, stretched out full length next to David and kissed him on the shoulder. "The sunrise will be incredible over the mountain. Wake up, you slacker, you promised. It'll be worth it."

"There's only one thing that would make it worth it," he said, still half asleep, wondering what had possessed him to agree to this plan. Her skin was warm against him, and an immediate surge of sensual pleasure made his pulse quicken. *Let's not go*, he thought, as he responded to the feel of her soft, bare skin against his. "I don't really see how anything could be better than being here with you, a little early-morning loving, watching the sunrise through the window and sharing the best part of life."

"I didn't say it would be better," Giselle said as she rolled away, got up, and padded into the bathroom to brush her teeth, take a quick shower, and get dressed.

"Okay, okay, but you'll have to make it up to me. I'll get up. But once we get to Rennes-le-Château, I want to renegotiate."

He made a show of sounding disgruntled, although he knew she wasn't buying it. There were many nights—and mornings—ahead with nothing to divert them from each other. *Being with a woman who wakes up in good spirits is a gift,* he consoled himself. Crowds made her feel a little nervous, she'd confided, and though he didn't really understand, it was far better to get an early start than to cause her any uneasiness.

"Emerson wrote 'give all to love,' and that's my plan," he called to her. "Don't turn off the shower, I'm getting in."

"These switchbacks are treacherous," Giselle whispered, as if speaking in a normal voice would plunge them off the side of the mountain.

"They certainly are, but no need to whisper—it's not a secret."

"You can't even imagine how crazy anxious this makes me. I'm actually screaming, silently, and I feel like I might faint."

"I heard you breathe in, but then, nothing. I think you're holding your breath, which actually could make you faint. At least that's what I've heard. Anyway, breathing is always a good idea."

"When I was a kid, my parents had friends who lived in a village called Grimaud, in the mountains, but not too far from the sea. They invited us to visit whenever it was convenient; so one spring break we took them up on it. My parents were in the front of a little Peugeot they rented, and my sister and the dog and I were crammed in the back. Just like now, we had to drive on the outside, no guardrails, a narrow little road not really wide enough for two cars, with these hairpin turns, over and over and over and over..."

She took a deep breath. "I really thought we were going to die. The whole time, hours, I guess, of being terrified, totally heart-pounding terror, and I promised myself I would never, ever, do anything like that again. And then, years later during a family trip to Saint-Maximin-la-Sainte-Baume—when it should have been a distant memory—Papa begged me to go to the Grotto. But when I heard what this road would be like, I wouldn't do it. He and my mother went alone, but the climb was too hard for her and she never made it all the way up, so of course he didn't either, and he never got to see it. I still feel guilty about that because if I'd been willing, well... Anyway, I know he'd be happy I'm finally going, but now, here I am again. I think I've suppressed exactly how terrified this makes me feel, so please, please, pretend there's a huge tortoise creeping up the road in front of us."

"Don't worry, I don't want you to have a panic attack, I don't want to make you scream out loud and, for your information, I don't want to die either. Maybe you should close your eyes."

"No, no, there's a tiny speck of control in seeing where we're going, and anyway, I don't want to miss this sunrise. At the risk of sounding a little flowery and syrupy again, I'd say it looks like the sky's been tie-dyed. Maybe by angels."

"Yes to flowery, but I get it. It's one of your anxiety-generated metaphors. So far as I'm concerned, you can be as flowery as you like."

A fuchsia-red sky lit the massif, making the quartz-shot limestone appear to be dripping blood.

"I see what you mean, it does look tie-dyed; reminds me of Arizona and the mesas where the Hopi Indians live. If Mary Magdalene actually found her way up there, she probably chose it for the same reasons they did. It's flat, unobstructed, and high enough to feel there's nothing separating you from heaven. And at this ungodly—forgive me—hour of the morning, well, I see why you're thinking of angels. We should be listening to the Hallelujah Chorus."

Without taking his eyes off the road, he gave her a quick smile, hoping the spectacular sunrise would take her mind off the repetitive hairpin turns as they zigzagged higher and higher.

"I actually never accepted that Marie-Madeleine lived up there," Giselle said, "particularly because we know she walked around preaching and spreading the Word. It would have been totally impractical. But you know, legend has it she survived there for thirty years, meditating, not eating or drinking, visited five times a day by angels who took her to the clouds, played music, and danced with her."

"Yes, I read some variation of that," he said. "I've never understood why people have to go that extra step and take the story into a supernatural twilight zone, but they seem to do that over and over. What nature, and people, have to offer in reality—that's the miracle, and that's what we should celebrate and protect."

Giselle was quiet, making David wonder if he'd been a little too blunt and dismissive. "What do you think of Mary Magdalene's thirty-year legend?" he asked.

"It could have been a local legend, but I wouldn't be surprised to find out the Church invented it to counter Pope Gregory branding her a prostitute in 591. She couldn't become a saint unless they created a way for her to earn forgiveness and repent. Some people still refer to her as a wanton dirty whore. It's incredibly upsetting because she was a remarkable woman who managed to leave a lasting legacy even though she lived at a time when women were pretty much nothing. So no, I don't think she fasted in a cave for thirty years praying for forgiveness for sins she never committed; but, finding her way up here to die, alone, closer to heaven, I can see that."

"You sound pretty angry," he said, "as if you take it personally."

"I guess I do, which is a little ridiculous, and I apologize. I told you she was a role model, and when innuendo damages someone's reputation, particularly someone like her, well…anyway, we're making a pilgrimage in her honor, and that's really all that matters today."

"People from the past—good and bad— people who breathed this air and drank this water thousands of years ago, send whispers on the wind. They have a lot to teach us if we're not afraid to know the truth. Objective truth can't always be known, but Mary Magdalene certainly made her truth heard."

"And I think she would've appreciated your support almost as much as I appreciate your driving. I feel much better."

"Thanks. That's probably because we're almost at the parking area."

19

THE GROTTO, SAINTE-BAUME

JUNE 18, 2013

A FEW MINUTES later they arrived at the small, empty gravel parking area that had been carved out of the forest at the base of the massif. Towering gray granite walls rose in front of them like a volcanic island erupting from a surrounding ocean of rolling green.

"What a great, old tree," Giselle said, pointing to the huge gnarled remains of trunk and branches pirouetting on a grassy strip at the edge of the gravel.

"Go stand in front so I can take a picture," David said, taking the camera off his shoulder. "I'd probably get a decent shot with my phone, but call me old-fashioned, I still like the real thing."

A wooden signpost bearing two arrows pointed in opposite directions, each labeled Grotto of Marie-Madeleine. The slightly more generous walkway on the left was covered with a thin layer of small, grey granite pebbles. David reached for Giselle's hand, and without a word they set off on the path that disappeared between the trees as it began to wind its way up the mountain.

Diamonds of dew sparkled on low-lying greenery. Moss and lichen-blanketed rocks, as well as wild mushrooms and ivy, carpeted the forest floor, and birds sang into the otherwise silent surround.

"There's something very sensual about this place," David murmured, "so lets take our time and savor it." Giselle smiled and nodded in agreement, as if this was an ordinary thing to say; of course it wasn't, but it described the experience perfectly.

"I think part of the sensuality is the sense of seclusion and hush," she said. "It's a fairytale enchanted forest glen, and I almost expect to see wood nymphs, or some sort of little prehistoric creature who's lived here thousands and thousands of years hiding behind a tree."

"They're all still sleeping," David whispered. "Maybe we'll see one on the way down."

Giselle gave him a look and was just about to remark that the climb wasn't as difficult as she'd heard, when the angle went from gentle slope to sharp incline, making it far less of a leisurely stroll as each step became more of an effort.

"Well, now I see why my mother couldn't do it, so shame on me for my ungenerous thoughts. This is making me feel old. But look at you. I'm impressed! You're carrying the backpack and I'm wishing for a walking stick," she said. "This is the price for my sedentary life."

"We can stop if you get tired; no shame in that," was his quick reply, "and if I see a loose branch, your wish will be granted."

He reached behind into the backpack, took out a bottle of water and offered it to her.

"I think I'm quickly getting used to being pampered."

"As I said before, you're easy," he said, and kissed her.

"Actually, I'm not. I'm sort of prickly." She paused, waiting for David to laugh and say he didn't believe it, but when he remained silent she added, "and I'm extremely stubborn and not very forgiving. So be warned." She unscrewed the bottle cap, took a long sip and handed the bottle back.

"I can see that," he said, sounding serious and shaking his head slowly up and down, "but I say bring it on—if you need to. I can take it, and I'm not pushed away so easily." He smiled, and the familiar mixture of amusement and mischief began to twinkle in eyes. "Even porcupine gentlemen find a way to, uh, cozy up to their womenfolk."

He opened his arms, and she stepped into his embrace as he wrapped his arms around her. "Don't worry," he whispered into the nape of her neck, "your Marie-Madeleine has plans for us."

Giselle kissed him and stepped back. "I can't argue with that," she said.

A few minutes more of gentle climbing brought them to a stone cistern collecting spring water where a small bird had stopped to take a drink. It quickly flew off and perched on the highest branch of a nearby tree, as if it was waiting for them to move along. Giselle was about to speak when David put his finger to his lips, and then to hers, pointing to a sign asking for silence. She nodded.

The dense, majestic forest was a designated holy place, just as it had been since the Middle Ages, protected by a royal decree and Papal Bull. Nothing was to be disturbed. Indigenous moisture-dependent plants, rare in Provence and unique to Saint-Baume, thrived and covered the mountainside with lush greenery. Venerable old trees with exposed roots thick as trunks kept the sharply tilted forest floor from sliding down the mountain and washing away.

They walked slowly, hand in hand, Adam and Eve in an ancient forest, ascending toward open sky as they might have at the beginning of time. *Countless others have made this pilgrimage, hiking to the Grotto and taking care not to leave a remnant of civilization*, Giselle thought, *and we are all connected by that thread, that reverence for nature's perfect creation.* The fragment of a poem she had memorized in an English literature class, *God's in his heaven—* came to mind. *Was it Robert Browning or Elizabeth Barrett Browning?*

David would know. The question seemed pressing enough to break the silence.

" 'God's in his heaven,' " she whispered in his ear, to which he replied, " 'All's right with the world.' *Pippa Passes,* Robert Browning. That sums it up for me too."

Giselle paused to translate the message appearing on a small sign planted along the path, but her whisper floated away on the breeze. David squeezed her hand; *no matter how old or how big you are*, he thought, *this sort of place is a reminder of how small and insignificant we actually are.* He pictured his eight-year-old self, sitting with his parents on Sunday mornings listening to Reverend Ward, who had preached in a hushed voice that encouraged the congregation to be absolutely silent. Those were the last years of innocence.

His mother's health began to fail when he was twelve, and he'd go to church with the sole purpose of striking a bargain with Jesus; he'd be the most obedient boy in the world, he'd never complain, he'd make any sacrifice, any, if only his mother could be herself again, without the cancer or the pain. She took a lot of years to die, but she suffered the entire time and was too weak and exhausted to attend church. His father had no interest in anything that took him away from the woman he loved, and David decided praying was a waste.

He shook himself out of his reverie and took a deep breath of the sweet, mountain air, thick with the scent of lavender and the unnamed, but unmistakable, fragrance of abundant foliage. He leaned toward Giselle and whispered, "I love you, and my mother would have loved you too, prickles and all."

As the angle of the incline became more acute, horizontally laid logs terraced the path into wide plateaus. After almost an hour of walking beneath the leafy canopy concealing the mountain and sky, Giselle looked up to see the massive gray wall of the massif looming above the treetops, the adjacent monastery an appendage hanging over its side.

"It doesn't look real." The awe Giselle felt was clear in her voice, as they began climbing the hundred and fifty limestone stairs carved into the stone. Saplings grew directly out of the granite stairway, and sparse vegetation emerged from natural crevices, crawling along the walls as if to announce nature could not be thwarted by man's meager attempts to civilize it.

They passed through a large wooden door and found themselves on a level platform in front of the cave.

"Absolutely spectacular," Giselle murmured. "Do you remember that scene in *The God's Must Be Crazy*, at the end, when he reaches the edge of the cliff to throw the Coke can off and he thinks it's the edge of the world?"

David nodded. "That's exactly how it feels. I could easily believe we had climbed to the highest spot on the planet if I didn't know better." He took out his camera and motioned for her to stand facing him in front of the entrance to the Grotto. Her pale cheeks were flushed and slightly damp from exertion, and the sunlight turned her hair to flame; his breath caught in his chest when he looked at the image through the viewfinder. Botticelli's Venus was staring directly into his eyes through the lens; disconcertingly beautiful, and fragile.

Throughout his years of traveling alone he had taken many great photos—landscapes, he privately told himself, that would be worthy of National Geographic. *But that was the art of the lonely*, he thought, as he snapped a few more shots with Giselle in the foreground of each. Taking photos of her, not just a place or a thing, felt normal; it meant something, it transformed a memorable vista into a shared experience.

On the mountainside adjacent to the plateau there were large painted statues easily recognizable as the Virgin Mother, Mary of Bethany; Mary Magdalene was sitting at the feet of Jesus on the cross, her long red hair streaming loosely over her shoulders and down her back. "That could definitely be you," he said, "the Renaissance ideal."

"You and my father would have had a lot in common," Giselle said as they climbed the small flight of stone steps that led to the wooden plank doors covering the gaping entrance to the cave, "he was always saying something that embarrassed me, just the way you do."

20

INSIDE THE GROTTO, SAINTE-BAUME

JUNE 18, 2013

"THIS ISN'T WHAT I expected," Giselle whispered, as she stood at the entrance, mesmerized by the sheer volume. "It's huge."

"Maybe the Saint was claustrophobic."

"You're making fun of me."

Seven stained glass windows cut high into the outer stonewall provided the only dim light, and droplets clung to the jagged stone high above, dripping occasionally and forming small pools on the floor. A drop landed on her head before she moved away.

"The walls are weeping," she whispered, pointing to tiny threads of water seeping out of invisible crevices and slowly trickling down over the face of the granite and into a cistern.

An elaborate chapel whose large altar displayed a relief of Jesus on the cross dominated the center of the cave, but was dwarfed by the soaring stonewalls. About twenty empty primitive wooden benches with kneelers faced the altar; a reliquary box containing Mary Magdalene's tibia and a lock of hair sat in a little glass box around the corner.

Toward the far back wall of the Grotto, almost hidden in the gloom, stood another white marble sculpture—this one of a beautiful, young Mary Magdalene being lifted up, dancing with angels in front of flickering candles.

"So beautiful," Giselle whispered, "and mystical. I want to dance with her." She and David lit votives and placed them in the iron stand. She stood still and closed her eyes, shutting out the art and artifacts, not thinking, only aware of a visceral response to this place. *She's here. I feel her presence. Maybe I'm losing my grip on reality, and conjuring this up, but she's here.* Giselle gave a little shiver, trying to shake it off; she imagined her father standing next to her, skeptical, but not dismissive. She knew what he'd say, "Spiritual people have spiritual experiences, and you are a spiritual girl. Don't confuse it with being religious. You can be that too, but they're not the same."

She opened her eyes and looked at the shadows cast on the cave wall by the flickering candles. "Let's go downstairs," she said, taking David's hand.

They descended to the bottom of the Grotto and sat on a small stone bench facing the third life-sized carved likeness of Mary Magdalene. The rough, jagged granite was an incongruous backdrop for the smooth, polished white marble. The Saint sat on the ground, legs curled beneath her, the large crucifix in her arms replacing and symbolizing the body of the man she adored; she was a portrait of grief, suffering, and sorrow. *She feels despair,* Giselle thought, as her eyes filled with tears, *and not just for herself—for all the loss and loneliness people endure, hopeless and helpless at the hands of the violent and evil.*

David quietly put his hand in his pocket and brought out a cotton handkerchief, neatly folded into a clean, white square, and offered it to her. Wondering if her father's spirit inhabited David's body, she took it and patted her eyes dry.

"Ready?" David asked. She nodded and stood, brushing her hair over her shoulder so her cheek could touch his. "I know whatever I experienced, or thought, while I was here was something I brought with me," she whispered, "but I would swear it was coming from her. She touched my heart."

The stone ramparts and steps outside the cave were crowded with people grateful for a place to sit after their arduous walk, enjoying their moment in the sun like so many lizards. David and Giselle moved to the perimeter and stood still, without saying a word. Giselle was reminded of a night, years before, when she had been invited to join a Jewish friend at the evening service that ushered in Yom Kippur, the sacred day of atonement and fasting that marked the end of one year and the beginning of the next. The cantor, a full, rich baritone, had sung the mournful prayer called *Kol Nidre* in Hebrew, a haunting five thousand-year-old melody that was clearly some sort of plea.

At the conclusion of the service she became aware that all the worshippers remained silent; no one shook hands or said good-bye as they went their separate ways. Several days later, when she inquired whether people were forbidden to speak, she was told it wasn't a rule, but came about spontaneously as people retreated into contemplation and self-reflection, *Of course. It's nondenominational spirituality. I'm not praying to someone, I'm praying with someone who inspires me to do some soul-searching as a member of the human race.*

"I hope it's easier going down," she said.

21

DRIVING DOWN FROM THE GROTTO

JUNE 18, 2013

"DRIVING DOWN IS not quite as death-defying as driving up," Giselle said, "but I'm still terrified, even on the inside next to the mountain when we wouldn't be the ones hurtling off the cliff into space."

"Also, I'm driving more slowly than a donkey cart." David laughed. "So, where did you get the red hair? Someone Irish, or Celtic, in your ancestry?"

"No, not that anyone knows about or admits to. Actually, people rarely ask me if I'm Irish. Anyway, I got my hair, my nose, and my reserve from my Mamie. I don't think I mentioned that my mother never liked her, probably because Papa adored her. Mamie tried to be tolerant, but I know she thought my mother was a vain, superficial woman and she hoped I would do something more meaningful with my life than shop. She thought we had some Greek ancestors."

"Aha. Perhaps you're descended from Cleopatra. She was actually a redhead, despite Elizabeth Taylor, and, need I say, smart as well as beautiful. Or, if it turns out Jesus and Mary Magdalene were married and had children…"

"I knew you were going to say that," Giselle said, laughing and shaking her finger. "None of that *Da Vinci Code* conspiracy for me."

"So, what's the latest on the *Gospel of Jesus's Wife?*"

"Well, you know, Karen King continues to believe it's authentic, but even she is open to further testing. Never before has such a tiny scrap been subjected to such scrutiny."

"Do the official Gospels say outright that Jesus wasn't married?"

"No. It's just an assumption people make. And if He was married to someone other than Marie-Madeleine, you'd think his wife would've complained."

David laughed. "The Hebrew fathers, like Abraham and King David, had many, many wives. That was the way, although in my experience the right woman can keep you pretty busy."

"You mind returns to sex like a boomerang."

"It's your fault; sitting next to you, feeling—anyway, it's normal, and that's why it's easy for me to believe Jesus was married. He wasn't afraid of love. It's too bad there's nothing written that comments on his marital status."

"Well, if the Cathars hadn't been murdered by the Catholic Church, we'd probably have a way to verify the truth, whatever it is. But the Albigensian Crusaders exterminated them, even more completely than the Nazis did the Jews. The Cathars had preserved a book they said contained writings of Jesus, called *The Book of Love;* it was the foundation of their church. They were tortured until they revealed where the book and all the writings were hidden, and then everything was burned. It's disgusting."

Giselle stopped speaking, opened the window, and inhaled. "The mountain air and the perfume of wild thyme and lavender always make me feel better. It reminds me of Mamie and carefree times. I've spent the vast majority of my life in cities, but even the ones with huge parks or green areas and gardens are cultivated—the seeds come from somewhere else, like immigrants." She took another deep breath and smiled.

"You know, my everyday life has a very narrow focus, and my colleagues and I constantly talk about minutiae we all think is important. But sometimes I wonder if I'm missing the bigger picture. For instance, I've never paid much attention to the plight of women in today's world, but recently I've been more aware that even if the world is a totally different place than it was two thousand years ago, a woman's place in it hasn't changed that much, relatively speaking, particularly for women of faith. We can become saints once we're dead, but not priests, bishops, or cardinals while we're alive."

"Cardinal Giselle Gélis, I see you in a long, flowing red gown. You'd be stunning and a huge distraction to all those men of the cloth."

Giselle started to giggle. “Maybe I should shoot for pope, because that’s the position with real power. Also, white is a little more elegant.”

“The world would be at your feet,” David said. “And I would write the Gospel of Giselle to prove to future generations that it really happened.”

“If only it were that simple.” She leaned her head on the window frame to let the rushing air blow across her face. “The fact is if the church didn’t like what some book or bit of writing had to say, well”—she gestured across her neck with the flat of her hand—“finis. The end. It would wind up like the Gospel of Philip.”

“I don’t know much about that,” said David, “except that it was discovered at Nag Hammadi in 1945.”

“It’s one of the Gnostic Gospels, but they’ve all been ignored and excluded, except by a few academics.”

“Why is that?” David asked.

“There are lots of excuses, but the truth is the Church didn’t like what they had to say. For instance, the Gospel of Philip refers to Marie-Madeleine as the *koinonos* of Jesus—translation: companion or partner.”

“I had no idea,” David said, noting the anger that had crept into Giselle’s voice. “It sounds like this is another one of those issues that gets under your skin.”

“I don’t like it when people in power promote misleading information. Like the weapons of mass destruction hoax, or making people believe that Gnostic means nonbeliever, or heretic. It’s just the opposite; it means someone’s who’s enlightened; gnosis, knowledge—anyone can see the root of the words is the same.”

“Of course. So gnosis is something like the Buddhist idea of enlightenment?”

“Yes, exactly. Where was I? Oh, the Gospel of Philip. He wrote that Jesus loved Marie-Madeleine more than the other apostles, and that he kissed her frequently on the mouth.”

“Wow! I didn’t know that. What do you make of it?”

“I don’t know. Nobody knows enough. And lots of people, including scholars, come with a preconceived idea, and if something doesn’t fit in neatly, they put a lot of effort into discrediting it. That’s the way it’s always been. Look at the battles in the States over climate change; people believe what they choose to believe. And by the way, I have no doubt that climate change is a man-made catastrophe, and Pope Francis does too."

"He's a remarkable man. I really admire how much he's speaking out, but the conservatives don't seem to be fans."

"Exactly. He's closer to Jesus's teaching—about women, humility, the immorality of wealth inequality. If Peter were alive today he'd be apoplectic. He was outraged that Philip said Jesus favored a woman over him, or trusted significant teachings to a woman, regardless of the fact that it's what Philip observed. Most people who've studied Marie-Madeleine think she was educated, literate, and articulate, but Peter didn't want to hear that."

David shook his head in agreement. "It might as well be several thousand years ago, as far as orthodox religious groups are concerned. None of them have woman in positions of authority. Look at the Muslims, or orthodox Jews. They basically refuse to acknowledge we've learned anything meaningful since the Bible was written."

"I know, but until I read what Dr. King presented in Rome, I just didn't think about it. Even if the fragment turns out to be a fake, I can't continue to ignore how the Church, my Church, views women. And treats them. It shouldn't matter if Jesus was married or celibate, should it?"

"Well, you know the answer to that. For some people he has to be celibate to be pure, uncontaminated by sex, or desire—like Adam before the apple. Of course, if Adam never took a bite, it wouldn't have been the beginning of the human race. It would have been the end." David laughed, but kept his eyes on the road. The cave had put Giselle in a feisty mood, and he was enjoying her diatribe, which needed no encouragement.

"You know," she said, "several popes were married and many more had mistresses and fathered illegitimate children, so obviously the celibacy laws were totally ignored. In fact, it's said that Pope Julius II advised his secretary to take three mistresses at one time, in memory of the Holy Trinity. It's so hypocritical. Look at the way they covered up for priests who molested little boys."

"Well, Professor, I think you're preaching to the choir."

"Oh, David, I had something like—I'll call it a mystical experience—in the Grotto. I guess it sounds like it's getting to be a habit, but I swear I felt Marie-Madeleine's presence. It wasn't a vision, or anything like that. I just felt her reaching out to me, reminding me of all she suffered, and that women have to stand tall. That's what my father used to tell me, stand tall. I plan to take it to heart and be less complacent about these things."

"Without making light of that, let me remind you that despite being the opposite sex, I fully support you and I'm here to help."

"I know, I know. Maybe that's why she sent you to me."

He laughed again and patted her thigh. "I'm willing to give her the credit. Some men feel threatened by charismatic, powerful women like her, but I think it's sexy, so feel free to let your inner tiger out."

They both started laughing, and the little creases that always appeared between her eyebrows when she was worried or anxious, disappeared.

"I'm hungry," David announced. "Perhaps we should go someplace where you can get red meat."

22

COUSTAUSSA

SEPTEMBER 29, 1891

OLD AGE HAD crept up on Father Antoine Gélis, although there were times he thought he had become old when other boys became adolescents. Autumn was in the air, and the changing seasons, even minor shifts in night temperatures, made his joints ache and his patience short. It had been only four years since his glorious trip to Italy, but as every successive summer gave way to cooler temperatures, and leaves began to dry up and return to the earth, he couldn't escape conceding his traveling days were over. Even the memories had become cloudy and seemed more like fanciful wishes.

Arthritis had set in early in life, as it had for generations of his family, leaving his knuckles disfigured and painful, and turning his knees to large knots of burl supported by bowed twigs of legs. The thought of walking long distances made him wince. Kneeling to pray, a bedtime ritual he felt compelled to endure, only made things worse, sending excruciating pain shooting into his hip and spine, precluding any slim chance of a spiritual experience.

The biting night wind chilled the marrow of his bones, and he lay in bed shivering, despite a warm flannel nightshirt, the gift of Bérenger Saunière, and a nightcap pulled tightly over his balding head. Men had wives to keep them warm in their old age, even stupid men with big bellies who didn't bathe and couldn't read. He had never known that comfort or companionship, although he still remembered being a young boy and assuming he'd have a girl in his life someday, someone like Emilie.

If he closed his eyes he could still picture her rosy-cheeked face and straw-colored hair, smiling at him when he'd walk past her cottage at the start of a new school term. He was proud of being the smartest boy in the school, and she'd always give him a shy smile, which he assumed meant she liked him. He was a stellar student, surpassing everyone in his village. He'd taught himself to read Greek, Latin, and Aramaic fluently by the time he was fourteen, and he became conversant with Aristotle's ideas on physics, biology, and philosophy. Those were the glory days.

Nodding his head to himself, he recalled the painful morning his father sat him down and told him the priesthood was his only viable option; that was when misery crept into his soul, and slowly, over time, displaced joy and hope.

Despite his bitterness, he had always been too proud and stubborn to reveal the truth to anyone except young Saunière. "I was conscripted," was the phrase he used with countless acquaintances over the years, "but it turns out to be a fine life for a poor country boy with no other prospects." Making people laugh and nod in agreement allowed him to present himself as a good-humored man who'd made peace with his destiny; and, over the years, there were times he almost believed it.

These days he barely remembered why it had ever mattered at all. His brain was as sharp as it had ever been, but the relentless repetition of his days made him feel dull. He doubted that any of his parishioners would know the difference, or care. He massaged his aching hands under the covers. *Lord, I've said Mass in Coustaussa for over four decades,* he prayed, *and I know it is Your will that I give thanks in all circumstances, but you must admit these years have brought me little but a shriveled body and shriveled dreams. I know it sounds like self-pity and complaint, but Lord, if I haven't mentioned it, I'm grateful you sent Bérenger Saunière. He is a ray of light in the murky obscurity of my old age.*

Several days before, a message had arrived from Rennes-le-Château, asking him to pick a date and have his presbytery prepared for an extravagant luncheon with a select group of neighboring priests, courtesy of young Saunière. They had both become men of the cloth reluctantly, but that superficial commonality didn't account for their like-mindedness, their interest in intellectual pursuits, or their distrust of Church hierarchy. Somehow, Saunière's spirit had not been crushed, and he infused their relationship with optimism and fearlessness. Along with Bishop Billard and young Henri Boudet, they had formed a secret brotherhood, and sworn allegiance to it and each other. They were confreres, united by unorthodox ideas they knew were better kept between them, and they confided in each other with total trust.

These luncheons were the highlights of Gélis' life, and he never inquired or allowed himself a flicker of curiosity about Saunière's ability to provide several bottles of good wine and a fresh rack of lamb, or something equally decadent for these occasions. Today, his old friend the Bishop of Carcassonne, Félix Billard, was invited along with the young priest from Rennes-les-Bains, Henri Boudet. Saunière's note said he had something to reveal that required advice and expertise, and the brotherhood would be gathering to share the secret.

Gélis woke at dawn feeling unusually energized. His joint pain was tolerable, and he was already salivating over the afternoon meal, the lively, stimulating conversation, and hearing about the mystery. At ten o'clock a messenger arrived with a note from Bishop Billard, saying he was indisposed, but was sending his thick-witted secretary, Guilliame Cros, in his place. It was an unfortunate turn of events, but the presence of that envious worm wasn't nearly enough to ruin the pleasure of the day to come.

At the appointed hour, Gélis waited at the threshold of the presbytery door despite the unseasonable chill. Saunière jumped out of the carriage before the driver pulled to a stop, and embraced the gaunt, older man.

"I'm anxious to hear what you'll need from me, but whatever it is can't possibly repay you for the feast you've provided. By the way, Félix is ill, but he's sending Guilliame, although I can't imagine what possessed him to do it.

"Antoine, I hope your heart is strong enough to see what I've brought with me today, but it's for you and Henri's eyes only. I'll inform Félix privately when I see him, but Guilliame is not to know. I don't trust him."

"Only a fool would, my boy, and you are no fool. He has the mind of a donkey, and he functions well in that capacity, but I think his envy of dear Félix's inheritance would lead him to be a Judas if anyone made him the right offer—and by that, I mean any offer—such a detestable creature!"

Henri arrived within minutes, and the three men walked into a small parlor where kindling and logs lay ready on the hearth. "Bérenger, perhaps you should light the fire, so it's more comfortable and appears a little more welcoming for Guillaume. I'll pour us each a glass a wine, and as soon as the donkey arrives, we'll excuse ourselves and see your astonishing treasure."

Saunière, who was kneeling and about to strike a match, began to laugh.

"You make it sound like some trinket a schoolboy brings home. Even you, a man well versed on the dark side of history, can expect his heart to feel as if it's been struck by a bolt of lightning." He lit the kindling, and the fire began to crackle.

"Don't worry, if my heart has withstood the banalities of the confessional, I think it must be made of iron."

Gélis knew how harsh he sounded, but the other men were used to his sharp tongue and jaded point of view, both of which they ignored with good humor.

"You'll change your tune in short order," Saunière said with assurance, totally unperturbed and relishing the moment he'd share his discovery and see their faces. The freedom to tease each other, the easygoing give-and-take, was part of the pleasure the brotherhood shared. They were the only ones who knew that Gélis belonged to the secret society of Rosicrucians, a belief system that transcended religion and connected him with nature, the greater physical universe and the spiritual world. It was a theology at the other end of the spectrum from the one into which he was ordained, philosophically closer to the Freemasons. The Church considered both of those groups evil adversaries, even though members of his subgroup, Esoteric Christian Rosicrucians, believed in Christ and prayed to him. It made no difference; it was forbidden, and if he was found out, the nuances would mean nothing to his congregants or superiors in Rome.

Cros arrived within minutes, making it impossible for the three to leave the room and offer any shred of diplomatic face-saving. Seeing no point in prolonging the inevitable, Father Gélis decided not to worry about the unavoidable bruise to Guilliame's ego and cleared his throat. "Bérenger, Henri. May I have your opinion on a very personal matter? Guilliame, please excuse us for just a few minutes, and enjoy the warmth of the fire and the wonderful cabernet Bérenger brought. We'll rejoin you shortly."

The three men left the room and followed Gélis, who limped down the narrow hall to his spare bedchamber and closed the heavy door.

Saunière reached into his cassock pocket and extracted two pieces of leather, independently rolled but tied together.

"Sit down, gentlemen," he said, motioning to the bed as he undid the ties and laid each piece of leather flat on the small wooden table standing against the wall. The yellowed letter and the small ancient parchment rested on top of each piece respectively.

"I am about to tell you a story, perhaps the most amazing story you will ever hear. One of our forerunners, Father Antoine Bigou, wrote a letter over two centuries ago and hid it in the wall of my church where I discovered it during the renovation. I have brought it with me today"—he indicated the single yellowed page—"and, as you shall hear when I read it to you, that letter directed me to a hiding place under the altar stone, where a concealed stairway descends to a sealed crypt. There, exactly where he said it would be among those buried in the tomb, was an urn which he knew, for a fact, contained two ancient documents. The urn itself is breathtaking, as intact as if it was newly turned on a potter's wheel in Toulouse. It was sealed with wax, which I carefully scraped away, allowing me the great privilege of examining both documents preserved inside. It was, without a doubt, the most thrilling experience of my life."

"You should write suspense stories, Bérenger. I'm too old to waste this much time on the prologue."

"Your patience will be well worth it, Antoine, and in any event, you have no choice. Where was I? Oh, yes, the larger document in the urn is an ancient papyrus, and though Father Bigou did not see it himself, he was told on the best authority exactly what it is and what it says. From the little research I could do on the Aramaic alphabet, I have no reason to believe he was mistaken. I've decided to share this stunning secret with you today, but the papyrus is sealed in the urn once again, and hidden away. However, there was another occupant of the urn"—he pointed to the parchment lying on the leather—"which I'm not able to decipher. Fortunately, you, Father Gélis"—he motioned dramatically to the older man—"will be able to apply your underused expertise in Aramaic, and if we're lucky, you'll be able to give us a hint of a translation. But before I read you the letter, I'd like your assurance that everything said in this room today will remain a secret of the brotherhood."

Saunière put out his hand, and each priest, in turn, laid his hand on top. "So sworn," each said in turn.

Saunière picked up Bigou's letter and stood next to the table, reading in a hushed voice until Gélis interrupted, "Speak up, Bérenger, my hearing isn't what it once was."

"Of course, Antoine," responded Saunière, beginning again many decibels louder, unaware that the increased volume of his deep, resonant voice could now be heard beyond the thick oak door where Guilliame, furious at being excluded, had positioned himself.

My Dear Monsieur,

I am Abbé Antoine Bigou, the parish priest at Rennes-le-Château since 1774 when I replaced my uncle, Abbé Jean Bigou, who left this life in the year of our Lord, 1776. My uncle had maintained a cordial relationship with the Hautpoul family, and I have continued that honored tradition. In 1781 I was summoned to hear the final confession of Marie de Nègre d'Ables, the wife of François d'Hautpoul, Marquis de Blanchefort, who had predeceased her.

At that time, she bequeathed to me, and not to her estranged children, the small remains of her estate and the entire archive of her family's ancestors. She also passed on to me the Hautpouls' family secret, which had been passed from generation to generation of Hautpouls before her, and, dear sir, it is that information I am now entrusting to you.

The Hautpouls have been landowners in the Languedoc since medieval times and have always been faithful to the Church. Members of the family took part in the Crusades with the Knights Templar. I tell you this to impress upon you that what is here revealed does not spring from disrespect for the Church, but rather from a deep love for it.

For hundreds of years, we in the Languedoc have had great reverence for Saint Marie-Madeleine, believing that after the crucifixion of our Lord, she came to France and lived here until her death. I have no reason to doubt this as the relics of this sainted woman were discovered in this land. But beyond that, I have the duty to present to you the evidence that Marie-Madeleine was the wife of our Lord Jesus Christ.

23

RENNES-LE-CHÂTEAU

CIRCA 1781

MASSIVE SWATHES OF velvet draped the windows, and had it not been for the light of a few flickering candles, the richly appointed sleeping chamber of Marie de Nègre d'Ables, the Marquise de Blanchefort would have been a tomb. She was already a ghost, propped up against layers of white embroidered cushions, her snowy nightcap disappearing into them, leaving only her pale face and dark eyes visible above the goose down quilt tucked around her. After a discreet knock on the intricately carved door, Abbé Bigou, her confidant and confessor, escorted by a ladies' maid, entered and sat down on a chair next to the bed. The Marquise motioned the servant woman away with a flick of her hand, and the door closed soundly, leaving the two alone in the shadows.

"Some water, if you would, Abbé." Although the Marquise's voice was weak, her tone was disconcertingly commanding. Bigou had attended others nearing death and expected to find a woman drained of will and spirit, but the impression made by the waxy skin stretched tightly between bony protuberances was misleading. She was frail, but her eyes were bright with life.

"Please let me assist you, Madame," Abbé Bigou said, quickly rising to his feet and pouring some water into the silver goblet beside the bed. She was bones in a nightdress as he put his arm behind her and offered the goblet. Sipping the water slowly, she forced herself to drink a few sips more than she needed, before indicating she was ready to be eased back against the large feather pillows.

"Thank you," she rasped. "There is much I must tell you and I fear I have precious little time left. Bring your head closer."

"Of course, Madame, but do not exert yourself. If I am meant to learn what you plan to tell me, God will provide enough time."

"That may be so, but Ecclesiastes says, 'there is a time for every matter under heaven,' and the time for this is now." The Abbé lowered his head to the level of the pillows, and the Marquise turned toward him and began to speak, determined to tell her story.

"One of my husband's more prominent ancestors was Bertrand de Blanchefort, the fourth Grand Master of the Templars. In the late 12th century, his grandson, Bertrand Raymond d'Hautpoul, left home to study theology at the University of Paris, but long before completing his studies, he lost interest, or so the story goes, and he turned his attention to science.

"When he returned home, he told his father he'd lost faith in the Catholic Church. As you know, the Cathar movement in the Languedoc was very strong, and though young Bertrand apparently didn't agree with all their teachings, he strongly supported their appreciation of women and shared their reverence for Marie-Madeleine, though the Church had branded her a sinner. And, of course, he strongly opposed the actions of Pope Innocent III."

The Marquise stopped and motioned for another sip of water. After helping her again, the Abbé, who knew the history of the Cathars well, said, "Yes, it was a terrible time of bloodshed. An Inquisition. After he was ordained—I believe it was 1198—he made it his mission to eradicate the Cathars and all their supporters, even members of the nobility. They were branded heretics, and all their sacred books and writings were burned."

The marquise nodded her head slowly in agreement. "Young Bertrand became a teacher, but, as the story was related to me, spent much of his free time exploring the caves around Saint-Maximin, hoping to find evidence that Marie-Madeleine had been there. This was perhaps forty or fifty years before the relics now at Saint-Maximin-la-Sainte-Baume were discovered. About a week after one of our small earthquakes, he was out walking on the mountain and noticed a cave he hadn't seen before, which he believed had been revealed by a shift in the massif. When he went to investigate, he found a small crevice deep in the wall, above a small pile of rocks that looked like they had fallen from the—"

The marquise began to cough and gestured for water. Bigou quickly reached across to the night table and poured a little water into the goblet as she reached out to take it from him.

"Thank you," she said. After several deep swallows, she handed the goblet back to him.

"Madame, perhaps you should rest now. I can come again tomorrow. This is clearly tiring you."

"No, I must finish." She was adamant. "I'm as strong today as I will ever be again." She took a deep breath and resolutely continued. "Bertrand lit a candle and looked in the space left bare by the rocks that had fallen away, and there, at the bottom of the crevice, he saw a clay jar sealed with wax. He suspected it was very old, and as it was told to me, he said he felt a divine presence had led him there.

"He brought the jar to Rennes-le-Château, scraped away the wax seal and removed the top. There were two ancient documents inside, a papyrus and a small parchment. He believed they were both written in Aramaic, which he'd studied briefly in Paris; obviously, he didn't study it well enough because he wasn't able to translate the small parchment at all. However, he could make out names on the larger papyrus, and he was certain it referred to a marriage; the remarkable thing is that the betrothed couple was Yeshua, the son of Joseph of Nazareth, and Miriam, the daughter of Cyrus of Magdala.

"Do you see what this means, Abbé?" she said, her reedy voice rising with excitement. "It proves what we here in the Languedoc have always believed—that Marie-Madeleine and Jesus were married."

Bigou sat back in his chair, stunned.

"Abbé, Abbé, say something."

"I apologize, Madame," he finally whispered, "but such news is…is… overwhelming. I am at a loss for words."

"You must listen carefully, for the times are just as perilous today as they were when these documents were discovered. Young Bertrand was afraid to reveal what he'd found, and rightfully so. Even without knowing what was written on the parchment, he had no doubt the pope would condemn and destroy them along with anyone who knew of their existence. He believed the only thing he could do was put them back in their jar and reseal it. Then, in the middle of the night, he went to our private chapel—of course, now it's the church of Maria Magdalena in Rennes-le-Château—found a secure spot somewhere in the crypt, placed the jar there, and had a large rock carved with some image moved to obscure the entrance to the stairway. Then, to be safe, he commissioned an altar to be built over it.

"As you know, the Hautpouls lost Rennes-le-Château to Simon de Montfort in the Albigensian Crusade when all the Cathars were murdered in 1212, and the property was given to Pierre Voisins. But the family was able to recover it in 1422 when Pierre Raymond d'Hautpoul married Blanche de Marquefave, a descendant of the Voisins family who received the Rennes property as her dowry. Even though the church had to be rebuilt after it was destroyed in the thirteenth and fifteenth centuries, the altar survived and never had to be moved; it is the same one that is there today. If the altar and stone are removed, the urn containing the documents will be in the space below."

"But Madame, this is not a good time to remove it; there is so much uncertainty: unrest among the peasants and poor, the rioting, the looting."

"Yes, yes, it is likely it will have to remain where it is during your lifetime," she said, "but now the secret is yours to guard and you must find the right person to pass it to before you die. God willing, there will come a time when this secret can be revealed."

The pupils of her eyes were huge, black orbs boring into his, imploring him with the intensity of a young, desperate, and impassioned woman, while wisps of silver hair escaped her nightcap as if electrified.

"I beg of you," she pleaded. "Help me die in peace with a free conscience."

Bigou sat absolutely still, head bowed. He was her confessor, her confidant, and friend. He had no choice; the burden was now his. "Yes, of course, Madame," he said slowly. "As our Lord Jesus Christ is my witness, I swear an oath to do what you request."

He crossed himself and smiled at her. "Put your mind at rest. Now, I will hear your confession."

24

COUSTAUSSA

SEPTEMBER 29, 1891

SAUNIÈRE PAUSED TO look at his stunned companions before continuing. "After a few paragraphs with instructions on where to find the clay vessel containing the documents, the letter concludes:

> *Finally, Monsieur, I pray that you are a man of courage and wisdom; I pray, too, that the age of Godlessness has passed, and you will be free to reveal the Truth of Our Lord Jesus Christ and Saint Marie-Madeleine.*
>
> *May God be with you and bless you.*
>
> *In the name of The Father, The Son and The Holy Spirit,*
>
> *Abbé Antoine Bigou"*

"Bérenger, I am stunned beyond reason," Henri said after several minutes of silence. "As you well know, archaeology is my hobby, and I go poking around as you do, always hoping to find some interesting remnant from the past, but I never imagined—couldn't imagine—can barely believe the papyrus you found in the urn is what this letter says it is."

"It takes time to modify your reality," Saunière replied, remembering he'd had the same reaction not too long ago, "but as best as I can tell, it appears to be what Bigou says it is. I've never studied archaeology, as you have, but I've consulted several fine books with drawings of first and second century urns, and the one left by Bigou fits those descriptions."

"Let me see the little parchment that has yet to be translated," Antoine interrupted harshly, slowly pulling himself to his feet and fumbling to get his spectacles on his nose. "Perhaps it will shed some light on this story."

With great care, Saunière lifted it from the piece of leather and placed it on the palm of Antoine's outstretched, gnarly hand. "Yes, it is written in Aramaic," he said with authority, bringing his head within an inch of his hand, as he began to decipher the tiny ink scratchings.

Saunière, whose eyes were riveted on the old priest's face, saw immediately that it was becoming as white as his sparse halo of hair. Gélis clutched his chest with his free hand, as he was overcome with dizziness and stumbled backward onto his bed.

"Dear Lord," he whispered hoarsely. "This cannot be true!"

25

ON THE ROAD TO RENNES-LE-CHÂTEAU

JUNE 18 - 19, 2013

THE MORNING AFTER they arrived at Château de Creissels, a spectacular medieval castle reincarnated as a charming luxury hotel, was the first leisurely one of the trip. It was exactly what David had been hoping for, and after lingering in bed, they barely made it to a late breakfast of flaky croissants and steamy cappuccino before the restaurant stopped serving.

"I'm so happy to be here with you," Giselle purred. "I don't think I've ever felt this content."

"My Madonna," he said, "you have a kind of glow that makes me wish I were a portrait painter. I'm lucky Titian isn't alive today to steal you from me. You know, we could just stay here, bypass our next stop, and go back to bed."

"You're incorrigible, but even if you've corrupted me and I'm tempted, Rennes-le-Château is not to be missed. Anyway, our next hotel is supposedly just as decadent and glorious as this one. We'll take the happiness with us."

He stood, took her hand, and put his arms around her as soon as she was on her feet. "A perfect interlude," he whispered before kissing her.

"It was," she whispered back.

Once they got on their way, he turned to her. "Okay. We're going to be on the road for quite a while, so regale me with the story of Rennes-le-Château. When's the last time you were you there?"

"I've been trying to figure that out; it's probably been about twenty years. I went with two of my girlfriends, Naomi and Greta, and we had a good time, but the strange thing is, I don't remember too many details. It's the mystery connected with it that makes it intriguing, but once you've seen it, there's no reason to go back…" Her voice trailed off. "Well, not unless you want to share it with someone," she added quickly.

"I'm glad the someone is me," David said, patting her knee. "And no matter where we've been before, doing it together makes it entirely different. I think I wrote something about the sensuality of sharing intense experiences in one of my letters."

"You did," she said. "But I don't think revisiting a village falls into that category."

"It might, if the place arouses some strong feelings. You know Masada? Coincidentally, also on a mountain."

"I've heard that," she said, laughing.

"Well, I've been there of course, but when you come to visit me, we'll go again, and I'll tell you the tragic story of the nine hundred souls who took their own lives rather than be conquered by the Romans. You'll be moved."

"So, you're expecting a visit from me?"

"That can't be a serious question," he said, glancing over and seeing the amusement in her eyes, "but just to be absolutely clear, yes, I'm expecting you to make the journey to the Holy Land. It's shocking that you've never been there, and I want to go on record as saying it should be a required journey for every biblical scholar. Also, I'm there, but if that's not enough of an incentive, there are some pretty amazing places to see."

Giselle gave his arm a little squeeze. "You're all the incentive I need, and you're right, I should have gone long ago, but for some reason I was never motivated. I don't know why. But now I'll have you as my personal guide, so maybe it was meant to be this way."

"In Israel they say 'it's beshert' when something is meant to be; and when someone—say me, for instance—finds the one—you, for instance—who's meant for him, he says she is his 'beshert.' "

"You mean like soul mates?"

"Exactly. But it also has the element of being fated, as if nothing happens by coincidence and there's a mysterious plan."

"What a great word; it describes us perfectly…beshert." Giselle lowered her voice. "But when it comes to mysteries, it will be hard to match the many mysteries and intrigue of Rennes-le-Château."

The neat little segue got a laugh from David.

"Ah, mystery," he said. "Taking bits of what's known and piecing them together until they reveal the ghost of the unknown. It's sort of what I do."

"I know, and it's why I'm sure the mystery of Rennes-le-Château will intrigue you. It's a real story, with dozens of clues and tantalizing fragments of information, but the most amazing part is, no one's ever figured it out."

"Well, as per your request, I controlled myself and didn't read up on it, even though I was tempted. But now the time has come. I'm prepared to be intrigued."

"Well, telling the story is something like trying to untangle a bowl of spaghetti, so bear with me. There are documented facts all mixed up with history, theories, rumors, and strange little morsels, but basically it all swirls around Abbé François Bérenger Saunière, the priest of Rennes-le-Château. Coincidentally, or maybe not so coincidentally, he and Uncle Antoine were friends, and I've always wondered if there's some connection to the murder."

"Interesting. And the mystery is…"

"Actually, there are two mysteries, both involving Saunière. First of all, he went from rags to major riches and no one has ever figured out how. Secondly, he scattered strange, provocative clues around, but no one's ever figured out what they mean. There's been endless speculation, of course, but it's been well over a hundred years…"

"Good grief woman, enough foreplay."

"Okay, just wanted to give you the background. So, in 1885 Saunière was sent to be the priest of Rennes-le-Château, which was a tiny, poor village—I think the population was about three hundred—at the top of an isolated mountain; there was a decaying medieval church—dedicated to Marie-Madeleine, by the way— but not even a place for him to live.

"I've seen photos of him, and he was very dashing, in a Latin lover kind of way, which may, or may not explain why a wealthy patroness—The Countess of Chambord—gave him a little money to fix up his church. He apparently had grand plans right from the start, and he had the workers move a large stone altar supported by two Visigoth pillars, and dig out a large boulder in the floor. Supposedly, the workers saw gold coins, either under the rock or in the wall, which Saunière may have taken."

"That doesn't sound like much of a mystery."

"True, but it wouldn't have financed very much either, and none of that's been verified. Anyway, here's where the intrigue begins. Supposedly, there were parchments hidden inside the hollow of one of the pillars."

Giselle stopped speaking and grinned.

"Yes, yes, and they said?"

"No one knows! As the story goes, Saunière couldn't decipher them and he was packed off to Paris to get a translation. Somehow, he met Emma Calvé, a famous opera singer at the time, and she was so smitten with him she visited Rennes-le-Château multiple times. In fact, she gave him a live monkey and a dog, and I read somewhere they carved their initials in a rock."

David laughed. "Any good story has sex in it, particularly a French story. Are you suggesting the priest and the opera singer got it on?"

"It's possible, although again, no one knows. He wouldn't be the first French priest to have a mistress. But that came before he met Marie, his housekeeper, who lived in the presbytery with him and was his lifelong confidant and companion. I think she was eighteen or nineteen when they met, and they were inseparable."

"So he was a man of passion."

"No doubt. He was certainly passionate about Rennes-le-Château."

"Now, back to the documents. What did they say?"

"Another of the unknowns. They disappeared without a trace, although some think they're still under lock and key in Paris at the Seminary of Saint-Sulpice. There's some speculation that they were a genealogy that traced the ancestry of Jesus to the Merovingian royal line."

"Leaving that aside for the moment, after he miraculously became a millionaire, what did he do with the money?"

"Most of it was spent on Rennes-le-Château, although he was very generous with great-great-uncle Antoine and another priest friend of his. The only thing the Church actually owned was the little church, so Saunière was able to buy up all the surrounding land. He designed and built his own presbytery with a private chapel, a tower, and a library; he planted elaborate gardens, and completely decorated the church interior after it was rebuilt.

And then there's the Orangerie, which is the thing I remember most clearly. It's a simple, extraordinary sort of a solarium, and he built it just so he could sit and watch the sun set over the Pyrenees. He gave banquets for the parishioners. He had bank accounts in Paris, Budapest, Toulouse, Vienna, and in the Hapsburg bank; the Duke of Hapsburg actually came to visit him."

"I'm impressed," said David. "The Hapsburgs were the most important family in Europe; if I remember my European history correctly, they ruled over the Holy Roman Empire for hundreds of years. Is there more?"

"Saunière used to walk the countryside and disappear for periods of time—and he and Marie used to dig in the church cemetery at night. When the parishioners complained, he built a wall around it, so they couldn't see what he was doing; then he built a secret room and a grotto in the garden."

"It's amazing that no one ever figured out how he became such a wealthy man."

"I know. The Church tried. They went to great lengths to explain it, and, more importantly, to discredit him. Their official position was he'd been selling masses, which he was, and they made him stop, but that's a ridiculous explanation; it's just not that lucrative. Others think he used information in the documents for blackmail; but he died safeguarding his secret. So, as I said, it's a mystery."

"It's really pretty incredible."

"I knew it would get to you. It's like a delicious, flaky pastry. Once you get a whiff, it's hard to resist. Every time I read about it, I discover some new piece I didn't know before. Anyway, he left everything to Marie, absolutely everything, including the secret. After many years, she sold the estate to a Neil Corbu, and promised to reveal the secret to him before she died; but she had a stroke and couldn't speak, except to whisper three words, 'pain, sel, vase.'

"Translation?"

"Bread, salt, and vase, like an urn, something you'd put flowers, or water in."

"What do you think she meant?"

"I have no idea," said Giselle, "nobody does. Saunière left a lot of stuff around that seems like pieces of a puzzle just waiting for someone to put them all together, but I'll just whet your appetite with one. He had an inscription carved over the archway leading into the church."

"And it said?"

" 'Terribilis est locus iste.' "

26

COUIZA AND RENNES-LE-CHÂTEAU

JUNE 19, 2013

"THERE'S NOTHING LIKE this in Rennes-le-Château," Giselle said, responding to David's question as they finished lunch in the enclosed courtyard of Château des Ducs de Joyeuse in the town of Couiza, about six kilometers from the hilltop village. "There's a little B & B but I knew you'd vote for romance and charm over tawdry and practical."

David grinned and held his glass of water aloft in a gesture of acknowledgment. "You've got my number," he said, "and I'd be happy to spend the afternoon here, relax, make love and enjoy our good fortune." He waited. Giselle smiled but said nothing. "Or, we can drive up to Rennes-le-Château, spend a little time in the church; then tomorrow, we can explore the rest of it and stay as long as we like."

"It's a hard choice," she said. "I'm tempted to stay here, really tempted; love in the afternoon sounds sort of...decadent, no, that's not the right word, maybe I mean illicit. I knew you were going to suggest it, but it makes me tingle even when I expect it. The downside is I know I'll doze off and then I won't be able to sleep tonight." She thought for a minute before adding, "How about a compromise? Let's go up to Rennes, have an early dinner without lingering over the wine or staring at the stars, and go up to bed."

"Sounds fine; you're always worth waiting for."

"I can't wait to see your expression when you open the door to the church."

"This is as treacherous as getting up to the Grotto," David commented, "I'm surprised you didn't mention it."

"I must have suppressed it," Giselle said, "because I wouldn't have turned down an afternoon of making love for an unnecessary, extra trip on this road."

"Now you tell me."

"Did you see that?" she shrieked, bursting into a fit of nervous laughter, and pointing to a little yellow graphic sign stuck in the gravel on the outer edge of the hairpin turn. A car flying off the side of a mountain said it all.

After paying two euros at the lower of two parking lots, they were permitted to drive further up the mountain, park, and climb an exceedingly long flight of open, weathered wooden steps that scaled the wall of granite and took them to the foot of the village.

"How on earth did he ever get to Paris?"

"If he was traveling with you, he probably never would have gone anywhere," David said, as he put his arm around Giselle's shoulders and gave her a quick squeeze.

Someone had painted life-sized portraits of Saunière and Marie on the outside wall of a small café, portraying them as nineteenth-century aristocracy, with her seated in a chair while he stood proudly at her side.

"Look at that!" Giselle knew she should be able to take some light-hearted teasing, particularly coming from David, but the trip up the mountain, and those steps had unnerved her. She moved away and stood in front of the portraits, trying to remind herself that her anxiety wasn't his fault, even if it was easy to blame him. "It's a good likeness, at least of him. He was courtly and tolerant, not like some people."

"I think I'll ignore that last part my prickly friend, but I see what you mean. He looks like an Italian movie star."

She smiled at him and the moment passed.

As they continued walking up the road, it became a brick-edged footpath, too narrow for cars, leading directly to the church, a modest fieldstone building set in red clay. A peaked, highly decorated wooden gable sheltered the front door and the small sculptural figure above bore the forerunner of a modern nameplate, identifying her as St. Maria Magdalena. Low stonewalls enclosed the walkway, preventing trespassers from trampling the grass, and iron gates kept intruders from wandering through the original arched passageways in the wall. High, spiked iron fencing lined up like honor guards on top of the wall enclosing the courtyard and cemetery.

"These gates were built by Saunière; actually, he designed them and had them made and installed by Marie's father and brothers. He was a secretive man."

"Yes, you mentioned that. I assume you've collected all these trivial details for my benefit."

"Of course, I hope you're impressed."

"Inquiring minds want to know," David said, and kissed her on the forehead.

As they got to the old, carved wooden door set into the arched entrance, David looked up and began to laugh. "Just as you said, 'Terribilis est locus iste.' It's quite a statement for a priest to have carved in stone at the entrance to a church."

"I think it's one of Saunière's little jokes. It could mean terrible, but it could also mean awesome; he left it for us to decide. Just guessing, but I think he must have liked the double meaning."

"I can't imagine the church hierarchy got the joke."

"Probably not. But even in the end, when they stripped him of his position, he kept saying Mass in the presbytery, and the parishioners were fine with that. I read a diary entry of his online where he refers to himself as a poet and dreamer; but who knows what he thought made the church a terrible place...Maybe he was just disillusioned with its—"

"Grandiosity?"

"Could be. I was going to say hypocrisy. Sometimes it's hard for the faithful to integrate personal beliefs with Church dogma."

"I assume you mean hard for you."

"Exactly right, Dr. Freud. For me and Saunière. The little bits I read about him made me wonder if he would have been a Cathar, if they still existed, and sometimes I wonder if that's true for me as well. They believed in Jesus as a spirit, but they didn't like all the middlemen or layers of pomp and hierarchy to pray to Him. And they had very liberal ideas about sex."

"Sounds good to me," David said, with an exaggerated leer, "but that must have been heretical as far as the Catholic Church was concerned."

"Absolutely," she said and laughed, "but need I say as popular with the people then as it is with you now. In fact, Catharism was the dominant religion here in the Languedoc. They were very progressive for their time, maybe for this time, too, but they were strict about following Jesus's teachings; they advocated living in poverty and absolute honesty. And then there are the Freemasons, which is a secretive group that requires its members to take a vow to be charitable. I've never exactly understood why, but the Catholic Church was threatened by both, and that's when they systematically exterminated the Cathars and forbid membership in the Freemasons."

"So if Saunière was a Freemason, or a Cathar sympathizer, the inscription makes all kind of sense."

"It's anyone's guess. Let's go in."

A garishly painted, grotesque wooden figure greeted them in the church vestibule, and David stopped and stared, more or less transfixed by the brightly painted wooden sculpture.

"The look on your face is priceless," Giselle whispered, "and I knew it would be! To me it looks like a smashup of Frankenstein meets the Marx Brothers in Disneyland. In any universe it's a pretty unique holy water stoup. I can only imagine how scary it must be for little kids—enough to give them nightmares, I bet."

"If I wake up screaming tonight you won't have to wonder what I was dreaming about. He'd be quite a sight anywhere, but as the welcoming committee to God's house, pretty bizarre. Who is he?"

"Well, the easy answer is the Devil, but at some point, a writer named de Sede made the case that it's meant to be Asmodeus, the demon of lust."

"How perfect. Abbé Saunière certainly had a wicked sense of humor."

"Very clever," she said, "but the real question is not who it is, but what does it mean? To me, that's part of the whole mystery. According to the Kabbalah—"

David interrupted; the look on his face had become familiar and predictable. He was about to tease her, but now there was something endearing about it, and she was grateful he wasn't easily pushed away. "Is that a book of the New Testament?"

"Maybe it should be," she said, unflustered, as she looked around and lowered her voice. "Can you imagine if one of my colleagues heard me?

Either you, or Saunière, or both of you have put me in a totally irreverent mood, and no, I'm not bi-polar. Just happy. Anyway, as I was saying before being rudely interrupted, the Kabbalah names Asmodeus as the spawn of King David and a succubus."

"King David supposedly had six hundred wives and two hundred concubines, so maybe a she-devil was a nice change of pace," he said, chuckling. "Or maybe he was so exhausted he didn't even notice. What do you think Saunière was saying?"

"I've seen two references that might be relevant. The Talmud connects Asmodeus with Solomon's Temple, perhaps as the one guarding his treasure, and then there's the seventeenth-century book of demonology titled *Ars Goetia* where it says something like 'Asmodeus showeth the place where treasures lie, and guardeth it.' "

"Those would certainly explain it—and be so damn clever! If I believed in an afterlife, which I don't, by the way, I can picture Saunière up there laughing at all of us. Do you happen to know what Asmodeus was holding in his right hand?"

The arm and hand in question were raised, the thumb and forefingers forming a circle, familiar to David as the customary contrivance of ancient statues carrying flags, spears, banners, anything that could be passed through the circle. The Egyptians and Chinese had used this device long before the time of Jesus. *A fierce-looking demon with huge bug-eyes, Spock-like ears and sharp, pointy fingernails—looks like the most likely thing he would have carried would have been a weapon of some sort,* thought David.

"Clever of you to notice that. Having my own personal archaeologist has its benefits. Want to hazard a guess?"

"Pitchfork?"

"That's what they think. And now is where having your own biblical scholar familiar with a multitude of ancient languages comes in handy. Do you see the inscription carved on the left wing?" She pointed to some barely imperceptible marks. "There—the runes—it says *zouz* in Hebrew. The people who translated it say it means crouch or liquid silver, but I think it refers to the ancient money used by the Israelites, one zouz, two or more zouzim. That makes much more sense to me. Saunière purchased all the other statues and reliefs from the catalog of a company in Toulouse, but Asmodeus was made to order."

"You know, his face reminds me of a Bernini bust of the Devil, it's the same profile and kind of menacing look."

"That would be interesting, and it wouldn't surprise me at all if Saunière was familiar with Bernini's work and used it as a model. I didn't know Bernini did anything like this. The piece I love is—"

David interrupted, "Can I guess? Apollo and Daphne in the Galleria Borghese?"

"It's the most beautiful piece of art in the world."

"Agreed," he said, "great artists live on through their creations. I think it's the closest anyone gets to immortality and eternal life. I guess this," he motioned to the interior of the church, "is Saunière's legacy."

"Rennes-le-Château was his Lazarus. Originally it was a Roman colony called Rhedae, taken over by the Visigoths around 550 CE. There had been a church, and Dagobert II, the last king of the Merovingian royal line was married here, but it was abandoned for about a thousand years, when it became the private chapel of the Hautpoul family. When Henri d'Hautpoul died in 1695, his will left instructions to bury him here in a crypt under the church he called the Tomb of the Lords."

"And then Saunière found his way down to the crypt."

"Exactly. But all the while he was resurrecting the church, adding gothic arches, stained glass windows, a new altar, everything, he kept the crypt a secret. He acquired all the art, and then he personally modified some of it."

"Is it a clue?"

"You clever man! Come over to the 14th Station of the Cross." She immediately pointed to the vividly painted piece hanging on a wall to their right. "I can't wait to hear what you make of it."

"Well, said David, "it's a beautiful little relief of Jesus. I suppose it's meant to show Jesus being dragged into a cave by the man standing behind him, whose arms are under his armpits. And I'd guess the one at his feet, weeping, is Mary Magdalene."

"Yes," Giselle said, "and it's known to be practically identical to one at

Jean d'Alcas Church, but Saunière made some important, telling, changes." She pointed to the sky.

"See, he painted a moon in the sky to show it was night. Jesus was crucified on a Friday, and because of the Jewish Sabbath laws, they would've had to cut him down after just a few hours. Ordinarily, people who were crucified were left in the sun for three days without food or water, and then all their bones were broken. Jesus didn't have his head put in a noose, so he wouldn't have strangled, and he wouldn't have bled to death because hands and feet don't bleed very much, certainly not enough for him to exsanguinate. They didn't break his bones, and being stabbed in the side isn't necessarily fatal unless it's directly into the heart..."

Giselle stopped and waited for David to say something, but he remained silent, studying the image. She had no doubt that Jesus had died on the cross, but it was clear that Abbé Saunière was convinced he had reason to believe otherwise.

"I'd call that a clue." There was nothing flippant in David's tone. "Jewish law says that burials must take place before the sundown, and obviously, a moon high in the sky screams the sun has set. It's definitely night."

Giselle pointed to Jesus's body. "Also, the blood dripping from the knife wound to his chest isn't dripping down toward his feet, it's running down his chest sideways as it would if he were still bleeding as he was carried horizontally."

"It's quite a statement," David said somberly. "The message of the moon seems unambiguous, at least to me. And blood doesn't flow once the heart stops pumping, so I think Saunière wanted us to conclude that he believed Jesus was alive the night after being cut down from the cross."

Giselle nodded and stepped back to make sure she hadn't missed some other detail. "It's not really such a unique theory, although it's not what the majority of Christians, myself included, believe; but there are some, more than a handful, who think He survived the crucifixion and had to leave the Holy Land to live unobserved. There are lots of theories; He went to India, or Spain, or came here, but all of them are unsubstantiated, or at least unproven. This seems different. Saunière didn't broadcast his ideas, but he obviously wanted people to discover he found something convincing and was afraid. I know I would have been if I were him."

David put his arm around Giselle and turned toward the long rows of empty, polished wooden benches. "Let's sit down for a minute," he suggested. "This is such a personal space, it almost feels rude to be strictly an observer."

Giselle was taken aback. "Do you mean you want to pray?"

"No," David said, sliding into a pew with Giselle beside him, "but this is the only church I've ever been in that was erected solely by one man's will, and I feel I owe it to him and what he accomplished to be part of it for a minute."

"David, your mother did a good job encouraging your softer side."

"Thanks. I'm pretty sure she would've approved of Saunière. Maybe he was a little disillusioned, but it never robbed him of his generous spirit or confidence in his own judgment. I hope the same can be said of me when I'm gone."

He looked at his watch.

"It's getting late. Let's take a quick look at the windows and the altar before we head down the mountain, and when we come back in the morning, we can visit the Orangerie, the Tour Magdala, and walk through the garden and cemetery."

He turned to get confirmation from her, expecting the usual bright smile, but her face had become solemn, and she was gazing off into middle space.

"Oh, David, it upset me to hear you talk about dying."

"Sorry, I was inspired by what Saunière created, and the kind of man he was. I have a lot of years left."

"I know." Sorrow had crept into her voice. "But think what he was up against; he couldn't speak out and be unafraid. None of the major religions teach hatred, but terrible things have been done in the name of religion to people who question, or challenge or think differently. Weapons get more sophisticated, but people are as primitive as ever. That's not what Jesus would have wanted."

David took her in his arms and held her close, stroking her hair.

"I know, I know," he said. "It's always horrifying to contemplate the brutality human beings are capable of."

She pulled away and looked into his eyes. "It makes me incredibly sad and helpless," she said. "When I see Jesus bleeding, and I think of the Protestants and Catholics in Ireland, Sunni and Shiite, Jews and Arabs. How can someone call out 'God is Great' and then blow up a marketplace or fly a plane into a building?"

David wrapped his arms around her again as if they could protect her from her thoughts. He completely agreed, but when he thought about 9/11, or a marketplace blown to smithereens, he was filled with rage. The human race was nanoseconds from cavemen in the existence of the cosmos, and still had a lot of evolving to do.

Her sad, little half smile was obviously forced. "This has been more of an emotional day than I expected, and that little painting is very unnerving. Anyway, it's out of my system and I'm recovered. We can go if you're ready."

They made their way out of the village hand in hand and started down the long flight of wooden steps built over the rocky face of the mountain.

"It's important to remember the past, but it shouldn't be allowed to destroy the present."

"Who said that?" she asked.

"I did," he said, "although I'm sure I'm not the first."

27

RENNES-LE-CHÂTEAU

JUNE 20, 2013

"THIS GARDEN WAS magnificent when Saunière was alive," Giselle said the following morning, looking for vestiges of plants that might have survived. "The Abbé had peacocks—can you believe it?—and a little cage for the monkey. Oh, and he had two dogs; Emma Calvé gave him one he called Pomponnet, and the other one was named—drumroll, please—Faust!"

"You're kidding me."

She put her hand over her heart. "The honest truth. Named for the man whose claim to fame was selling his soul to the Devil for the promise of unlimited knowledge and worldly pleasure."

"And Pomponnet?"

"Ah, not as obvious, but maybe even more interesting. There was a geographer named Pomponius Mela who lived and published books around 43 CE. He wrote about an ancient treasure placed in the mines of Pyrene in the Pyrenees, just south of Carcassonne, and you won't be shocked to hear Saunière had a translation of the book in his library. So not only was the dog named Pomponnet, but the monkey was named..."

"Don't tell me—Mela!"

"Yes! I love serving up these little tidbits; I can almost see you salivating. You're hooked!"

"Who wouldn't be? It just gets better and better. Anything else?"

"Well, Pomponnet was also a character in a French opera, a comic opera..."

"And did Emma Calvé sing in it?"

"I don't know, but the opera is called *La Fille de Madame Angot,* and I wouldn't be surprised if Saunière saw it in Paris when he was there. It was very popular, and coincidentally I saw a production of it a few years ago, which is why I recognized the character's name. He—Pomponnet—sings an aria that I really loved, called 'Elle est tellement innocente'— she is so innocent!"

Giselle's arms raised, palms facing the heavens, mimicking the dramatic gesture she remembered from that performance. She could have been offering the perfect soufflé, warm, airy perfection; the pleasure of it all couldn't be contained. David began to laugh, and she joined him, feeling like a triumphant Julia Childs. It was impossible to resist the trail of strange and tantalizing breadcrumbs sprinkled around and left behind by François Bérenger Saunière.

They walked over to the now infamous Visigoth pillar, which had supported the altar inside the church and had been placed upside down in the garden as a plinth for the statue, *Our Lady of Lourdes*. The original pillar had been removed and was housed in the Saunière museum, but the resin replica stood on the spot Saunière had planned for it in his carefully plotted landscaping. It was inscribed *Mission 1891*, and *Penitence! Penitence!*

"Ah, the famous pillar. I suppose there are theories about the inscription."

"I saw something about it, but it was too convoluted for me. When I read *Holy Blood, Holy Grail,* I was convinced the documents Saunière found inside had messages encrypted with the same cipher as the gravestone of Madame Hautpoul. Have you read the book—no? It's fascinating. According to the authors, one of the documents had an inscription about Arcadia, another said something about the genealogy of Dagobert II..."

Her voice trailed off as she tried to remember what was on the other two.

"Look," Giselle said after a while, "I don't want to give you misinformation, and there's so much that's factual, it's silly to mix it up with someone's conjecture. I just have one more fact tucked away that I'm sure you'll enjoy. The Merovingian royal line I mentioned—famous for Dagobert II, who some believe may be connected with Jesus, or Marie-Madeleine—all had red hair."

She looked at David and smiled slyly, picturing the gears turning in his mind and knowing where his thoughts would go.

"So, you've been holding out on me, and you look like there's more."

"A little arcane information courtesy of my father. Dagobert was kidnapped when he was five and exiled to Ireland by the mayor, who put his own son on the throne. When Dagobert grew up, he returned and married Giselle de Razes, who was the niece of the king of the Visigoths—a fact I relished as a kid. The marriage was supposed to cement an alliance between the Visigoths and the Merovingians, of course. And, as I already told you, they were married at the Church of St. Maria Magdalena in Rhedae, now called Rennes-le-Château, on the very same spot this church was built a thousand years later."

"In the words of Alice, this gets curiouser and curiouser. Are you named after her?"

Giselle laughed and shook her head. This was one of the stories she loved to hear when she was a little girl, and she'd created an elaborate fantasy for herself in which she was a Merovingian princess placed in the temporary care of her mother, to keep her safe until her true identity could be revealed. She wondered if her father ever suspected what she had created out of his Tales of Brave King Dagobert.

"No, I'm named after my Mamie. I don't think I mentioned she fought with the French Résistance in the war. I told you my mother was always a bit resentful that I loved Mamie so much, and that we were so close. She wore a scarf wrapped around her head during the war to hide her hair."

David decided not to ask how many generations of redheaded woman had been named Giselle before her, although it was the obvious question. Maybe some other time, he thought—or not.

They climbed the steps to the belvedere, the graciously wide, raised walkway that connected the Tour Magdala with the Orangerie.

"Left, or right?" asked David, walking to the rear of the stone wall that followed the contour of the mountain. "The view is absolutely spectacular."

"Let's go to the Tour Magdala first. The Orangerie is so beautiful I want to save it for last."

They turned left toward the gothic chess piece of a tower, built at the very edge of the mountain, its round turret appearing to be suspended in space.

"What an amazing architectural feat," David said. "I can picture sitting here in the sun with a good book on a chilly afternoon and looking out at dusk to watch the light change on the mountains. Saunière obviously didn't think he had to hide his windfall."

"Well, he paid the price. The Church finally summoned him to the ecclesiastical tribunal in Carcassonne, found him guilty of misappropriating funds and suspended his right to administer sacraments, though he wasn't excommunicated. That's when they replaced him as the priest here, but he refused to leave, and kept saying Mass in the presbytery. He owned it, and nobody went to Mass with the new priest, who eventually left."

"I think you're a little sweet on him, Dr. Gélis, but it's understandable. And now, if you're ready, let's go sit in the Orangerie; it gets my vote as the most romantic spot in the civilized world."

"It is, isn't it?" Giselle sighed. "It's otherworldly. When people build greenhouse rooms like this next to mansions, they're always the most wonderful part of the house, but this one, alone at the edge of the mountain, with its peaked roof and turret on the side, belongs in a fairytale."

The large glass-paned building, connected by an interior circular stair to the room below at ground level, was a poetic masterpiece; heart-shaped iron curlicues punctuated the perimeter of the roof and crenellated peak. Benches invited visitors to sit and be awed by the vast expanse of rolling countryside, a patchwork quilt of small farms stretching in every direction.

"It's like being suspended in the clouds," Giselle sighed. "It's exhilarating, breathtaking. I mentioned that Saunière described himself as a poet and dreamer, and I guess this is the evidence." She gestured around. "He dreamed a sonnet; then he found a way to translate it into this, on a mountaintop. I'm in absolute awe."

Minutes elapsed as they sat quietly, shoulders touching, lost in the magic. Giselle's eyes remained focused on the shadows dancing over the distant mountains when she finally broke the silence.

"Well, my darling David, what do you make of it all?"

He spent a minute silently gathering his thoughts before he spoke. "I think Saunière discovered something, and whatever that something was, it filled him with courage and allowed him to live life on his own terms. He didn't try to convince anyone that his ideas were right, or better than theirs, and he lived by a moral code that allowed him to feel at peace with himself.

He loved someone who loved him in return, and they shielded each other from whatever cruel winds blew their way. Like I said yesterday, I'd take that."

"As long as you take me with you," said Giselle.

"I wouldn't have it any other way," David whispered softly, and began to stroke her wrist. "I didn't know anything about Saunière before I met you, but the more I find out about him, the more I remember that the superficial facts of life, where you're born, or what job you wind up with, really isn't what defines who you are or what draws us into each other's orbits. Just by being here we've become part of what Saunière dreamed, beyond the perimeters even he could imagine."

"And you see yourself in him?"

"I do. Langston Hughes wrote, 'Hold fast to dreams / For if dreams die / Life is a broken-winged bird / That cannot fly.' My dream has been of you, although I couldn't have said so. Of you, of sharing the joy of where I am, and what I see, and what I think with you. Of listening to your thoughts and fears. Of love that is understood in silence."

Looking up through a frame of glass in the Orangerie roof, a few wispy clouds hung motionless in the clear azure sky, making the reality of a spinning earth seem like fiction. All was silent. Giselle leaned her head on David's shoulder, and moved slightly to bring her arm and the length of her thigh in direct contact with his; she wouldn't have been surprised to be told their hearts were beating in synchrony, or that waves of energy were ebbing and flowing freely between them. *This is the dream to hold fast,* she thought. *This is beshert. I pray I don't ruin it.*

28

CHÂTEAU DES DUCS DE JOYEUSE COUIZA

JUNE 20, 2013

"THAT MUST BE him." With a subtle nod, Giselle indicated a short, balding man sporting a precisely trimmed and waxed gray mustache, who all but disappeared into the wallpaper of the hotel reception area.

She and David had lingered at Rennes-le-Château far longer than either of them anticipated. The spell it cast stayed with them as they made their way down the mountain, and neither one had the slightest interest in talking about a murdered relative, but there was no way to avoid it. She'd checked for a message at the desk on the off chance he'd cancelled, but no such luck; and here he was, a little early.

"I'm sorry about this," she whispered to David as she approached her guest, hoping he wasn't discerning enough and she wasn't transparent enough for him to know how she really felt.

"Monsieur Pages?" she inquired, in French. "I apologize if we kept you waiting."

"Not at all. You are Dr. Giselle Gélis?"

"Yes, and this is my friend, Dr. David Rettig," she said, extending her hand quickly, short-circuiting any attempt to kiss her. "Dr. Rettig is an archaeologist, and you may remember I mentioned he'd be joining us. I've told him about our relative, Father Gélis."

The little group headed for what was once an austere Renaissance cobblestone courtyard, but now served as an open ultra-atmospheric dining space. David had made reservations and they were immediately seated at a linen-covered round table, canopied beneath a pristine, white market umbrella. The sky was somewhere between indigo dusk and moonless dark, but the candles were lit and glowing, adding to the sense of being on a private island where conversation wouldn't be overheard. Giselle glanced at David, hoping her look was able to communicate how much she wished they were alone to enjoy the bottle of Château d'Or et de Gueules he ordered.

"We greatly appreciate that you were willing to travel here this evening," Giselle said.

"It is my pleasure," Gilbert responded, with a courtly jerk of his head, which was only slightly higher than Giselle's shoulder. "It is a short journey for me, and I don't have the opportunity to meet a new blood relation very often." Continuing in English, he said, "If for you, it is easier," motioning to David, "my English is not the best, but I hope, good enough. It is something necessary to function in the real estate business in this part of France. The Brits are fond of coming to the Languedoc-Roussillon region to take their holiday, and my clients appreciate that I speak their language. Many return to me to book summer rentals."

"Of course. Speaking English must be a great asset in your business, and I appreciate it as well," David said. "Listening to a French conversation without the benefit of subtitles would totally leave me in the dark."

Gilbert did not smile.

The waiter returned and poured some wine into a fragile goblet for David to taste. "Superb!" he said to the waiter, giving it the French pronunciation and adding, "one of my five French words," in an aside to Gilbert. After the wine was poured, David elevated his glass.

"In Israel, where I work, we say *l'chaim*, to life."

"To long-lost relatives," Giselle toasted, noting that Gilbert appeared extremely ill at ease; his eyes darted around the room and he was strangling the corner of the napkin he'd put on his lap. "My father spoke about you before he died; he regretted that he'd never met you in person. In his last years he wanted to make sure I knew as much as possible about our ancestors, and it saddened him to think how uninformed I was. He said he'd been negligent as an historian, telling me the sagas and travails of strangers, but not about my own relatives, especially great-uncle Antoine and his murder. Of course, it was over a hundred years ago, but he thought perhaps you knew more of the story. Can you tell me exactly how you are related to Antoine?"

"I am surprised your father didn't explain. Antoine was my great-great-uncle, the same as for you. There exists a family tree. We are cousins, but I am not an expert in the—how do you say—degrees? But that is no matter."

"Of course not," said Giselle.

The conversation had an unmistakable edge, and Giselle was relieved that David decided to interrupt. "I don't know about you two, but I'm starving. Would you mind if we order dinner before the conversation gets serious?"

As they studied their menus, the owner approached the table, introduced himself, and wound the umbrella down, suggesting they take a minute and admire the star-studded sky overhead.

"I must make you a compliment," Gilbert said seriously. "I would never have the privilege to dine in such a place as this without your invitation, but I regret I have nothing of value to offer you in return."

"Not at all. I promised my father I'd travel here and meet you, but I never expected to learn anything new. Papa thought of Antoine's murder as a black mark on the Gélis family name, though I don't know why he saw it that way."

Gilbert made no attempt to hide his exasperation. "Perhaps it was the way he was found—posed flat on his back with his arms crossed over his chest; he was laid out for burial, as if he deserved to die. It is said many people did not like him."

"And at least one who *really* didn't like him," David said. Gilbert's face was a mask.

"True," Giselle continued, smiling at David, grateful he was so comfortable being himself and trying to interject a little humor. "But the chain on the presbytery door was unlocked when he was found, and it was common knowledge Antoine didn't open it for strangers, so everyone assumed he knew his killer, and it was personal. And then there was the cigarette paper with the strange note written on it."

"And he did not smoke," Gilbert interrupted. "Yes, so strange, and it is true that it must have been personal. Some think it was a warning to others. The note said, 'Viva Angelina,' which means"—he turned to David with an air of superiority—"long live the messenger. In Latin."

"Sounds like a P.D. James mystery," David said, " 'Murder in the Presbytery.' "

Giselle laughed softly and added, "Too bad she can't solve it. Although when you put that together with all the mysteries and intrigue surrounding Rennes-le-Château and Abbé Saunière, she'd be tempted to imagine, as my father did—as I do—that Antoine's murder may have been connected in some way."

"I don't know the writer you speak of, but the connection to Saunière is possible, of course; it was not a topic of conversation in my house. You may not know," he paused dramatically, "my grandfather was accused of being the killer, and the police arrested him. Once, when I was fifteen, when Rennes-le-Château was receiving much publicity, I asked my father whether there was a connection to Antoine's murder. He said it was best not to ask any questions. That was the only time we spoke of it, and I took it to my heart."

"So," Giselle continued, "even after all the interest, the information on the Internet, the books, you never thought about it?"

"I put it out of my thoughts, and I think there is nothing more to know," Gilbert said. "This is such a beautiful summer evening, a beautiful setting, charming companions—what I'd like is to know more about is you. If you don't mind, I'd prefer to enjoy the wine and the meal before we speak further on this subject."

"Of course," Giselle said, "as you wish." Gilbert's discomfort couldn't be more obvious, and Giselle was convinced there was some kind of elephant in the room, but there was nothing she could do about it. *It's probably more of a chipmunk than an elephant anyway*, she thought. *A strange chipmunk.*

The conversation became more relaxed. David began telling stories about Israel and his olive pits, while Giselle and Gilbert sipped wine and allowed themselves to be entertained without adding much to the conversation.

After the waiter put their cappuccinos on the table, Giselle decided to ask one final time. "Gilbert," she said, changing the tone to signal she hadn't forgotten or given up, "we are family. I would not have bothered you and stirred up unpleasant memories had I known, but I would be grateful for anything you can tell me that would allow me to honor my father's wishes. If there is nothing further to say, I will accept that."

"There is not much to say that isn't already public," Gilbert responded quickly. "For an example, Father Antoine was a mentor to Abbé Saunière, and they became good friends. Six years before the murder, Antoine, Saunière, Henri Boudet, priest of Rennes-les-Bains, and Guilliame Cros, secretary to Carcassonne's Bishop Billard, met at Antoine's home. Afterward, Cros told many people that Saunière brought some valuable documents for the other priests to see, but that he was treated as an untouchable. The four priests, the three I mentioned plus Bishop Billard, had some kind of secret society."

"I've never heard that story," said Giselle, "but how would it be connected to the murder?"

"Many believe Cros was angry and resentful. Humiliated. He was never allowed to hear the secrets he knew they had. It is possible to imagine Cros murdered Antoine out of jealousy, and tried to find the document he knew was hidden there. Perhaps he succeeded. Since you are a reader of mystery books you must know jealousy is always a good motive. The thing is," he added with a hint of triumph in his voice, "it wouldn't explain the other deaths and death threats to people associated with Rennes-le-Château."

Giselle was obviously startled, and made no attempt to pretend otherwise.

"I see that surprises you," Gilbert said. "It is all—how do you say—circumstances, of course, still, so many coincidences..." The sentence trailed off, as if he was uncertain how much more he wanted to divulge, and his mustache twitched slightly as he chewed his lip. He remained silent.

"Could you elaborate?" David prompted.

"Yes, please," Giselle added. "This is quite a bombshell. I've never heard any mention of other murders or death threats."

Gilbert cleared his throat and took a sip of water. He was a cartoon, subtitled, "itching to tell what he knew but reluctant to succumb to the prodding." Giselle smiled but thought it best to say nothing more, hoping the wine would make him want to scratch the itch.

"You know the name Hautpoul?" Henri's upward inflection made it sound like a question.

"I do," Giselle said, "they were the family that owned the church at Rennes-le-Château in the 1700s."

"Then you may know that François Hautpoul, who had the title Marquis de Blanchefort, was married to Marie Nègre d'Ables."

"I'm sure I've seen her name connected to Rennes-le-Château, but what does that have to do with any murders?"

"Marie was the daughter of the Lord of Niort, who owned the Pays de Sault. She was orphaned early in life and became the ward of her uncle, François de Montroux. Bernard Mongé, Abbé of the village Niort–de-Sault, her original home, was found murdered, exactly like Antoine; his skull was bashed in by fire irons and his arms were crossed over his chest. Montroux, her uncle, was convicted, but then he convinced the court he'd been falsely accused, and they set him free."

"I can see some similarities in the way both were killed," Giselle said, "but I don't really see a connection. Are you implying some sort of conspiracy?"

Gilbert tilted his nose up as if he were sniffing the air, a rabbit creeping out of its burrow and checking for predators. "I imply nothing, cousin. I relate only the similarities and the fact that both men were connected to Rennes-le-Château and Saunière."

"I see the relationship of Marie de Nègre and Rennes-le-Château, which became her family's ancestral church. But I don't see how Saunière could possibly be connected to Abbé Mongé's murder."

"Saunière's first parish was in the Pays de Sault," Henri responded with a flourish, as if he'd pulled the rabbit out of a hat.

"That's really reaching for it," David said. "You make it sound like you think Saunière carried a curse, or something like that."

"Maybe I do," Henri admitted, "but it's probably just a coincidence, as were the others."

"What others?" Giselle asked, impatience creeping into her voice.

"Though the official cause of death was cancer, it has been rumored that young Abbé Henri Boudet of Rennes-les-Bains, one of the compatriots, died of poisoning two years before Saunière, and his successor, Abbé Joseph Rescanières, died within a year of his appointment. Then there was Noel Corbu, who bought Saunière's domain from Marie Dénarnaud, and spoke to her on her deathbed; he died in a suspicious auto accident in 1968."

"These all sound like unfortunate accidents," Giselle said. The connections her cousin was trying to spin into a weird conspiracy theory made her feel like she was watching a bad spoof of a horror movie and couldn't look away.

"Perhaps. But as I said, there has been a great deal of speculation through the years that both priests were poisoned. There are even some who think Saunière himself was poisoned. After all, he had no known illness and he was a fit sixty-four years. As for Corbu, automobile accidents are easy to arrange, particularly when it involves a failure of the brakes. But this isn't only ancient history."

He drew himself up and looked Giselle directly in the eye. "There are those today, among the living, who have not been immune to threats of death."

"Wait a minute," David said slowly, "are you suggesting that there are people, people you actually know, whose lives are being threatened because of their association with Rennes-le-Château?"

"No," said Gilbert, making no attempt to contain his irritation. "I am not, as you say, 'suggesting.' It is a fact. Chantal Buthion—someone I actually know—daughter of Henri Buthion, who bought the entire Saunière estate from Corbu, received a death threat in 1990, as did her father before her." He stopped, took a deep breath, and lowered his voice. "His car received many bullets. It was never discovered who did this terrible thing."

"Oh my God! That's horrible." Giselle had no idea what to make of this information, if it was true, but it clearly frightened Gilbert, who furtively glanced around to make certain he hadn't been overheard.

"I thought it best that you know."

David was far less unnerved; his impression was that Gilbert was something akin to Jacob Marley's ghost, trying to frighten Giselle as if he wanted to teach her a lesson. "Are you suggesting, and I mean suggesting, since you haven't said outright, that speaking to you puts Giselle in danger?"

"I suppose I am. I would not like it to be on my head, so I must say no more. I have never received a threat, but I—how do you say—keep my head down."

David was tempted to ask if he had forgotten to take his medication today, but said instead, "Sounds like a plan. It was good of you to join us for dinner, in public. I see now why it must have been difficult for you. We appreciate it."

"Merci, and now I must ask you not to contact me again." Gilbert removed the napkin covering his knees, wiped his mouth and mustache carefully, folded it, and placed it on the table. "I am going," he said curtly as he pushed his chair away from the table and stood. "I wish you the best of luck. Au revoir."

Without waiting for a response, he made a courtly half-bow again, turned, and left.

"All I can say is thank God my father never met him," Giselle murmured. "Do you think any of it is true?"

"Probably all of it. But what he makes of it is crazy, poor guy. It must be awful to go through life imagining people are out to get you, but who knows, maybe it makes him feel important. What he doesn't know is that we've got Mary Magdalene watching over us."

"I'm glad you reminded me. It actually makes me feel better."

David laughed and looked at her with amusement and tenderness written across his face. "Stick with me, kid," he said.

"I intend to," she answered, turning her head up toward the magnificent diamond-studded navy sky. "I think we should have an after-dinner drink and see if we can find Cassiopeia."

"To paraphrase Shakespeare, it is not the stars that hold our destiny, but ourselves. For tonight I'll be happy to get lost among them with you."

29

RENNES-LE-CHÂTEAU

SEPTEMBER 1904

THE FIRST HINTS of autumn were in the air. The roses that had wilted in the August heat were offering their last bloom of the year, and the garden bench provided an unobstructed view of the distant countryside and the first hint of the dramatic autumn show to come. Marie reached over, entwining her fingers with Saunière's, hoping for some sort of acknowledgment, some sign—a smile, no matter how fleeting—that this spectacular day was lifting his spirits. But he was focused inward, and she suspected he was remembering the terrible October day, seven years ago, when Antoine Gélis, his dearest friend, had been murdered.

The weeks before the murder were the happiest time of her life. Saunière's mind was alive with plans, and his enthusiasm and passion about what he planned to build infused the entire village with optimism. He'd look up from his drawing board when she entered the room carrying his mid-afternoon glass of wine and say, "rejoice in hope." And she did.

It was just this time of year when he'd returned from what would be his last luncheon with the brotherhood, buoyant, affectionate and excited, eyes as bright as a schoolboy who'd discovered where the Christmas gifts were hidden.

"Father Gélis was able to read the little parchment," he'd told her as she lay in his arms that night, "at least well enough to conclude it was actually a note, saved, no doubt, by Marie-Madeleine. And"—his voice dripped with excitement—"he was able to pick out some key words."

"And what does it say?"

"I think I'll tease you with that until an absolutely accurate translation is complete. When I told Antoine I'd leave the parchment with him as long as necessary, his eyes actually filled with tears; he declared that afternoon the highpoint of his life."

Marie shuddered, remembering. November 1, 1897 had changed Saunière, perhaps forever.

Father Gélis' body had been found that horrible morning. He'd been bludgeoned to death, his presbytery had been ransacked, and the ancient parchment had disappeared. Neither she nor Saunière had any doubt it had been stolen by the assassins, and was gone forever, as was the pleasure he should have gotten from his life. Seven autumns had come and gone; seven autumns when the sight of leaves turning to brilliant reds and golds put the priest in a melancholy frame of mind, and there was very little she could say or do to change it.

"The Lord is my shepherd. He restoreth my soul," Marie said quietly, squeezing his hand.

"Ah, Marie," he sighed, "but since Antoine's vicious assassination—right in his own presbytery—I can't say I shall fear no evil. I fear men without conscience or humanity who carry out evil acts, and I fear the forces that encourage them."

Marie could only nod in silent agreement. Last night she had prayed to Saint Marie-Madeleine, fervently asking for a way to bring the joy and fire back to Saunière's eyes, to help him delight in watching his dreams take shape.

His heavy sigh could easily have brought her to tears, had she not been unwavering in her resolve to be his rock. "Have you heard from Antoine's cousin, the one who creates gardens?"

"I did. I never knew anything about the Gélis family but it seems like the hand of fate that Antoine's cousin is a prominent landscape designer and architect; he's agreed to create a garden on that wasteland in front of the Villa Bethania. The sketches he sent were magnificent: flowers, color bursting in the spring and all through the summer, and palm trees from the south of Italy. Ah, how I wish that Antoine could have been here to see it, and Félix, of course."

"You've had many losses these last few years."

"Yes, the brotherhood has been cut in two. And the new bishop is a different sort entirely." Saunière smiled at her ruefully and dropped his hand to his side. "I think I'd like a cup of tea," he said, standing and starting back toward the presbytery. "I've made a big decision I want to tell you about."

Once they were seated at the kitchen table, sipping hot, fragrant cups of chamomile tea, the priest seemed less dejected. "You know," he began, "I was distraught and depressed after the murder, but I didn't feel vulnerable while Bishop Billard, dear Félix, was alive. But Bishop de Beauséjour is a different sort entirely. I think he genuinely believes it's his holy calling to meddle in my business, and I think it's only prudent to take some precautions."

This was the first time Saunière had confided his personal views of the new bishop, and though it was clear she wasn't being asked to offer an opinion, Marie decided to seize the opportunity.

"Bishop Billard was your friend, and he celebrated your good fortune. Monsignor Beuvain de Beauséjour is a man whose eyes are clouded with envy. We were there when he learned that Bishop Billard owned the church of Notre Dame de Marceille in Limoux, and I can honestly say I've never seen hatred instantly distort a man's face as it did his that day." She brought her napkin to her mouth and fell silent.

Now that his two closest friends were gone, her support and advice were needed more than ever, even if he didn't say so. "Yes," he said sadly, "you're right, as usual. Sometimes the righteous masquerade their bitterness and jealousy as a virtue. He'll try to bring me down, that's obvious already. I know I see danger lurking behind every tree since Antoine was murdered, but my safety, and even yours, pales next to protecting the urn. It must survive when we are returned to dust."

"It is a sacred trust."

"Indeed. While the construction is underway here, you and I will walk the mountains and look for a suitable hiding spot; perhaps we'll have to create one, much as Bertrand did. Then, in the spring, we'll part with our treasure. I never actually thought of it as mine to keep, only to keep safe."

Marie smiled at him with unabashed, and genuine admiration in her eyes; a few strands of silver were now mixed in with his thicket of black, and only made him more desirable. Their intimacy was more than physical: she knew his secrets, his hidden feelings and fears. She was his Madonna. A man, even a man of God, might share his bed with a passing stranger, but she had his heart, and wanted nothing more from life.

30

COUIZA AND RENNES-LES-BAINS, FRANCE

JUNE 21, 2013

STEAMING WATER PROJECTED forcefully, one notch below scalding, just the way Giselle liked it. Some people sat on the floor to meditate, and she'd be the first to admit practicing yoga had been good for her, but standing still under hot water ushered her into a kind of reverie. It was liquid acupuncture. Maybe needles of hot water and thin metal needles inserted into the right places could both bring reflective states and curative triggers. Anything was possible.

David had held her in his arms for a long time last night, stroking her hair and replaying the day's events. "I always wanted to be important, or make an important discovery," he confided, "but meeting your cousin reminds me that living life in the sunshine and loving with your whole heart is more meaningful than having the world acknowledge your importance."

"And to be loved in return."

"Absolutely. T. S. Eliot said, 'Half the harm that is done in this world is due to people who want to feel important.' So, taken to the next level, I'd say that if we can make each other feel important, we're not likely to do harm."

She laughed. "That's a leap Mr. Eliot probably didn't intend, but it sounds good to me."

The week had changed her perspective more than she ever imagined was possible, and her previous life was beginning to seem constricted and maybe a little humorless—certainly without poetry. The days—had there only been six—had a rhythm, and dancing to it had been effortless. She trusted and depended on a man she'd met in Amsterdam only a year ago and, despite their differences, she couldn't imagine any scenario that could possibly make her reconsider, long-distance or not.

In retrospect, there had been moments she regretted, but that was her own critical eye, not David's. She could hear her mother's nails-on-chalk-board voice saying "a little self-control, please," when she had begun weeping after dropping her ice cream cone or when joy propelled her into a fit of twirling on the banks of the Seine. David was tolerant and relaxed; he listened to her point of view but felt no need to convince her he was right when they disagreed. She was even learning to accept a little teasing with something like grace. *Face it, girl. He has his own convictions, and he's at peace with them and himself. He's not bothered by your beliefs. He loves you, anxiety and all, and he doesn't expect you to change. What more do you want?*

The hot water wasn't going to last forever, and David should have a chance before it ran cold. The Gélis family reunion was over, and now they'd have ten leisurely hours a tour guide would have labeled a free day. On the horizon: a little exploring, a picnic near what remained of Château de Blanchefort, some quiet, private time sans agenda, lazy with a romantic vibe. The New York universe would be a whirlwind of dinners, family, theater, old friends—all exciting and fun, but certainly not private.

She stepped out of the shower and wrapped herself in a thick towel. Taking a second towel she bent her head forward and deftly wrapped her long mane into a turban. The vanity mirror was steamed up, but she knew without looking that David would make some complimentary, perhaps a little suggestive, comment when she opened the door. *I'm already spoiled rotten*, she thought.

Everything about the Château des Ducs de Joyeuse was perfection. The grounds were magnificent lush stretches of lawn and carefully tended gardens that led down to the bank of a little river with bubbling waterfalls. It didn't take much to imagine unicorns emerging from behind the beds of roses, playing without a concern in the world. *Heaven,* she thought; *God's in His heaven.*

"I think the fragrance is stronger every day," David commented, inhaling the mountain breeze wafting in the window as they drove toward the ruins of Château de Blanchefort. "It's imprinted in my brain, and I'll never smell lavender or thyme again without thinking of this week with you. I wonder if anyone ever studied them as aphrodisiacs."

"That would explain a lot," she said dryly.

He gave her a sly, sideways glance. "I hope you know I was kidding, but let me spell it out: You are the turn-on, the blossom with the irresistibly sweet nectar. I wish I could write something about us, something that hasn't been said before, but I think better men— and women—have already used all the best words."

She laughed. "There are probably some good words left. Why not give it a try?"

"Maybe, when I have something unique to say, I will. In the meantime, I'll say, 'You have witchcraft in your lips. There is more eloquence in a sweet touch of them than in the tongues of the whole French council.' "

"You are taking advantage of my ignorance, sir, and what's worse, I think you're trying to make me blush."

"Ah, if you blush it's because of where your mind has taken you. In my own simple words, you are the love of my life, my beshert."

"Well, that's poetry to me. I don't know why you feel that way, but I believe it, like anything else I accept on faith. Kierkegaard said, and I'm paraphrasing, 'Faith sees best in the dark.' "

"Ah, so true. But here we are, in the brilliant light of the Languedoc, and I have faith—in us. And, I might add, my eyes are open."

"I certainly hope so!"

"That reminds me, after you fell asleep last night I couldn't stop thinking about Rennes-le-Château, so I looked online and tracked down the GPR reports. They leave no room for doubt that a crypt exists, perhaps a double crypt dating back to the ninth century, maybe even earlier. It could be a Tomb of Lords, from Carolingian or even Visigothic times, but so far, and despite what seem like very reputable archaeological researchers, the government hasn't given approval to excavate."

"GPR?"

"Sorry, Ground Penetrating Radar."

"Of course. I didn't realize you'd gotten up. I must have been dead to the world," Giselle said. "So if the crypts are there, what do you think the holdup is?"

"It's way more complicated than you might think; the French government has to have a reason they think is compelling, and, at least for now, they don't. Apparently, there's a parish registry from the eighteenth century in the possession of the City Council, which certifies the existence of a tomb under the church. And someone named Saussez, S-A-U-S-S-E-Z—am I pronouncing it correctly?—recently made impressive 3D computer renderings of the church and the crypts, which, by the way, seem to have three entrances."

"The French establishment isn't interested in exploring outer space, the oceans or the center of the earth. They don't like to have their old beliefs challenged."

"Too bad. I'd love to know what's in those crypts."

"This could be a little bit of a challenge," David said, looking up through the trees, after they parked the car in Rennes-le- Bains. They planned to look for the remnants of the Château de Blanchefort, but only because it seemed more fun to aim for a destination; neither of them really cared.

"Surely not for someone as fit as you."

"Very funny, princess. I was thinking of you."

"You could be right, but you're not supposed to point out my deficits."

"I don't see it as a deficit, it's a strength—and I mean that. You don't profess to be athletic, but you're willing to try. In my book, that's admirable."

"Okay, okay. My bruised ego is soothed; anyway, it's not a contest. Let's take our time and remember we may not pass this way again."

"Words to live by," he said, and kissed her.

31

THE RUINS OF CHÂTEAU DE BLANCHEFORT

JUNE 21, 2013

THE BIRDS WERE calling to each other, as if they were complaining at the intrusion of humans into their wild domain. A woodpecker tapped in bursts, like a visitor waiting for an answer after knocking.

"I used to go on walks like this with my father," Giselle mused, stepping over a large fallen tree trunk. "He loved being in what he called 'the wild,' and I think my mother was glad to get rid of us for the day. I always thought his alter ego was someone like Jacques Cousteau, having adventures, exploring places most of us never get to see. His life was so—I don't know—civilized and predictable, and mine isn't very different. I've thought about the Galapagos, but that's as far as I ever got."

"Well, maybe we'll get further together," David said. "Sometimes the idea of something is appealing, but not enough to make it happen for yourself. I suspect your father got a lot of pleasure out of his time with you, regardless of where you were or what you were doing. I know I do. I bet we would have really liked each other."

"Definitely. I think I told you my mother resented that I was so close to him, just as she did with Mamie, but she never said so. The thing is, I had more in common with him, and—it's hard to admit—I liked him better. I lived on his imagination. He always had a story ready: Marie-Madeleine gets lost at the market, or the country witch comes to Paris." Giselle's face lit up.

"Even the witch turned out to have a good heart. He called her Greenie, and she understood how hard it was to be different."

" 'It's not easy being green,' " David said.

"No, it's not, and my father made that up long before he knew about Kermit. It's not easy to be different in any way. My mother cared a lot about what people thought of her, and me, and I understand that, but I..."

She hesitated; her father didn't approve of her criticizing her mother, whatever he may have thought privately, but she wanted David to understand. "It wasn't just the fashion stuff; we never really clicked like other mothers and daughters. I was never social enough. She thought there was a proper way to do everything, and maybe you wouldn't guess it now, but I used to be more of a free spirit; she was always focused on things that didn't matter to me at all. She would have been horrified that I didn't pack beautiful shoes when I went to Amsterdam. I know she thought she loved me, but she never understood me or accepted who I am, so how is that possible? If you always want someone to change, you can't really love who she is. At least I don't think you can."

"That must have been so sad for you."

David immediately pictured his own mother, his number one fan, sitting through countless little league football games, there to encourage, offer a helping hand, or let him fly on his own. It had never occurred to him to question his mother's love. He took it for granted, which was exactly what she wanted him to do. Instead of a lullaby at bedtime, she had sung *Always*—'I'll be loving you, always, with a love that's true, always'—and he knew she meant it, no matter what he did or didn't achieve, no matter where he washed up. "I can't imagine how someone could share a home with you, and watch you grow up and not love you with all their heart."

Giselle looked down at the ground, determined not to become tearful. She was always taken by surprise when these old wounds, ones she thought she'd come to terms with long ago, were still so ready to cause pain and bleed.

"It's very sweet of you to say," she said quietly, recovering her composure, "but it's something I've known for a long time. She tried her best."

David took her hand and brought it to his lips, as he had many times before, and she looked up at him with a smile meant to say thanks for the Band-Aid. His courtly gestures had surprised her at first, and she'd wondered if it was an affectation he'd copied from one of his mother's favorite musicals, or from his father, but now it seemed totally him, and totally endearing.

They continued up the mountain without conversation, David walking slightly ahead with her hand in his, pushing any bramble or branches out of the way and helping her over the rocky outcroppings and loose stones underfoot. Every now and then they'd stop, as one or the other pointed to a cluster of wildflowers starting to peek out of an inhospitable crevice, or a bird nesting in the crook of a pine tree branch. Large golden eagles flew so high above they were no more than black specks in an otherwise perfect turquoise stretch of sky. A green-and-yellow head peeked out of a bunch of twigs and leaves, practically hidden in the brush covering the ground.

"Look," whispered Giselle, pointing at a bird the size of a goldfinch. "It's an ortolan. They used to be a delicacy, drowned in cognac and cooked whole, eaten by men with napkins draped over their heads. Now they're protected by the government."

"Ah, yes, I've never seen one in person. They're mentioned in the movie *Gigi*, when the aunt is educating her on the right way to eat them—whole, including the bones, how to light a cigar and…"

"Yes, and how to tell if pearls are dipped, and the color of the best emeralds. It must have been one of your mother's favorite five."

"Astute guess," he chuckled. "Another improbable romance, though I think what she liked particularly was the romance between the grandmother and Maurice Chevalier. But I'm surprised you know it."

"I practically memorized *Gigi*; it's sort of a risqué French Cinderella story. You can't imagine what a thrill it was when my nephew Trevor started calling me Gigi in that sweet baby voice."

She stopped, imagining her father's voice floating through the trees. "Papa used to tell me soul mates float around, each half looking for the other, and if I was patient we'd find each other. He'd be so happy for me."

"And your mother?"

"She would've been impressed with your dashing good looks, and maybe with your publications, but since you don't speak French, she'd have called you a barbarian."

"Never been called that before."

"I guess you haven't been exposed to very many Parisians."

"And then there's you."

"You know I pride myself on being from Toulouse."

She flashed him a dazzling smile and they proceeded up the massif until David braved it and asked if she wanted to take a break.

"I sort of understand the strategy of building so high up a mountain," Giselle said, shaking her head 'no' as she continued to climb, "but it reminds me of Rennes-le-Château. You know, they both seem a long way from everything and make it difficult to…let's say, go see a sick friend. Or get pizza." She laughed at the image of a nineteenth-century family setting out for fast food. "Not that I eat much pizza," she added quickly, "and I understand it makes it difficult for would-be attackers, but living in these remote places, even with servants running the errands, must have been a major challenge. There's a photo of Saunière's Marie looking very fancy in a Parisian dress, and the first thing I thought when I saw it was, did she order it by carrier pigeon? My mother never would have survived."

At a plateau about halfway up the mountain, David pointed to a barely visible path that seemed headed toward a rocky outcropping protruding through the foliage. As they got closer it was apparent they were approaching the mouth of a small cavern. The question in his eyes was clear as he looked at Giselle and she held out her arm, indicating he was welcome to go exploring while she waited.

David stood at the entrance, sweeping his flashlight beam over the rock, obviously startling several large black spiders who quickly scurried across the webs decorating a large portion of the cave walls.

"Want to look around?" David called over his shoulder.

"I'll stand guard." Giselle gave an exaggerated shiver. "Just being here is enough of an adventure for me."

"Why am I not surprised?" David said, as he made sure his hat was on securely and his collar was covering his neck. "I won't go far. Just want to take a peek."

He slipped through the narrow opening and reappeared after only a few minutes. "Nothing much to see," he said. "There's a small crevice off to the side that I can't fit through, lots of spiders, not much else."

Giselle nodded, relieved she wouldn't have to confront anything that crawled.

They continued up the mountain, finally reaching a small ruin that was little more than remnants of rough-cut chunks of limestone. A large circular hole filled with cement dominated the center of the enclosure. Nearby, a less-formed semicircular wall, no more than shoulder high, was the only vestige of its former self. Whatever else might have been there was buried, overgrown, blown away, or tumbled down into a heap of rubble below. Giselle sat down on the ground and leaned against the wall, as David paced it off, reaffirming his first impression that it couldn't have been the footprint of anything vaguely as large as a château.

"A tower for wayward women?" Giselle suggested. "Wayward priests? Saint Barbara?"

"I have to admit I don't know Saint Barbara," David said, joining her.

"Well, as the story goes, she was locked in a tower by her father, who also built a small bathhouse for her nearby. He was a pagan and she converted to Catholicism—secretly, of course."

"Of course."

"But she must've wanted her father to know, because she had the workers put three windows in the bath tower. Want to venture a guess why?"

"The Holy Trinity." He gave her the look of a man overly proud, throwing his arms in front of him as if he expected applause.

"You can stop gloating now, Dr. Rettig; it wasn't that tough a question. Anyway, when she admitted she was a Catholic, he drew his sword to kill her, but her prayers allowed her to escape and be transported to Arcadia, watched over by shepherds. There's more about being betrayed and tortured, but her faith remained strong and she performed thirteen miracles. In the end her father beheaded her and then he was struck by lightning. Maybe Zeus intervened."

"Mixed mythology, my girl. Love those mashups." He patted the stone. "Anyway, I think we should name it after her. How about the Tower of Saint Barbara? Actually, it's coming back to me. I knew someone, a U.S. marine in the Field Artillery Division, who was in the Order of St. Barbara. It's a great honor, from what I remember. So," he said, pointing to a mountain easily visible in the distance, "Saint Barbara could have looked out of her tower that way. I think it's Cardou. And"—he pivoted slightly, and pointed—"over there is Rennes-le-Château. It's hard to tell how old these ruins are, but I'd guess not more than several hundred years."

"Well, whatever it was, I'm glad we got to see it. I think Saint Barbara would've been happy to invite us to her place for a little lunch."

David pulled the sandwiches the hotel had been kind enough to prepare out of the backpack, along with bottles of water. Giselle had stuffed the large cloth napkins they'd used at breakfast into the backpack and, after shaking them out with the flourish of a headwaiter, spread them on the ground. They had discussed the pros and cons of wine, and Giselle had yielded to David's reluctance, although she still thought a cold glass of chardonnay would have been wonderful.

David lightly tapped her bottle of water with his. "To a perfect week, to life and to love."

"And what we have yet to discover."

They lingered over the meal, relishing the rare opportunity to be nowhere in particular, have no commitments and no schedules to keep in mind. After some grapes and almond biscotti, they stretched out as carefree as lizards sunning themselves on a rock.

"This truly is Arcadia," she whispered, "a little piece of paradise. When I'm in a place like this, it's hard to imagine that right now, somewhere, there are people scheming to destroy vast swathes of the world, you know, unable to find a way to live a happy life without crushing someone else."

"That seems to be on your mind a lot."

"I know. I start to feel guilty when I'm so completely at peace. When I was a kid, I thought I'd do something to make the world a better place. But I wasn't brave enough to take on the dragons. In my world, its like we're all wearing blinkers; we speak pretty much the same language and argue about trivialities that seem urgently important, but really, no one cares but us, and it doesn't change anything."

"I know what you mean. When I look back on the years I played football at Wisconsin, you'd think we were playing for world peace. The total focus of the team, me included, the whole school really, was on winning those games, and we felt courageous, in a way. Thousands of people cheered for us like we were heroes, and the whole week before a game, complete strangers would slap me on the back and say, 'counting on you, buddy.' It was everything. Don't get me wrong—I still enjoy watching college football when I get the chance, but when I do, it's just a game. Sometimes the broadcasters call a player 'courageous,' but now, well, that sounds ridiculous to me. It's the people who face real danger, or take a stand for some principle, they're the ones with real courage. That's the kind of courage I'd like to know I have."

"It takes courage to die with grace," Giselle said.

"Yes, it does. I guess we've both seen that. But it also takes courage to go on when you're the one left behind."

"If you mean me, I'm doing fine," she said and smiled at him. "Better than fine."

David kissed the top of her head and sat up. "It's funny," he said, "that's exactly what my father said to me the summer after my mom died. At first I think he wanted to crawl into the coffin with her, but then he asked me to go to New Mexico with him, on the trip he and Mom always talked about but never got around to. We sort of did it in her honor."

"And what made him feel better than fine?"

"I think it was being in the Carlsbad Caverns, with me, and knowing it's what would have made Mom happy. That's when he said it, and that's when I decided the two of us should become amateur cavers."

"Tell me about caving with him. Don't they call people who explore caves spelunkers?"

"No, not anymore…just plain old cavers. It was a long time ago, but it gave me a real appreciation of the history of the earth, and what a tiny fraction of time human civilization's been part of it. I wanted to do something that honored and preserved the planet we've all inherited, and for a while I thought I'd go into politics, but I'm not pushy enough for that."

"I don't know. I seem to remember you finessing that group of men, including Charles, at the bar in Amsterdam."

"Ah, that was about you. My heart made me brave."

Giselle rolled over and said, "Let's head down a different way, what do you think?"

"Why not?" he answered. "There's still plenty of daylight and I have rope if we need it. I wonder if being foolhardy is some corollary of courage."

32

THE CAVE AT THE RUINS OF CHÂTEAU DE BLANCHEFORT

JUNE 21, 2013

AFTER INCHING THEIR way down for half an hour, they stepped out of the overgrown vegetation onto a rocky plate that offered a new, equally spectacular vantage point. At his request, Giselle posed for several more photos with the made for Hollywood background. Finally, shaking her finger to indicate she had done all the modeling she intended to, she sat down and stared at the sky, wishing the day could last forever.

"Take some shots of the scenery," she suggested, as she reached for her smartphone, intending to snap a few candid photos of David.

"Okay," he said, taking his 800 mm telephoto lens out of the backpack, unwrapping it and carefully screwing it onto the camera. He scanned the landscape, hoping for something worthy of the lens—a bird hiding in the dense forest beyond the rocky ledge, a salamander basking in the sun—and then he saw it; a massive, upright slab of rock that appeared to be directly in front of, and parallel to the side of the mountain. An accumulation of rubble, perhaps five-feet high, seemed to be spilling out from between the two, as if a truckload of chocolate M and M's was being squeezed out of a stone sandwich.

A rush of adrenaline heightened all his sensations as his heart began to race. "Let's look over there," he said with obvious excitement, pointing and reaching for his flashlight. "I'm not one hundred percent sure, but I have a high index of suspicion that it's a cave."

"But of course, chéri," she responded, with an exaggerated French accent, "eet eez the 'ighlight of the tour!"

As they got closer, it was obvious to David that the mountain wall had split, most likely the result of an earthquake or a shift in the tectonic plates.

Another surge of adrenaline.

A concealed cave, or at least an obscure one, he thought, scrambling up the heap and directing his flashlight beam in the space between the towering slabs of limestone.

"I'm going to take a quick look. If it's a cave, and I can squeeze through the entrance, I'll come back before I go exploring," he called to her as he slid down to the mouth of the crevice.

He was well aware that the caves of southern France were favorites of treasure hunters searching for gold, but that wasn't the sort of prize that did it for him. It was the possibility of discovering evidence of earlier civilizations, like those discovered in the Chauvet Cave, a cavern in this very region that had the earliest known and best-preserved cave paintings in the world. The spectacular prehistoric fossilized remains and footprints of creatures now extinct were breathtaking discoveries that had been carbon-dated and shown to be 30,000 years old, and they had remained hidden until 1994—practically yesterday! The French archaeologist Jean Clottes had published a fascinating book making a case for the connection of these surprisingly sophisticated paintings and shamanic practices.

It wasn't beyond the realm of possibility that this cave, in the same geographic area, might also have fossils, perhaps not as historically momentous, but significant enough. He made a mental note to ask Giselle if her path had ever crossed with Clottes, who, if he remembered correctly, had taught at the University of Toulouse and was about the age her father would have been.

Within a minute, he was scrambling back up the pile of rocky debris that obscured the cave's entrance, hoping Giselle would understand his exhilaration.

"It's a huge cave, maybe bigger than the Sainte-Baume Grotto, and I'd really like to take a look around. Not expecting anything in particular"—*not expecting, but wishing*—"so it's hard to pass up such an amazing opportunity.

If you'd rather not go with me, I totally understand—lots of spiders for sure and who knows what else. I promise I won't stay more than half an hour, at the outside."

Giselle hesitated; the thought of going made her skin crawl, but she didn't want to sit outside waiting by herself either. She'd always had a horror of little crawling things scuttling around: spiders, bugs, vermin of any variety. She thought of second grade, and a little boy—Pierre—and recess in the church schoolyard when she'd seen a daddy longlegs and began to scream. She could still picture Pierre gently picking it up and letting it crawl on his hand. "Look at the size of it as compared to you. You silly goose," he'd said, voice dripping with adult-sounding scorn. *Okay Pierre*, she thought, *I'm getting too old to act like a silly goose.*

"You're not going in there without me. One minute and I'll be ready."

After tucking her hair tightly inside her hat and making sure her collar was protecting her neck, she edged up the pile of rocks and took hold of David's extended hand, as he pulled her to the top.

They skidded down the other side of the loose mountain of gravel, forcing some of the dislodged stones to skitter down to the bottom. The crevice formed by the limestone walls was no more than ten feet long; David slung his backpack over his arm to protect his camera equipment and shimmied through crab-style with ease. The narrow alley opened into a visually infinite black space; water dripped onto the clay floor and formed small puddles, reflecting their flashlights' beams.

"It's spectacular," David whispered, standing at the mouth and rotating the light around the perimeter. "Did you know there are hundreds, maybe thousands, of limestone caves around the world that have never been explored."

"I've never given it a thought—before now. Does that mean mountains aren't actually solid as a rock, they're hollow?"

"Exactly. God's original housing solution—hence, our ancestors were known as cavemen."

Giselle's laugh created faint echoes as it ricocheted against the cavernous walls. "The ghosts of our ancestors are laughing at my ignorance," she said, "and it must've made socializing a challenge."

"Actually, some people think there could be a network of tunnels that connects them to each other right through the mountains. Like one huge ant colony."

"Oh, look over there." Giselle's apprehension had given way to a sense of awe. "Do you see where the ceiling slopes down? It looks like someone hung draperies."

"It's actually not an uncommon formation, but that doesn't make it any less awesome."

"I guess caving with your father paid off. What's it called?"

"Would you believe—draperies? Maybe this will be our new hobby."

"Don't count on it," she said, aware that her neck had begun to tickle. She quickly ran her fingers along the edge of her collar, praying she found nothing, and reminding herself that even if she did, it couldn't really hurt her. At least she didn't think so. Nothing there but a wayward strand of hair.

"I think I see a little tunnel to the left of the speleothem—that's stalactite formation to you. Stand right behind me and I'll keep my light focused directly ahead; you sweep yours over the walls and ceiling. We'll go very, very slowly. Tortoises again."

"I wish I had my shell."

David led the way to a narrow passage where the ceiling height decreased to about four feet. He dropped into a crouching position, leaving Giselle little choice but to do the same. Occasionally a shadowy form scurried across the wall and it took all her self-control—and memories of Pierre—not to scream. *I am ridiculously riddled with fears*, she thought: *spiders, the dark. But I'm here now and I'm certainly not going back by myself.*

They crawled slowly through the claustrophobic space, barely wider than David's shoulders, for some distance, until he stopped and said they had come to a chimney.

"A what?"

"Not a chimney someone built," he said chuckling a little at her alarm. "I'm sorry. It's a natural formation. I estimate it's about three feet deep, but I can't be sure. I'll go first, and if I think we'll have trouble getting back up, this will be the end of the line."

She reluctantly agreed, and lit the interior for him as he put his arms and feet on either side of the interior of the rock chimney, and slowly lowered himself down.

"Okay," he said, from below, "sit on the ledge and dangle your legs. It's only a short drop. Now put your hand on the inside of the walls and brace yourself against them. I'm right here to catch you."

She did as instructed, trying not to think of what might be on the walls waiting to crawl onto her, and within seconds his arms were around her waist, helping her down. It was another crawlway, only minimally wider than the one above, which seemed to be sloping downward, although it was impossible to actually know in the pitch black of the enclosed space. They inched forward, like large bugs crawling through a rain gutter. After a minute the crawlway emptied into a cave with a ceiling high enough to allow them to straighten up. The intimate, womblike space enclosed them in absolute silence, and David turned to face Giselle, wrapping his arms tightly around her.

"I love you," he whispered, "more than ever. I had no idea you were such a good sport. After we look around here, I'll be ready to start back. It would've been exciting to find something, maybe some bones, something old and amazing, but I think the only amazing thing in this cave is you."

"I'm glad we did this," she whispered back, meaning it with every fiber, "and I'm sorry you're disappointed. I was hoping you'd find something too. I guess we both secretly thought, maybe—but maybe next time. Maybe when I come to visit you in Israel."

They stood quietly in the middle of the space, which seemed at most eight feet high and no more than fifteen feet across at its widest point. A stalactite and stalagmite had grown together to form a pillar in the corner, where water continued to drip down its length.

"Wow!" David pointed his flashlight at a formation along a ledge of the far wall. "That's extraordinary. It reminds me of the honeycombs at Wind Cave in South Dakota, which are totally spectacular, but these are no slouches. They're called boxwork formations, for obvious reasons, and I have to say this one really looks like a honeycomb of post office boxes projecting from the wall."

They moved closer, both flashlights focused on the intricate network of calcite plates protruding like a sculptural relief.

"That's very odd," David murmured, as much to himself as to Giselle, pointing to a large, smooth pale gray rock positioned on the ledge, framed by the delicate projections. "I'm no expert, but that looks sort of contrived."

He held the flashlight closer, examining the stone and trying to see behind it. "Normally I wouldn't consider disrupting a natural creation, but this doesn't look natural or accidental." He stopped to question himself and his motives, as he did routinely on an excavation. "I think I should move the rock," he said tentatively, as if waiting for Giselle to object.

Every sensation was on alert, and he found himself counting each breath she took, as he became exquisitely aware of the slight pressure of her shoulder and the warmth of her body. "It's your call," she whispered, taking one step to her right, leaving him ample space to reach for the stone.

"Okay," he said firmly, as his heart began to pound in his chest, "that rock is free standing, and it didn't get here by accident. It might as well be labeled 'move me,' and that's what I'm going to do." Without disturbing the crystalline blades, he grasped it firmly and cautiously set it down next to his left foot while Giselle focused her flashlight beam on the exposed cavity. "Well," he whispered," I knew I was right, but it's still hard to believe; someone hid something in there."

Giselle's voice was husky and faltering. "It's some sort of earthenware, David, and something else, something shiny. Do you know what it is?"

His thumping heart had become a jackhammer and beads of sweat began to trickle down the back of his neck. Someone had gone to great trouble to hide something in this obscure place. They both stood completely still, as if they were staring at a mirage that would disappear if they averted their eyes.

"No, I don't, but there's only one way to find out," David said, extending his hand between the crystalline shards forming the pigeonhole. Muscle memory took him to his first time in Rome when, after visiting the Coliseum he'd taken the route his guidebook suggested, and wandered down a busy thoroughfare to the *Mouth of Truth*; his anxiety then, as now, seemed irrational, but unavoidable.

He extracted the clay-colored object first which, on cursory inspection, appeared to be a narrow urn of some sort. Giselle had put her flashlight between her knees to free up her hands, and he passed the vessel to her before reaching for the second, a tube-like case covered in some sort of reptile skin. The flashlight beam bounced off the silver fittings that held it closed, creating little mirrors of light dancing across the cave ceiling like a disco ball.

Giselle sat on the ground and cradled the urn in her lap, spiders be damned. She unzipped the backpack and felt for the napkins she'd brought from the hotel. The whimsical afterthought had been a nod to some romantic image in her mind; now it seemed like brilliant prescient planning. Or kismet. Or luck.

"So clever of you to bring those." David's voice was barely audible. "Let's wrap the vessel, get both these things in the backpack and get out of here."

He had no idea what they had, but he would have staked his life on the fact that someone thought they were important, needed to be hidden and were worth preserving; with that in mind, he felt obligated to take possession of them. The next cavers might not be as trustworthy, or as knowledgeable. Irreplaceable Nag Hammadi codices had been burned for warmth by a shepherd's mother and were gone forever. Whatever they'd found would be safest with the two of them.

They descended the mountain slowly and silently, like kidnappers with an infant in a carrier might, eyes focused on the rock beneath their feet. When they finally reached level ground and began walking briskly to the lot where they'd parked the car, the driver of the vehicle parked next to them was just locking his doors. He looked up, saw them, and waved in recognition.

"Giselle, what a coincidence. I knew you were on holiday, but I assumed you had gone off to visit your sister. Oh..." Switching to English, he extended his hand to David. "From the look on your face I suspect you don't recognize me in the daylight. We met a few years ago over a glass of wine, and then again in Amsterdam when you whisked Giselle away from under my nose. I believe the last time was just last week...at the airport in Marseilles, but I suspect I'm easy to forget. Charles Abrison."

"Nice to see you again, Charles," David said brusquely, "and of course I remember you. I was just surprised to see you here."

"Well, I'm not stalking you, if that's what you think. I enjoy visiting this area, just as Giselle does. We have very similar tastes and we share a lot of history." The bald insinuation was delivered with a forced smile.

Giselle saw David's jaw muscles tense, and she quickly interjected, "Unfortunately, we don't have time to chat, Charles. David and I are running a little late and we have to get going. I'll see you another time." Small talk would have been out of the question with anyone, but Charles didn't qualify for one minute of effort or diplomacy. On the few occasions they had dinner years ago, something about him always struck her as a little sleazy; even now he was looking her over as if he planned to make a bid and wanted to be sure she wasn't chipped before he raised his paddle.

Without further niceties, David opened the car door and waited for Giselle to get settled and snap the seatbelt before handing her his backpack and closing the door firmly.

As soon as he had walked around to the driver's side, Charles approached Giselle's window and tapped on it, leaving her no choice but to roll it down. His fair complexion had developed the big, red blotches she'd seen on another occasion when a colleague had humiliated him at a faculty meeting, as well as at the bar in Amsterdam.

"Where are you staying?" His tone was falsely congenial, like a prosecutor trying to soften up his suspects.

"Sorry," David said, making no attempt to sound gracious in return. "It's the last day of our brief vacation and we have to make a quick stop in Toulouse before we leave for New York. Maybe another time."

As they pulled onto the road David could easily see Charles in the rear-view mirror, rooted to the spot and glaring at their car. *It's beginning to be a tradition.*

33

COUIZA AND TOULOUSE

JUNE 21, 2013

"THAT WAS MORE than a little unnerving," Giselle said, as David hit the accelerator with more force than he intended before shifting into second gear. "I don't mean your driving, I mean Charles. There's always been something—I don't know what exactly—a little slimy about him, and I can't help wondering if he suspected something." Realizing this sounded somewhat paranoid, she added, "I know, I know, he can't read minds and there's no way he could have even an inkling. I barely have an inkling. It's just my guilty conscience."

"If he's thinking about us at all, he's probably picturing us going back to our hotel and falling into bed," said David. "Trust me, the reptilian part of his brain is overdeveloped."

Whenever she heard that phrase she pictured a snake curled up inside a skull—a strange, graphic image that didn't even make sense. She'd never see Charles again without picturing some sort of scaly, slithering creature— maybe a cobra, or a python— wound up in his head, ready to hiss and strike. Strange that his resemblance to a viper hadn't occurred to her before now. She began to laugh. "You're right," she said. "It's always good to have a man's perspective."

"Much as I wish his lizard brain could predict our afternoon, I think we'd better pack up quickly, check out, and head for Toulouse. Agreed?"

"Absolutely."

"We should find a place to buy some surgical gloves before we get to your flat; also, tweezers. Do you have a small paring knife?"

Giselle nodded. "Anything else?"

"No, not until we know what we've got. Right now I'm anxious to be somewhere private, lock the door, and take a look. Then we'll have to make some decisions."

"You mean about who we notify?"

David shook his head in the affirmative, although he'd already decided that if the vessel or something in it were historically important or valuable, he'd want to authenticate it personally. He'd never thought of himself as a control freak, but the French had a different way of doing things, and whatever that way was definitely wouldn't include him. If he were in charge, the crypt below Rennes-le-Château would have been opened long ago. And what could they do to him—nothing, not once he was on American or Israeli soil, but for Giselle it was an entirely different story.

"Do you have dual citizenship?" he asked.

"I do," she said. "I'm a genuine natural-born American citizen with a U.S. passport, although I usually travel with my French one; easier for me when I return. Why do you ask?"

"Thinking about possible scenarios." He stopped speaking. No reason to examine the options until they knew what they were dealing with, and, in any event, he couldn't make decisions for anyone but himself.

"Look, it seems to me you think we've stumbled onto something important." She waited, but when he neither confirmed nor denied the implied question, she continued, "and since this is your area of expertise, I guess we'll talk about it when you have a chance to form some opinions. But please keep in mind I don't want to wind up in a prison. Agreed?"

"Yup. It all comes down to what prize we find in the Cracker Jack box," he said.

Once they pulled onto the gravel at the hotel, Giselle handed the backpack to David, and quickly made her way up the small circular stairs to their room, feeling more and more like she was in the middle of a bank robbery. She flung her empty suitcase on the bed and, grabbing her belongings by the handful, heaped everything into it, threw her toiletries on top, zipped it and rolled it to the car. He left as quickly as a team member in a relay race, and she sat guarding—whatever it was—while he gathered his things and checked out. The entire maneuver took fourteen minutes.

The route to Toulouse took them through farmland where forests of huge sunflowers were beginning to reveal their golden faces.

"If we came here a couple of weeks from now, it would be like driving through a van Gogh painting," Giselle said. "Did you know all the flowers face the same way? It's quite a sight. People come from around the world to photograph them. The French word for sunflower is *tournesols*, which literally means turning to the sun. When they're still growing, they face east in the morning and track to the west by the end of the day. Then they reset. There's something so innocent and simple about that, starting fresh every morning, exactly the opposite of how I feel right now."

"I'm sorry this is making you anxious, sweetheart. We haven't done anything criminal"—*yet*, he thought—"but if you want to escape for a little while, close your eyes. The route on the GPS is pretty clear and if French Siri says something I don't understand, I'll wake you up."

"I think I will," she said. "You once told me you're a little thick-skinned, but even if you are, you could probably use a break too. From me, I mean."

Within minutes she was asleep.

Without the distraction of conversation, David's imagination and, he couldn't help but admit, wishes, were on steroids, generated by the feel of that earthenware vessel in his hands. Of course it could be some sort of hoax, but that seemed totally improbable. After handling, smelling, and looking at these vessels his entire adult life, when one in particular made the hairs on the back of his neck stand up, he paid attention. The minute his fingers touched that familiar texture and he withdrew it from the pigeonhole formation, obviously chiseled away to hide it, he knew. Unburnished. Red-colored clay. Not a ceremonial vessel. *Caution... Caution... There's a long process ahead: carbon dating, maybe in two laboratories, analysis of the clay's composition.* But the similarity to vessels he'd uncovered in Israel from the first century CE was striking. It was like falling in love; you felt it right away, but it took time to verify.

He didn't want to say anything to Giselle until he could examine it more carefully, but the long cylindrical shape was reminiscent, *remarkably reminiscent*, of the scroll jars found at Qumran. *There I go again,* he thought, *always dreaming of the find of a lifetime*, as a slide show of the Dead Sea Scrolls paraded across his brain. Lantern light could cast strange shadows, but he was pretty sure someone had tampered with the wax seal, because it looked like there were multiple colors. When the wax was scraped away and the lid was removed he'd be shocked to find nothing inside—wax seals had a purpose. And that interesting little case, perhaps a few hundred years old, probably hidden away at the same time. What could they have in common? Strange bedfellows. The scroll jar—the designation was already fixed in his mind—will have to come second. Best to open the little leather covered case with the silver fittings first—nothing tricky about that. It could have been used to hold a small spyglass, or a bone. *You're a strange man, David Rettig. Most people would probably hope for jewels.*

When the beautiful Pink City came into view, David reached over and stroked Giselle's cheek.

"Wake up, beautiful, I'm going to need your help," he said as soon as she opened her eyes. "I forgot to mention that besides the gloves and the tweezers, we'll need a small, soft paintbrush, like you'd use for moldings."

"Okay, let me think, it's a little tricky. We'll stop at my pharmacy for the gloves and tweezers, and there's a little hardware store a few blocks away where we can get the brush. Do you think it matters if we go where I'm known? I was dreaming something—it doesn't make sense, really. I was wearing a mask—it was gold and jeweled—and my father didn't recognize me. He thought I was Cleopatra. And I kept saying, 'No, no; she was killed by an asp.' How crazy is that? Anyway, what do you think, I mean about where we buy supplies, not about my dream."

"It doesn't matter. The most convenient place, as long as I can wait in the car. It doesn't look like it'll be easy to park anywhere."

"Okay. I never realized how paranoid I am—sorry. Oh, turn right here."

After quickly collecting what they needed, they found a spot on the street, which Giselle deemed "a miracle." With David carefully cradling his backpack in his arms and Giselle wheeling both suitcases, they walked across the broad plaza and entered 9 Place de la Daurade. The flat was stifling and close, and as soon as she opened the windows and let some air in, they both sat down on the sofa on either side of the backpack; Giselle unwrapped the surgical gloves, handing a pair to David before putting on her own. At his request, she took a bed sheet out of the linen closet and draped it over the cocktail table in front of them, preparing a comfortable place to recline for the elderly guest and the little case, still dressed in the white hotel napkin.

Laid bare, the case bore some resemblance to a miniature thermos bottle, perhaps six inches long, covered in waxed animal skin. On closer examination in the light it was clear the top was hinged, and, if the mechanism worked, would likely spring open with a push on the silver button.

"I think I may know what it is," said Giselle tentatively. "I'm not a hundred percent sure, but I saw something in the window of a local antique shop a few years ago, and I thought it might be a great gift for Simone, so I went in and asked about it. The dealer said it was a scent case. In the eighteenth century, upper-class women, titled aristocrats, for example, kept a small bottle of parfum inside when they traveled. The one I saw was lined with fabric but the price was ridiculous, so I left it there. This one looks very similar."

"It makes sense," David said, as Giselle smiled to let him know she appreciated his pun.

"Let's find out. Here we go." David compressed the silver button, and the top snapped open effortlessly. The entire case was lined in faded pink silk, and in the center, in the space designed to cradle a bottle, there were two slightly yellowed sheets of paper. He extracted them carefully, flattened them enough to determine they both had been written in French, and handed them to Giselle.

She was a translator of old documents by profession, but there was nothing personal in that; these letters seemed more like getting mail from a two-hundred-year old ghost, and she began translating into English with something akin to reverence. "The first page is a formal letter from Abbé Antoine Bigou, meant to be read by whoever finds it," she said, reading slowly and carefully until she got to: *I have the duty to present to you the evidence that Marie-Madeleine was the wife of our Lord Jesus Christ.* She stopped, and heard the sharp intake of David's breath, but he, too, sat silent for several seconds before saying in a suddenly hoarse voice, "Are you sure that's what it says?"

She nodded. Her throat had become intensely dry, and her tongue was sticking to the roof of her mouth. Her voice cracked. "Yes, I'm sure…and there's more…but I need a minute to absorb…to wait until my heart stops pounding. I'm afraid I may faint"

Without another word, she handed David the letter and closed her eyes.

34

TOULOUSE

JUNE 21, 2013

"I CAN BARELY breathe," Giselle whispered.

"I'm not surprised," replied David, "I'm a little shaken up myself, but this is just the hors d'oeuvres. So if you're ready, read the rest of the letter, and let's prepare ourselves for the main course."

He held out the letter, and Giselle began reading again, struggling to keep her hand and voice steady.

> *So Monsieur, that is the secret of the Hautpouls. Though I have never beheld these Holy documents with my own eyes, you may be assured they are secure in the Church of St. Maria Magdalena in the exact location described, and may be retrieved by removing the altar and the stone on which it rests.*
>
> *It is God's will that I will never have the joy of touching or even seeing these sacred items as it is clear that I am no longer safe in France. It is now the year of our Lord 1792 and the peasants and bourgeoisie remain out of control, using the Revolution as an excuse for the wildest and most outrageous attacks. Everyone believed the priesthood would remain exempt from such hostility, which is the reason so many nobles and aristocracy forced to flee France in the early days of the Revolution entrusted their valuables to me. Sadly, men of the cloth are now targets,*

and I have no choice but to pass responsibility for all that was left in my care. A list of these fine noblemen and an inventory of their precious belongings follows this letter, along with the specifics of where their valuables have been secreted for safekeeping.

Due to circumstances necessitating my hasty departure, I will place this letter in a scent case left to me among the effects of Madame de Nègre d'Ables. With Divine guidance, you have found it in a small space behind a loose stone in the Church wall, where it was hidden for safekeeping.

Finally, Monsieur, I pray that you are a man of courage and wisdom; I pray, too, that the age of Godlessness has passed, and you will be free to reveal the Truth of Our Lord Jesus Christ and Sainte Marie-Madeleine.

May God be with you and bless you.

In the name of The Father, The Son and The Holy Spirit,

Abbé Antoine Bigou

Giselle put the letter down on the table next to the scent case, the fragile yellowed pages like jaundiced skin against the freshly laundered cotton. *I've led such an uneventful life*, she thought. *Most of the things that excited me were small and insignificant; even things I was proud of will fade unnoticed into collective history. My dreams of changing the world or discovering the cure for cancer are reveries from another lifetime. Ordinary, predictable and anonymous are my safe haven; graduate school in New York was probably the most courageous thing I ever did.*

"Ç'est trot," she croaked, before David's puzzled look reminded her to switch back to English. "It's too much. I'm overwhelmed. This has to be what Saunière found when he renovated the church. It explains why he had the stone under the altar lifted; he was looking for the scroll jar." She took a deep breath and sat quietly for a minute, as the information started to make sense. "I wonder if he told great-uncle Antoine? Maybe all four confreres knew. This could be the reason Antoine was murdered. It gives me chills. Really."

She started trembling, and David put his arms around her, as she knew he would. The information, astounding as it was, wasn't the primary reason she was so shaken. It was having possession of the urn—the urn Marie-Madeleine had carried from the Holy Land— here in her home. All her faith, her mystical, irrational belief that Marie-Madeleine was with her, suddenly seemed validated and unequivocally true.

After a few minutes of quiet contemplation, she kissed David on the cheek and whispered, "I'm okay now. I'll read you the other page; it's not actually a letter, more like a list."

"Whenever you're ready. There's no rush."

The following page, in the same neat hand, was neither addressed to anyone, nor signed. Rather, a list of names spilled down the page, paired with a list of objects and where they could be found: engraved gold urn, silver hand mirror with relief of Saint-Marie-Madeleine, etc. It was extensive and detailed, but, relatively speaking, boring and trivial.

"Saunière's wealth doesn't seem so mysterious anymore," Giselle said, as her heart returned to its normal rhythm.

David laughed. "Elementary, my dear Watson. I think the mystery of Rennes-le-Château may be solved. Two days ago, I would have gotten pretty excited about that, but right now all I can think about is the scroll jar; the rest of the intrigue goes on the back burner. The value of what's retrieved from the past can only be measured by its impact on the present and future. I would say that puts jewelry and gold coins in the category of irrelevant."

"Who said that?" she asked.

"I did," he said. "Let me know when you're ready to move on."

"Should we?" she asked. "We know what it is. Maybe it's time to notify someone."

Without saying anything else, David stood and walked to the windows, staring at the charming pink city glowing in the afternoon sun. The Garonne River was clearly visible, and he could easily make out groups of people, probably students, sitting on the wide grassy areas along the banks, enjoying what he imagined was a carefree afternoon and watching the huge Ferris wheel slowly rotating on the opposite bank. He wasn't the man Bigou had intended to pass his burden to, but via Saunière it had fallen on them, on him, and he felt simultaneously euphoric and like Atlas, carrying the entire weight of the world on his shoulders. If the document in the scroll jar was what the letter said it would be, the earth was going to shift on its axis, and he'd be the one shifting it. It was a grandiose and dramatic way to think about it, but true nonetheless. He had no intention of handing any of this to a nameless bureaucrat or Church intermediary.

He pulled the drapes across the windows, shutting out all natural light, and turned to Giselle, who was still sitting on her sofa, "One step at a time," he said. "Let's verify the contents of the scroll jar, and then we'll decide what to do. But as I said before, I have no hidden agenda. I trust my intentions and my instincts. Do you trust me?"

"I do," she said hesitantly, "but I'm not sure that's the point. I agree we'll open it before we make any other decisions."

"Fair enough," he said as he walked into the little kitchen and found a paring knife where he expected it to be. *I may deny it, but I've never given up on finding something with a larger meaning, something that's not only part of the mountains of accumulated knowledge, but also stands alone in its own right. I guess that's the essence of grandiosity. Who've I been kidding? I haven't changed. I wanted to be the one the guys carried on their shoulders after the game, the one who makes the defining touchdown. Hubris,* he chided himself, *the downfall of mortal men. But, if your number is called, and you're lucky enough to pick up the fumble, you run for the end zone as fast as you can.*

"Can I bring you something to drink—water, wine?" he called to Giselle.

"Water, thanks."

As he handed her the glass, he saw the Bigou letter had been returned to its little pink nest in the scent case. She took a few sips, handed the glass back, and smiled.

"I'm ready as I'll ever be," she said, "or maybe, more to the point, as I need to be. I don't think there's a way to actually be ready—not for something like this; at least not for me. But now that I'm over the initial shock and we've agreed on the next step, it's pretty exciting—in a good way. What can I do to help?"

As instructed, she removed the soft down pillow from the head of her bed, put it on the kitchen table, lay a white pillowcase over it, and pulled on a new set of surgical gloves. David carefully removed the scroll jar from his backpack, unwrapped it and, after creating a little indentation in the center of the pillow, lay it down. The small, cylindrical, clay-colored vessel capped with the bulbous stopper looked like a surgical patient, already anesthetized, waiting for the first incision.

"Pots made in this shape in the centuries before and after Jesus was born were specifically meant to house and protect written documents, scrolls. Even without wax, this would be a tight seal, but putting wax around the collar finished off the job. When it was done properly it made them essentially air and watertight. If we accept the facts in the letter, we know when it was originally sealed; Bertrand opened it and resealed it, and then Saunière. But there's a fourth wax layer, so either someone else opened it and resealed it, or one of the three we know about opened it twice—and that could have been any time during the last two thousand years..."

"Right now I don't even want to contemplate the possibilities, although it could have been Saunière. Maybe he unsealed it a second time to show Antoine."

"Maybe," said David, "but why attack Antoine? If this was the motive, then Saunière would have been the target."

"I guess so. It's otherworldly that you and I are the ones to find it. Even a skeptic like you has to admit it's possible that Marie-Madeleine thought it was time the world knew, and decided we should make the announcement."

"It's as good an explanation as any," David agreed.

Scraping wax seals off earthenware objects wasn't new to him, but he was finding it hard to exhale, as if the awe that filled his lungs was a sticky substance adhering to the inside of his chest. The importance of what he was doing—he briefly considered that Giselle could be right and he shouldn't be doing it at all, but quickly pushed the thought away—made him work more slowly than usual. A few more minutes after two thousand years meant nothing, and, he reminded himself, patience always pays.

He carefully rotated the pot another quarter turn and brushed the loose wax crumbs from the clay. When he was certain the entire circumference of the neck was free of wax, he gently began twisting the broad, mound-shaped top. It yielded with minimal struggle, and he carefully lay it down. They walked to the head of the table and peered into the vessel, where a rolled papyrus was clearly visible.

"The moment of truth," he said, as he gently grasped the edge with the rubber-tipped tweezers, and slowly eased it out.

35

TOULOUSE

JUNE 21, 2013

"IT'S SMALLER THAN I imagined," Giselle said. "Just goes to prove size doesn't matter."

"Very funny," David said, "small but extraordinary." He stared at the piece of papyrus, which he guessed was seven or eight inches long at most and four or five inches wide. It lay curled on the white cotton pillowcase and appeared to be in remarkably good condition, except for a small piece missing from one corner. At first glance it was similar to the Dead Sea Scrolls. It didn't appear to be brittle, making it likely they'd be able to unroll and read it—assuming it was in a language familiar to one of them. *Do people run out of adrenaline,* he wondered, as his skin began to tingle.

"I've never really understood what people meant by an out-of-body experience, but I think I do now. I feel as if I'm outside myself, watching some doppelganger, as if it's not me touching this document," David said, as he placed the papyrus on the white sheet covering the cocktail table, and gently held the leading edge down with his right-gloved hand as he unrolled the body. Bold black letters marched across the thick fragment, written in a firm, practiced hand.

"Aramaic," he said.

"As anticipated," she responded, leaning over, touching nothing, all attention fixed on the papyrus.

"Extraordinaire," she whispered in French, positioning the magnifying glass at a distance that brought the letters into clear focus.

She read and reread the first line slowly and silently. Although she'd seen these Aramaic words and names many times before, she needed to convince herself she wasn't making a mistake or inventing something; that all her years studying ancient writings had been in preparation for this moment.

Unaware she'd been taking only quick, shallow breaths, she was suddenly overcome with dizziness and backed away, landing on the sofa. "Don't worry," she managed to say, between taking several long, deep lungfuls. "I'll be fine. I felt like the earth was tilting and I was falling off, but I think I was hyperventilating a little. It happened to me once before. It's a scary feeling, but it doesn't last. Just give me a minute."

She sat very still, consciously inhaling and exhaling slowly, while she waited for the prickly numbness in her fingers to disappear.

"The whole thing's so crazy, right? I know exactly what you mean about out of body. Sometimes when I'm having a dream, I'm there watching, and this is like that but we're awake and this is really happening. I've seen other documents from that time period, and even though none of them were marriage contracts, there's no question in my mind that this is a Jewish marriage contract between Miriam, daughter of Cyrus of Magdala, and Yeshua, son of Joseph of Nazareth. It starts off with a date, 'On the 7th day of Nissan in the year 339 in the city of Cana.' "

"I don't understand. 339?"

"They were using the Seleucid calendar."

"Oh, of course. So if we subtract 311—"

"We get 28 CE, the year of our Lord on the Gregorian calendar. That was the year of the famous wedding at Cana, attended by Jesus and his mother Mary, where he performs his first miracle, turning water into wine. Lots of scholars have speculated about it. No one's ever had a good explanation for why Jesus had the responsibilities of the host, or why his mother was even there—it's been painted many, many times."

"Well, I guess we have the answer to that now." Giselle was still staring, but not prepared to try to decipher anything else on the page.

"Well, let's not rush to judgment; after all, it could be a fraud. I don't know of any other marriage contracts that have survived from that time, but—I can barely say it—on the face of it, there's no reason to believe it's not the genuine article. If you think the names and date are clear and unmistakable, I assume the rest of it will spell out the details of the contract. The Jewish people wrote a *ketubah* as protection for the bride, and it usually stayed in her possession."

Giselle carefully removed her surgical gloves, and put her arms around David's neck. "I love you very much," she whispered as she began running her fingers through his hair. "Did I ever tell you how happy I am that you haven't lost your hair? No? Well, I am."

She kissed him softly and sank back down onto the sofa.

"I don't know if I'm up to the task," she said seriously. "I don't mean whether I can translate it. I can do as good a job as anyone, as soon as I gather my wits about me. I mean the rest of it—going public, facing the Church, the government, my peers. Overwhelmed is the only way to describe what I feel. It's all overwhelming. You know I'm not very good at confrontation—don't laugh—okay, that's an understatement. And I can't think of a bigger confrontation—with the whole world—than this. Talk about needing courage!"

"I hope you know I'm not laughing at you. I was just seeing the humor in the two of us planning a quiet holiday, hoping to get to know each better without the stresses of everyday life, and as soon as we settled in and got comfortable—this. I'm as overwhelmed as you are, I just don't show it," he said, "but, as I told you, I'm fine with confrontation and taking the lead on this if you'd rather not be involved. I won't think less of you."

"I never thought you would. That's not what's bothering me."

He sat down next to her on the sofa and reached for her hand. "Of course not, I wasn't thinking about what this means to you, personally or professionally. You're French, you're Catholic, your faith is part of you, and you've made it clear that you believe—profoundly."

"I don't know why, but when Dr. King presented her codex, it didn't shake me like this. Maybe being in the middle of this tornado isn't for me."

"Maybe not, and maybe you shouldn't go any further; but as for me, I can't, in good conscience, turn this over to anyone else now." His voice was quiet, calm, and unwavering. "I feel obligated to shepherd the ketubah through a careful and thorough authentication process, and I can't, and won't, leave it in a stranger's hands."

Giselle leaned her head on David's shoulder, listening without comment. He wasn't giving even a minute of consideration to informing the government or the Church, and she couldn't force him to. He was clear and resolute, but she still had a lot to consider.

"I don't want to be rushed into a decision I might regret," she said softly.

He moved away a little and took her face in his hands.

"I would be lying if I said I'm sorry this fell on us," he said, trying to penetrate the veil that suddenly obscured her eyes, "but whatever you decide won't affect our relationship, at least not from my end. Your name doesn't have to be involved. You can say you begged me to turn it over to the government or the Church, and I refused. Everyone would believe it."

"What exactly are you planning to do?"

"I've been thinking about that since the cave," David said slowly, "and I haven't come to any firm conclusions; there are a lot of factors to consider."

"I haven't even considered that you might take it out of the country..." Giselle's voice began to rise with alarm. "Are you thinking of taking it to Israel? I know you're the one who noticed the cave, and decided to go exploring, and found it, but you wouldn't have been there at all if it weren't for me, so I think my opinion should count for something."

"Absolutely," he said, startled by her combative tone and change in attitude. "It's been a long time since I had to consider anyone's opinion but my own. I'm sorry I sounded as if your opinion is irrelevant, and, of course, I want to hear what you think, but I've been toying with all the possible scenarios for hours, and from my perspective the papyrus should go to the U.S. I want to guide it through the process, which I have no way of doing in France. Before we announce anything, or make any claims, I want to get it carbon-dated as discreetly as possible. Once we tell the French government or the Church, it's totally out of our hands. So many people, starting with Mary Magdalene, have taken extreme measures to keep it safe. I don't want to be the weak link."

"I see your point," Giselle said, somewhat mollified, "and I accept your apology. I don't take well to being disregarded. The thing is, what you want to do will actually make us thieves, won't it? No matter what we think, isn't France the rightful owner?"

"Well, it's hard to say who the rightful owner is; the land the cave is on may still be owned by the Hautpoul family, or some other private citizen, and then there's Israel, France, the Catholic Church, the Jews. They could all have lawful claims, but the way I see it, the rightful owner isn't necessarily the lawful owner. Since I'm not as wise as Solomon, and I don't think his famous solution applies anyway, you may be surprised to hear I've been wondering what Jesus would do."

"Shocked is more like it! And pray tell—I couldn't resist—what do you think he'd do?"

"Somewhere in the New Testament it says Moses brought the laws and Jesus brought the truth."

"It's in John 1:17; the law was given through Moses, but grace and truth came through Jesus Christ. A pretty profound statement."

"Yes, it is, and I think this should be about the truth, not the law. Assuming the ketubah is authentic, you and I have become the guardians of a piece of historical truth, and I think we have an obligation to protect what's been entrusted to us."

"I see your logic and…" She hesitated. The rightness of David's arguments did nothing to dispel her confusion. Documents had disappeared before, and there was no guarantee it wouldn't happen again. Breaking the law, helping someone else break the law, cheating on her taxes or lying on Customs forms was something other people did, and she wasn't sure she was ready to become one of them. But if anything was ever meant to transcend the laws of government, this was it.

"Look, sweetheart, this is a really big decision, and there's nothing to be done tonight, so why not give yourself a little more time to mull it over."

"It's moments like this I realize what a comfort the Bible is, at least to me, even taking all my trepidation and irritation into account. John 8:32 says, 'You will know the truth, and the truth will set you free.' He was preaching about spiritual freedom, but I think it's the same principle. So I don't need more time to decide what's right, but getting comfortable with it—that's another thing entirely. I agree, the papyrus should go to the States. But what about the scroll jar? How will you get it through Customs—without documents?"

"I was thinking we'd leave it here for now, if you're good with that, and we can deal with it after the papyrus is authenticated. I travel back and forth using GOES; it's a U.S. government program where you get preapproved, but then you clear Customs more or less automatically whenever you travel. I put my passport into a machine, scan my fingerprints, and hum *God Bless America*. Anyway, I don't think it's going to be a problem."

"The way you say that makes me wonder if you're some kind of international jewel thief posing as an archaeologist. If so, now's the time to come clean."

"Ah, I see a flowery phrase in my future."

Giselle started pacing back and forth in her little parlor, laughing nervously. "Oh my God, it's really bad when I can't even think of something flowery to say."

"Let's do some practical things, and maybe by the time we're finished something will come to mind. We should get the ketubah between two pieces of acid-free Plexiglas as soon as possible and tape it closed; the same for the Bigou letters."

"Maybe I should carry the Bigou letters, you know, in case...in case things don't go well."

"Look, it's not necessary for you to take that risk. It's your call if you want to, but there's no point. Once I clear Customs, I'm home free. I don't know how that works for you, so—just a suggestion—mull it over 'til the morning." He kissed her and stood up. "I know that no matter what happens, I won't have one minute of remorse. Maybe using remorse is a good barometer. Do nothing that has the potential to cause you remorse."

Giselle shook her head. Her life was filled regrets, things she wished she'd said, or not said, paths not taken and choices that turned out to be mistakes; but there was no way to predict that sort of thing. You could be rolling along and roll off the side of a mountain, you could be dancing in the rain and be struck by lightning. Maybe David had some way of being certain, but she did not.

"While you're thinking, I can get the Plexiglas. Is there something like Staples, or a framer, even an art supply store nearby?"

"There's a great arts and craft shop only a few minutes' walk from here. They'll probably have what we need."

"Tell me how to get there, and while I'm out, I'll get us something to eat. After we take care of our treasures, we deserve some wine, bread and cheese—and some decompression. Then it can percolate in our heads overnight. This morning seems like it was two centuries ago, and I feel like I've aged appropriately. You can refer to me as the ancient archaeologist. If you'd open the bottle of red wine I saw in the kitchen, I'll run out and be back by the time it's breathing."

"You don't speak French," Giselle protested weakly. Not that she wanted to go and ask for the telltale Plexiglas; or have to look the boulanger, Jacques, in the eye as if nothing unusual was happening and ask for the crusty baguette she always did, while he laughed at what a creature of habit she was. He loved to tease her, pointing to chocolate éclairs, beignets, pain au chocolat, apricot croissants straight from the oven, their fresh-baked aroma so hard to resist, but no, it was always the same plain baguette for her. "French women are faithful," she'd chide him. "It's French men who like variety." No doubt he'd ask about her holiday. She didn't know if she had it in her to banter with him in the usual way, or if she even wanted to try.

"I can't be the first American tourist to walk into an art supply store, or to buy cheese and bread in this city," he said. "They may turn their noses down at my limited vocabulary but they'll take my money. I'll manage."

She put her arms around him and whispered, "Thank you," before going to her desk and taking a piece of paper out of the top drawer. "It's not very complicated. When you leave the front door, you are in the plaza of Place de la Daurade. Turn left and walk toward Notre-Dame de la Daurade, the Basilica. I was planning to take you there, it's such an interesting building, with an interesting history; originally it was a morgue for dead people fished out of the river—maybe next time—anyway, you'll continue past..." She continued drawing the diagram of little crooked streets, hoping it was accurate.

"You see," she said, holding up the paper, "you're making a little circle. If you get lost, anyone can point you back here." She hesitated before adding, "I hope we're doing the right thing."

He took the map and pulled her tightly against him. "Think of it this way," he said. "If we're right, and this ketubah is the real deal, Mary Magdalene will be able to take her rightful place in history. And, I have no doubt it's what Jesus would have wanted. So, despite my personal beliefs, or lack of them, I'm willing to do whatever it takes to make that happen."

He kissed her on the mouth, the American way, and left.

36

TOULOUSE

JUNE 23, 2013

GISELLE WOKE BEFORE sunrise and quietly slipped out of bed, hoping David didn't sense her absence and would be able to sleep a little later. He'd probably be shocked to find out she wasn't usually an early-morning person since getting up and out early every morning the previous week had been at her insistence. Firing on all cylinders usually required at least two cups of coffee, and she padded into the kitchen and put some up to brew.

As the coffee began to drip, her mind drifted off to the previous evening. Before placing the ketubah between the Plexiglas sheets, David had picked up the urn and turned it upside down. "Let's see if the missing corner of the ketubah is still in there," he said.

Two corner pieces floated out.

One completed the papyrus like the last piece of a jigsaw puzzle; the other belonged to an unknown parchment, which set them guessing again.

"Well, we know where this came from," he had said, pointing to the papyrus, "but this one? Obviously it came from a document that's already been removed; I can't even imagine what it could have been, but it's intriguing."

"That's putting it mildly. Maybe it has something to do with the fourth wax seal."

"That's definitely one possibility. Anyone who sealed it could have reopened it, put in the parchment, and then resealed it. But that doesn't make any sense. Why would Saunière or Bertrand open the urn, seal it to put in the parchment, reopen it to remove the parchment, and then reseal it? I can see one of them removing the parchment but not putting it in there. No, I think someone did that before either one found the urn."

"So someone else, someone we don't know about, found the urn and sealed it after removing the parchment."

"Certainly plausible, but there's another explanation—crazy as it might seem."

"And that is…?"

"Mary Magdalene. Maybe, after she arrived in France, there was a parchment that had special meaning for her, something she considered precious, that she wanted to keep safe. Or she wrote something and wanted to preserve it. Putting it in with the ketubah would be the obvious thing to do."

"But why? What could have been so important?"

"I have no idea. But in the words spoken in the *King and I* by Chulalongkorn, the great Siamese king, 'Is a puzzlement.' "

Giselle had come to love David's ability, and inclination, to reference movies or poems or Shakespeare or song lyrics; it was like watching electricity zoom from the switch to the light bulb. She'd smiled at him. "Yes, is a puzzlement. Let's sleep on it. I'm too tired to imagine anything but how great it will feel to have your body next to me in my bed."

"Well, let me remind you that the real thing is much better than anything you imagine," he'd said.

Everything was where they'd left it the night before: the papyrus, the two corner pieces and the Bigou letters were sandwiched between two Plexiglas sheets lying on the dining room table. The scent case and scroll jar, each wrapped in a white pillowcase, remained on the cocktail table. *Too bad I didn't put Papa's cell phone in his pocket,* she thought again. *I'd text him in heaven. He'd be tickled.*

They'd had a ritual. She'd stand beside the front door, waiting for him to arrive home from the university; as the clock chimed six, the hinges on the heavy wooden door would creak as he pushed it open, hang the fedora he always wore on the hat rack, kiss her, and ask, "What's new, different, and exciting?"

"Nothing." It was her unwavering stock answer and was always followed by him shaking his head in disbelief. "Something must have happened today," he'd say, but she always repeated, "No, nothing." *Finally, Papa, I have something new, different, and exciting to report*, she thought wistfully, and *I wish I could tell you about it.*

Things seemed clearer this morning, now that her mind wasn't muddled with shock, anxiety, and fatigue. Last night she'd been frightened, torn by doubt, and regressed to second grade. *Not that there aren't real concerns*, she consoled herself, but she didn't have to fly off to the worst scenario, picture them being apprehended by the gendarmes and disgraced forever. David didn't seem plagued by self-doubt, but that would never be her. She had to run all the possibilities by the panel of judges in her head and wait for their verdict before she was comfortable with her decisions.

As thoughts of the man sleeping peacefully in her bed flickered through her mind, she walked over to the bookshelves and took down a book she'd purchased after seeing the Renaissance painting *The Marriage at Cana* at the Louvre. It was a monumental, thirty-foot long canvas, and it was thought that Veronese, the artist, had included himself as a musician, along with Titian and Tintoretto. Its scene was crowded with wedding guests, a hundred and thirty or so, in addition to nobles and royalty, certainly not a faithful depiction of the modest celebration recounted by John. The painting had been commissioned by Benedictine monks in the mid-1500s to commemorate the time and place Jesus performed his first miracle, and the artist had embellished the scene, ostensibly to inflect splendor into the event.

The book she'd purchased, a thick tome on Giotto, contained a much earlier image of the marriage, and portrayed a scene much closer to the version in the gospels. After scanning the index, she quickly found the beautiful, high-resolution reproduction. There, presiding at the head of the table was a woman who easily could have been Marie-Madeleine, wearing a festively embroidered red gown sitting next to a haloed Jesus.

During graduate school, Giselle had participated in discussions about this wedding, and she knew all the rationalizations scholars presented to explain the presence of Mary, mother of Jesus, and why she took it upon herself to act as the hostess. As the story is told, she's the one who goes to Jesus to tell him the wine has run out, which is usually explained as her tacitly suggesting he should perform a miracle—but now, Giselle realized, it could be both. It would have been his obligation as the bridegroom, particularly because

Joseph, Mary's husband, was believed to have died many years before. *And it was traditional for a wedding to be held in the home of the bridegroom's family.* No one agreed on the exact location of Cana but it was in the Galilee where Mary and Joseph had made their home.

She stared at the Giotto fresco through fresh eyes, noticing Marie-Madeleine's enigmatic expression—her half smile not unlike the Mona Lisa's—sitting between her groom, also in a lavishly embroidered robe and matching head covering, and an older woman—*Mary?* And the man with the white beard and hair—a halo around his head—*the same face as Giotto's fresco of Saint Paul. It's not a photograph*, she quickly reminded herself, *more of a Bible story illustration. Still…*

David stood at the bedroom door and cleared his throat to signal his presence. "Good morning, beautiful," he said, smiling broadly. "I smell coffee brewing. Reading something juicy?"

"It's all in the eye of the beholder," she said, grinning at him. "I was just looking at Giotto's *Marriage at Cana*. The bride is a redhead, by the way."

"Well, he got that right. Did he paint any portraits of our girl? Should we look on the Internet or do you think they'll be in the book?" he asked, as he sat down next to her on the sofa.

"It really doesn't matter; we have the definitive answer, right? See what there is while I pour us some coffee and then we can sit and talk about our plans," she said before she left for the kitchen.

"You know how they make room fresheners that are supposed to smell like vanilla or spring mist? They should make one that smells like fresh-brewed coffee," she called out as she carried two mugs of steaming café au lait into the living room. "Find anything?"

"It would knock your socks off, that is if you were wearing any," he said. "Look at this."

The book was open to a full color reproduction of Mary Magdalene and Cardinal Pontano, a fresco painted for the series done to immortalize Saint Francis. Mary Magdalene was a bit older, but the face was unmistakably the same one he painted for the bride at Cana.

"Not hard to tell what Giotto thought," David said, "unless all women looked the same to him. And he was right. How are you feeling about all of it in the light of a new day? Any revelations in your sleep? I don't mean to make light of your feelings," he added quickly, "but you look so much less troubled this morning. Those little creases between your eyebrows are gone."

"Observant devil you are," she said with a laugh. "Maybe I should consider Botox. But yes, I am, as you put it, less troubled. Marie-Madeleine is counting on me as well as you, and I am up to the task. And once again, though I may appear bipolar from time to time—and it may look that way—I'm not. When I saw the papyrus last night and touched the scroll jar she touched, the implications seemed monumental—they are, of course—and they made me feel like a timid child, afraid of disapproval and, well, just plain afraid. But I hate feeling like Jane Eyre, and I'm not going to let it ruin my chance to be part of something so exciting and important. I'm still afraid, but I can't let that paralyze me. Maybe that's what courage really is."

"I seem to remember you getting all worked up over the place of women in the Church—was it only last week—that didn't sound very meek."

"True. But those were only words. Last night I was lying in bed forcing myself to make a list of all the terrible things that might happen: I could be denounced by the Church or fired from my position. I pictured my head in the guillotine."

"You're kidding, right?"

"No, I truly thought it. Papa always said, 'No one can do to you what you can do to yourself,' and as usual, he was right. And you're right. I don't like people who obscure the truth, and I don't want to give anyone the opportunity. I prayed last night, not something I do very often anymore, but I asked Jesus to help me, to give me strength, and I think he's answered my prayers. So, bottom line, I want to be your partner in this in every way, if you're willing to have me."

David's answer was to take her in his arms and hold her.

"I think we're a match made in heaven, a miracle," he whispered into the crook of her neck, "so let's sip our coffee, get ready to go and talk about our plans. First thing is to get it to the AMS lab in Tucson for carbon dating, and come up with a control."

"Be kind to the ignorant. AMS?"

"Accelerator Mass Spectrometry. They did a great job with my olive pit, to say nothing of the Dead Sea Scrolls."

"That seems like a pretty good recommendation."

"Only the best for the Saint."

"I hope you realize I don't know anything about the mysteries of authenticating ancient artifacts. Some things just have to be accepted on faith."

"Some things, I guess, but not this thing—this is really more about science than faith. There's been so much data collected, and so many advances in technology, not much is left to guesswork—or conjecture—these days. The equipment is calibrated to recognize Nano changes that have taken place in the atmosphere's carbon-dioxide content over the past 50,000 years. The information it generates is pretty precise."

"It's sort of unbelievable, but don't worry, I believe it. I'm not a science denier. I think you can believe in God and evolution; if Tucson is good enough for your olive pit, well, this will be a piece of cake."

David laughed, but his eyes quickly lost the lighthearted glimmer that always accompanied their bantering. "You know that no matter how many experts see it, no matter who does the authentication, there'll be those who ignore it, or dismiss it and decide it's a fraud."

"Yes, I know." She shook her head somberly and took a deep, audible breath. "I'm very well aware that some biblical scholars, as well as lots of ordinary churchgoers, don't like to let science get in the way of their beliefs."

"When I first met you, I was afraid you were one of them, and I'm very grateful you're not. So many people, of all faiths, are trying to keep civilization frozen in the past, afraid if they don't, everything will melt away into a puddle of water."

"I may be afraid of many things—spiders, the dark, condemnation, and ridicule come to mind—but not of my beliefs melting. Oh, I am afraid of the glaciers melting; but everyone should be."

37

NEW YORK

JUNE 23, 2013

DESPITE BEING A high-profile attorney who took media attention in stride and whose friends were either public figures or insistently anonymous in the world of extreme wealth, Edward Chrystal felt a pulse of pleasure when Matthew Harper's name popped up on his caller ID. The men had been friends since college and had remained in touch over the decades, in spite of traveling in New York social worlds that rarely intersected.

"It's been too long." Edward leaned back in his chair and muted the news talk show he'd been watching. "Is Simone still channeling Dolly Levi and hoping to match me up with one of her lovely friends?"

Matthew laughed. "Women, and my wife is no exception, can't see a handsome, smart, successful, single and, most prized, straight man without trying to figure out which of her friends is the yin to his yang. It's against their religion. But no, Edward, I'm calling on business. My latest movie is about to go into post-production."

"And you forgot to ask me to do a cameo."

"Not exactly, but it's good to know you think as highly of yourself as you did thirty years ago. Actually, the producers, including yours truly, would like to hire you as a combination legal consultant, spokesman, advisor—title to be determined—but generally, to represent us to the press and the public, if necessary."

"Sounds like you're expecting a major problem."

"It's a definite possibility, and you're the perfect guy to stand between us and the righteous," Matthew said, becoming serious. "The movie's a little, well, let's say controversial. But it's a great love story."

"I'm a sucker for a good love story, Matt, but I'm pretty busy these days. Aside from our friendship, which is no small thing, what makes this an offer I can't refuse—and I don't mean the money?"

"The issues. The issues you write about, and speak about and have cared about as long as I know you. Your brand is atheist/First Amendment expert, and I want to know we've got the best guy in the country to frame the issues and sound reasonable. This love story could upset some people."

Edward laughed. "You know, I published a book before 9/11 called *Religion Kills*—and there were some religious folks who wanted to kill me. Does the movie have a working title?"

"It's called *Devotion,* written by Talia Benjamin, who's very respected in the industry—great script, by the way. She says she started salivating in 2009, when she happened to spot a brief mention in the *Times* about a Jewish synagogue that had been discovered barely below the surface in Magdala, which was a first century port city on the shores of the Galilee.

"According to Talia, there was a priest in Jerusalem who dreamed of creating a retreat for pilgrims there, because that's where Jesus supposedly performed many of his miracles."

"Good God, Matthew. I'm rethinking this friendship."

"Just bear with me. This is really amazing stuff. This priest raised enough money to buy land near the Sea of Galilee, and Pope Benedict XVI arrived and blessed the cornerstone."

"I guess that made it kosher."

"You have the tolerance of a mosquito, Edward. Pay attention. There's an Israeli law that says before breaking ground for any new building, an exploratory excavation has to be done, and lo and behold, barely twenty inches—twenty inches!— under the sand they found a two-thousand-year-old synagogue. Talia says it's only one of seven known to exist from the Second Temple Period, which was somewhere between 50 BC and 100 AD. They uncovered stone benches around the perimeter, and a large stone, probably used to read the Torah, engraved with a seven-branched menorah in its center. According to her, Jewish and Christian scholars believe Jesus probably preached there."

"Okay, that's interesting stuff, although I'm not tempted to fall on the floor and shout hallelujah. Can I assume this is the setting for the cute meet?"

"Edward, you are incorrigible, but yes, it's where Jesus meets Mary Magdalene. "

"And it was a match made in heaven."

"Talia thinks it was. And do you want to know why people will be outraged?"

"No, this is enough of a shock for today. I'd like to read the script if I'm going to defend it and all you heretics who brought it to the silver screen. In the meantime, I'll just have to live with the suspense."

38

PARIS - NEW YORK

JUNE 23, 2013

"YOU KNOW, BOARDING a plane these days reminds me of hurdling," David said, thankful to put the police, border, and Customs checks behind him and have a few minutes to reboot before their flight was announced.

"You can't imagine I know what that is." Giselle was seated in the lounge next to David, facing the windows and the activity on the tarmac. When she turned to face him, she noticed that the way he was stroking the backpack on his lap could easily make someone imagine there was something live inside. She put her hand on his.

"It's a track event that was part of my preparation for football season," he said, smiling at her. "The name says it all."

"Oh, I get it." She narrowed her eyes as if she was assessing a piece of art. "You know, if I didn't know better I'd say you were a little nervous. Maybe you're not totally ready to step into 007's shoes."

"Ah my beautiful co-conspirator. He was a spy, not an antiquities smuggler; you, on the other hand, look as composed and innocent as Eve before the serpent enters the garden."

"That's particularly apt," she replied. "I've been thinking about the Garden of Eden and the tree. You probably know scholars have interpreted the story many ways, but the most common is Eve tempts Adam after she eats the fruit, and then they're expelled from paradise. But if we take all the elements apart, it starts with God creating a tree whose fruit will give knowledge of good and evil, a tree of wisdom; then he tells Adam not to eat the fruit. That's never made sense to me. Aren't people supposed to learn how to evaluate good and evil, you know, develop a conscience? Anyway, He creates Eve to keep Adam company. And then he sends in the serpent"—an image of Charles flashed through her mind, but she ignored it—"who convinces her to eat the fruit; of course, she offers some to Adam.

"Ultimately, they all blame each other for disobeying God and they're punished. My recent conclusion, a little out of the mainstream, is that they were cast out—punished—because they didn't take responsibility for their own actions. Also, it becomes a rationale for shunning wisdom and righteously ignoring science. Maybe this is my way of justifying what we're doing, but I'm comfortable taking responsibility for my part and seeking wisdom. It's a good thing, and I want to be sure that no matter what happens, you know I don't blame you for any of the consequences."

She leaned over and kissed him, feeling totally at peace.

"Well, as far as I'm concerned, you're doing the right thing and so did Eve. The human race wouldn't exist if they'd stayed innocent in paradise and never had sex—or children. And of course, you have to be able to weigh good and evil in order to make ethical decisions. Eleanor Roosevelt—a very wise woman by the way—said, 'Do what you feel in your heart to be right, for you'll be criticized anyway.' We're doing the right thing."

The Air France Airbus was the largest plane in the skies, and in deference to David, Giselle had booked Preferred Seats for the flight to JFK. Crossing the Atlantic had always made her uneasy, and she'd expected her anxiety to be heightened on this trip, but after a little food, wine, and some silly movie, she was surprisingly relaxed.

"Okay with you if I take a little nap?" she asked, putting her head on David's shoulder.

"Sweet dreams. I'll be on guard duty." With a quick jerk of his head he indicated the overhead compartment. "In all these years I've never had a backpack or a piece of carry-on luggage stolen, or taken by mistake, but it seems careless—idiotic—to take the chance, no matter how infinitesimally small the odds. I'll wake you up if I need an alternate."

"My hero," she said, and closed her eyes.

He'd plotted it all out in his head but hadn't yet contacted anyone, not in Arizona or at Columbia University, where they used micro-Raman spectroscopy to determine the chemical composition of ink, and had vast experience with manuscripts from the ketubah's time period. He also planned to talk to a chemistry professor at MIT's Center for Materials and Engineering and ask him to do infrared spectroscopy on the ink. Then there were the people at NYU to contact. Getting as many experts as possible to weigh in before any announcement was crucial to establishing the legitimacy of the papyrus. *And even then, there will be naysayers who won't be satisfied or convinced. Some people can't admit they're crying even when tears are rolling down their face.*

Although he hadn't mentioned it to Giselle, he'd given a lot of thought to the wisdom of unrolling the papyrus. If it had looked brittle, or been much longer, or fragile in general, he wouldn't have done it. But the decision wasn't difficult once he saw it, and his estimate of eight inches was spot on. Not the length of some scrolls, but there'd be no reason for a ketubah to be very long. *Maybe I've been out in the sun too long*; *maybe someone devised some sick prank, but that makes no sense*; *the parcel in that overhead bin is probably the most precious item ever to cross the Atlantic.*

Giselle shifted in her seat, opened her eyes, and smiled.

"How long have I been sleeping?" she asked, stifling a yawn and kissing him on the cheek. "I was dreaming about, let's see, my mother, wearing a long black dress and a black leather glove, holding her arm out like a falconer, but there was no bird." Giselle laughed. "It must be about the papyrus because that's the only thing on my mind, but I don't get it right now. No matter. Are we almost there?"

"As a matter of fact, the pilot announced he was starting our descent. You slept right through it."

"Well, I can't say the sleep of the innocent, my blinders are off. Oh, maybe I'm the falcon, flown off, hunting for prey. That's a horrible image."

"You don't look like a bird of prey to me. Maybe it's a bird that prays, p-r-a-y-s."

"Clever. I guess it could be both, but I was thinking of all the people who will be disillusioned, feel hurt or betrayed—those are our prey."

"I'm sorry you see it that way. I'm not out to hurt anyone. It's like you said before, accepting the Bible as a literal story and ignoring the advances made by science, and concepts like evolution, that's hurtful to all of us who share the planet. I loved what you said about Eve. Acquiring knowledge isn't the sin, it's using it for evil. Turning your eyes away from knowledge or wisdom, that's the sin."

"You're right, you're right. Simone is going to love you, David. She's been telling me the same thing for years. She doesn't understand how I can devote my life to trying to find the exact meaning of every word in a book she sees as allegorical at best. I can't wait to tell her, and Matthew, of course. He's producing a movie about Jesus's life, but according to Simone it's pretty hush-hush. They'll probably tell us about it when we're there, and we'll tell them about—well, you know."

"I do. I can keep their secret if they can keep ours."

"Oh, my sister can keep a secret. She's kept many of mine, but I'm not telling what they are."

As the plane rolled up to the gate, David stood, retrieved his and Giselle's carry-on suitcases and slipped on his backpack.

Giselle queued up with other foreign nationals waiting to clear Immigration, while David walked to the kiosk, slipped his passport into the machine, scanned his fingerprints, and got a GOES receipt. Wheeling his carry-on bag, backpack securely on his shoulders, he handed the receipt to the Customs agent, who took it, smiled, and welcomed him back to the United States. As he exited the doors, he walked up to a uniformed driver holding a white cardboard sign with the name 'Gélis' written in black marker pen.

"It'll be a while before she's here. But don't worry; you can't miss her. She's the most beautiful woman in the world, and I'm the lucky guy who's traveling with her. I'll let you know when she arrives."

39

NEW YORK

JUNE 23, 2013

THE DRIVER OPTED to cross the East River via the old Brooklyn Bridge, entering Manhattan at the southern end, heading west across Chambers Street, turning right on West Street and then north to Greenwich Village where Giselle's sister, Simone, lived with her family. Every time he made this trip, David got a little charge as the city revealed itself from the vantage point of the middle of the bridge, its century-old network of ornamental iron a stark contrast to the silver skyscrapers in the distance. New York wasn't nearly as elegant as Paris, as charming and romantic as Rome, or as exotic as Marrakesh, but it had a palpable energy that made his pulse quicken.

Giselle sat on his right, his hand over hers on his knee, as he absentmindedly continued to stroke the backpack on the seat to his left. Being back in the U.S., imperfect as it was, still filled him with the sense of safety he'd gotten playing hide-and-seek, and streaking for the tree, Olly, Olly, in come free, without being tagged. The mist blowing past the Statue of Liberty and rising from the East River carried away the vigilance he'd worn like body armor. He squeezed Giselle's hand and whispered into her hair, "land of the free and home of the brave."

"Let's keep it that way," she whispered back.

Matthew's driver was familiar with the narrow cobblestone streets that followed no particular pattern and, as it was a late Sunday afternoon, traffic was minimal. Most of the four-story row houses lining the arbitrarily assigned one-way streets were privately owned, and the labyrinth automatically discouraged the idle driver. Mature trees filled with vibrant greenery provided a canopy over the parallel sidewalks, giving no hint of the skyscrapers that were the hallmark of the city. The car turned right onto Perry Street and four blocks later, as they crossed Bleecker, Giselle pointed to a slender blonde woman and two children halfway down the block, sitting on the stoop of the only white limestone townhouse among the brownstones, just as they saw the car and began to wave and run down the steps to the sidewalk.

"We're here!" Giselle's voice was filled with joy as she waved furiously through the window she'd quickly rolled down.

"No way to mistake that," David said. He'd never seen Giselle so unabashedly exuberant, and her uncharacteristic lack of reserve prompted the fleeting thought that he'd missed out on something that might have added dimension, and happiness, to his life.

Giselle flung the door open the minute the car came to a stop, and the kids who had been hopping up and down on the sidewalk threw themselves on her. David slung his backpack over his shoulder, got out on the street side, and walked around the back of the car.

Before he could offer a handshake, Simone put her hands on his shoulders, kissed him on each cheek, and said, "Finally! It's lovely to meet you in person. Giselle has told me all about—well, perhaps not all, but enough for me to know how happy you make her. Now, let me extract the two little groupies from their beloved Gigi, and we'll go inside." Her French accent was far more prominent than Giselle's, but their voices shared the throaty, musical quality he loved. Their resemblance was striking despite the difference in coloring, and David felt an immediate bond as he followed Simone up the steps and into her home.

"And that's why we decided to live in the West Village," Matthew was saying as he refilled David's wine glass. After a relaxed al fresco dinner, the kids put on a little talent show and then reluctantly agreed to get ready for bed if their Aunt Gigi read them a chapter of *Harry Potter and the Goblet of Fire*. That had been well over an hour ago, which, he was informed, was routine for these visits. Along with the host and hostess, he had adjourned to the secluded and beautifully landscaped garden beyond the living room's French doors.

"This smells like the south of France." The now-familiar aroma of lavender drifting through the June dusk was unmistakable. "Not a coincidence, I assume."

Simone laughed. "But of course, chéri. I can sit back here, close my eyes, and imagine I'm in the Languedoc visiting my grandmother, while I live the lifestyle of a New Yorker with all that implies. I have the lights of Broadway, the museums, the jazz clubs, the restaurants and stores, but my home is a nineteenth-century townhouse on quiet, charming Perry Street. A huge social world or, if I prefer, solitude, are at my fingertips. I have the best of both, thanks to my very indulgent husband."

Matthew, who was standing near a small, wrought iron table set with a cheese platter, crackers, and a bottle of red wine, walked over and kissed her on the top of her head.

"A happy wife is a happy life," he said.

The western sky had lost the last of its flaming afterglow, Simone's cue to light a dozen candles placed on ornamental stakes around the garden. Small spotlights focused their beams on branches and leaves, casting shadows on the tall brick walls that framed the perimeter, and little lamps set close to the ground lit the path that led from the house to the courtyard. Discreetly camouflaged heat lamps warmed the evening chill enough to make it feel unseasonable balmy. It was silent.

David lifted his glass in a gesture of approval. "It's hard to believe I'm in New York City. You've created something magical back here."

"Would you ever consider living here?" asked Simone, who tried, unsuccessfully, to make it sound like an offhand question, and added, chuckling, "I apologize. That was a little heavy-handed, and my sister wouldn't be happy if she heard—"

"If I heard what?" Giselle had quietly closed the French doors behind her and was about to join the group in the garden. After pouring a glass of wine, she sat down next to David, as relaxed and content as he'd ever seen her. "If I heard what?" she repeated.

"Never mind," said David. "Are the kids asleep?"

"Yes. I stayed until I was sure, and I almost fell asleep myself. They were still so excited and it was hard to get them settled down. They wanted to know all about you, and they've already invited themselves to Israel so they could go on a dig. I think Trevor is a budding archaeologist. He told me who

Heinrich Schliemann was and what he discovered. I told them they could wake us up at seven, and I promised we'd make them pancakes." She turned to Simone. "I hope you have pancake mix."

"I'm sure I do, but you shouldn't have told them they could wake you at that ungodly hour. You'll be exhausted. And I see you assumed David wouldn't object, and he didn't even blink, making it even more obvious why you're crazy about him. Since you've already promised...well, I know better than to get between you and *mes poulettes*. It's such a beautiful night, I was hoping we could sit around and catch up, but that can wait if you're getting up at the crack of dawn." Her smile had an oblique, but obvious, message to her sister that she assumed would be understood. "I won't take offense if the two of you want to go to bed."

Giselle looked at David, who nodded and turned to face Simone and Matthew. "Actually, we have something to tell you," he said, "and this is the perfect time."

Simone's face lit up as if someone had plugged her into a high-voltage line. She gave them a huge grin, obviously anticipating a different sort of announcement, and she held her wine glass high, ready to make a toast, when David held up his hand.

"Sorry, Simone," he said, "I should have realized what that would sound like, which is not to say that kind of announcement isn't a possibility sometime in the future, but what we have to tell you tonight isn't personal. However, it is huge, and a secret for now. Giselle assures me you both can be very tight-lipped, but I'd like your personal assurance, if you don't mind."

The relaxed, celebratory mood shifted immediately; Matthew reached for Giselle's hand and asked quietly, "Are you all right?"

"I'm fine," she said, smiling, but feeling some anxiety creep back into her chest. The distraction and pleasure of the kids and the familiarity and comfort of her sister's home had put it all out of mind. Now, as soon as David made eye contact, the monumental weightiness of those fragile documents bore down on her. With some effort, she took a deep breath and said clearly, "It's nothing like that. Nothing terrible has befallen me, us, unless you put knowledge in that category and think I've taken a bite of the forbidden fruit.

"David will explain in detail, but succinctly put, we discovered a—I'll call it a document—very old, which is potentially explosive, and we smuggled it out of France." A sound, some combination of choking and sputtering came from Matthew, and even in the dark the startled look on her sister's face was obvious, so she repeated the words, enunciating slowly and clearly, "Yes, smuggled. What we smuggled must be examined and scrutinized by the experts and authenticated, but we believe it to be genuine. And since it's here in your house, we thought you should know."

Simone turned her attention away from her sister to David, and said, "You've certainly cast a spell on my sister, and I haven't decided how I feel about that, but in the meantime, I can assure you I won't reveal anything you tell us, whether I agree with you or not; I don't give a hoot if you've done something illegal. We're family, and nothing is more important to me, to us," she added, taking her husband's hand. "Whatever your secret is, it's safe with us for as long as you want it that way."

Matthew nodded in agreement, waiting to hear what David had to say. Simone kept his secrets, and he would have no trouble keeping hers if that's what she needed of him.

"Cheer up," David said, smiling his lopsided grin. "I'm going to tell you a story, a great story: of passion, conflict, good, evil, intrigue, tragedy, excitement and, primarily, love."

And in the quiet candlelit urban oasis, a world away from mountainous caves, he began.

Most of the candles had burned to stubs and extinguished themselves by the time David finished speaking, turning the foursome into inky silhouettes.

"Je suis sans voix," murmured Simone, adding, "blown away. I can't believe you two have been so relaxed. It's the most remarkable story I've ever heard."

"Really. Extraordinary," Matthew said, "and eerily coincidental. My current project is a movie called *Devotion*, and my friend Edward Chrystal— you know him, Giselle— has been hired as outside counsel and press liaison. He says he should be listed as Chief Guardian in the credits. Anyway, he's forbidden everyone to talk about it until we go public But assuming you'll return the favor of secrecy, I can tell you it's the love story of Jesus and his wife, Mary Magdalene."

"That gives me chills," Giselle said, "It's like being in the *Twilight Zone*. Do you show the wedding?"

"We do. The screenwriter did a lot of research. She's going to be out of her mind when she hears about your evidence."

"Not until it's got the official stamp of authenticity and has made it through the process," said David quickly.

"No, no, of course not. Talia, the writer, told me there are scholars who think Jesus, biblical Jesus, never really existed at all, so this will give them something to chew on." He started to laugh, thinking about his docile sister-in-law disturbing the tectonic plates of religious academia and creating a tsunami. "Having his name on a contemporaneous document is unprecedented, right, Giselle?"

"Well, most of what's been written about Him, the gospels, for instance, weren't written contemporaneously," Giselle answered, "and weren't formalized into the New Testament until hundreds of years after his death. Josephus, the Jewish historian, lived in the first century and mentioned him, but there's a lot of controversy over how much of what he wrote was subsequently changed by Christian scribes after Jesus was long gone. So, to answer your question, there hasn't been direct proof of anything. But if what David and I discovered proves to be genuine, it would be definitive confirmation he lived—and married Marie-Madeleine."

Before anyone could say anything else, David stood and offered his hand to Giselle. "Thanks to both of you for the wine, the cheese, and the attentive ear." He bent down and kissed Simone on each cheek, noting that she and Giselle must use the same shampoo. "Your beautiful sister has gotten me up at dawn the entire week, and obviously tomorrow isn't going to be any different. I'd like to get a couple of hours before the kids get up."

"Of course, chéri. Visitors get special privileges in 'the city that never sleeps.' "

40

NEW YORK

JUNE 24, 2013

GISELLE ROLLED OUT of bed the minute she heard Trevor knock on the guest room door.

"I'm going to make the pancakes," she whispered, "and I know it's early, but come down and have a cup of coffee with me before I take the kids to the park. It's not what I had in mind, but it's better than nothing."

David had lingered at the breakfast bar after she left, sipping his coffee and mentally organizing his plans, when Matthew stumbled into the kitchen. "So, where do you start, Dave?" he asked, as he poured himself a cup of coffee and slid onto the adjacent bar stool.

"There's a lot I have to set in motion, some here in New York, some in Massachusetts, and some in Arizona. When I pulled the papyrus out of the urn, I saw that a small piece was missing from the upper right corner, and luckily for us it came out when I shook the urn. The strange thing is there was another little piece, completely different, that obviously wasn't part of the ketubah, but tells us something else was in that scroll jar at some point. Of course, that doesn't change anything for us right now. Having the ketubah corner will make everything much easier, because I can send it to the University of Arizona for carbon dating, and the researcher there can do an independent analysis at the same time the people at Harvard and Woods Hole do theirs. Even though it's really short notice, I'm hoping the folks at Columbia are willing to clear some time for me this week so they can analyze the ink."

"What do you mean—analyze how?"

"They have a special piece of equipment called a micro-Ramen spectrometer that's able to verify the age of the ink by running it against established control papyri. It's just the first step of a long and complicated process. A lot has to happen before we're confident enough to go public."

"Of course. To a layman like me it all seems sort of magical, but, on the other hand, so does the Internet. I'm a movie guy myself, and even that is half tech-generated special effects these days. Do you understand all this stuff?"

"Well enough to know what needs to be done, and as things move along, people will point me in the right direction. I'm starting off with the basics, doing what's been done in the past to establish a date and verify authenticity. MIT has a—let's just say an amazing Star Wars contraption—that adds microscopic data to what they get from the mass spec, and it doesn't damage the papyrus. An incredible piece of equipment. In Arizona, they'll look at the exact composition of the papyrus, you know, figure out exactly which grasses it's made from and where they grew, so they can be identified and carbon-dated using an accelerator mass spec. The new technology is pretty fantastic; they can pinpoint the date to within thirty years."

David leaned against the granite counter and took a long swig of his coffee. He didn't want to be giving a pompous-sounding lecture full of technobabble, but he couldn't think of another way to explain it, and Matthew seemed genuinely interested. For someone who'd finished his doctorate in the Dark Ages, keeping up with all the mind-boggling advances had been a challenge, but he'd tried to know what was available, even if he didn't understand most of them.

"It sounds a little like science fiction to me," Matthew confided. "I'm totally fascinated. How are they able to come up with a date?"

"Ah, a low-tech question I can actually answer. There's a species of pine in the White Mountains of California that have been growing for about four thousand years."

"You mean there are trees that are four thousand years old? I had no idea. How do they put that together with technology?"

"Well, you know every year a tree forms a new ring, and that ring incorporates the specific amount of carbon that was in the air that particular year. It's like the Rosetta Stone of carbon history. Some very smart people figured out how to use that information to calibrate the machines. Of course, it's infinitely more complex, but that's the basic idea."

"I think I get the broad outlines" Matthew said, "but what I find really unbelievable is the synchronicity—it blows me away. My movie and your papyrus, happening at the same time is pretty remarkable."

David shook his head and took another sip of coffee. It was a strange coincidence, and he could see why Matthew would be focused on it, but at the moment, it seemed insignificant. He needed to start contacting people.

"Look David, I may be able to offer some help, that is, if you want it," Matthew said. "No offense taken if you don't. I don't know how much Giselle's told you about me, but—I'll cut to the chase—I have access to my company's private jet. I can have my assistant fly down to Arizona, if I have that right, and hand deliver that little piece as soon as you make the arrangements."

"Rich or poor, it's nice to have money," David said, laughing. "What's not to like? It would solve a huge problem for me. But before I do anything else this morning I need another piece of acid-free Plexiglas and acid-free tape for the fragment. I bought Plexiglas in Toulouse, but not enough to protect the fragment separately. Any thoughts about where I can get that?"

Checking the clock hanging on the kitchen wall, and noting it was only a quarter after eight in the morning, Matthew stood and said, "Let's plan to meet in my study around nine. I've had some thoughts I'd like to run by you, and while we talk, my assistant, Sundar, can go and get whatever you need—no questions asked."

"Having your help is going to make everything so much easier. Thanks, Matthew."

"My pleasure. Now I'm going to bring some coffee up to Simone, who's been waiting for me to fill her in on the morning's headlines. She had a hard time falling asleep last night. When you get to know her better, you'll see she's a little more excitable than her sister.".

David stood. "It's a plan. Again, Matt, I really appreciate everything."

Simone had obviously gone to great lengths to make the guest bedroom and bath as comfortable and luxurious as any five-star hotel, and she'd succeeded, as far as David was concerned. He was looking forward to this shower, hoping the hot water would soothe the tightness and pain in his shoulders that had announced itself this morning. He stepped in and stood still, allowing the five strategically positioned jets to come at him. The last forty-eight hours—*could it be only forty-eight hours*—he'd unconsciously lived by the same rules he had in the weeks leading up to a big football game, never allowing himself to be distracted by fatigue, tension, or minor aches and pains. Coach always told the team they knew what they had to do—*a silly thing to say*—but it had always increased his confidence. *Well, I know what I have to do now,* he thought.

One week ago I was sitting with Giselle at a little table in the courtyard of Le Courtesie, under a canopy of glittering stars. 'Bend low again, night of summer stars. / So near you are, sky of summer stars, / So near, a long-arm man can pick off stars.' Carl Sandburg, you are a genius.

That was the night Giselle confided, like a mystic fortune teller, that she believed Mary Magdalene had a reason for bringing us together. She might as well have said it was written in the stars. Maybe her spirituality gives her a sixth sense. I certainly wouldn't vote against it.

The towels were oversized, thick and absorbent, making the very act of drying off a hedonistic experience. He was vaguely curious about what Matthew wanted to discuss with him, but he'd find out soon enough. After they spoke, he'd wait for the Plexiglas, photograph everything completely, and start making calls.

During the previous year, he'd briefly been in contact with a renowned papyrologist, the director of the Institute for the Study of the Ancient World at NYU, who'd been very generous with his time and extremely thoughtful in his opinions. Assuming he was willing and available, he'd be the perfect person to consult with first, and NYU was an easy walk from Perry Street. The complete translation would be a long, tedious process, and he knew it couldn't possibly be done while they were in New York, but he hoped Giselle could arrange to be at the initial meetings. If Mary Magdalene had arranged all of this to make a believer out of him, she was certainly off to a good start.

41

TEL AVIV, ISRAEL

JULY 1, 2013

WHEN HE WAS informed in mid-June that a location crew would be going back to Israel for additional footage, Edward cancelled his holiday plans in the Hamptons. A few scuffles with the Israeli government in the past made him particularly cautious, and even in the best of circumstances, it wasn't his nature to leave anything to chance.

Matthew had called several days before to let him know about the ketubah.

"My, my. What a stunning development! Hard to believe your beautiful, retiring sister-in-law has become an international smuggler of religious artifacts, but I always thought there was more to her than meets the eye. This ought to rock the foundations of the church."

"They're going to need your help Edward—and I'm not referring to the church. Too bad you were out of the country when they were here, but Giselle's boyfriend is an archeologist and he works in Israel; so I thought they could come to you."

"Works just as well. Matthew my boy, this is going to make things very interesting."

"I've thought about all that, but for now just do your best to keep them out of jail."

"I'm sure you're aware that whatever you tell me is held in strictest confidence," Edward assured the couple once they'd settled onto the sofa in his hotel suite's sitting room. "I currently represent Steele Productions, Matthew's production company, but that is an entirely different matter and I don't see any conflict. However, if you have the slightest hesitation, I'll be happy to refer you to a colleague."

He stopped speaking, took a sip of his Perrier, and waited.

"You're the best, at least according to Matthew, and that's good enough for me." Giselle said without hesitation. "If you can represent us both, that's ideal, and if not, well…" she saw David's sideways glance, but ignored it, "we'll talk about it." She had given this a lot of thought, and there really was nothing to talk about, but now wasn't the time. David would inherit Edward.

"I see no reason to think of severing at this time. So, I suggest we get started. Tell me everything from the beginning."

Like an Aboriginal elder passing along an oral history, David slowly recounted the details of the day.

"That's quite a story," Edward said, when David finished. "I know a couple of screenwriters who'd love to have the rights to it. I'm not an expert on French law, but it's a pretty good assumption that you've broken one or two. Have you looked into it?"

"I did a little reading online," David said, "and it's pretty clear that under French law, all antiquities found in France become the property of the French government. So, in the eyes of France, I've committed a crime, and there's no way around that. The scroll jar is still in Giselle's flat, so we haven't done anything illegal with that yet, although a case could be made that we stole it from whoever owns the cave—probably descendants of the Hautpoul family."

Edward sorted the pieces of information for several seconds.

"Okay," he said finally, smiling at them and refilling their glasses. "There are several issues we'll have to deal with, but it's unlikely that either of you will wind up in prison. I don't like to guess about these kinds of things so I'll wait until I've consulted a French attorney who specializes in this field, and be guided by his or her advice. There's nothing to be done until then, but it shouldn't take more than a couple of days. I assume you don't want me to start any negotiations until the ketubah has been authenticated."

"Exactly right," David said.

"I just want to clarify," he said to the two silent scholars. "You believe the marriage took place in what is now Israel."

"Yes, and it's not just our belief. The ketubah says so," said David.

"Actually, knowing what I know, my guess is that the State of Israel will consider itself to be the rightful, original owner; but I can't imagine the French will see it that way."

"True enough, but it gives us some potential leverage. Israel can certainly lay claim if they choose, particularly because it's not physically in France anymore, so we have a couple of negotiating chits that hopefully will keep the gendarmes from your door. Right now, there's no reason to tell anyone where you found it, and I suggest you don't. Once it's been authenticated to your satisfaction, and you think you're on firm footing, let me know and I'll start the negotiations with the French. How long do you expect this to take?"

"It could take years, but hopefully, we'll have a sense of it by the autumn. If it's an outright fraud, we'll know quickly."

Giselle had met Edward a number of times, and knew he had a reputation for being a scrupulously honest control freak and rabid defender of the First Amendment. Today, as she walked into the hotel lobby, she was flooded with the same fear and apprehension she'd felt in fourth grade entering Sister Jean-Marie's office after being caught whispering to her best friend. But Edward apparently had no intention of judging them.

Giselle smiled with obvious relief. "I'm so grateful for your help, particularly because I know you're busy putting out fires over Matthew's movie."

"No fires yet, but the potential is there."

"Simone said Matthew really fell in love with this script, so something must make it more compelling than another run-of-the-mill Jesus movie, but with all the excitement over the ketubah, we never got around to discussing it."

"I'm trying to keep the buzz to a minimum, but given your discovery, I'd say it's the perfect example of art imitating life. Basically, it's a love story. It starts off in India and Tibet, where Jesus spends his youth learning from the monks and becoming a holy man they called Issa. In time, he returns to his mother's home in the Galilee, and begins preaching in a Jewish temple in Magdala. He sees Mary Magdalene and it's love at first sight. She's descended from royalty, educated, very strong-willed and outspoken, unlike other women of the time, and he is besotted with her beauty, her quick mind, and good heart. She convinces her father to allow them to marry, and they become inseparable. She travels with him, supports him with her inheritance, and becomes his favorite disciple."

"That's amazing," David said, "it's probably not far from the truth."

"So it seems, according to your ketubah. But there's more. He's crucified on a Friday morning after Judas betrays Him, but cut down before sunset. Joseph of Arimathea and Mary Magdalene stop the bleeding and dress his wounds, but they carry him to a secret hiding place, leaving an empty tomb. Because they are so recognizable as a couple, Jesus and Mary Magdalene make the wrenching decision to part; she sails west across the Mediterranean and arrives in the south of France; he sets out on foot, walking the 2,500 miles across what is now Iraq, Iran, and Pakistan before arriving back in India."

Giselle stared out the window, watching the gentle waves of the Mediterranean lap onto the sand after Edward stopped speaking, wondering what had possessed her sweet brother-in-law to think producing this movie was a good idea. Of course he was expecting fireworks. His movie was an affront to people of faith; he had trashed her beliefs and treated them as pure fiction. Simone must have known how distressing it would be, but she was disgusted with organized religion after the Boston Globe exposé of the pedophilic priests and the systematic Church cover-up.

I should have more of an open mind, Giselle thought. *After all, Jesus and Marie-Madeleine were married; but no, Matthew took it too far, and for what? To create a sensation and make money.* She closed her eyes for a few seconds, hoping the love she felt for her brother-in-law would temper her anguish and shift her perspective, but when she opened them, nothing had changed.

"That's going to create quite a stir," she said evenly, sitting up straight and smoothing her wrinkled summer skirt over her knees.

Her devastation was none of Edward's business. "After all, the Resurrection is the foundation of Christianity. I certainly understand the power and pathos of star-crossed lovers like Romeo and Juliet, and plots like one of David's favorites, *Casablanca.* But this movie, *Devotion,* makes a mockery of what millions of us believe. Paul says in Corinthians that it's futile to have faith if Christ wasn't raised, because there'd be no way to be saved."

"I'm so sorry I upset you." This was the first time Edward had discussed the movie with anyone who didn't have a positive, or at least neutral reaction, and he was clearly taken aback. "As a confirmed atheist it's hard for me to fully appreciate what this means to you and how personally you take it. I had no idea—Matthew didn't warn me—but I'm one who believes the messenger is responsible for the message he delivers of his own free will, so I apologize."

"No, no need. Matthew doesn't see it the way I do, and for all I know, he enjoys thumbing his nose at the church. The thing is, I thought they respected..." She paused, aware that her eyes had filled with tears and there was nothing she could do about it. "I'm just disappointed that people I love are involved with this."

Matthew, it's sort of ironic that it was your namesake who preached about forgiveness; it's in Chapter 6, but right now I can't remember what he said. She carefully placed her glass on the table, stood up, and smiled weakly at Edward.

"If you can represent this movie and the uproar it will cause, I trust dealing with the problems of two insignificant academics will be child's play," she said, brushing away the tears rolling down her cheeks as she walked toward the door.

David stood and hurriedly shook hands. "Thanks for everything," he said, striding across the floor and reaching for his handkerchief. "We'll be in touch."

42

JERUSALEM

JULY 2, 2013

THE TROLLEY DROPPED them at the foot of Yafo Street, across from the promenade that led to Jaffa Gate.

They had one extra day to spend in Israel, and, in deference to Giselle's mood, the whirlwind tour David had planned was postponed; they were limiting themselves to the Church of the Holy Sepulchre and the Western Wall, both within the confines of the Old City of Jerusalem.

"It's only a movie," he'd repeated several times during the course of the previous night, "and there's definitely a bright side—Mary Magdalene is a tragic heroine, not a whore. Let's not let it ruin our first visit to Jerusalem together."

"David, you should write a book about persuasion," she said, lying in his arms and trying to take his advice to heart; she couldn't, but he didn't have to know.

"I think the title is taken."

"Pity. But say no more. I'm persuaded. *Devotion* has nothing to do with us and we have nothing to do with it."

As they passed through the Jaffa Gate, he said, "David Street bisects the city into unequal sections: Christian and Muslim Quarters on the left, Armenian and Jewish Quarters on the right. The Western Wall is the farthest point from here, so I suggest taking in the sights and going there first. Then we'll backtrack and wind up at the Church of the Holy Sepulchre and we won't have to rush."

David Street was more bazaar than street, a crowded alley of ancient stones, punctuated every few feet with steps going down into the bowels of the city that had remained unchanged for thousands of years. Shops on either side, from tiny to grand, offered everything from T-shirts and souvenirs to antiquities and fine jewelry. Color, babble, confusion, and excitement bombarded visitors from every direction.

"You were right, David. Every biblical scholar should be required to walk this street; it oozes ancient world, and I'm glad to be here."

"So, do I get the credit for bringing you, or does it go to the Saint?" David asked as he put his arm around her and steered away from a man carrying a huge stack of brightly colored fabric.

"I can hear her calling to me." Giselle stopped, pushed her hair behind her ear and cupped it with her hand.

"And what is she saying?"

"She says I should thank you for arranging this visit, especially because you're not a true believer."

"As I've said all along, she was a woman of great wisdom, and good manners."

"I'd like to see if we could find a little gift for my sister. She may be colluding with Matthew where that movie is concerned, but I love her anyway."

"Of course. And don't forget, Matthew's been great. Men are people too, you know."

Giselle smiled ruefully and shook her head. "No, I'm not ready to forgive him yet, but maybe we'll see something for Trevor and Laila."

"You know, he didn't really do this to you."

"I know." Giselle's anger and resentment was obvious, "but I get the feeling you're defending him, and believe me, he doesn't need your support."

David stopped walking and turned to face the woman he loved, who looked on the verge of tears.

"I'm not defending Matthew," he said quietly, pulling out his handkerchief and handing it to her. "And he hasn't done anything that requires a defense. I understand that you take this to heart, but I can't imagine you would condone censorship, or limiting freedom of expression. No one will be forced to see the movie."

"Well, I'm not in favor of issuing a fatwa against my brother-in-law, but

I don't like or approve of what he chose to create." She handed the handkerchief back and gave him a little smile. "Let's just go directly to the Wall. I don't feel like shopping, and I don't feel like fighting and ruining my first trip to Jerusalem. Truce?"

"It's a plan," David said, but he could see Giselle had retreated behind her eyes again.

"There it is." With a sweeping gesture David motioned through an ancient archway, one of the many entry points into the plaza housing the exposed portion of the 187-foot-long Western Wall.

They found a place to sit on a low stone wall behind the men's section, where they could watch male tourists, students, and the black-garbed orthodox in tall fur hats walk past the checkpoint. Small skull caps stamped 'Kotel' were automatically handed to anyone whose head was uncovered.

"It's true that I'm glad I decided to come," Giselle said after several minutes, "but I'm really not in a good frame of mind. I think I warned you that I have a hard time getting over this kind of thing."

"You did, but it would be clear even if you didn't. The thing is, giving Matthew this much power over you, over us, and our ability to enjoy this day together, isn't fair to me."

"I know, I know," she said. "I'm trying, but I just can't shake it. Papa always told me I take things too personally and I'm overly sensitive. It's just been so easy to be with you, I wasn't expecting you to, I don't know, gang up on me."

David was stunned. "You're creating something in your mind that doesn't even have a seedling of truth," he said. "You're right, I don't see the movie the way you do, or the implications, but I'm not ganging up on you. The last thing I want is for you to be hurt. I love you."

He reached over, covered her hand with his, and began to stroke her wrist.

They sat quietly this way until Giselle finally relaxed and put her head on his shoulder.

"When I come to the Wall," he whispered into her hair, "it's not to pray, but to honor a place where people were slaughtered for their beliefs; where the place itself was destroyed over and over in the name of religion, as if that could change what people believe. If murder can't change people's beliefs, what harm can a movie do? It used to be called the Wailing Wall, and I prefer that, because I like to think the Wall itself remembers and weeps, as if those who come, touch it and listen can prevent horrible things from happening again."

"David, I'm sorry. Sometimes I forget how wise you are." She stood up and smiled at him. "I'll touch it and listen, but I'd also like to leave a note for my father, just in case."

"I thought you might," he said, fishing a piece of hotel stationery out of his pocket and handing it to her along with a logo stamped pen. "I'll go to the men's side and be back here in fifteen minutes, but take as long as you like. We're not in any rush."

"My hero," she said taking the paper, tearing it in half, and heading for the sequestered women's area on the right side of the divider.

David headed to the left, where scores of men stood with prayer books, shoulders draped with prayer shawls, white tassels with blue threads peeking out from beneath their jackets, swaying forward and back as they prayed. *God's army.*

I might as well be a ghost, he thought. *If the earth were spinning backward, or I arrived here in a time machine, I'd find the same men, thinking the same thoughts, reading the same books. Carbon dating, the lessons of science and technology, the insignificance of this planet in the universe have no meaning for them.* He bent his head and touched it to the Wall. *I hope*; *I hope we don't blow ourselves up in the name of religion before people evolve and give up creating magical solutions for everything they don't understand.* He stood that way for several minutes, before backing away and returning his kippah.

It was at least twenty minutes more before Giselle made her way to the meeting point.

"I was wondering if I should start to worry."

"Worry that I'd run away or worried that I'd been abducted by some Orthodox women who convinced me to convert and pick out a wig? No, I'm feeling better, but I did have some sort of experience."

"What do you mean? Do you want to go sit down somewhere and tell me about it while we get a coffee, or while we're walking to the Church?"

"Let's walk. This is my kind of wandering."

"Was it a mystical experience?" David didn't exactly roll his eyes, but his tone gave him away.

"Don't make fun, certainly not today; it was, sort of. While I was standing at the Wall, I couldn't get Marie-Madeleine out of my mind—I expected to think about my father, and Mamie, of course; I left them both little love notes, but I kept thinking about Her. She might have walked down David Street before it had a name, buying vegetables or visiting a friend. She was here in this city, and I swear I could feel her presence just the way I did in the Grotto.

"Maybe she didn't touch that part of the Wall, but it was there in her lifetime, and you're right, there's something almost alive about it, like an ancient animal, a dinosaur maybe, who lived in the murky past and now stands there to be petted and soothed. It's a Wall with a heartbeat; you said it weeps, but it's the same idea. As soon as I touched it, I felt a visceral connection to my ancestors, all the unknown and unnamed people who lived and grew up and had families thousands of years ago, maybe right here in Jerusalem. I told them I was proud of them, and that we've come a long way, although I'm not so sure that's true for those who haven't changed over the last two thousand years."

"It sounds like a profound experience. I think you have a remarkable capacity for spiritual insight that I don't have and never did. It's a gift."

"And you are a gift," she said, taking his hand. "I have a very hard time forgiving people, but you have some way of making me want to forgive you."

"That's good to know," he said, smiling, "but please keep in mind I didn't really do anything that should require forgiveness. I hope you don't think we'll never disagree about anything. I'm easy to get along with, and I try to be supportive, but I'm not without my own convictions and ideas from time to time."

"I know, I know," she said again, but David wasn't at all convinced.

When they were finished with their visit to the Church of the Holy Sepulchre, Giselle whispered, "I heard there's a cave in the back of the church that some people think contained the tomb of Joseph of Arimathea. Are you willing to take a look?"

"Of course," David whispered back, "caves are sexy places."

"Good grief, David. Think about where you are."

The far reaches of the sprawling building had a small, unadorned, empty room that acted as an entrance into a desolate granite space that would have been in total darkness had it not been for the shadowy light cast by a small oil lamp.

"Some people think Jesus was the one entombed here, not Joseph of Arimathea, because it was found empty; but it's all conjecture." She looked around and sighed in a way David interpreted as somewhere between loss and defeat. "In the end there's no way to ever know what really happened."

David nodded. "Ultimately, all that really matters is what you believe and the meaning you make of what you discover; after all, nothing can be proved—or disproved. I think it's sort of futile to try to bake abstract creations of the mind and concrete things you can touch into the same soufflé. All I believe in is us and the power of the human spirit."

They stood, arms around each other, together in the dark, neither one wanting to face the sunlight, the hordes of bustling humanity and especially not the trip to the airport.

"You are my beshert, and we will find a way to be together. It's written in the stars," he murmured, kissing the crook of her neck and tasting the salty residue from the drops of perspiration under her hair.

"Oh David, when I'm in your arms all that sounds inevitable. But once I'm home, I know I'll start thinking about Matthew, and that movie, and I'll feel isolated and alone. Once that happens I'll doubt everything, especially how it feels right this minute. This is why I vowed never to be in a long-distance relationship."

"Shakespeare wrote, 'Our doubts are traitors, and make us lose the good we oft might win.' If you just remember I love you with all my heart, we'll be fine until we figure it out," he said.

43

OCTOBER 19, 2013

NEW YORK

DAVID AMBLED DOWN the stairs and stood under the archway leading to the living room, admiring the perfect tableau Simone had created; the dancing flames in the hearth, a bottle of red wine breathing on a cart next to delicate crystal goblets, a selection of cheese and crackers on a side table away from the heat of the fire. Each element combined to create the ambient glow of camaraderie, however contrived and misleading.

"Giselle is still with the kids, and she'll be down in a while," David informed Simone. "She said to tell you she feels like she's surrounded by clones of Judas."

"And I'm sort of trapped in the middle," Simone said quietly. " The best I can offer is neutrality, which never makes anybody happy."

"Don't worry, she can take care of herself," Matthew quickly interjected, "after all, she's the big sister."

David remained silent as he walked over to the fireplace, rubbed his hands together, and stood with his back to the room staring at the blazing logs. They had arrived last night, happy to be here together for Trevor's birthday weekend, but Giselle's entire mood changed this morning when Simone told them about the dinner plans.

"She asked to borrow one of my dresses," Simone said as she joined David, "an expensive one, and she only does that when she feels particularly vulnerable. It's like armor. And she said some flowery thing I barely understood when she went down to Laila's room; you know, that thing she does when she's anxious, so of course I'm worried. She's my sister."

"She'll be fine." Matthew reiterated, not sounding concerned in the slightest. "Let me pour you a glass of wine; what about you Dave?"

David nodded yes and added, "Please tread lightly. This is a very sensitive topic for Giselle, and I'm sure you know she hates being taken by surprise."

"Look, Dave, Edward and I aren't bullies; it's obvious Giselle is a little uncomfortable with the movie plot, but we haven't had any unpleasant words about it."

"Let's keep it that way," Simone said over her shoulder as she hurried to answer the doorbell.

"You get more beautiful every time I see you," Edward said by way of greeting. "You are the only woman who's ever made me regret my bachelorhood. I hope Matt appreciates you."

"I think he does, but feel free to remind him how lucky he is. Oh, the flowers you sent are gorgeous. Come in, have a drink, and make small talk until Giselle escapes the clutches of my little ones; she won't want to miss anything, and I promised we'd save any serious conversation until she joins us."

Edward took off his coat and scarf and handed them to Simone. While she was placing them on a hanger and getting ready to put them in the guest closet, she said quietly, "Matthew told me what a masterful job you did negotiating with the French government and the Israelis, and I want you to know I'm personally grateful."

"I was glad to do it. It still astounds me that a discovery like this is getting so little recognition. It only goes to prove people don't like to be confused with the facts."

"Well, even with all the skeptics and naysayers, the French weren't willing to give it away."

Edward laughed and patted her arm. "They were hedging their bets. They're still on the fence, but they wanted control, and if there turned out to be glory, they wanted that too."

"People here don't seem as impressed and excited as I thought they'd be, but the movie, #devotion, or some derivative, is consistently trending on Twitter," Simone said. "But let's not mention that to Giselle. She's upset enough."

Giselle arrived almost an hour later, mindful of making her entrance with graceful, perfect posture. The sisters at College Stanislas de Paris had been relentless when it came to what they called "good carriage." Slumping, for any reason, was unacceptable—*a dictum I never fully appreciated until tonight,* she thought. No one in the room, not even David or Simone, understood how deeply abhorrent it was to her to link Matthew's movie with the ketubah—the precious ketubah that had been entrusted to her.

She'd spent the entire day gripped by the same horrible, unrelenting agitation she'd felt in Jerusalem. Idiotic as it might be, she was hoping her sister's black Chanel dress would embolden her, especially combined with a pair of Louboutin red soled stiletto-heeled pumps—shoes she never would have purchased—that announced, "don't mess with me." Maybe her mother was right about the power of shoes.

David brought her a glass of wine and whispered, "You are stunning." She gave him a pro forma smile that announced she wasn't interested in having her attention diverted.

"Sorry I kept everyone waiting," she began. It was the same lie David used in the Amsterdam bar. "Simone tells me you two"— indicating Matthew and Edward—"want to talk to us about our ketubah and your movie.

Simone held up her hands, palms out, and Matthew, who was about to say something, remained silent. "Let's move into the dining room," she said softly, " dinner will be ruined if we don't get started, and I for one, think sitting around a dinner table will remind us we're a family." She sent a piercing look to Giselle, who nodded.

"So," Edward began after they were all seated at the table and dinner had been served, "I thought the *Times* writer did a nice job with the announcement. It was understated, professional, and I suspect most people won't notice that it doesn't say where the ketubah was found."

Matthew raised his glass in a toast. "To Edward, for keeping my favorite sister-in-law and her co-conspirator out of prison, and for his help in bringing my movie to safe harbor. Thank you."

"We're grateful too, Edward," David added. "We know it was a tricky negotiation, and besides being a super smart, diplomatic lawyer, Matt bragged that you have a particular talent for being wily—but remaining on the right side of the law. I know that must have worked to our advantage. So, I—we—are in your debt."

"My pleasure," Edward responded, looking directly at Giselle. "I hope you're pleased with the plans for the ketubah."

"I am," she said evenly, meeting his eyes across the table. "The new wing of the Louvre is the right spot, and even though we won't be acknowledged, we'll be at the opening; seeing it safe is all that really matters."

"It will be an understated exhibition, and, from what I can gather, somewhat equivocal, but maybe it's better that way, for now."

Giselle smiled at him, feeling slightly more relaxed, until he continued, "I hope, since our meeting in Israel, you've made peace with the plot of *Devotion*."

So it begins, she thought, as she steeled herself for the confrontation. "No, actually I haven't, but since I don't expect to be personally involved, except for the fact that I'm related to Matthew, it hasn't been on my mind."

"Well, I'm proud of being related to you," Matthew said with a smile she didn't trust as entirely as she had in the past. "Your discovery of the ketubah is monumental, really earth-shattering, and Christians of every denomination throughout the world should have the opportunity to hear about it and rejoice in what it means."

"Matthew, I've known you a long time, and I love you, but it irritates me when you do this. I don't know what to call it exactly—trying to butter me up, pitching an idea, spinning, manipulating—it's beneath you, and it's certainly beneath me. It's so Hollywood, and I can't believe you think I'd fall for that kind of approach."

"But I mean it. Sure, the ketubah helps legitimize the movie; I don't deny it would be priceless publicity for *Devotion*, but, as your sister has pointed out to me, it would also force the Church to rethink its position on women and marriage for priests. If there were no celibacy requirements, maybe there'd be fewer child molesters among the clergy. Who knows where it could take us."

"If you're sincere, I apologize," Giselle said, offering a wary smile and reluctantly giving him the benefit of the doubt. "But let me be clear. I'm adamantly opposed to using the discovery of the ketubah to promote your movie. It diminishes and trivializes what you just described as monumental. The ketubah is real, with real implications. Your movie is fiction."

The more she spoke, the more amazed and impressed David was. They had taken the kids to the park after school, and while they sat and watched Trevor do tricks on the jungle gym, she'd carefully explained her position again. She felt duty-bound to protect the memory and legacy of Marie-Madeleine; any link to the movie was a non-starter. There was no wiggle room. He'd never seen her quite as earnest and intense, and he wished he could support her unequivocally, but he vehemently disagreed. Matthew and Edward were owed a huge debt, not only for help in expediting all the physical machinations; not only for negotiating with the French, Israeli and U.S. governments, but also for carrying the burden of it. They weren't asking him to lie, or endorse the premise of the movie, and he didn't see the harm in talking about something he was so proud of. Was that hubris? Rationalization? Maybe, but it was more than that.

Everyone at the table remained silent for a few minutes. The candles, sparkling crystal, and autumnal arrangement of red, orange, and gold gave the illusion of a warm, festive gathering of friends and family, enjoying a good meal and interesting conversation; but a definite, palpable chill had settled over the room.

"Look, everyone, in case it's not clear, my sister doesn't want to participate in a movie tie-in. It could have been an unexpected bonus, but we weren't counting on it, and the movie will do fine without her help. So, let's move on." Simone smiled at Giselle, who smiled back with relief.

"Okay, I accept that," Matthew said, turning his attention to David, "but what about you?"

"Oh, mon Dieu, you're such a troublemaker." Simone's tone had an edge as sharp as a sword. "Can't you let it go?"

David cleared his throat and said quietly, "It's fine, Simone. I don't have a problem with hearing what Edward and Matthew have in mind. We haven't even seen the movie, and maybe we should. Matthew, maybe you can clarify what would make the movie acceptable to people of faith."

Matthew said, "Let me try again. *Devotion* is a story of love. It's a story of hope. It's not meant to say the basic message of the New Testament is wrong; it's meant to say that even if Jesus was married, which we now know he was, even if he survived the crucifixion, he was here on earth to spread a message of love and teach humanity how to live together in peace. He could still be the Son of God, for those who believe. Those whose faith depends on the premise that Jesus dies for our sins—well, this isn't the movie for them. *Devotion* isn't a comment on religion or religious principles, although some folks may see it that way. It may not be the narrative of the Gospels, but He is the Jesus of the Gospels."

David persisted. "Okay, but why upset people like Giselle and deny the crucifixion took place? Is there any basis for that?"

"A reasonable question," Edward said, "and one I asked early on, just out of curiosity. And, by the way, the crucifixion does take place, but Jesus is cut down before he dies, and is tended to by Joseph of Arimathea with aloe and myrrh. His wounds are healed and he recovers; but they realize that if he's found, he'd be nailed up again, so he has to disappear."

"Why India? Why not France with the woman we now know was his wife, and his friends?"

Matthew said, "I can speak to that. The writer did a lot of research and discovered that villagers in Kashmir claim their history books refer to Jesus living and dying there. There's a hill called Temple of Solomon that has an inscription in stone commemorating the year 54 CE, when Yuz Asaaf, as they pronounced it, revealed he was Jesus, the prophet of Israel. According to them, his mother, Mary, was with him and died in a small town named Mari, where she is buried.

"They believe Jesus died in Kashmir in 80 CE and His tomb, which was built in 112 CE, points east-west in the Jewish tradition, while the other Muslim grave points north-south, toward Mecca. So, *Devotion's* premise shouldn't be totally dismissed."

"I didn't know that," David said, "although I know there are many contemporary biblical scholars who believe Jesus was alive after his crucifixion." He looked at Giselle apologetically, but continued, "And Abbé Saunière, the priest who had possession of the ketubah, and hid it, never said so outright, but he alluded to it by altering a little painting in his church. The thing is, the important thing is"—he looked at Giselle again—"it didn't change Saunière's faith."

"Interesting," said Edward, "I really don't know anything about Saunière."

He looked pointedly at Giselle. "I hope you don't reject what David's saying totally out of hand."

"You are an atheist, Mr. Chrystal, and I don't expect you to understand how painful this is," Giselle said coldly.

"You're right, and please, please, call me Edward. We may not agree on this, but I hope we're not enemies." Giselle gave a curt nod, but she had no interest in either animosity or friendship; in fact, she didn't really care what Edward did or didn't understand; her statement was meant for David.

"Look, Giselle," Edward continued, "You're right. I make no pretense at being a believer, but if I were in a position to save a life, particularly of someone I admire or love, nothing would stop me. It makes all the sense in the world that Joseph of Arimathea or Nicodemus, or Mary Magdalene, or all of them would have tried to save him, and very well might have. It certainly makes more sense, at least to me, than his rising and disappearing into a black hole in the far-off universe; after all, people come back from near-death experiences all the time and their family and friends rejoice."

"Yes, that's how an atheist would see it," Giselle said, "but there are a billion Christians around the world who have faith that He rose on the third day. We don't need it to make sense. It is our truth and salvation."

"That's a lot of people, but there are more than one and a half billion Muslims and, it may surprise you to know, over a billion atheists, who don't buy it. There was a time children were taught the sun revolved around the earth, and it was accepted as truth. The truth in India and Israel is not the truth in Rome. But the thing is, I'm not only a nonbeliever. In general, I've come to see religion as a source, or an excuse, for hatred; for people trying to prove that what they believe is better than what their neighbors believe. People possessed with religious fervor have been responsible for more death, torture, rape and pillage than ever caused by atheists—think of the Crusades, the Salem witch trials—"

"Excuse me, this is taking us far afield from the movie," David interrupted forcefully. He could see Giselle disappearing behind her eyes the way she did when she felt attacked and needed a hiding place.

"Right, I apologize. This isn't the time or place."

Giselle looked stricken, and Simone threw Matthew a look meant to say, "enough."

"Sorry, Giselle," Matthew said sincerely. "I know where you stand on this, and we won't say another word."

He turned and looked at David. "It seems to me you and Giselle see this differently. If that's the case, I wish you'd consider doing a couple of late-night talk shows; there's nothing cheesy about them. Or maybe *Ellen*, or *The View*. Even a news show is a possibility. You could talk about how you found it, or what you did to prove it's authentic; any part of the story you're comfortable with." He paused, but David's face was impossible to read. "It would mean a lot to us, not just financially—but if you talked about the real ketubah, maybe showed a photo of it, it would really legitimize the love story, which is the essence of the film and what makes it unique." He paused again, but getting no reply, or indication of any kind, he added, "Look, I can't speak for all the producers, but I'm willing to donate some part of the profits, something substantial, to a charity of your choosing: Catholic Charities, Women's Health, something archaeological, whatever you want."

"I'll think about it," David said, reaching for Giselle's hand. She pulled away, stood up, excused herself, and headed upstairs.

44

NEW YORK

OCTOBER 20, 2013

DAVID PUSHED BACK his chair, put his napkin on the table, mumbled a quick thank you and left. He took the steep staircase one step at a time, as slowly as a three-year-old, grateful for the few minutes of contemplation provided by climbing four flights of stairs. His hand slid over the gleaming, carefully restored and preserved banister as he marveled once again that two sisters growing up in the same home could be so different. There was nothing he could think of saying that was likely to make an impact; whatever Giselle was responding to meant exponentially more to her than the sum of its parts.

Anyone who knew him, even vaguely, would have attested to his adaptability; it was as automatic as breathing, and Giselle had come to expect it. Accommodating her schedule and desires had been easy, and capitulating on this issue should have been a no-brainer, if that's what she needed from him; but something, some undefined, amorphous principle, made him unable to do it. The debt he owed Matthew and Edward was huge, but just as important was his belief that the ketubah should be presented to the public by a reputable, serious, person; namely, Dr. David Rettig. *Maybe I'm just on a big ego trip,* he thought again, as he started up the fourth and final flight. *Do I need my fifteen minutes of fame so badly? That's probably part of it, but how often is there an opportunity for an archaeologist to communicate directly with the larger world—even Dr. Karen King has limited her audience to subscribers of closed circuit TV and arcane publications.*

He tapped quietly on the closed guest room door, aware of the kids sleeping one floor away, and tried the knob. Unlocked. Giselle was sitting on the edge of the bed, staring down at the carpet, dry-eyed. He knelt in front of her and took her hands in his.

"I love you," he said. "I love you to the depth and breadth and height my soul can reach."

"But that won't keep you from doing it," she said, challenging him; her voice conveyed cold anger laced with distress, an anguished child accusing someone who revealed there was no Santa Claus. "I don't understand. I just don't. It's so important to me; it has significance for me, and I know it doesn't really mean that much to you."

David teetered on the edge for a fraction of a second. It was painful to hear her sound so wounded and know he was the knife. But she was wrong. This did mean something to him. "I know you don't understand, and I don't know what to say that will make you. It's rare that I try to convince anyone about anything, you know that, but I have my own point of view about this, and I'm asking you to try to see it. Edward and Matthew have gone out of their way for me, for us, big time, and this is a chance to reciprocate and do something for them no one else can do. That's one part of it. But the bigger issue is…" His voice had gotten louder and more argumentative. He stopped, took a deep breath, and continued in a low, steady tone, "I think this is an opportunity to tell the world who Mary Magdalene was and the place she had in Jesus's life. We have a chance, maybe even an obligation, to illustrate how uncovering the past and learning the truth enriches humanity."

"I know; I see that, but that's a separate issue. Doing it this way would sensationalize the ketubah and link it to the story in the movie. That's how people would hear it. Don't you get that?" Giselle sounded shrill, and her frustration was obvious.

"I don't agree with you," he said sadly, shaking his head. "I know you're used to me going along—it's my M.O. And that's fine with me. It's not my way to be in a war of wills; when I have a different opinion it usually isn't important enough to me to make it into an issue. But this—this is different. I'm not trying to convince you to go along with me; you're free to do whatever you think is right, and I respect your decision, but—"

"Are you going to say I don't respect yours?" She made no attempt to disguise or control her anger. "You're right, maybe I don't. But who's right or wrong isn't really the point. If you know, really know, really understand how upsetting this is to me, how painful, how awful it is that my own brother-in-law, a man I love, would want to promote a story that shreds the basis of my religion—and that you want to help him—don't you see what a betrayal this is?"

Tears of fury and despair held in check finally welled up, and she began to tremble with pain stripped of reason. Her naked desolation pushed him to the edge again, but the words she wanted to hear stuck in his throat.

He had remained sitting on the floor at her feet, but as soon as she started to cry he stood and sat next to her on the side of the bed, wishing relationships and life in general could be simpler; but they never were. "I don't want to hurt you," he said, smiling into her eyes with tenderness, "but there will be times, like this, when I have to do what I think is right, even if you don't agree. We're two separate people. I love the woman you are, even though you think about the world differently than I do. I love our differences; I celebrate them. It's not that I don't understand, I do; I just don't agree."

The tears were silently rolling down her face, and David took out his carefully folded white cotton handkerchief and patted her cheeks before handing it to her.

Through her staccato breaths she said, "And I love the man you are. I just don't think I can forgive you. You say you understand, but I don't think you do, and actually, I don't think it should matter if you do or don't. You shouldn't be willing to participate in something when I'm so opposed to it."

There was silence. David tried to put his arms around her, but she shook her head and moved away just enough. She loved that handkerchief and the man who carried it, who looked at her through the kindest of eyes. But this wasn't the way it was supposed to be, and she couldn't reconcile the David she loved with the one who could hurt her and ignore her feelings this way. "After Trevor's party I'm going to go home; I need a little time, and space, to think about this. Alone."

"What does that mean, exactly?"

"It means I think we should take a break. I'm not trying to punish you, or manipulate you, but I don't think we have what it takes to be a couple. Maybe we've each been on our own for too long, or maybe neither of us knows how to compromise and never did. I'm confused right now, and I need time without you." Giselle dabbed at her eyes as the tears came again, without her consent. "I thought we were perfect, but…"

David leaned over and put his arms around her, wanting, hoping, his physical being would penetrate to a place his words couldn't go. She pressed tightly against him, holding him, getting the comfort she always did from being in the warmth of his arms; neither one wanted to separate and relinquish the pleasure. David whispered, "Don't do this. We are perfect. You're perfect for me; you are the woman I would have invented, the woman I've spent my life looking for. You were meant for me, and I was meant for you. We are beshert."

"But," she said sadly, "I hear a disclaimer in that."

"But you have to accept who I am, and our differences. You have to accept I have to do what I think is right, even when you're opposed."

She pulled away and looked at him, feeling as devoured by grief as she had the day her father died; it expanded and consumed her, replacing every other sensation and thought, and for the second time in her life she wondered if people could die from heartbreak.

"And this is another thing we don't agree on," David said. "I like to talk about problems and try to work them out together. Silence is okay if you're listening, but if you're silent and deaf, it's like the other party doesn't exist. I can't believe you want to just wipe me out that way."

"No, that's not what I want, but I don't want to hear about *Devotion*, or what talk shows you appeared on, or what you said, or the movie opening or anything about it. So, I don't want to hear from you. We rushed into this relationship, and our time together has been mostly a vacation, without the stresses of everyday life, or the conflicts. You're a wonderful man, and this will be excruciating for me. But I hope you'll respect that I need to be alone for a while; everything goes out the window when I'm in your arms or we're in bed together."

"Do you want me to go to a hotel?"

"No," she said, "I don't want to have to explain to the kids why you left.

It's Trevor's birthday tomorrow, and I don't want to spoil it for him. I'll go down to the sofa where I used to fall asleep watching a movie."

"You stay here." David got up and began gathering the things he'd need. "Trevor will be knocking on the door in a few hours anyway, and my absence will barely be noticed. But don't think for a minute I've surrendered. I don't intend to lose you; I just need to come up with a better strategy for the second half."

45

RENNES-LE-CHÂTEAU

OCTOBER 1910

THEY STOOD SIDE by side in the quiet church, surrounded by painstakingly chosen art—sculptures, bas reliefs, paintings, frescoes, stained glass windows, and polished wood, created and maintained by the willpower of the recently defrocked Abbé François Bérenger Saunière. Marie pointed to the relief they were facing, the 14th Station of the Cross.

"Do you think anyone will understand why you put a moon in the sky," she asked quietly, "or will it be chalked up to your habit of thumbing your nose at the Church and general irreverence?"

"Someone will figure it out someday." He remained unmoving, staring intently at the colorful scene of Jesus being dragged out of the cave by Joseph of Arimathea and Nicodemus, blood flowing from a wound on his left side, spent, perhaps comatose, but alive the night after being cut down from the cross. "Perhaps there will be some other proof in the years to come, but our evidence is gone. Even after all these years, I wake in the morning and regret leaving the parchment with Antoine. Years ago, before I met you, he had something like a premonition, and I thought he was a little crazy. I shouldn't have told anyone, not even him; it was the greatest mistake of my life."

"You had no way of knowing," Marie said, "but at least you held it in your hand. You saw it with your own eyes. Even though it would have looked like chicken scrawl to me, it would have been a thrill to touch the note that said our Lord Jesus was alive."

He put his arm around her as if she needed protection from her wish.

"You would have been the one in danger if that parchment were here; you might have been thrilled, but you are an exceptional woman in every way. Most people wouldn't want to find out Jesus survived the crucifixion and wasn't resurrected. Even the brotherhood was shocked, especially Henri, although Antoine felt positively vindicated. He was always outspoken about his beliefs."

Saunière paused and fixed his eyes on the altar, where a painting he'd commissioned of Saint Maria Magdalena hung above a Latin inscription that read 'Jesus you remedy against our pains and only hope for our repentance, it is thanks to Magdalena's tears that you wash our sins away.' He pointed to it. "Some say it's blasphemy to suggest anyone but Jesus can wash away our sins, but they don't know the truth. Poor Antoine knew, and he paid the ultimate price."

Marie shuddered and shook her head as if she could physically cast off the terrible memory. She hadn't had a carefree day since November 1, 1897, the horrible morning after Antoine's murder, and no matter how many years rolled by, every knock on the presbytery door made her heart pound in fear. Saunière didn't broadcast what he knew, but the clues were perfectly obvious to anyone who could add two and two. Every Station of the Cross was surrounded by a gilded frame featuring a prominently carved Masonic Rose-Croix, exactly like the one on Antoine Gélis' tomb, making his allegiance to the Freemasons obvious.

The Stations themselves were hung in reverse order, opposite to every other Church in France except Saint-Sulpice. The two inscriptions over the entryway read 'This place is terrible' and 'My home will be called a House of prayers'; only a few devout scholars were familiar with the entire sentence in Matthew, which continued: 'but you made it a den of thieves.'

"You look lost in the cosmos," Saunière said before kissing her on the forehead. "Contemplation is an admirable state, and as you know, it's been my life's ambition to understand and improve myself. But if I had to guess, I would say you're more worried about my soul than your own."

"I don't worry about your soul. It is your life, your precious life, and therefore mine. Without you I have no future, only memories. Bishop de Beauséjour is determined to destroy you out of his envy. He doesn't know you or what you've given the people of this village. And, I don't think he cares. He doesn't know all the greatness in you." She began to cry.

"The world is full of small-minded men whose greatest pleasure is punishing those whose minds are free of pettiness. Plato and Aristotle wrote about these ethical and moral issues in ancient times, and Rousseau, only a hundred years ago, wrote about individualism, an idea I—" He stopped abruptly and smiled at Marie. "No reason to cite philosophers. Plainly said, don't worry. The new bishop cast a net with holes so large I swim right through them. I will continue to say Mass in the Villa Bethany, and the new priest will soon grow tired of hearing his voice echo in an empty church."

"You are one of the great men, my love. With all you know, do you still believe?"

"I do," he said, taking her hand and walking toward Asmodeus, the holy water stoup at the church entrance. "Our Lord Jesus Christ married Marie-Madeleine and was forced to live most of his life alone. He didn't die for our sins, but he suffered at the hands of the cruel, the pious, the righteous, the betrayers, and the hateful. She did as well. But they left behind the beauty of their love and a design to show us all a way to be human. I believe in the message."

A little boy who'd been sitting at the entrance, exactly where he'd been told to wait, jumped up and threw his arms around Saunière's legs. The priest bent down and in one graceful and practiced motion lifted the child onto his shoulders.

"Have you been a good boy, Abdon?" Saunière asked playfully.

"Yes, Father. Very good."

"Well then," Marie said, running her hand over the bare leg dangling over the priest's chest, "we'll all go home and have some apple pie and milk."

46

TOULOUSE

OCTOBER 22, 2013

THE DOORBELL BUZZED, insistently, irritatingly, zzzzzzzzz, zzzzzzzzz, as if someone knew she was there and wasn't taking no for an answer. The buzzer had been shrill the entire ten years she'd lived there, a long time to put up with that annoying sound, but her friends had learned to give it only a quick tap, so she never bothered to have it changed. Someone, a reporter, perhaps a Good Samaritan trying to return something she'd dropped, was being annoyingly persistent. She could ignore it—but she couldn't. At the very least she should open the door and say thanks or no thanks. "No comment" would be her response to any journalist brazen enough to accost her at home without an invitation.

"Charles! What a surprise."

Despite the big smile he flashed, a news reporter, a neighbor, in fact just about anyone else, would have been preferable. But he was a colleague she'd have to see at the university and at meetings; difficult as it was to be pleasant, there wasn't any alternative.

"I was strolling by the river, contemplating the relationship of faith and perception, when I noticed you approaching your flat, and I thought, well, I wondered, if it was a sign. The article from *The New York Times* was posted on Yahoo, and I hoped I'd have an opportunity to congratulate you privately, and there you were. It's quite a bombshell, and to think I've passed you in the halls and even sat next to you at a conference and you never breathed a word.

It's so like you; but just now, when I saw you were alone, I thought, why not ring up and seize the moment? Hear about it from the primary source."

Charles smiled again, and Giselle immediately thought of a snake, a cobra, waiting to strike; but then, the image morphed into something else. *Ah, yes, that statue of Asmodeus, the demon of Lust, at the entrance to Rennes-le-Château.* They bore a striking resemblance to each other she hadn't noticed before.

It was no secret at the university that Charles had always been sweet on her; thinking of it that way, as if it was something adolescent and innocent, helped to counter both his reptilian image and the darker, more ominous Asmodeus. She glanced down, half expecting to see sharply pointed fingernails, but there were the same carefully manicured hands she'd seen many times before.

If David hadn't smoothly orchestrated her escape that night in Amsterdam, she would've been trapped into having dinner with Charles, and now there was no one to intercede. If the discovery of the ketubah was out there in cyberspace, maybe soothing his ruffled feathers was a good idea.

"I'm sorry I couldn't say anything about the ketubah to you, Charles, but I'm sure you realize we had to wade through a pretty exacting process before submitting the paper and going public. Originally, we were going to wait until the paper was presented, but this sort of thing is hard to keep under wraps, so we gave the *Times* interview, hoping it would minimize any distortions. And I'd love to tell you all about it, truly I would, but, well, this isn't the best time. I haven't unpacked and I have some calls to make. I've only just returned from New York," she added lamely, hoping he'd be discouraged and gracefully, if reluctantly, leave with the promise of lunch in the next few days.

The awkward silence made it clear Charles planned to stay.

"Perhaps you could come in for just a few minutes and have a cup of tea—and I'll tell you as much as I can for now."

"That would be lovely," Charles responded, as he quickly stepped across the threshold.

Giselle motioned him to the sofa and walked into the kitchen to put a kettle on to boil. Even if he was Asmodeus or a King Cobra in disguise, he was no fool, and she'd have to be very cautious answering his questions, walking the fine line between evasive and circumspect. She had no good explanation for the sort of questions any scholar would ask, and she planned to follow

Edward Chrystal's advice and not discuss anything that wasn't already public information. The water seemed to be taking a particularly long time to boil, and she called to the living room, "I don't have milk, but I do have lemon and sugar—how do you take it?"

No answer, no one on the sofa. Walking quickly back into the room she saw her overly familiar and curious colleague had wandered over to the objects displayed on the wooden bookshelves standing against the far wall. A cold fear surged through her; the empty scroll jar was sitting on the shelf in plain sight, and Charles was standing and staring at it, practically sniffing it.

She could say it was a replica, but she never would have purchased a replica, and Charles knew her well enough to know that. In fact, they'd had a conversation once, years ago, about her buying original, if virtually worthless, art. She had made the bold statement that she didn't like owning reproductions. Well, she was about to pay for her arrogance. And would he put two and two together? Of course he would. And what if he did—why did it matter? She immediately wished David would walk through the door, but he wasn't going to rescue her tonight, or any other night, ever; getting involved had been a mistake and breaking it off now was so painful she didn't know how she would bear it, but it was for the best. They didn't understand each other, and she was better off on her own. Again. She hated Charles for intruding on her and her misery, forcing her to be pleasant and evasive. It was too much.

"This is extraordinary," Charles said, pointing to the red clay vessel. "I don't remember seeing it when you hosted the committee meeting last year. When did you get it?"

"Just last summer—it was a gift."

"That's quite a gift, if I may say so. You seem to be full of surprises. How old is it?"

"It's thought to be"—she was aware of speaking in the third person, but it was the only way to say something mostly truthful—"very early, but the date hasn't been verified."

"Just a wild guess, but might it perhaps have contained a scroll—maybe *the* scroll, the one that will turn the Church on its head? It must have slipped your mind when you met with the *Times* reporter. I'm sure he said you couldn't reveal where the ketubah was found. I assume it was a gift from your friend Dr. Rettig?" He waited, but getting no response, he added, with some measure of taunting pride, "if memory serves, you used to have a little ceramic object sitting in that exact place, one you said was precious because your nephew made it. Obviously, this…replacement…is even more precious."

I'm not as bad a liar as I thought, she congratulated herself. "Yes, it is precious to me, and one might say it's a gift from Dr. Rettig. Unfortunately, I'm not at liberty to reveal more about it or to comment on whether it did or did not contain any documents. Well, the water must be boiling by now. Sugar? Lemon?"

"As for the tea, I'm a man of simple tastes. But you can't seriously expect me to accept your answer about the scroll jar, and yes, I'm not an idiot, although you insist on treating me like one; I'm a religious scholar and I know a scroll jar when I see one."

He followed her into the kitchen and stood so close the putrid odor of garlic and anchovies on his breath overwhelmed her and made her feel sick. Although she thought her hand might tremble, it was steady as she poured water into the porcelain teapot, but acid burned her stomach and began to rise to the back of her throat, bringing on a wave of nausea.

"Look, Giselle, you know I've always liked you…" He held up his hand to indicate he didn't expect or want a response. "I don't know what you've gotten yourself into with Dr. Rettig, but clearly, something isn't on the up-and-up. Is he stealing from his archaeological sites and using you as a go-between? Is he smuggling? Did he smuggle the ketubah out of Israel and leave you holding the pot, if I can make a little joke? Is he planning to sell it on the black market? Whatever he's doing can't be legal and you're making yourself an accessory to a crime. Your whole career is in jeopardy, maybe even your entire future." Clearly frustrated by a lack of response, he bellowed, "People have been murdered over things like this."

Again, he waited for a reply, but the last comment put Giselle into full panic mode, and it was all she could do to keep breathing, while her heart raced and her fingers began to tingle.

Charles lowered his voice. "The ketubah, if it's authentic, is an earth-shattering discovery; don't ruin it by getting involved in some dirty scheme. You're not cut out to fence antiquities—and the international authorities will come after you. I have always been a man of discretion, patience, and good manners. You have treated me poorly, but I am willing to put that behind us. Please, let me help you."

His mustache hairs grazed her nose, and when he put his hand on her shoulder, she felt the vomit begin to burn the back of her throat, about to splatter over him and his polished brown shoes.

"Maybe you were led astray by Dr. Rettig and his swashbuckling pirate persona, but I, for one, never trusted him, and it's not too late. I won't say a word to anyone, I promise, but you must sever your relationship and stop participating in whatever scheme he's cooked up. I see how nervous you are; you look positively green, although you may think you've got me fooled. You're not cut out to be a thief. I know you. I understand you. I,"—he emphasized the I—"am the right sort of man for you."

As he turned his head in an awkward attempt to kiss her, Giselle backed away and shouted, "Stop! Stop, Charles. It's nothing like that, and even it is, it's not your business. I have no interest, none at all, in a relationship with you, and I must ask you to go before this goes any further."

Backing away, she heard her father's voice so distinctly she almost expected to see him standing at the door, reminding her to "stand tall." He'd started saying it when she'd wave good-bye and walk toward the school entrance; in those days she thought he was reminding her not to slump and shrink. When she was older, he'd say it when she had an important class to teach or meeting to attend, and she thought he was saying she should be proud of herself. Today, as his words came to her, she realized what a nuanced piece of advice it was; a strategy for dealing with bullies, as well as her own strict, punitive conscience.

Without another word, she turned and indicated the door.

"Ah, Giselle, Giselle. You always thought you were too good for me, but I hoped, for your sake, that you would see the light." Spitting his words, he added, "Clearly, you're not as smart or upstanding as I once believed you to be. Obviously, my loyalty to you is strained, and my admiration is tarnished. You are a Gélis, and perhaps you can't escape the family temptation to hide things you have no right to possess."

Giselle was stunned. His last words, "no right to possess," reverberated in her head like an ominous drumroll at a military funeral.

Charles sneered at her with unmasked contempt. "Yes, of course I know all about Father Antoine Gélis. Who in the Languedoc wouldn't have heard the story? He was involved in something dark and illicit, and he paid the price. Your name will be besmirched as well, and you'll likely wind up in prison, where you belong. Perhaps one day you'll come to regret this, but it will be too late. I shall see myself out."

The instant she heard the latch on the heavy wood door click into place, she walked over calmly and slid the deadbolt, before collapsing into the soft, enveloping down cushions of her father's easy chair. She felt more alone and vulnerable than she thought possible to endure. *The Lord is my shepherd* she began to recite in her head, hoping the familiar words would bring her some comfort and help dispel the terror that gripped her.

47

KHIRBET QEIYAFA, ISRAEL & TOULOUSE, FRANCE

LETTERS

DAVID TO GISELLE

JANUARY 1, 2014

My Dearest Giselle,

You asked me not to contact you until after the movie premiered, and though each day felt like Asmodeus had played a cruel trick and added extra hours between sunset and sunrise, I've kept my promise. I expected to spend New Year's with you, but here I am alone, wondering where you were when the clock struck twelve, and wishing you would call. Then I realized this is a time people make resolutions, not wishes.

Soon it will be spring, and I hope these letters, like new leaves unfolding, will remind you of all there can be for us again. When a heart becomes hard, it stops beating, and everything that depends on it dies. Please, don't let your heart become hard.

Because of you, and despite our differences, I discovered I believe in miracles. You and I finding each other was a miracle, and I can't believe the woman I have come to know would walk away from something so extraordinary. I accept that you are wounded, and that I took part in inflicting the wound. Even so, I hope that time has healed you enough to forgive me, because love can't always be perfect, but even with a few dings it's the best life has to offer.

Perhaps Shakespeare's words will carry more weight:

The quality of mercy is not strain'd
It droppeth as the gentle rain from heaven
Upon the place beneath. It is twice blest:
It blesseth him that gives, and him that takes.
Your forgiveness would be a blessing.

Love,

David

DAVID TO GISELLE

FEBRUARY 2, 2014

My Sweetheart,

It's hard not to hear from you, but 'Hope springs eternal in the human heart,' especially mine.

There is always meaning in silence, for both sender and receiver. Since I'm the receiver, I'm left to guess. Is it fear, or hate, or love or anger? Is it what I dread the most, the antithesis of love—cold indifference? That would be a dagger to my heart. I don't believe, won't believe, that's what it means. So, I'm waiting.

I was going through the photos of last summer's trip. There's one I took just as we finished the climb to the Grotto, your face is flushed with pleasure and triumph and there is love in your eyes. I am desolate when I think there may not be more of those moments.

Here in the Middle East, young people blow themselves up for something they believe in, and even though it's horrifying and fills me with rage, it's always profoundly sad as well; life is fleeting enough, and we should be celebrating our good fortune every day, together, not destroying something precious. Love, that incomprehensible connection between two souls, is a gift some mortals never experience; and as far as I'm concerned, it should be considered a sin to squander it.

Please, my darling, let's not throw happiness away.

David

DAVID TO GISELLE

MARCH 3, 2014

My Dearest,

I came upon a small round piece of glass today. When I held it up to the light and closed one eye, I was a ship's captain. looking through a spyglass, and there you were as I remembered you, sitting on the bench in Saunière's Orangerie. The sun lit you in a theatrical way, splaying through the glass panels of the roof and walls, your face glowing like a burnished Madonna. How I wanted to make love to you that glorious day in Rennes-le-Château, right there on top of the world. I wanted to dance with my angel and toss the conventions of civilization aside, as Saunière did. I remember thinking, 'You've opened heaven's portal here on earth for this poor mortal,' and it seemed to have been written especially for us.

Come back and dance with me in the clouds.

I have not loved, truly loved, many people in my life, but in that select group, I have never unloved a single one. Nor do I think it's possible. At this moment, I'm picturing you as a firefly, a magical, flittering burst of light that has brought unexpected joy to the dark landscape of my mind. When we met, I knew nothing about you, but even then, I knew.

That is the magic.

You are a believer, and I am a dreamer, always chasing rainbows, but as a practical matter, I don't think you'll ever find anyone who will be willing to drive more slowly.

You once said that when I had something unique to write, I'd be motivated. Well, here it is. It's a little hokey and sentimental, but what else would you expect?

We are beshert,
without volition, will or plan,
beyond the reach of
what we understand.

But this I know;
miracles are not illusions.
Love too is real,
and serenades the soul.

My heart hopes still
that you will hear the melody,
and yearn to dance
again, with me.

We have spoken many times about mysteries, coincidences, miracles, kismet, fate, and beshert. The human capacity to understand these things, these winged inscrutabilities, is limited and earthbound. Whether it was the spirit of Mary Magdalene or some cosmic force beyond our comprehension, we were brought together. You are my koinonos. Call it what you will, a miracle such as ours is a gift, and should be treasured.

Your David

GISELLE TO DAVID

MARCH 15, 2013

Dear David,

You're right. Silence has layers of meaning, but all I can say for now is that I'm confused about us, and it seems better to say nothing until I have some clarity. But I wanted you to know that no one's ever written a poem for me before, and I know it was from your heart. Thank you.

Now here's something strange. I was in a bookshop that happened to have an entire section of English-language books, and one of poetry. Normally I wouldn't have thought to reach for it, but of course with you on my mind, I couldn't resist. By some serendipity I opened it to a Walt Whitman poem you may, or may not, know; but once again it was one of these occasions that seem more than coincidental. I've copied it out for you:

Miracles
Why, who makes much of a miracle?
As to me I know of nothing else but miracles,
Whether I walk the streets of Manhattan,
Or dart my sight over the roofs of houses toward the sky,
Or wade with naked feet along the beach just in the edge of the water,
Or stand under trees in the woods,
Or talk by day with any one I love,
Or sleep in the bed at night with any one I love,
Or sit at table at dinner with the rest,
Or look at strangers opposite me riding in the car,
Or watch honey-bees busy around the hive of a summer forenoon,
Or animals feeding in the fields,

Or birds, or the wonderfulness of insects in the air,
Or the wonderfulness of the sundown, or of stars shining so quiet and bright,
Or the exquisite delicate thin curve of the new moon in spring;
These with the rest, one and all, are to me miracles,
The whole referring, yet each distinct and in its place.

To me every hour of the light and dark is a miracle,
Every cubic inch of space is a miracle,
Every square yard of the surface of the earth is spread with the same,
Every foot of the interior swarms with the same.

To me the sea is a continual miracle,
The fishes that swim—the rocks—the motion of the waves—
the ships with men in them,
What stranger miracles are there?

I cried when I read it, although I have to admit I cry easily these days, like I did after Papa died. I don't want to be mean-spirited toward you, and you don't have to convince me of your love. I know you love me, and I love you. That's exactly what makes this all so painful. I agree. Our love is a miracle, both ordinary and extraordinary. But lovers can be star-crossed, and maybe people who are beshert can be too.

I think our differences, not only on religion but also on how couples should be in the world, make us incompatible. I see now I would be angry with you often if we were together; things that matter to me don't matter to you, and that would make life together ripe for disagreement and unhappiness—because you don't really understand me, even though you think you do. I'd rather remember what we had than ruin it, with each of us making the other unhappy.

I've tried, but I can't get over you cooperating with Matthew and validating his movie. Your letters are beautiful, and I know you are doing in writing what you do in person; you are being charming and stroking a sensitive spot, but as soon as I melt, I remember. I'm sorry, but I'm stuck there.

I still love you, but sadly, that doesn't bring me to the same conclusion as yours.

Giselle

DAVID TO GISELLE

APRIL 2, 2014

My Darling,

T.S. Eliot wrote, "April is the cruelest month, breeding lilacs out of the dead land, mixing memory and desire." I hope to prove him wrong. I'm heartened by your willingness to write, and I believe memory and desire can foster hope. The Paris exhibit opens in only eight weeks, and even though we won't be staying together, my spirit soars at the prospect of seeing you.

I had a thought I want to share with you, and though it reeks of pop psychology, I hope you'll at least consider it.

I've come to believe that your relationship with your mother has had a big impact on what's been going on between us. For instance, you think she didn't understand you, and that is the same accusation you levy against me. You've told me she expected you to see the world through her eyes, and you've been blaming me of doing the same thing. I think you're responding to me as if I'm her, which isn't fair, or accurate, because I have no interest in you being like me. I love you for who you are, and I don't want a clone.

And there's more. During the past few months, since I started writing to you, I get the impression you're treating me the way your mother treated you. In other words, you're behaving the way she did. She was disappointed in the kind of girl you were, and let you know it, and then you started to feel like a disappointment. Well, now I'm the one who feels like a disappointment.

I hope this makes as much sense to you as it does to me, because I know you don't want to become your mother and push me away because I walk to the beat of my own heart, as you did and still do. In fact, I thought you liked that about me.

Did I mention I've been seeing a therapist? I needed to talk to someone because the pain was almost intolerable; it's genuinely helped. However, just so you know, all these constructs are mine, not his.

Like Walt Whitman, I see miracles every day in everything, but I believe the greatest miracle is unseen; it's the emotional/spiritual/mystical/magnetic/mental force field that we call love.

We have that. It is the greatest miracle, and you shouldn't let your mother cast a shadow on it.

Your David

GISELLE TO DAVID

APRIL 10, 2014

Dearest David,

I gave your letter a lot of thought. In fact, it sort of tortured me. I know people unwittingly turn out to be like their parents, even hated parents (I'm not saying I hated my mother), but I never thought I was anything like her.

But I think you may be more right than you could know. When I was a little girl, maybe five or six, Maman punished me by making me stand in the corner. I think it was when I threatened to run away if we moved to Paris. And, it's sort of funny now, in an ironic way, but when she said I could come out of the corner, I wouldn't. I stood there for hours and hours, the entire day, while she was begging me to have lunch and go out and play. I didn't come out until Papa came home, sat down next to me in the corner, kissed me, and explained that what I was doing wasn't nice.

I felt helpless, and it was the only revenge I could get, but it wasn't nice, and I don't want to do that to you, or anyone.

How my mother felt about me is moot. As far back as I can remember she treated me with a certain disdain, and she couldn't tolerate that my ideas were different than hers. My relationship with you is so different, but to my horror I realize I have the same expectations of you she had of me. It's strange, but I think I'm also responding to you as if you were her, making myself feel better by being stubborn and punishing you for doing something I'm opposed to.

My beliefs are important to me, and that's not going to change. I know you struggle with what you believe as far as religion goes, but I think trusting in the existence of beshert, or kismet, as you do, is a way of saying you believe in something unknowable, however you want to name it. I don't know how the Church will make peace with Jesus and Marie-Madeleine being husband and wife, but that doesn't change anything for me. I still don't agree with what you did, but I see now you had a right to be guided by your own conscience and values, not mine. It's that simple.

Whatever our disagreements may be, you are not a disappointment to me. You have a heart full of love and compassion and humor and generosity; you are moral, trustworthy, romantic, and reasonable. You make me feel like the most desirable woman in the world, and the most loved.

Whether it's written in the stars, or whether it was Marie-Madeleine's plan, or whether those are the same thing: 'You were meant for me, and I was meant for you.' (I got a DVD of Singin' in the Rain and I've watched it too many times to count these past few months.)

It is pathetic and self-defeating to stand alone in the corner. I want to be with you, to see your grin when I wake up in the morning, to feel your thumb stroking my wrist under the table, and to celebrate our differences.

Of course, I'm wondering if this is what Marie-Madeleine wanted me to discover. Maybe she did, but even that doesn't matter.

I've figured it out. I love you with all my heart and I always will.

Your Giselle

48

PARIS

JULY 1, 2014

HOW COULD I ever have considered refusing this offer? Giselle wondered, recalling her conversation with Simone as the doorman at the Plaza Athénée escorted her to the front desk.

"I'm not going to elaborate," Giselle had said firmly when she telephoned Simone, "but we're back together. Or at least we're planning to be. I was going to stay with a friend, but now I have to find a pension for the two of us; the Paris hotels have become exorbitant."

"Haven't I taught you anything?" Simone sounded genuinely horrified. "Why not stay at a convent and be done with it, for heaven's sake; give me the dates and I'll call Hubert at the Plaza Athénée."

"That's ridiculous. We can't afford that and we don't need it."

"It's not about need. It's about the sensuality of decadence. Surroundings matter; even you enjoy beautiful restaurants, so why not hotels? Anyway, I won't waste my time trying to convince you. I'm booking it, and if you choose to stay in a hovel with cockroaches and rats, it will go unused."

It had always been pointless to argue with her little sister, and Giselle had no urge to try. "You're impossible, but I love you," she had said. "Thanks."

"Why would I object?" David asked while they were face-timing, when Giselle explained the reason they were booked into one of Paris's best hotels. "She's happy for us, she believes in hedonism, and we may never get this chance again."

"You're right, you're right."

"And it's a great idea to arrive the day before the opening. It will give us a little time to get reacquainted, you know, stir the sugar in and let it thicken into syrup."

"Good grief. Don't you forget anything?" Giselle was laughing, but a little red blush was creeping up her neck. "You're embarrassing me."

Well before the usual check-in time, Hubert, the hotel manager, personally escorted Giselle to an opulent suite with a charming Juliet balcony on the fifth floor. Her beloved flat in Toulouse seemed like a hovel compared to these spacious, beautifully furnished rooms and sybaritic bath, and it was likely the charge per day was more than she earned in a month. *And what if it is,* she lectured herself, *it's perfection, and I'm going to relax and wallow in it.* Room service was at the touch of a button. She called down and requested a modest bottle of wine and a cheese platter, despite cocktail time being several hours away.

His knock came only moments after she replaced the phone in the cradle.

"You'll never know how many times I've dreamed this," he said as he walked in, dropped his overnight bag, and pulled her tightly against him.

"You've gotten more gray hair," she whispered into his ear, "and it makes you even more dashing. Oh my God, it feels so good to be in your arms. Never, never let me go."

"Never," he said, "never again. I didn't think it was possible, but you're even more beautiful than I allowed myself to remember. A little too thin, maybe, but the only way to describe how I feel is, 'all's right with the world,' with my world, when you're in it."

"*Pippa Passes*. I remember."

"Yes. Great loves send echoes through eternity." He stepped back an arm's length and took her hand. "Don't ever do this to me again," he said. "No more standing in the corner. No matter what the issue is, we'll talk, about anything and everything. Wasting time should also be one of the deadly sins."

"I promise," she said, leaning in and kissing him again before making a sweeping real estate agent gesture toward the room. "Pretty spectacular. Simone doesn't do simple, but she does extravagant with the best of them."

"And she means well. My mother used to say accepting a gift with grace is a gift to the giver. Obviously, this is a gift straight from her heart, and I'm going to make the most of every minute."

A circumspect tap announced the arrival of the room service waiter, who set out his platters on the sideboard in the adjacent sitting room before uhmmming discreetly at the open connecting door. "Est-ce que je peux ouvrir le champagne?" he asked.

"I didn't order champagne," Giselle murmured so quietly only David could hear. "I ordered an ordinary red wine. Do you think it's a mistake—or a Simone?"

"I'll bet on your sister; she knows how to get a reunion party started, even from thousands of miles away." He turned to the waiter with a smile. "Oui, s'il vous plait," he said before quietly adding, "And that's not all I've added to my meager French vocabulary. I don't want you to have to do all the talking for me, just in case I have reason to spend more time in France. You'll be surprised at what I've added to my arsenal. After all, it's the language of love."

"I don't know whether to be pleased or apprehensive; I hope you have a firm grip on which are public and which are private phrases."

She pressed her body against his, and as he engulfed her in his arms the warmth of his breath on her neck sent a little shiver of pleasure coursing through her body. Every point of contact, her wrist, the small of her back, her breasts against his chest, sent messages of desire to her brain. "Je t'aime," he whispered in her ear as he ran his fingers slowly down her body. "Do I have that right or should I translate?"

"Oh, you have it right," she breathed, as the excitement spread through her like a wildfire, making her weak with desire, "and, for your information, I'm not the girl I was in Saint-Maximin-la-Sainte-Baume. I heat up faster and the syrup has started to flow, but it's a criminal offense in France to waste a good bottle of champagne, so let's have a glass or two before we take off our clothes and I get to lie naked next to you."

"Je t'aime, je suis fou de toi, je ressens un amour fou pour toi," he whispered.

"And I'm madly in love with you, too," she whispered. "In any language."

49

PARIS

July 2, 2014

THE LARGE RED digital numbers glaring from the nightstand were jarring when David's cell phone rang and woke him from a deep sleep at 2 a.m. He fumbled for it, assuming he'd mistakenly set the alarm, before he realized someone was calling.

"It must be Simone." Giselle had gone directly from a contented slumbering state into alert anxiety. "Something terrible must have happened."

"No, it's Edward Chrystal." David didn't allow himself to sound as alarmed as the assortment of tragic possibilities whizzing through his mind made him feel.

"Sorry to wake you in the middle of the night," Edward said quickly, "but I thought it best not to wait until morning."

"Is it Simone? Matthew? The kids?"

"No, no, they're fine as far as I know. It's the ketubah."

David kissed Giselle's bare shoulder, and positioned the phone between his ear and hers. Hearing whatever Edward had to say over a speaker, like a public service announcement, struck him as incongruous in the hush of this bedroom.

"What about the ketubah?"

"It was stolen."

David was stunned into silence.

After months of bitter negotiations and intense committee meetings, the

Ministry of Culture and Communication, the ultimate protector of national treasures, had selected the Louvre as the place the ketubah would be displayed.

While the exhibit was in the planning stages, the scroll, protected in its acid-free and airtight housing, had been placed in storage along with other museum treasures not currently on view to the public. The permanent collection of the Department of Greek, Etruscan, and Roman Antiquities was to be its final home, where it would be the only acquisition not discovered in the Levant, a vast geographic swath of land that included modern-day Israel. David and Giselle were told not to expect any acknowledgment at the discreet, understated opening scheduled for the next day, but they had been thrown the bone of an invitation. The plaque on the exhibit would be unequivocal, saying only, "believed to be," leaving room for future deniability from anyone and everyone, especially the museum's board of directors.

"What do you mean, stolen? I don't understand," David said as he tried to read Giselle's expression. It was impossible from his angle, and he reached across his body and felt for her, laying his free hand on her leg. She put her hand over his, but said nothing.

"Do you know what actually happened?" David asked finally.

"More or less. They had their lawyer call me, and even though his English is excellent, at best it's still a secondhand story. What I learned was that when a new exhibit is in the preparatory stage, they close that section to the public. Eight days ago, the ketubah and scroll jar were moved from storage into the display area; when workers arrived the next morning, which was exactly a week ago, they found the display case demolished and the ketubah gone."

"I'm having a hard time processing this—it's unbelievable." David could hear Giselle beginning to cry, and feel her trembling next to him. "There's so much that doesn't add up. There must be alarms, sophisticated safety measures of all sorts"—he took a deep breath, remembering the awe he felt when Giselle read the words at the top of the little papyrus—"but what I really can't wrap my head around is that they've known about this for a week, a whole week, and nothing's been said publicly."

"As it was explained to me," Edward said calmly, "the police and Interpol were contacted immediately, but everyone agreed to keep it hushed up, at least until they ran out of road. It wasn't until today that people on the guest list were notified; I'm told they wanted to warn you off, but didn't know how to reach you directly, so they called me."

"And now it's a whole week later—they must know something."

"Yes, they do, quite a bit actually, but not the whereabouts of the ketubah. According to the fellow who called me, there's no question that it's an inside job because all the surveillance cameras had been disabled, and electricity for the entire area was cut off."

"Well, that narrows down the suspects…" David patted Giselle's leg in what he thought was a reassuring way, although he was painfully aware that there was a very small window of time to retrieve stolen antiquities before they disappeared on the black market.

"Right again," Edward said. "Of the two thousand plus people the Louvre employs, only one, a guard, didn't show up for work the morning after the robbery."

"So they must assume he was hired by someone, or some group."

"Possibly. The ketubah will be worth millions on the black market."

Edward sounded much more tentative than David thought he should about something that seemed so obvious. "Look, Edward, you're making me think there's something else you want to say, and if so, say it. We're entitled to know everything." David was getting angry at this spoon-fed doling out of information. The news couldn't get worse, and if Edward was hesitating because he was concerned about Giselle's reaction, he'd have to get past it.

"What I have to say falls into the category of speculation, according to the man who called me, and he said it's not going to be released to the press. But you're absolutely right; you're entitled to know. The security guard they identified as being the likely perpetrator was the victim of a hit-and-run accident in the early hours of the morning on the day after the theft. When the police managed to piece the two events together, they thought they'd find the ketubah in the dead man's possession. But a team of investigators went to the morgue, looked in every possible place, including the lining of his clothes, his shoes, body cavities—everywhere. He didn't have it. I'm sorry. I know how much this means to you both, and—and, all we can do right now is wait to see if it's recovered."

"Thanks, Edward. I hope whoever has it is smart enough to keep it protected. Please let us know if there's anything we can do, or if you find out any more information."

"Of course. Oh, one last thing, I almost forgot to mention. Does the phrase 'Viva Angelina' mean anything to you?"

Giselle's entire body stiffened, and he heard her sharp intake of breath as his heart began pounding.

"Why do you ask?"

"There was a note scrawled on a piece of tissue paper left in the spot where the ketubah had been. That's all it said. 'Viva Angelina.' Apparently it means 'long live the messenger.' "

"Yes, that's what it means," David said, and hung up the phone.

50

PARIS

July 2, 2014

SLEEP WAS IMPOSSIBLE. They lay cardboard still, silent but fully awake, until Giselle murmured, "Maybe Gilbert wasn't as paranoid as we thought he was."

David turned on his bedside lamp. "Are you frightened?" he asked, immediately regretting the absurd question. Irrational as it was, even he was shaken. Whoever wanted the ketubah already had it, and there was no incentive to come after either of them, but this was no frivolous theft orchestrated by a collector of antiquities or some cabal hoping to make millions.

"You know," he said, giving voice to thoughts that had been swirling around in his head while he desperately tried to put things in perspective, "you've changed my outlook on everything. I'd made peace trekking through life as a bachelor—and then I met you. When we fell in love my world went from black and gray and white into brilliant Technicolor. I love being in love; having you to care about gives my life meaning that transcends success, or fortune or fame. We wandered into that cave as if some divine presence was guiding us right to the ketubah, then we smuggled it to New York, and it turned out to be the real deal. It was written about, and questioned and argued about, and the whole time the only thing that really mattered was that you had left me. Discovering love, discovering the ketubah, each took on the elusive quality of a dream; reality began to take on the uncertain haziness of fantasy. The memories were almost like ghosts."

"I'm so, so sorry," she said quietly, moving her hair out of the way and kissing his shoulder. "And now, I'm here, but the ketubah has vanished. Probably forever."

"Maybe. But if I can only have one in my real life, I'd choose you in a heartbeat. The world may forget, or deny that the ketubah ever existed, or was genuine, but some know the truth, including us. Those with fixed convictions were never going to believe it anyway."

"And the messenger?"

"Let's talk about that over breakfast," he said, rolling toward her and running his hand along the curve of her waist and thigh. "And after I make love to you, we'll decide where to spend the rest of our lives. But first things first."

Their original plan had been to find a charming sidewalk patisserie and bask in the moment, but neither of them was in the mood for anything that reeked of celebration, and Giselle decided the hedonism of room service should be postponed for a more appropriate time.

"Let's just eat downstairs," she said sadly. "Even that doesn't seem right, but I need some coffee to soothe my soul."

They followed the maître d'hôtel, who led them to a small table set for two, protected from the sparkling morning sunlight by a vibrant, red market umbrella. Fresh, fragrant coffee was poured without a word being spoken, and menus were delivered.

"The umbrellas should be black," Giselle said quietly, "and it should be raining. This reminds me of that wonderful courtyard where we had dinner with Gilbert, but this is more festive and exciting." An inadvertent shudder shook her. "I never thought…"

She stopped speaking, suddenly aware that someone was standing inches from her right shoulder. Assuming it was the waiter being overly attentive, she looked up, forcing a smile.

It was Charles. His face was contorted into something reminiscent of a grin, or at least the corners of his mouth were upturned, but to Giselle he was Asmodeus, the grimacing water stoup, with fiery hatred glaring from his eyes

"Charles! You startled me." Her voice was a shrill alarm bell in the serene setting, and David immediately dropped the menu he'd been looking at and stood up.

"Back off Charles!" It was the guttural growl of a wolf about to lunge at his prey, and Giselle had no doubt David was prepared to attack.

"David…David," she shouted, grabbing his arm, "I'm fine. Please, sit down. I'm sure Charles doesn't mean us any ill will." She could barely believe she had said something so reasonable, and so at odds with how she felt, but much to her relief, David returned to his chair.

Charles remained rooted to the spot, inches from Giselle, tilting his head as a taunting smirk replaced the grimace.

Praying that she could keep the panic from creeping into her voice, Giselle tucked a loose strand of hair behind her ear, pulled her shoulders back and looked directly into those tiny, glinting reptilian eyes. "Nous avons une conversation privée," she said automatically, before realizing and switching to English, "We, David and I, are having a private, um, chat, and I can't ask you to join us." She couldn't imagine Charles would make a scene, or do anything in public that compromised the image he liked to present, but she wasn't in the mood to find out.

"I have no expectation of joining you, nor do I wish to," Charles said, drawing himself up straight with a scornful toss of his head, apparently unaware that a few telltale red blotches had suddenly blossomed on his face. "I simply wanted to extend my regrets."

"Regrets? About what?"

"About the ketubah, of course. I assume you've been informed that it was stolen."

Giselle thought her heart had stopped. She hadn't told David about her encounter with Charles because she knew it would have upset him for no good reason, but now she regretted it. Bile and coffee began to rise and burn the back of her throat, reminding her of that horrible afternoon; Charles knew about Uncle Antoine and the note left with his dead, bloody body. She didn't trust herself to speak, and hoped David understood the look she'd given him, signaling that he should take over.

"Yes, we know about the theft." David had regained his composure, and his words were delivered with deliberate calm, "but why do you know? It hasn't been made public. And you still haven't said how you happened to turn up here."

Charles kept his eyes focused on Giselle as if David was invisible

"You," he said and stared only at Giselle, thrusting his index finger at her face, "have always vastly underestimated me. You have never appreciated how well connected I am, or that I am held in high regard, very high regard, by extremely influential, important people. I have long been a consultant to the Louvre, and I was one of the first to be informed of the theft."

He turned to face David. "Rumor had it that Giselle was done with you. Obviously, that's not the case, but I'm not surprised; her judgment has always been questionable, which is exactly what I told the department chairman before he decided to terminate her faculty position. And knowing how corrupt a man you are, I found it hard to believe the ketubah could be authentic," he said, spitting his words out. "But there are those less skeptical than I who don't see it the way I do. I hope you realize you've put Giselle in a terrible position, a dangerous position."

"What are you talking about?" David growled again, louder, making it apparent he was having a difficult time controlling himself. "What danger? Are you threatening her?"

Charles obviously meant to laugh, but the sound came out as a sniggering gurgle more suggestive of someone choking.

"I sir, don't threaten. That is not my place. I am merely the messenger," he said, making an awkward bow, turning, walking past the other tables, and disappearing into the hotel lobby.

51

ALEXANDRIA, VIRGINIA

JULY 1, 2015

"IT'S REALLY GREAT to have you here…finally," Giselle said with obvious pleasure, as she sat down across from Simone at her new kitchen table. "The photos don't do it justice, do they?"

"No," Simone said, "they don't, although when you did the walk through and face-timed, I got a real sense of how light and airy it is. And I had no idea you have such a gift for making it look comfortable, and happy. But the best part is you're only a car ride away. Funny how things work out."

"Thanks for saying that. Happy is actually a good way to describe it. I know I don't have your touch, and it's not exactly your taste, but this suits us. When we stepped through the front door the first time, and David saw the sun streaming through the windows lighting practically every corner, the beautifully preserved wide plank floors gleaming and the old copper hood over the grill in the kitchen, he looked at me and said, " 'God's in His Heaven.' " It's sort of a little joke between us, but I knew he was feeling exactly the same thing I was. This was the place. Our place. I feel so lucky that—" She stopped as Trevor came running in the kitchen door, barefoot and dripping with pool water.

"Be careful not to slip," Giselle said, "Are you done swimming?"

"No, no, Gigi, it's the best pool ever, and Uncle David taught me how to dive," he shouted, practically dancing with excitement. "Come and see. Bring your phone so you can post a photo."

"We'll be right there my little sweetheart," Giselle said. "Tell your Dad to take a video. He's supposed to know something about making a movie."

"I'll tell him," Trevor said, and was gone.

More days than not, Giselle felt like magic dust had been sprinkled over her, creating an alternate universe for her to inhabit. David said her attitude had changed, that the 'slings and arrows of outrageous fortune' weren't all lodged and festering in her heart anymore. She hoped it was true, but she had to be on guard because who knew what could come along and bring her demons to life. No exorcism was ever that complete, but these past many months she'd been floating in a bubble of contentment, *and who wouldn't be,* she wondered.

A sunbeam illuminated Simone's hair, transforming it into molten gold cascading around her face, reminding Giselle of Marie-Madeleine in the crypt at Saint Maximin la Sainte Baume. A different lifetime in another galaxy. Someday she'd go back and say thank you, face to face.

"Simone, Song of Songs says, 'you are altogether beautiful, my darling; there is no flaw in you.' And that's what I see when I look at you. I just want to say again that I'm grateful from the bottom of heart, and I love you dearly."

Simone put up her hand, as if to say stop, but Giselle ignored it. "You put David in touch with the right people at the Smithsonian, and I know you whispered in an ear or two. The position couldn't be more perfect, and it wouldn't have happened without the personal introduction, no matter how qualified he is, or how many credentials he has. And then, there's the rest of it. I've always complained that you're too pushy, but sometimes I need a push, and I don't think any of this"—she made a sweeping gesture with her arm—"would have happened without you."

Simone got up, walked over to the French doors and stood still, watching her children.

"You know the Smithsonian was Matthew," she said finally, turning to face Giselle, "with a little help from Edward."

"I know, I know. You may not be on the stage yourself, but you're the one who's orchestrated the entire production. I don't think I've ever told you how much I admire your can-do spirit, and your kindness. You may be my little sister, but you grew up first, and I've learned a lot from you. I don't ever want you to think I take anything you do for granted. Merci."

Simone was teary as she walked across the kitchen to Giselle. "After all the horrible things that went on in France, you know I would have moved heaven and earth and black holes in space, if that's what it took for you to make a life here and be safe. Maman would have been happy about how things worked out, even about you living in the U.S., no matter what you think."

Giselle rose from her chair and enclosed Simone in her arms. They stood together silently, embracing the way they used to when they were little girls. Finally, Giselle kissed Simone's cheek and walked over to the granite counter where she had left her sunglasses and the baby monitor,

"Well," she said, "you knew Maman better than I did, so I'll take your word for it that she'd be happy, but I don't give her the credit."

"Nor should you," said Simone. "I know—we all know—who you give the credit to, and…who I am to say otherwise?"

"Last month, when Madeleine arrived from Haiti, I was flooded with all sorts of totally incompatible feelings, all competing for my attention; fear, of course, terror, really, and doubt, and something I'd call absolute, irrational joy. And love, but in a way I never experienced before, in a way I can't really put into words, and it was the same for David. Remember I told you he practically attached her to his chest for the first two days. All he did was watch her face, and sing the songs his mother sang to him. But then I began to worry that Trevor and Laila would be jealous. You know, they've never had any competition for my love."

"Mes poulettes? There's nothing for you to be concerned about. They were over the moon when they heard they were going to have a little cousin. Trevor can't wait to read to her, and Laila plans to give her some of her Barbies, although I'm not so sure she'll be able to part with them. But I know where to find more if it comes to that."

"I'm so blessed," Giselle said as a little squeak coming from the monitor signaled the baby was awake, and the screen image began to squirm.

A circus of color waved at her from just beyond the edge of the patio when she opened the door. It wasn't the scent of the Languedoc, but the fragrant lavender mountain lilies, firecracker flowers and yellow, red, white and purple butterfly tulips planted by the previous owner lent the summer day their own distinctive perfume. *Your works are wonderful and I know that full well*, she thought, as she heard the children begin to shriek with laughter at some silly thing David was doing. “Dry off and come inside you two,” she called out. “Madeleine is awake and after you meet her, and I change her diaper, she can come outside with us and see your dive too.”

“That’ll be great!” Trevor quickly swam to the side of the pool and scrambled out with his sister. “I want to tell her welcome to the family.”

ACKNOWLEDGEMENTS

Just as it takes a village to raise a child, it takes a village to get a novel ready to go out into the world. And authors, like parents, need their village to help them survive the process. I've been fortunate to have years of support and encouragement from my community of family and friends who read, and reread and reread with unflagging interest and enthusiasm. There is no village in this world better than mine.

And then, in an entirely different universe, there is my husband, Bob Miller, the best in every way, and therefore saved for last.

Because I believe in thank-you's and acknowledgments, this note can't help but be long, as well as genuinely heartfelt.

Hundreds of publications and websites, train schedules, hotel brochures and newspaper archives were consulted to add depth and nuance to the background. Countless hours were devoted specifically to researching the history of Rennes-le-Château, Father Saunière, Father Gélis, and the various theories regarding the place of Mary-Magdalene in Jesus' life. I am indebted to all who communicated their ideas, shared arcane information, and reported the fruits of their research. I'm grateful to those who posted little YouTube videos of their trips to Holy sites, and while I can't possibly list every article or book, I'd be remiss if I didn't specifically credit *Holy Blood, Holy Grail* by Michael Baigent, Richard Leigh and Henry Lincoln, *The Gospel of Mary Magdala; Jesus and the First Woman Apostle* by Karen King, *The Gnostic Gospels* by Elaine Pagels, T*he Woman with the Alabaster Jar* by Margaret Starbird and Ben Hammott's informative website *Rennes-le-Château Research.* My husband, Bob, did meticulous research on early Christianity to provide context and an historical scaffolding for the story.

My sister, Emily Andelman, and our dear friends, Jean and Don Donahue, read several early versions of the book, offering invaluable insights, questions, and thoughtful comments that pushed me to reach deep and try to become a better writer. Rick Schwabacher and Mary Ann Rametta, dedicated, special friends, read several later drafts willingly, and each time added helpful, perceptive and unique points of view. Special thanks to Jean for knowing I would love the Tennessee Williams' quote, and to Rick for introducing me to *Miracles*. Each one has been a source of tremendous encouragement, patience and support, which is appreciated enormously.

Thanks to the magic of the Internet—and the stars aligning—I found Lourdes Venard, editor extraordinaire, who lives five thousand miles, and many time zones, away. She offered a wealth of expertise, organization, fact checking, suggestions, criticism and encouragement with a gentle touch. Her generosity went above and beyond anything I ever expected, and I have been enriched by her guidance and friendship. Thank you.

On our travels through the Languedoc region of southern France, Bob and I met many people who took the time to help us understand the local myths surrounding Marie-Madeleine. It is where we learned they firmly believe she wandered the countryside preaching love two thousand years ago, and the longer we were there, the more credible it seemed. Pilgrims making the hours long climb up to the grotto, and their reverence for that holy place is contagious, making it a spiritual experience for people of all faiths. We are grateful they shared it with us.

To Loren, Jen and all the family members who read the earliest versions and continued listening without a hint of boredom to how it was progressing, heartfelt thanks.

I am deeply indebted to my patients, who courageously share their stories and inspire me with their insights and perseverance. I am humbled by their willingness to shine light on their darkest fears and struggle to become the people they'd like to be. I have learned so much from you, and each of you has had a part in the creation of this book.

The children in my life are a constant source of joy and love, which has been essential in creating this novel, my love song to the world. Trevor, you are the only child I've ever known who could sit and listen for as many hours as I was willing to tell you a story; you reminded me of the enormous pleasure I get from creating imaginary worlds. Thanks also for alerting me to the recent vandalism in Rennes-le-Château. Lily, Trevor, Talia, Steele, Sundar, Ben, Greta, Naomi, Laila, Max and Elliot—your idealism, imagination, enthusiasm, confidence and basic belief in the goodness of humanity fills me with hope for the future. Because of you, I want to create bright futures and happy endings.

And then there is my beshert, my husband Bob. We had written a previous book together and started out to write this one together as well. He is the one avidly interested in the history of early Christianity, and many of the pivotal ideas and circumstances originated with him. Like David, he has romance in his soul, and is the most generous spirited person I have ever known, but he is not a writer of romance. As the book took shape and I took ownership of it, Bob graciously stepped aside as I obsessed over every word. However, he remains intimately involved with sending *Discovery* out into the world, and I consider myself blessed to be his wife and share my life with him. Did Mary Magdalene bring us together? Who can say?

AUTHOR'S NOTE

If you've read *Discovery*, it will be obvious that I've intentionally blurred the boundary between real and imagined, fact and fiction, possible and impossible, literally making the actual past a prologue to the fictional present. It's been a great joy to create this story and blend the fruits of my imagination with historical facts, people and places my husband Bob and I have learned about or visited. To see photos of our travels in the Languedoc, and learn more about the underpinnings of the story, please visit my website, lesliesmillerauthor.com.

Abbé François Bérenger Saunière, his companion and housekeeper, Marie Dénarnaud, Father Antoine Gélis, Bishop Billard, Father Henri Boudet, and other clergy mentioned all lived and died in the Languedoc region in southern France at the times stated. The people of Rennes-le-Château did, indeed, refer to Marie Dénarnaud as "Saunière's Madonna;" she wore Parisian finery, dug in the cemetery at night alongside the priest, and her brothers built the wall around the cemetery. Father Saunière did spend time in Paris, and it is believed he brought a document to St. Sulpice. While there, he got to know the opera star Emma Calvé, and it is thought by many that she visited Rennes-le-Château and carved her and the priest's initials in a stone. I didn't see the stone first hand, but it's likely that she presented Saunière with a dog and a monkey, as I describe.

Father Antoine Bigou, Marie de Nègre d'Ables Hautpoul, and the Marquise de Blanchefort all played a part in the historical mystery surrounding the village of Rennes-le-Château. Father Saunière amassed a fortune worth millions, deposited money in many banks, was visited by Hapsburg royalty and fashioned an elaborate estate that survives to this day. Sadly, Father Antoine Gélis was brutally murdered in his presbytery, as I depict; the perpetrator, who left a note saying 'viva angelina,' was never found. A little boy named Abdon, reportedly the son of Marie Dénarnaud's adopted sister, lived in the presbytery where he and Father Saunière had a close relationship.

On the other hand, Dr. David Rettig and Dr. Giselle Gélis have never lived anywhere but in my imagination and the pages of *Discovery*. However, they meet at the Conference of International Biblical Scholars, which actually took place in Amsterdam during the time stated, although David was not a featured speaker the previous year. Just as they note, Seasons is a lovely restaurant and the Hotel Toren cocktail lounge is a jewel. During the conference, they learn that Dr. Karen King will be presenting a paper, *The Gospel of Jesus' Wife*. She is, in fact, a renowned biblical scholar and the Hollis Professor of Divinity at Harvard Divinity School. Her paper, describing a piece of papyrus that implies Jesus was married, was presented at a conference in September 2012 in Rome. Based on subsequent research, it is generally accepted that the papyrus is a forgery.

Though I have taken literary license in describing the documents and items attributed to Bigou, found and then hidden by Saunière, and subsequently found by David and Giselle, there is a great deal of factual evidence to support the premise that some such documents did, in fact, exist. However, those documents have long since disappeared, and it's anyone's guess what they revealed and why they were never made public. Abbé Bigou was the parish priest at Rennes-le-Château from 1774 until he fled France in 1792, and while his letter is pure invention, the Marquise is believed to have entrusted him with secrets long held by the Hautpouls. One of the oldest families in the Languedoc, its ancestors include Bertrand de Blanchefort, the sixth Grand Master of the Templars. On the other hand, Bertrand Raymond d'Hautpoul, the relative who discovers the urn and papyrus, is a pure creation of my mind.

Many people have speculated on the source of Saunière's fortune, but I believe the explanation presented in this book is as valid a hypothesis as any. It is very likely he discovered the valuables left with Bigou by local nobility, who opted for exile at the time of the French Revolution. As recently as December 2017, vandals dug a huge hole in the walkway leading to the entrance of Saunière's church, hoping to find the buried treasure that is still believed to lie beneath in one of the crypts identified by ground penetrating radar. The mystery continues to intrigue many people.

Pope Innocent III (1161-1216) shamefully called for a crusade to eradicate the Cathars in the Languedoc region in what was known as the Albigensian Crusade, during which time the Hautpouls lost Rennes-le-Château, only to subsequently recover it in 1422 upon the marriage of one of their descendants to a family member of the then-owners.

Among the archaeological finds, those discovered at Nag Hammadi remain an amazing source of information about early Christianity. The Gospels of Thomas and Philip discovered there, as well as others, such as the Gospels of Mary and Pistis Sophia discovered elsewhere, were deemed heretical by the Church and ultimately excluded from the New Testament. They comprise the "Gnostic Gospels," and those who are interested can learn more about these fascinating documents from *The Gnostic Gospels* by Elaine Pagels, a professor of Religion at Princeton University, or any of her other books on this subject.

Khirbet Qeiyafa, where David works, is an active archaeological site, though no one there has ever heard of him. His comments about King David are reflective of the controversy concerning the historical significance of that site. The Talpiot Tomb, discovered in 1980, was documented in 1994 in the "Catalogue of Jewish Ossuaries in the Collections of the State of Israel." Just as Giselle remembers, the conclusion that this is Jesus's family tomb remains highly controversial, but is thought to be a good possibility by many reputable historians.

Talia Benjamin, the writer of the fictional screenplay *Devotion*, doesn't actually exist. However, she accurately describes the real discovery of a Jewish synagogue in Magdala, a first-century port city on the shores of the Galilee, before construction could begin on a retreat for pilgrims planned by Father Juan Solana of Jerusalem.

To soak in the flavor of the region, Bob and I drove the same 500-mile journey devised by Giselle, beginning in Marseilles with the first stop in Saint-Maximin-la-Sainte-Baume, visiting the Basilique Sainte-Marie-Madeleine and descending into the crypt to view the gold-sheathed skull of Mary Magdalene. It took several wrong turns through small villages and mountain roads before reaching the parking area for the Grotto of St. Marie-Madeleine—we were surprised at how many locals had never heard of the Grotto. We then made the pilgrimage up the steep mountain trail to the Grotto. As we were coming down, a woman climbing up offered to buy the branch Bob found for me as a walking stick. We toured Saunière's breathtaking domain in Rennes-le-Château, climbed the belvedere and sat awestruck in the Orangerie, contemplating the sort of man who imagined and built such a romantic structure on an obscure mountaintop well over a hundred years ago. We stayed in the beautiful hotels mentioned, and traveled the nerve-racking switchback roads up and down the Pyrenees in the newly named regions of Provence-Alpes-Côte d'Azur and Languedoc-Roussillon-Midi-Pyrénées. Getting lost became inevitable; fortunately, we were rescued and redirected by lovely people along the way. If Bob weren't fluent in French, I might still be trying to get back home.

Washington Square Park took many years to renovate, but the fountain is finally operational again, although now the roads surrounding the park are torn up. Perry Street in Greenwich Village is as quaint as it's been since the original row houses were first constructed; however, no one named Simone lives in the limestone house in the center of the block, nor does Giselle live at Number 9 Place de la Daurade in Toulouse, although I think it would have suited her.

Much has been written about Rennes-le-Château and Abbé Saunière, and I gratefully acknowledge all the authors who have shared their research and ideas in books and on the Internet. Theories are plentiful, but no one has managed to put all the pieces of the puzzle together in a definitive way. I believe the explanation for Saunière's wealth I present in *Discovery* is as plausible as any, but in no way do I suggest I have the corner on historical accuracy or the truth. The mystery lives on.

The fascinating book *Holy Blood, Holy Grail* by Michael Baigent, Richard Leigh, and Henry Lincoln, first published in 1982, hypothesizes that historical Jesus married Mary Magdalene and had one or more children before Mary and her offspring emigrated to southern France. Though the book became a bestseller and was roundly condemned by the Catholic Church, the people living in southern France have long believed that after the Crucifixion, Mary Magdalene arrived either at Marseilles or in what is today know as Saintes-Maries-de-la-Mer, and lived in the region until her death. The evidence for this is very compelling, and its connection to the mystery of Rennes-le-Château spurred my curiosity and impetus for writing this story.

About the Author

LESLIE SCHWEITZER MILLER is a psychiatrist and psychoanalyst with an active private practice in New York's west Greenwich Village neighborhood. In addition to a passion for writing, she paints and shows her work in Gallery23, a small, charming country gallery in New Jersey. The cover art for Discovery is adapted from one of her paintings, aptly titled Rennes-le-Château.

She lives in New York City's Greenwich Village and Blairstown, New Jersey with her husband Bob.

To learn more please visit: lesliesmillerauthor.com

CPSIA information can be obtained
at www.ICGtesting.com
Printed in the USA
BVOW08s2012230418
514210BV00001B/2/P